Other Fictions by Curt Leviant

The Yemenite Girl
Passion in the Desert
The Man Who Thought He Was Messiah
Partita in Venice
Diary of an Adulterous Woman
Ladies and Gentlemen, the Original Music of
the Hebrew Alphabet and *Weekend in Mustara*
A Novel of Klass
Zix Zexy Ztories

KING OF YIDDISH

CURT LEVIANT

[signature]

Livingston Press
The University of West Alabama

isbn 13: 978-1-60489-160-7, trade paper
isbn 13: 978-1-60489-161-4, hardcover
ISBN: 1-60489-160-2, trade paper
ISBN: 1-60489-161-0, hardcover
Library of Congress Control Number 2015941912
Printed on acid-free paper.
Printed in the United States of America
Publishers Graphics
Hardcover binding by: Heckman Bindery
Typesetting and page layout: Joe Taylor, Amanda Nolin
Proofreading: Teresa Boykin, Joe Taylor, Amanda Nolin,
Sidney Kessler (with special thanks from the author)
Cover design: Leora Chefitz

This is a work of fiction:
any resemblance
to persons living or dead, especially dead, is coincimental.

Livingston Press is part of The University of West Alabama,
and thereby has non-profit status.
Donations are tax-deductible:
brothers and sisters, we need 'em.

first edition
6 5 4 3 3 2 1

KING OF YIDDISH

CURT LEVIANT

The flood continues, time rains down on us, drowns us.

Jose Saramago, *The Year
of the Death of Ricardo Reis*

The first rule of history is not to lie.
The second is not to be afraid of the truth.

Cicero

For Erika

פאר עריקא

די קיניגן

I

NOW ...

1

WHAT WAS KNOWN, OR RATHER "KNOWN,"
ALL OVER JERUSALEM

JERUSALEM, it was known all over Jerusalem, the holy city, that Shmulik Gafni, Overlyfull Professor, Chairman and Distinguished University Researcher of Yiddish language, Literature, Culture and Folklore on the Mendl and Sadie-Yentl Eizenbahn Chair of Yiddish Studies at the University of Israel, the most famous scholar of Yiddish in the world, not only by his own estimation but in the estimation of others, for instance a fellow scholar, Sh. Meichl-Rukzak, who was himself a leading candidate for that honorific, in an interview with *The New York Times* (with the help of a translator) called Shmulik Gafni "Mister Yiddish" (but everyone, aware of their rivalry, said it was just a sarcastic jibe), married for more than forty years was he, forty not being the mythical forty of the Bible, a ubiquitous Biblical cipher, but a metaphor for a long long stretch of time, which by all objective accounts a forty-year marriage truly is, married not to two or three women, mind you, like most non-Yiddish scholars, with a graduate assistant and/or secretary on the side (the female side, to be sure), for Yiddish scholars tend to be more conservative (one to one-and-a-half wives at most), forty not being an aggregate of marriage years, a sum of various unions, but the number of years he'd been with one woman, Batsheva was her name, and for her there was only one man too, a goodlooking, bright and witty man was Shmulik, who had attained the Biblical three score and ten (he loved Biblical numbers, and names too, witness his choice of mate) in good health more or less (the less was a minor heart attack some years back for which he briefly took medications and, reluctantly, after much coaxing by Batsheva, now grumblingly wore an electric monitor called the *Chaver* or friend, based on the American model known as the "Companion," which he never yet had to use, didn't know the workings of, except maybe press a button), with sparkling grey eyes compressing a gleam that could be ironic, sardonic, impatient and disarmingly affectionate in rather quick order, a mellifluous baritone speaking voice, which even when he spoke privately at home rang out with a lecturer's boom whose authority, charm and fluidity of nuance excited all his girl students, especially when he smiled and his powerful teeth shone and the

laugh lines at the corner of his wolf-grey eyes crinkled and he ran his
hand through his full head of wavy steel grey sprinkled hair, hair that
once years back when he was on a research trip an old Italian barber
in New York held up like a bunch of asparagus and said to him, "You
gotta healthy heada haira, you never ever gonna getta balda," a
prognostication that held true, even forty years later, and a look in
his eyes that combined boyish shyness, even at seventy, and worldly
assurance, with a thirty-four-year-old son, Yosef, twin daughters,
Rivka and Rachel, forty-three, and twin granddaughters, Penina and
Zehava (one from each daughter, explanation coming), one of whom,
the elder, though both were born precisely at the same second, now
had a one-year-old son, which made a great-grandfather of Shmulik
Gafni, a name he hadn't had of course back home in Warsaw, his
pre-World War II hometown, but which he changed from Weingarten,
"wine garden" (easy enough, right?, who says you don't know
Yiddish?), an imposing name with rhythm and élan, with tri-syllabic
balance and a triad of different vowel neumes, even a tone-deaf man
saying "Weingarten" sounded as though he'd just finished rehearsing
for a lieder recital, Shmulik dropping the Weingarten after being told
privately, discreetly, but in no uncertain terms that the authorities in
Israeli higher education, 1950 was the year, just two years after
Independence, not too keen on Yiddish in the first place, in fact, truth
to say, because we offer here no make-believe, but the whole truth
and nothing but the truth (see Epigraph, the second one, by Cicero),
as American court clerks state with such grandiloquence, the Israel
bureaucrats (all born in Eastern Europe and Yiddish-speaking)
looking down their quintessential Jewish noses at this Diasporic
Yiddish language that threatened (so they asseverated) to compete
with the ancient Hebrew, even though all the founding fathers of
Israel were born into that supple, juicy, evocative, folk-saturated,
wise, witty and image-laden Yiddish tongue, and greedily imbibed,
yes, sucked it in with their mama's milk, and spoke it more naturally
and felicitously than Hebrew, which was strong on verbs but weak
on modern nouns and the subtleties of adverbs and adjectives, and
how can you run a nation just on verbs anyway?, but run it they did,
in fact race and gallop in it, around it and through it with verbs,
moxie, faith and smuggled weapons too, Shmulik was told that these
higher ed officials would look more kindly on his efforts to establish
Yiddish studies at the University of Israel if he wouldn't have such a
blatantly *potch-in-pawnim* (slap in the face, for the handful of you
out in the boondocks who haven't yet mastered Yiddish) Diasporic
Jewish name but a more acceptable Hebraized one, Gafni, for
instance, remember this was two years after Independence when
nationalism was so intense it bordered on jingoism, although in

Israel they hadn't heard of the word and wouldn't know what it meant even if they heard it, but words are created for situations, movements and moods and not vice versa, and the mood then in Israel rejected all foreign-sounding (read: Jewish-sounding) names, hiding it under the protective purple cloak of Hebrew, when everyone knew that Weingarten had been around for two hundred years or more and Gafni hadn't even been around the block yet much less around the corner, and anyone who ever met a Gafni would at once say, "You used to be Weingarten, right?," just like if anyone met a phony concoction of a name like Har-paz, he'd smirk and say, "Ah, né Goldberg, hill of gold," but you know that from Bach's famous *Variations*, but Gafni it was, folks, and Gafni it had to be, Gafni, meaning "my vine," close enough, but that wasn't what was known all over Jerusalem, it won't be too long before you do know what was known, or rather "known," all over Jerusalem, and a juicy bit of knowledge it was — close enough to his paternal family name, but this Gafni business, as far as Shmulik Weingarten was concerned, was merely part of the "i" suffix name syndrome that most Israelis succumbed to and which most Europeans assumed were Italian, surnames like Gafni, Magdani, Zehavi, Caspi, Crispi and Crunchi, modern stand-ins for all the delicious, age-old, authentic Jewish names which the goyim had imposed upon the Jews and which the Jewish goyim in Israel were imposing on Ashkenazi names. (Question: What was the difference between the goyim there in Europe in the 1700's forcing you to take a name and the Jews here gently twisting your forearm to take a name? Answer: here you didn't have to pay for it). But there was a price, mind you, a mighty awful price to pay anyway, far costlier than the gold the Jews had to fork over to Christian authorities two-hundred-fifty years ago for their new Jewish family names, for now if a family member, let's say a Holocaust survivor or a Russian immigrant came to Israel and sought you out in the telephone book or on the population list of the Interior Ministry, he would never find you, for fine old Jewish names like Ginsburg, Brandenburg, Silverberg, Goldberg and Iceberg all became Hebraified, deracinated, a kind of nose job on the paterfamilias monicker, but Shmulik Weingarten reluctantly agreed to gafnify his name if it would help, and indeed it did, due to him and his passion for everything Yiddish, and thanks to the Yiddish supporters he mustered all over the land, The University of Israel Global Yiddish Department developed into a world center, perhaps *the* world center for Yiddish, competing with and even superceding the superb one at the Hebrew University, an "address" as he laughingly called it one day many years ago during his own interview with a foreign correspondent for *The New York Times* as he held his little twin daughters (one of whom, grown up now of course, had become a grandmother just a year ago) on his knees, but it was the other twins, a score or so years later, who were called a medical miracle, still being written up by doctors and parapsychologists and of course photographed, for they were two daughters born, one each to Shmulik's twin girls, Rivka and Rachel, at precisely the same time, at 7:16 AM, which aroused the curiosity of geneticists who found that the little sweety pies had the same DNA, hence they were twins, even though emanating from two different wombs, the which were presumably inseminated at the same time by two different men, but enough of medicine and magic and the hocus pocus of DNA, which science, important as it is, impertinent wags and wits have dubbed Don't Know Anything, for it is Yiddish and sex — not as unlikely a twinning, or coupling, by your grace, as you might assume — that here interests us, entwines us, betweens us, to coin a wordploy, which by the way is what fiction is all about, wordploy, although what is being said here, what was known all over Jerusalem, and remember, what's known isn't always true and what's true isn't always known, so what was "known" all over Jerusalem is neither fictive speculation nor imaginative rumination, but pure unadulterous truth (truth in the sense that it truly was known but not necessarily true) that Shmulik Gafni was reportedly plucking grapes from a wine garden not truly his own, having been seriously involved, so it was stage-whispered all over Jerusalem, which in fact meant all over Israel, via telephone, fax, telex, rooftop shouts, and tell-all-over-café-au-lait-tongue wagging which zipped all over town quicker than all the modern miracles of communication and, inter alia, let's not forget the Internet nor short-sell e-mail, which is only a trice slower than the pre-electronic instant mode of communication, you guessed it, it rhymes with e-mail and speaks in a higher-pitched voice and laughs when tickled; or, if the preceding obfuscates rather than clarifies, then let a hint to the wise suffice, so let's not beat around the bush (no offense to the former Prez Pere or junior), we're happy to repeat, let's not forget the Internet, e-mail and female, which was quicker? hard to say, which is more reliable?, let's not play dumb, okay?, that Gafni was involved, envalved, invulved with a blonde, full-chested, slim-waisted Polish Catholic *shikse* exactly half his age, thank God she had a couple of flaws, including pencil-thin eyebrows and vermicelli lips and slightly uneven teeth on an otherwise attractive face, because if she'd been perfect people would have jumped out of their skins, which in any case were already stained a deep envy green, but what Shmulik Gafni, né Weingarten, was thoroughly raked over the coals for was not that he was old enough to be her father (and maybe was), not that she wasn't Jewish (but could become), not that she was Polish, although her Polishness was an awfully bitter pill to swallow (given the Poles' endemic anti-Semitism and how, with few exceptions, they helped the Germans and did no small amount of killing themselves, during and even long after the war, a fact which Gafni knew only too well, and was one of the reasons he went back to Poland so often — about this more, much more, later — but accident of birth wasn't her fault), individually her flaws were excusable and even taken in toto they (that amorphous "they" out there) didn't mind that she was a young, pretty blonde (the fact that she was interested in Jewish history just made them roll their eyes), very busty, how busty? a straining-at-the sweater busty, a lump-in-the-throat, swallowing-with-difficulty chesty Polish *shikse* busty, and not even that she was young enough to be his daughter, which we've already mentioned in inverso fashion, but that for God's sake, how could you do this to us, Shmulik Weingarten, because that's who you really are, forget that glib Gafni disguise, Shmulik Weingarten, guardian of Yiddish, laureate of the Yiddish language, faithful amanuensis of Yiddish folklore, editor of Yiddish drama, anthologist and preserver of Yiddish poetry and prose, harvester of Yiddish humor and expert on earthy Yiddish expletives, for God's sake, Shmulik, the blonde bitch, to quote her own surfside confession after the linguistics conference in Nice, a remark that was typed, faxed, whispered and shouted in all the above-mentioned natural, artificial and telecommunication modes hitherto listed: the blonde bitch *doesn't even know a word of Yiddish!*

TRUE, Shmulik Gafni didn't want it known all over Jerusalem that he was involved with a *Poilishe*. Because the truth was — never mind the gossip, the malicious palm over mouth sotto voce that went from office to market to bus stop to e-mail to female (quicker than e-mail, see supra) but slower than light (Question: was there anything that traveled quicker than light? Answer: Yes! Lies!), and what was quicker than lies? Rumors of sex — that he was not involved with her. Let's repeat that, given the interruption of long parenthesis and double dashes: he was not involved with her. To those skeptics, mockers and doubters who think Gafni was after Malina (now you know her name) know ye that for years he had dreams that he was not married to Batsheva, but for Gafni they weren't dreams, oh no, they were nightmares in which he felt an awful depression, an emptiness that could only be sensed, never described, an irredeemable loss. In those dreams he was single, alone, lonely, and he felt a discomfit of mysterious origin, a disequilibrium, his wholeness compromised. Salvation came like sunshine breaking suddenly through clouds only when he woke up to find that he was indeed whole, two halves perfectly melded, Batsheva his. Still, there was no doubt in Shmulik's mind and in the minds of others that Malina was an attractive woman. The mystery in the rumor mill was why this lady named Malina Przeskovska (anyone who pronounced her name correctly was assured of her loyalty and friendship* and 5000 bonus miles on the other Polish national airline, Less, which had no frequent flyer mileage plan), who already had a PhD in Polish Linguistics from Lodz University, was interested in studying Jewish history in Jerusalem. Was it because she had met Gafni at the International Linguistics Conference in Nice and later, as gossip had it, continued their discussions about the niceties and subtleties of comparative linguistics on the finely pebbled beach of Nice where 80% of the women were 50% naked 100% of the time and the other 20% were 100% naked 10% of the time, engaging in their disquisitions in the international lingua franca (pace, France and French), English?

It began this way.

AT the conference Malina gave her paper in English as if she had lived in London for years; actually, she had never set foot in either that country or in the USA. She even took questions in English. So when Gafni approached her in person with a question he didn't want to ask publicly (no, not What's your phone number?) and began at once in Polish, accompanied by his engaging smile, he noticed her surprise, astonishment, pleasure. There was no joy like the joy of hearing your language far away from home, and there was no surprise like the surprise of hearing your native tongue when you did not expect it. She smiled with pleasure at the sound of his words even before she digested the tenor of his remarks. And even as he spoke he saw she was just as pretty up close as she was far away, for beauty at a distance can vanish when blemishes are seen up close.

Gafni studied her face, not for its innate, broad-boned prettiness — she had a large face, with everything in proportion, big eyes and flaring nostrils which for him was always a sign of womanliness, even overt eroticism, an animal hunger — but also for its air of familiarity.

"Your face looks familiar. I think I've seen it before."

She thought for a moment.

"Perhaps at a previous linguistics conference."

"Perhaps," he said. But if so he would have remembered the face and dispensed with that vague ill at ease feeling akin to a metaphysical headache. No, he decided, he hadn't seen her at a conference, and the fluttery feeling that her face or a likeness of her

---

*and, if you spelled it right, she was yours.

face, or a likeness of a likeness had made an impression on him somewhere remained imprinted on his memory.

Let's get the facts straight. Their chat did not begin on the beach. It began by one of those stone ledges behind the beach, by the promenade. After the conference, when Shmulik still wore jacket and tie and she a business suit, Malina merrily told him she hoped he wouldn't mind if she sunbathed. "I have a bathing suit on under all this," she said in her Polish-accented English, gesturing balletically. Remembering how she brightened when he spoke Polish to her, Gafni courteously suggested speaking Polish, but she, hurt, countered with: "Is my English that poor?" which made him feel bad and prompted him to say that her English was excellent, much better than his, in fact. Gafni confessed that although he read English, he did not lecture in English. His English was fair, not good. Then wondered aloud if perhaps his unused, perhaps even outmoded, Polish offended her ears. But looking at her made him quickly forget about the language; he only half heard her protestation about his magnificent, literary Polish. Later, upon reflection, Gafni realized that the slow demure striptease she did for him was a kind of non-avian mating dance. She turned modestly and took off her jacket and stepped out of her skirt, rolled down her panty hose, unbuttoned her blouse, still her back to him, doing the sort of undressing gestures done in a hotel room and not on a beach, then, her back still to him, she took out a terry cloth tunic from her bag, put it on, popped her clothes in a plastic bag that emerged from her pocketbook and lo, she stood before him, turning to face him now, practically naked in her bikini and her nakedness was all the more stark against his full sartorial elegance and she girlishly said to him, taking him by the hand (if indeed she did take his hand and he gave his to her. But if she did extend her hand to him, which still is problematic, and if he took it [even more of a question], if both these suppositions are true and questions of fact, veracity and malicious rumors are resolved and all doubts undone), then Gafni felt a brief electric thrum in his body, an inexplicable warm jolt which sent a message of no specific linguistic content running in all directions, for she had a firm, assertive clasp that he at once interpreted as goyish, it was a gentile hand clasp, a strong *shikse* womanly hold, and he followed, seeing and not seeing the half-naked girls sunbathing, even older ones who instead of baring their sagging wrinkled dugs should have covered them in shame with layers of clothing, but even so despite her bikini and the nakedness of the girls on the beach, Gafni felt that she was nakeder than they, it was hard to explain, but if pressed and if he thought about it, the word "sexy" would have come into play, for in the bared breasts there was stasis, nothing provocative or sexy, but in Malina, in that raspberry-colored bikini, Malina bikini, there was something sexy, taking him by the hand for a moment with a flirtatious tilt of her head, "Come to the water," and he followed her, undoing first his tie jerkily as he walked toward the water, left and right, a difficult manipulation when you're working only with one hand, as the white caps rolled closer and closer, lapping over the sunning ultramarine sea, the white caps breaking here and there like a cupped hand, and then his jacket and shirt, with two hands now, for he thought he'd look funny with only half his jacket and half his shirt off and finally he rolled up his cuffs until at least in spirit, if not in fact, his nakedness matched hers. He didn't realize she'd put his tie into her bag until she'd done it.

"I need sun," Malina sang. "I need sun and light, especially after that gloomy darkness in the lecture halls." And she removed her little terry cloth tunic.

Shmulik remembered reading once in an American novel a description of a woman with a "luscious body," and he recalled the phrase perhaps because the first syllable of "luscious" — lush — was the first syllable too of *loshn*, the Yiddish word for "tongue" and "language," and he repeated to himself, "What a luscious body."

Heads turned when Malina took off her terry cloth tunic and the sun shone on her deep raspberry red bikini top. Traffic stopped. The Nice-Monte Carlo helicopter shuttle hovered in midair. Storks carrying babies on their way over the Alps to nest in Morocco's Atlas Mountains swooped down, leaving some half dozen Eskimo tykes homeless. For a moment Shmulik was blinded by the size, shape, pitch, timbre, mode and musicality of the large ripe Galilee melons, first image that came to his Israeli mind, recalling the stacks of melons in the Jerusalem outdoor market, fruits that were popping out of their baskets, so small were the restraints — we're back to Malina's melons now — so large the countervailing force. And all this in contrast to her slim waist. Women of intellect weren't supposed to have bodies like that, Gafni thought, rubbing the sunlight from his eyes. His *loshn* cleaved to the roof of his mouth, as the phrase in the Psalms had it ("If I forget thee, O Jerusalem, may my tongue cleave to the roof of my mouth"), and even though he hadn't forgotten Jerusalem he was, temporarily, as the Yiddish proverb had it: *ohn loshn*, without tongue, or speechless.

He swallowed, although swallowing was difficult, what with his tongue stuck up there somewhere on his palate (I guess he had forgotten Jerusalem), and the everlasting springs of spittle as dry as the Negev desert in August. Temptation was like a snake slithering in the grass, ready to strike, then retreating into serpentine slumber:

temptation flashed its venomous wet fangs. Temptation, blood-filled, pounded its hammers on both sides of Shmulik's head, no syncopation here, rather perfectly timed right and left. He looked away, looked to the calm blue sea; tried to breathe in the blue of the water, the azure of the sky. In the lecture hall he had seen her in a business suit where she wasn't exactly flat-chested, but he attributed some of the fullness to the cut of the jacket. He couldn't imagine then that he would see later what he was seeing now.

Rather than say something stupid, he sought to steer the conversation back to linguistics. In such situations, *loshn* (hope you haven't forgotten, *loshn*, like *lingua* in Italian, means both "tongue" and "language") always comes in handy.

"Do you know what your name means in Yiddish?"

"No. I don't know. I don't even know one word of Yiddish," she said apologetically, but with a seductive little tilt of her head. The slight musical whine of her words delared: Teach me. I'm willing to learn.

"It means 'berry.' "

"Ah," Malina brightened. "Also in Polish and Russian."

"Yes, of course."

Malina frowned. "How could it be the same in Yiddish and Polish?"

How could "telephone" be the same in Russian, Yiddish, Polish, English, Dutch, Swahili, and Hebrew? he was about to lecture her, but then supposed it was a purposely naïve question, a come-on. She had a degree in linguistics, for goodness sake. Surely she knew.

So without condescension he told her, "Because Yiddish has influences from many language groupings, including Slavic."

Suddenly Malina sneezed. It was a little daisy of a sneeze, a demure little flower of a sneeze, "haptsee," and she giggled.

"Bless you. What's funny?"

"Nothing. I always give out a little giggle when I sneeze."

"Are you cold?" He was about to give her his jacket. Later, recalling his remark, Gafni wondered if he was being sarcastic or gentlemanly.

"No no no … It has nothing to do with cold … Just a sneeze. Don't make anything of it."

He didn't, but he would hear that sneeze, followed by a giggle, quite often in time to come.

And so all these rumors of "what was known all over Jerusalem" ("I mean, you know," folks would say, "it's known all over town.") was utter and absolute nonsense. They were colleagues and friends, Malina and Shmulik. She said she had always had a fascination with Jewish history, like many of her post-War-born, intellectually-minded friends. And since there were advanced fellowships available, it wasn't hard for Malina, that pretty little berry — once her name became known, it was the subject of a whole series of, God preserve us, fruity jocular concoctions — to get admitted to the Jewish history graduate program for a second PhD at the University of Israel. And guess who was helping her with beginners' Hebrew and Yiddish?

Where there is a suspected triangle, even though as they say in Hebrew, "the rumor has no legs," it would be remiss, when two sides of a triangle are being discussed, not to mention the third. We think you also ought to know that Shmulik's Batsheva was not well. She was ailing, in fact, at home, diabetic, and Shmulik would not compromise his affection for his wife by carrying on with another woman, luscious very berry though she was. In fact, Gafni hadn't wanted to go to the Nice Conference but Batsheva urged him to go. "You were looking forward to this trip," she said. "Go to Nice. Don't worry. I'll be all right."

That's the sort of woman she was. And he told her what you have already learned:

"Sometimes I dream that I'm a bachelor and in my dream I feel an unease. And then, still in my dream I wake up and realize I'm married to you and I'm so happy I have you and found you."

"And I love you too," Batsheva replied, her face glowing, "darling, handsome Shmulik."

Strange. As soon as Gafni thought of Batsheva and her illness Ezra Shultish popped into his head. Shultish, an older colleague from America, was a man with whom he had been acquainted for years (Shultish had written the classic work on the style of S.Y. Agnon, Israel's Nobel laureate.) Shultish, rather his fictional alter ego, Zera Tishler, was actually the hero of Agnon's seminal masterpiece, his last work, *Ha-na'ara ha-temanit*, which was translated into thirty-three languages and appeared in English as *The Yemenite Girl*. Now by no means should Ezra Shultish be confused with Zera Tishler, but all those who do will be forgiven. For Tishler, like Gafni, had an ailing wife. And there were other parallels, most of which he wasn't thinking about right now.

In short, Gafni went to Nice. If he hadn't gone, he wouldn't have met Malina and the rumors would not have begun. But Malina or no Malina, with Gafni there was always room for gossip. He knew of course that women looked admiringly at him. Although he was not tall, he was of robust appearance, solidly built, no flab. Despite his mild heart attack, he swam, he could walk backwards quicker than most people could walk forward, played tennis in a city that hadn't developed the sport, even skied when he went to winter conferences in Switzerland. His grandfather lived to his 93rd birthday; his father would have too, had he not been murdered by *them*. So, despite the occasional fibrillations, the chances were good for Shmulik Gafni too and he worked hard on his longevity.

And, of course, his mental acuity matched — what do you mean "matched"? it easily surpassed — his physical vigor. By the age of seventy, when he had been awarded Israel's highest honor, the Israel Prize, for his life's work, presented at the President of Israel's residence, Shmulik had already won the Bialik Prize for his study of Alsatian Yiddish; the Tel Aviv Prize for his book on 19th century Yiddish in Jerusalem; and an honorary doctorate from Oxford for his edition of the collected works of a hitherto unknown 16th century Venetian master of Yiddish. In addition, among his 111 books and monographs, there was a rather slim anthology of Yiddish jokes in Sicily; an edition of neglected 20th century Yiddish writers in Albania and Herzegovina; a study of early Swiss variants of the verb "to be," which he proved were derivatives of Old Yiddish.

Gafni's Latin-Yiddish, Yiddish-Latin dictionary was a tour de force. And his Latin translation of one of Sholom Aleichem's comic monologues was the hit of the International Latin Scholars Conference, the famous ILSC, held on Capri, for Latin conventions, like Yiddish conferences, always chose perfect locations and ideal weather for their week-long *festa festorae*. It put Yiddish on the map. When Gafni quotes Cicero's "A room without books is like a body without a soul" in his Yiddish — "*a tzimmer ohn a sefer is azoy vi a guf ohn a neshomeh*" — it sounds natural, homey, heimish. You would have thought Cicero grew up in a shtetl, and perhaps he did.

Of course, such productivity and fame sparked envy, and envy gave birth to criticism that soon degenerated to petty carping. (You see what I mean. Malina or no Malina, the carps are always there to nibble and quibble.) They criticized Gafni for his frequent trips abroad (trips they'd rather have taken). Why can't he stay home and teach? They skewered him for publishing so much. Why doesn't he rein in his pen (creating in their envy a mixed metaphor)? (By the way, with that hex they succeeded. See Chapter 3.) Why didn't we think of this first? Why does he dance all over the globe? Sicily, Alsace-Lorraine, Switzerland, Tirana, Shanghai. Next thing we know he'll be writing about Yiddish in Timbuktu. (Which, incidentally, he was working on already.)

Again lies and malignation. He did stay home and teach. But the carps would not cease nibbling, the pirhanas their petty carping: Why did he, that is Shmulik Gafni, always manage to find a Yiddish connection in world-class resorts? No one else but pleasure-garden-seeking, wine-bibbing Weingarten; no one but globe-hopping Gafni could find Yiddish in the Canary Islands, the Azores, Palma di

Majorca or Malta, where the last Yiddish speaker had died peacefully
in his sleep in the year 22 of the Common Era, a total, unwarranted
exaggeration, as the addendum at the end of this chapter will prove.
And what possible link could there be between Yiddish, continued
the carpers, or anything remotely Jewish for that matter, and the Taj
Mahal, yet Gafni was able to come up with an article only semi-
tongue-in-cheek entitled, "The Taj Mahal, the Pink Elephant, and
the Jewish Question." Success breeds envy, period. What next,
Gafni? Yiddish in Yemen? Jargon in Azerbaijan? *Mame-loshn* in
Mozambique?

On a bus in Jerusalem one day, he overheard two men sitting in
front of him speaking (No feline will be freed from the sack, as the
Russians say, if I tell that Gafni will meet these same two men again
in a bus discussing Malina a year or so from now.):

"And those trips of his to Poland. Every year, sometimes twice a
year, for weeks on end, as if he wants to establish residence there in
that idiotic and inhumane communist state."

"Yes," said the other man. "As if he has some secret about living
there that nobody else knows about and doesn't want to share with
anyone."

If I don't want to share it, Gafni thought, it's obviously a secret.

"Maybe he's getting reparations from the Polish government."

"Fat chance! A communist regime giving money away — and
to Jews!"

"Still there must be something. Something that explains all his
trips to exotic places to do his so-called research, places that have as
much links to Yiddish as my bobbe's beard has to bagels."

Gafni smiled. About establishing residence in Poland, gentlemen,
you're absolutely right. And how I want to establish residence there!
Yes, Shmulik had good reasons for going to Poland, which he didn't
want to talk about.

And neither do I.

Not yet anyway.

But how about fairness, balance, eh? That's the Jewish way. His
students thought he was a gifted instructor. His teaching assistants
adored him. He always took one or two along and managed to find
international grants and fellowships for them. And ask the members
of the various Polish *landsmanshaftn* in Israel how often Shmulik
would appear before their groups and reminisce with them about
pre-war Jewish life in Warsaw and other cities and never charge a
lecturer's fee.

Given all of the above, it is no wonder that Shmulik Gafni did not
want known all over Jerusalem what was known all over Jerusalem,
a so-called "known" that, according to Gafni, had no connection to

fact, but facts, as is well known, no quotes around that word, facts had as much connection to truth as cabbies to cabbage or cribs to cribbage. You've heard this before, but a truism — like a juicy lie — is worth repeating (in fact, Gafni himself liked to use this line and would ascribe it to various 18th century philosophes): a truism, like a lie, gets better with each repetition. Mere fact, mere access to truth, did not prevent lies from growing like a golem out of control.

The truth was that Shmulik Gafni was never alone with Malina. Giving her an occasional lift home in his car — a six-minute ride — to save her a forty-minute bus ride does not count. He drove; she sat next to him. Gafni looked down at her short skirt and bare, pretty legs and in his mind he stretched out his hands and touched, stroked her smooth, tanned skin, a tan and a bare that reminded him of the tan and the bare when he walked with her on the Nice beach to the water of the Great Sea, as the Bible called the blue Mediterranean, and even though she was partially clothed then she was nakeder than the 98% naked women on the beach. But all this was in his head; his hands on his lap he kept (and if I were Chaucer I would add: and Shmulik Gafni was he yclept). Looking at his calm hands and tranquil fingers, one would never have imagined the tremble in his fingers, the quake in his heart, the shake in his soul, the agitas in all of Gafni.

So then, Gafni was never really alone with Malina. And even when by pure coincidence Malina registered for the same conference, she always stayed at a different hotel.

But this didn't satisfy them (the "them" out there previously cited as "they"). They figured that precisely, *davke*, because the two of them were in different hotels it actually confirmed their suspicions. Why different hotels? Just because it's different hotels, they argued Talmudically, was all the more reason to believe that something was going on. It was such a transparent ruse, that different hotels ploy (there's that "ploy" again), even more revealing than if they'd been in the same hotel. Who are they (a different "they" this time) fooling with that two hotels monkey business? If vox populi makes up its mind, even truth can't come to interfere, as Cicero sagely observed.

And so with this — we now paraphrase a remark in one of Kafka's meta-fictions — we have come to the end of our investigation as to what was known (remember Pascal's apothegm: all knowledge is either Platonic arrogance or wishful thought) and not known in the holy city of Jerusalem, may it speedily be rebuilt in our day, Amen, by presenting all the facts as we (that is, I) know them.

Which means that we can now move on with Gafni and tell his tale, unencumbered by malice or gossip, which in a non-Euclidian universe are actually synonymous.

AFTERCHAPTER 1

SOMEWHERE in Chapter 7 of the great poet-philosopher Yehuda Halevi's masterwork, *The Kuzari,* the author states that men want always to be someone else: workers, poets: doctors, soldiers; barbers, waggoners. And everyone, he continues, wants to be somewhere else. If you're here, you want to be there; if you've reached there, you want to be back here again. Landlubbers want to sail the seas; sailors long to farm the land.

Ditto Shmulik Gafni. A simple professor of Yiddish was he, yet he yearned to be active in world politics, to be at the center of events. And that meant only one thing. American politics and the American president. Then one day his wish came true.

It was only after dreaming for months that he was at presidential press conferences, sitting in the back, not saying a word, just happy to be there, hoping that in some good-luck magical way his innate wisdom would be discovered, that he decided to become a presidential advisor.

Shmulik Gafni got his first opportunity to engage with world history during the Cuban missile crisis. His advice to John F. Kennedy came from his experience in the Israel Defense Forces where he served as a major. Act, never react. While others advised JFK to tough it out, make strong pronouncements at first, verbal threats later. In other words, while the Russian missile ships were heading for Cuba, wage a war of words and warnings with press conferences and lots of blather.

Gafni advised simply: They're sending ships. We'll send ships. Move a flotilla of four battleships and two aircraft carriers loaded with jets and accompanying warships westward to meet the eastbound Russian missile ships. Gafni predicted — correctly — they'll turn around well before the US Navy draws near, much less fire a shot.

His career as a presidential advisor was made.

Addendum to Chapter 1

THE LAST YIDDISH SPEAKER IN MALTA

WHEN the last Yiddish speaker, Gimpl Getzl Gottlieb, died in Malta in 1849, his family was at his bedside. His last word was "sholem," and as many interpretations abound as to the subtext of that remark as there are commentaries on the Bible.

Gimpl Getzl might have said "sholem," goes one analysis, and simply meant "peace." But, says another, it could have been the first word of a two-word phrase, the second of which he was not able to utter because the first word was his last. If he meant to say "sholem aleichem," it could have been his last goodbye, "peace unto you." However, as the keepers of standard Yiddish will tell you, no one says goodbye in Yiddish by saying "sholem aleichem," a phrase that is used only for greeting. It's like saying "Hello" when leaving. Or, so goes another commentary, Gimpl Getzl might have departed with the name of the famous Yiddish humorist, Sholem Aleichem, on his lips, although that's a stretch, seeing as how the last Yiddish speaker in Malta died about ten years before the legendary Yiddish humorist was born. Or Gimpl Getzl may have wanted to refer to the famous Friday evening Sabbath song, "Sholem aleichem" (note the lower case "a" in this case) that Jews sing upon returning home after synagogue services. Since that lovely hymn bids welcome to the angels who accompany men home from shul, it was perhaps appropriate for Malta's last Yiddish speaker to say hello to these angels who would welcome Gimpl Getzl Gottlieb to their supernal abode. As is well known, up there, in the celebrated celestial stratosphere, it is always Sabbath, as the Talmud teaches, and everyone rests (in peace or not, depending on location, for location location is everything). Up there, everyone always rests, except God, angels, doctors, cops, firemen and other emergency personnel.

Another school of thought posits that it is not "sholem" that Gimpl Getzl Gottlieb, the last Yiddish speaker in Malta, uttered. They feel that those who heard "sholem" heard it wrong. My, my, a dozen graduate students could have built solid careers in academia (not to be confused with Macademia, where nutty professors go when they retire), analyzing the myriad possibilities of that last word he uttered, not to mention the reams of comments that could be created on the few dozen overheard, misheard, underheard words Gimpl Getzl said in Yiddish to the nurses in the hospital corridor before he was taken home, not one word of which he understood. What the revisionists substitute for "sholem" is "shalem" or "shaleym," meaning "pay up." These new critics assume Gimpl Getzl was addressing members of his family, telling them to pay the long overdue hospital bill. But "shaleym" also means "whole" or "perfect," and it could have referred to his sense of the wholeness of his life, a nice positive thought don't you think?

It should also be added that the phrase "last Yiddish speaker in Malta" means just what it says. Even his children could not speak the language, although they had a faint understanding of it, because linguistic assimilation works its same patterns everywhere. Just one question remains. How did this "last Yiddish speaker in Malta" get there? It's not one of the desideratum locales for East European migrating Jews. It so happens that in the 1830's Gimpl Getzl bought a ticket to the Land of Israel. He knew, from readings, what the topography and landscape of the country looked like. But after a series of long horse-and-buggy rides he was not brought to the Land of Israel. He was misled. Corrupt and mendacious travel agents, after a short boat ride, dropped him off in Valetta, Malta, telling him it was Haifa. When he told the local agents that no one seems to understand his Hebrew, they said it was his accent. And when Gimpl Getzl hired a horse and wagon and saw the area up in the hills around the port city, he could have sworn it was the outskirts of Jerusalem, for indeed the topography is about the same. But enough of this unsung and perhaps even apocryphal man.

Let us return to the main story.

2

LIFE IS GOOD, SUPER, BUT THERE'S ALWAYS A BUT

SOAKING in a warm tub at night, Gafni saw a reflection of himself in the curved chrome spigot, a nut-sized mini-Gafni. Immersed in the warm water, he mused: he loved life; not just life itself in all its minutiae, or *pishtchevkes*, a super Yiddish word he loved, but the very fact of living itself. As someone who knew first-hand what it meant to have life cut short, he became a one-man advocate for longevity. The longer he lived, the more he would be able to accomplish for others. He sighed with pity thinking of men like the Spanish composer, Joachin Arriaga, who died at 19; the Jewish artist, Moritzi Gottlieb, who died at 22; Aubrey Beardsley at 26; and Mozart, poor Mozart, at 36.

A Delightful Little Man

Once, when I was at the Café Mozart in Vienna, during a stopover on my way to Warsaw, I met a delightful little man. I had ordered an iced coffee with whip cream. Atop the *schlag* rested a thin wafer on which sat a rather large pecan. I was about to pluck the nut off the biscuit and bring it to my mouth when the pecan began to speak.

"Forgive me for startling you, but if I hadn't spoken you'd have swallowed me ... Yes, you're surprised. Who wouldn't be? People like me are found only in folk stories. But, alas, I'm quite real."

In that "alas" I heard a slight note of pain, a sad musicality that I would not hear from him again.

"And, by the way, your mouth is still open," he said.

I took a closer look at the tiny man. He was well-dressed, but a patina of the eighteenth century clung to him, just like the sugary coffee aroma clung to the air of the elegantly wood-panelled Café Mozart with its cut glass chandeliers and marble tables. His tailor, the man later told me, was an excellent miniaturist who lived down the block, a doll couturier actually.

Before I could say a word, the man, now standing on the wafer, gesturing, quite agile and expressive, continued:

"I don't socialize with many people, but when I saw your eyes, your laughing grey eyes, and the pleasant crinkles at the edges of your eyes, I said to myself, I want to speak to him, so I told the waiter to put me on the floating biscuit in your *eiskaffee*."

I didn't know what to say. I didn't believe I was seeing what my eyes beheld. A little *Gadiel ha-tinok*, a tiny Tom Thumb, of Jewish folklore.

"Pleased to make your acquaintance. I'm Professor Gafni. Shmulik Gafni."

I thought I heard him say, "And I am William Amadeus Mozart."

"William Amadeus Mozart?"

"No, no. I said Wolfgang Amadeus Mozart." Then his tiny eyes constricted as if anticipating some blow to come.

"Are you *the* Mozart?"

I heard a little hissing noise. The whip cream suddenly melted, the air sucked out of it. Evidently, my question made Mozart so hot under the collar that the *schlag* melted at once. Mozart still floated precariously on the little cracker which had lost its protective cushion. He bent forward, broke off a piece of the wafer and paddled to the rim of the cup. Then he nimbly vaulted onto it and there he sat comfortably, his feet dangling over the edge of the fine porcelain. At first I thought his face was red because of the exertion.

"The the the," he sputtered. "That's all I hear. The the the. The minute I say my name it's the the the," Mozart said sarcastically. "These the's are the words I hear most often. The the the. Not, how do you live? Not, what do you think? But the the the, as if by saying that they're subtly reducing my individuality. If by the the the you mean am I Wolfgang Amadeus Mozart ..."

(to be continued)

GAFNI lay back in the tub; the back of his hair got wet. He

closed his eyes, remembering how he would look at obituaries and biographical notices, zero in on the parentheses. He saw the years, was glad for those who had long lives — Chagall, 98; Irving Berlin, 103. In his field it was a *mitzva* to live as long as possible. Never in one lifetime could one man accomplish all the things with Yiddish that Gafni set out to do. That's why he went to Poland as often as he could to listen to the Yiddish of survivors. That was the official, the academic reason, the cover. In reality, he sought two things. One was to build up credit for residence there (yes, those two men on the bus had correctly intuited it); the other gnawed like a disease at his soul: to find his father's murderer.

Both were difficult missions, but it was hard for him to assess which one was more unattainable. For Gafni thought he knew what others didn't know, what the surviving Jews in Poland did not speak of. But Gafni sensed, he felt, he got the hints. And then, on a recent visit to Warsaw, the full truth of the phenomenon of present-day Polish Jews was revealed to him. As stated, Shmulik longed for life. It wasn't for himself that he wanted to live so long. It was for the destroyed Yiddish culture.

As a child, Shmulik wanted to build bridges when he grew up. Read it as a metaphor or symbol, if you wish. After the war, when Shmulik returned from a partisan unit as a young fighter, he quickly gave up the idea of becoming an engineer. They, the vast numbers of theys out there. The Germans and their helpers destroyed his people, and even after the war the Poles continued to kill Jews. But Shmulik Weingarten survived. How? Because his life was always a blend of magic and reality. For "magic" read miraculous events, like the time he survived a German raid that killed his fellow Jewish partisans when the Germans left him for dead. They had been tipped off by a Polish resistance group whose members were captured and then told the Germans about the Jewish group. But despite the six million Jewish dead, Shmulik felt that the Jews were a living organism, and one of the limbs of that organism was their language. He decided he would devote his life to that language and its culture. That they would never destroy. The beasts almost succeeded, but just like the world can't wipe away the Jews, so they cannot wipe out the Jews' language.

And there was another thing he loved to do as a child.

In shul on Sabbaths he liked to see the Torahs and their silver adornments, especially the big, ornate crowns. These are the same crowns, he thought, that a king wears, and little Shmulik had a fantasy of putting a crown on his own head and making himself the king. Once, on Simchas Torah, when the entire congregation was outside for *hakofes*, dancing with the Torahs, Shmulik went back into the now empty shul, took a crown and, heart beating, placed it on his head. It was too large for him and it slipped over his ears and touched his nose, covered his face. Still, he had enough time to say, I am the king. Of what he did not know. He couldn't think of a kingdom he would rule.

Despite what the Poles had done to his father and uncle more than a year after the war, he found a special affinity for the few decent Poles, who were honored by Israel for being Righteous Gentiles for selflessly saving Jews, and he loved the ones who radiated humaneness. Oh, if only the whole world were like those kindly Poles, like his elderly friend, the document forger, who had helped Jews during World War II, what a lovely place it would be for Jews and non-Jews alike.

In the tub he thought of Malina by the water in Nice, in that astounding bikini, and the helicopters and the storks diving lower to get a better look, and he felt a stirring within him and he didn't want to look at his loins lest his thoughts give further encouragement to his flesh.

Yes, it was good in the bath, good to be alive, glad he had grown up with Yiddish, as if it were another skin.

As much as he loved Yiddish can we say it surpassed Shmulik's love for Batsheva? No, that would be an exaggeration. Love of language is one thing; love of wife another. And, anyway, in the ripe field of metaphors, and a rich thick grassy field it is, as green as the emerald tea leaf fields of Nepal, a deep green the like of which you've never seen except on canvas, where ecstasy was walking barefoot in that lush green velvet meadow, the metaphors of love exist only in love for man and woman, hence an erotic love, a pull as powerful as lust, for strong as death is love. But if there is such a thing as spiritual or intellectual love, why then that's what Gafni had for Yiddish. But maybe there was something physical here too. Like a girl he had once known who said she loved Jersusalem so much she could press it to her heart and embrace it, he too could have embraced not only all of Yiddish, but each of the letters, one by one. Like the great Hasidic storyteller and leader, Nachman of Bratslav, in the novel *The Man Who Thought He Was Messiah*, who loved the Hebrew alphabet, the unique architecture of each letter.

With six million Jews dying martyrs' deaths, crying their last cries in Yiddish for help that never came, Yiddish too had become a *loshn koydesh*, a holy tongue, like Hebrew. And Yiddish itself was martyred, the verbal lifestuff of a thousand-year-old civilization, it too was murdered. Yiddish went up in smoke along with its speakers and was buried in unmarked graves. The Holocaust was more than the death of a people, Gafni felt. It was murder in four, five, even six dimensions: it was also songs and jokes, word plays, folk expressions, foods, recipes, games and ditties, insults, proverbs, riddles, lullabies, gestures, future works of art and literature, inventions, cures. It's not for nothing the Talmud says: he who murders one man murders an entire world. And he who saves one man saves an entire world. That's what the murderers did, they murdered an entire world, worlds, a civilization that was — and would have been. And that's why Gafni felt he had to do dozens of tasks. One man against the world. That's why he was put on this earth, that's why his life was spared. He was Don Quixote and he would take on the windmills. All of them.

Now it was time to add more hot water to the tub. He looked at his tiny image on the chrome spigot, smiled as he thought of tiny Mozart, they'd make a nice twosome sitting on a wafer, and used his toes to start the flow. Just then, seemingly out of the wall, three little Hebrew letters materialized and hung in the air. Two *yuds* and one *daled.* They spelled the word Yid, which meant Jew. Or they could be the first three letters of the word Yiddish. Gafni stared, blinked. The letters remained hanging in the air. He stretched out his hands to grasp them. But they slipped away and vanished as eerily as they had come.

ONE morning in Warsaw, when Shmulik was about six or seven, a slight boy, he looked like five, wearing a black yarmulke, he went off by himself to *cheder*, to school, as he did every day. On his way to the cheder in the synagogue he had to pass a church. As he passed the gate a big Pole bounded out of the church and grabbed Shmulik. With one smack of his big hand he sent Shmulik tumbling to the ground.

"You dirty little zhid," he shouted as he beat him. "Why don't you take your hat off when you pass our church? You dirty little Jew."

Seeing Shmulik's yarmulke, the man kicked it further away, then walked back into the church. A man and a woman came out of the church but did nothing to help the sobbing Shmulik, who stood, picked up his yarmulke, and ran to the *cheder*. His head and shoulders hurt. There were other people, non-Jews, on the street. But no one came to help him. Even as a little boy he knew that the Christians taught that their religion was a religion of love. Where was the love? he wondered. And why should a big man hit a little boy? And why didn't people on the street who witnessed what had happened come to help a little boy? And why doesn't anyone make a Christian man take off his hat when he passes a synagogue?

Gafni shook his head. Why was he pitying himself when he should sympathize with someone closer to home? Because of her diabetes, Batsheva, poor soul, could no longer do housework. A full-time helper was with her most of the day.

In bed, his wife was half asleep, but he snuggled into her. To express his love for her, he pressed his chest into her back, his legs molding into hers as if they were one body just barely divided into two. Convex shape to concave, concave to convex, curve in to curve out, but damn that evil inclination, that negative impulse, that insinuated himself (or it is herself, a mute, invisible she-demon Lilith?) into Gafni, and as the curves of his and Batsheva's flesh were touching from shoulders to toes, Malina intruded.

3

WHAT CAN BE DONE ABOUT WRITER'S BLOCK?

MALINA was coming. Malina was coming. Malina was coming for a lesson, continuing with the Hebrew alphabet. When she came, he pulled a chair over to his desk for her and traced with his fingers the ever-so-slight but crucial difference between the shape of a *resh* and a *daled*. As his fingers moved over one letter and then another as if they were Braille, the shape of the entire Hebrew alphabet flashed before his eyes, in script and in print, all graceful, beautifully sculpted, every single letter a work of art, dancing while standing still. And as Gafni admired their form, he couldn't help thinking of another form that was also a work of art.

"Look, look, do you see the tiny difference?" He gazed at her face.

"I do," she said musically. And that music made him uncomfortable, gave him a vague feeling of loss, of deeds not accomplished.

"Remember I told you in Nice you look so familiar. Are you sure we haven't met before?"

"Pretty sure. Or perhaps we met in another life," Malina said. "I have a strong belief in mysticism, in the occult, you know."

"Because every time I see you, I also see the outline of your face, as if in a little mirror in the corner of my eye, like a photographic imprint. I don't know if it's the cut of your face or the bone structure — it's sort of indeterminate, like a taste you try to recall and can't seem to succeed."

Malina shrugged. "It's a Polish face, a common face. What can I do?"

She said it so helplessly he wanted to, he resisted the temptation, to hold her face with both his hands and tell her, No, no, no. Not common at all.

"It's not a common face at all," he said softly. "In fact, it's a very unusual one and maybe that's why I remember it so well and see you in double as it were."

You know, he told Malina in his thoughts, our conversations are like a passacaglia — one melody is the main theme, what we usually talk about, language and literature, and the inner workings of Yiddish; while the other melody is like a Bach ground bass that fuses imperceptibly with the main theme and adds dimension, tension and harmonic beauty. But in our conversation, only one of the melodies is heard, the one each one of us utters in a kind of bird-like dialogue; but the other, unlike in Baroque music, dare not be sounded out. It's this other melody, which is the beautiful one, the one I'm not singing to you. But in my thoughts these words are being said, while the more banal ones about Yiddish and language and linguistics are being spoken as a coverup, a subterfuge, a camouflage to the real melody.

Shmulik was about to tell Malina the words he really wanted to say but was cloaking them in the light banter of the profession that bound them. He looked at her attending his remarks about the shape of the letters *resh* and *daled,* saw the slight frown, three tiny vertical lines above the bridge of her nose coming together like the Hebrew letter *shin* and didn't say what he wanted to say.

What Gafni wanted to say was, How come we never say what we want to say? To our wives we always say what we want to say, because to them we don't hold back, whether praise or criticism. But to others the mask of politesse wins out and we sculpt the words to either hold back truth or to avoid giving offense. What I want to say, Malina, and what I'm not saying, is that you are one of the most beautiful girls I've ever seen, maybe not meaning it wholeheartedly because her lips were too thin and he loved luscious, fuller lips, but if he was already going beyond the bounds of shyness, he might as well tell her something that would make her feel good. Not only are you beautiful but there is an easy flow of talk between us, it seems like I've known you for much longer than I have, as if our conversations began a long time ago and we're now just resuming them, old friends meeting again as if time hasn't passed between us. So the truth of the matter is that only in thoughts does one tell the truth, for the truth is, Malina, I can't keep my eyes off your astounding chest, why if there was a Polish edition of *Playboy* you could certainly be a centerfold candidate, that is if that centerfold could accommodate your figure.

As Malina pressed closer to see the tiny difference between *resh* and *daled* one of her beautifully sculpted big breasts grazed his right elbow, whether on purpose or accidentally, he could not tell. But he did not move his hand and she did not remove the source of her pressure, whether consciously or abstractedly, because she was so involved in trying to distinguish between the subtle curvature of the printed *resh* and the straight horizontal ligature atop the vertical of the *daled.*

Gafni took a slow, deep breath, careful not to move. The palpitations of his heart, were they fibrillations or just excitement?

Who can explain his attraction to her, beside the physical one of course? Could it be a love-hate relationship? Maybe. He knew what the Poles were like. What they had done in Kielce to his father, uncle and other Jewish survivors of death camps in July 1946, more than one year after the war ended.

But sexual allure subsumes both emotional loyalty and scholarly objectivity. Or, put another way, the bright, seductive light of sexual allure drives emotional loyalty and scholarly objectivity into an umber corner. We'll try once more: when sexual allure enters, it scatters emotional loyalty and scholarly objectivity to the winds like seeds of a blown-upon dandelion.*

Sometimes, in the high of a good mood, Gafni thought life was just all opera, with violins in the background and a beam of bright light on him as he takes Malina in his arms while his wife smilingly assents in this operatic world of *The Merry Widow* where norms are suspended and all is possible until the applause brings down your dream.

Suddenly, Malina looked into his eyes and said;

"How come your pupils are so big?"

"Because I teach graduate students," Shmulik said and laughed, hoping she would laugh too. But she did not.

As his own broad smile vanished, he said, "That's funny, Malina, how come you're not laughing?"

She said she didn't get it, and he wondered why, if her English was so much better than his. Only when he explained that in English pupils are both in the eyes and in the classroom (she was used to the word "student"), did she roll with laughter, removing the pleasant pressure from his elbow.

Then Malina had to leave and there was a vacuum in his office, like an insatiable hunger. Oh, he could have written an entire excursus on temptation, if only his creative thoughts would not have been blocked lately. From his office window he could see her waiting for her bus. He couldn't move ahead with anything except his Warsaw streets project which, he was the first to admit (to himself, of course) was not scholarship but memoir in the guise of scholarship, and as a veteran academic, he knew quite well how to palm off anything, even the purchase of a *beigele*, as scholarship.

DESPITE his fame, his enormous bibliography, the sad fact was that Shmulik Gafni had no more ideas. He had run out of intellectual steam. All along he had had enough steam to propel ten locomotives, but now poor Shmulik had scholar's block, popularly known as sb, not even enough energy to run a toy electric train. Why a block?

---

*whose leaves, boiled, Sicilian friends tells me, make an excellent soup.

Could it be that his attention was divided, maybe torn is a better word, between his sick wife and a graduate student, erstwhile friend and colleague who beckoned him in his dreams? That could give anyone a block. And so he was reduced, alas, to listing the streets of his native Warsaw, block (and let psychologists and other pseudo-masters of the soul's complexities judge if the choice of one block was intended as a charm to unblock the other block) by block, the long-gone Jewish streets, first destroyed by the Germans, later bulldozed by the Poles, streets so Jewish even their Polish names rang Jewish for the Jews and maybe for the gentiles too, so Jewish the Yiddish shop signs loomed larger in his memory than the shops themselves, as if in some surrealist painting, as if his brain were one enormous total recall camera that saw those black-and-white Hebrew-lettered Yiddish signs, entire streets made of so many Hebrew letters a child could have learned to read just from the signs, since every letter of the *alef-beys* flew through the air. Life was so Jewish that even the walls spoke Yiddish, a memorable remark made by his martyred uncle Henekh Dusawicki (pronounced Dusavitsky), olev ha-sholem: *"Dos leben is geven azoy Yiddish az afileh di vent hobn geret Yiddish."* Rest in peace, dear murdered Uncle Henekh and Aunt Regina and cousins Idek and Shlomo, whatever rest your ashes may have. So Jewish that even now, some fifty years after he had last seen his Jewish Warsaw, Gafni could close his eyes and still smell the foods offered by the street vendors, the hot potato and kasha knishes with their savory smells filling the air, and garlic-spiced pickles from an old oaken barrel sold by women with babushkas over their hair, and freshly baked bagels peddled by a man carrying a long stick on which the crisp, slightly salted bagels slid and a deep pocket apron filled with onion *pletzlekh* — all this still tickled his nostrils and brought saliva to his mouth. He could put his hands into his pocket to withdraw a few zloty to buy the goodies, but by the time his hand emerged they were all gone in a mist.

Gafni interviewed old people from Warsaw who remembered the streets and lanes and alleys, the stores and peddlers, and slowly Shmulik re-assembled these memories onto a map. He knew quite well that the longer the name of a project the thinner its intellectual concept, the more fragile its scholarly underpinning. So he wasn't too proud of the longest title for an academic study he'd ever seen: "Reconstructing Jewish Warsaw: a Study of the Jewish Quarter, its Streets, Alleys, Lanes, Shops and Street Vendors, According to Personal Memories, Letters, Memoirs, Fiction, Archival and Personal Photographs and Interviews with Scores of Former Residents."

Still, any re-creation of Jewish Warsaw was a kind of resurrection — and resurrection was a mitzva, a good deed, a moral obligation.

And mitzva was more important than scholarship any day, ran Gafni's beneficent thinking, as he spread his working map before him on his large desk. He moved the chair on which Malina had just sat, the wood still warm, to the other side of the room. He had different colored pins — color-coded according to trades — dotting his map. He relied on memory, as his mile-long title indicated, and on books and people. Gafni was always on the lookout for informants. He traveled all over Israel. Even talking to them was a mitzva. Invariably, during the reminiscence, tears would well up in the person's eyes, and Shmulik too was often in tears himself, still mourning his murdered family, his destroyed Varshe, the Yiddish for Warsaw.

How many survivors had he freed of depression with the flow of their memories! Even if they contradicted each other — one said that on the southwest corner of Malawaska and Mila there had been a tailor shop, the other swore it was a tinsmith — no matter. A third, a fourth, would resolve the difficulty, stating that for a few years a tailor had been there but then he moved to Lodz and a tinsmith came. For real contradictions majority ruled, was Gafni's opinion, just like in the Talmud. He glanced out the window again. It was a bright, sunny day. Noontime; shadows hardly visible. Students crisscrossed the paths, their shadows close as paper clips. Was that Malina walking toward the building? Had she forgotten something? He glanced quickly around the office. Heart racing, he stood for a closer look. He opened the door so she wouldn't have to knock. He waited, three, four, five minutes. It wasn't her I saw, he concluded, and sat down. And he inhaled the scent of her departed presence for which surely she would not return.

GAFNI picked up a postcard from one of his informants. A word had to be clarified. As he opened one of his old dictionaries and the pages lay flat, he felt as if a flower were spreading its petals especially for him. Each word was a world unto itself and, like stars in a solar system, inextricably linked. Yes, he loved words. That phrase would make a nice epitaph, he thought, but he was in no hurry to make use of it.

Again Malina came to mind, even when she wasn't there, like music heard but not seen. While planning his project he didn't want to think of Malina, of her nearly perfect body, tried to block her from his mind so he could think of other blocks, tried not to recall that moment of glory as she took off her terry cloth tunic in Nice a year ago and made the sudden transformation from scholar to bathing beauty, distracting helicopters and storks carrying Eskimo babies on their way to nest in the Atlas mountains in Morocco.

Yes, Gafni thought, he was human too, and a great-grandfather. For who says that one's human-ness and one's desires decrease or disappear with age? Didn't Father Abraham have children when he was one hundred? On the contrary, the soul's desire gets stronger, richer, more condensed. When young, desires are spread all over the body. As man grows older, the desires specialize, like doctors, splitting into two regions. There they sizzle like switches about to be turned on: in the mind, the driver's seat of all desire, and the gonads, its faithful engine.

Back to work. Once he undertook a project, he devoted all his energy to it. In his persistence Shmulik was like his older colleague, Ezra Shultish, who for many years had taught modern Hebrew literature at the Manhattan Hebrew Teachers College. Again Shultish. Why Shultish kept popping into his head when he hadn't seen the old American Hebrew professor in a couple of years Gafni could not fathom. Why he didn't think of shoeleather, Abyssinians or roast goose was another thing he didn't know. Although Gafni had a reputation for knowing everything, he was modest enough to know there was plenty he didn't know — but he didn't shout this from the rooftops. Rather, he often said, and people believed him, that there were only three things he didn't know: first and foremost, how they made the crisp crust of potato knishes; second, if there was a God; third, the etymology of the Yiddish word *davenen*, to pray, which had eluded Yiddishists for centuries. People with a good sense of humor understood the self-mocking absurdity of the remark and its odd admixture of the serious and ludicrous; fools just nodded.

So then, why Shultish? The thought went through the bramble bush of the mind. First, Yiddish. Logical. What else would he think about? The great Hebrew writer Agnon. Although Agnon wrote in Hebrew, Gafni knew that lurking behind the Nobel Laureate's Hebrew was Yiddish. It was Gafni who had tossed off the famous remark which the wily Agnon later muttered was first said by him: "Although Agnon writes in Hebrew, he thinks in Yiddish." And this brought to mind Ezra Shultish's book on Agnon's style and diction. So there it went, from Yiddish to Shultish.

Gafni wasn't going to break his head analyzing why he thought of Shultish. Like he wasn't going to analyze why one wakes up in the morning and there's a hunger somewhere for something you can't put your finger on. Or why he didn't think of Malina, who he could have sworn was walking across the campus with that provocative hipswaying stride that made heads turn, men's and women's. Not a Jewish walk, he judged. Jewish girls didn't have walks, or bodies, like that, yes, that hunger you can't put your finger, much less a hand, on.

Gafni didn't want to admit it, but sometimes he felt like the old Hebraist. Not that he looked like Ezra Shultish at all. Gafni was about 5'8" and broadfaced; Shultish was about 5'4," maybe 5'5," on the slim side, a small oval face. Shultish was balding, his hair — whose wouldn't at eighty? if he was eighty; no one was sure — what little he had left, had turned white. Gafni's was steel grey. Shultish had a tentative, sometimes mocking smile, that clever, witty man, while Gafni's was powerful, energetic. That smile was his secret. A smile that came from deep within him. And all his teeth were there, healthy, solid like a colt's. He wasn't sure about Shultish's. Gafni's age was seventy but the vigor in him and the beauty of his smile said fifty.

Still. But. Nevertheless. He did sometimes feel like Ezra Shultish. The first time Gafni felt like this it was a shock to him. My God, the parallels, Shultish, a linguist, a writer, a scholar, a professor, a married man. In Agnon's novel, *Ha-na'ara ha-temanit, The Yemenite Girl,* the hero, modeled on Ezra Shultish and called Zera Tishler, fell in love with, or at least was infatuated by, a Yemenite girl. If someone would write a novel about Gafni, linguist, writer, scholar, professor at the University of Israel, a married man who was infatuated, allured, by a young Polish woman, the parallel would be complete. Did Shultish have any secrets like his? Was he too an advisor to presidents? In the Agnon novel, the demure, shy, withdrawn Tishler loved to dance in private to the stirring dance music of Louis Moreau Gottschalk, that half-Creole, half-Jewish American composer. He could just see Tishler begin to flail his arms, feel the itch of the music in his legs, and then take off to the seductive rythms of the Cakewalk or strut to the strains of Mozart's Turkish March.

A Delightful Little Man (continued)

"If by the the you mean am I Wolfgang Mozart, then I am the the, for that is what I am called. If by the the you mean am I the famous 18th century composer — to that I can only give out a little laugh. There is such a thing as mortality you know. For life, but not for names. I am the 16th in line from my famous forebear. And music still runs in our blood — and our soul." He sang the last few words to the tune of *Exultate Jubilate.*

I named the composition he was quoting. Mozart was impressed.

I wanted to ask him if he played an instrument, then I bit my tongue — how could such a person his size play anything? But, then again, since everything on him was in such fine proportion, maybe still …

"Do you play an instrument?" I asked. I didn't want to sound tentative or condescending, but I guess it was.

"Yes, viola and cello. But it is getting more and more difficult to find violin makers to fashion in mini-miniature a viola or a cello that will resonate. But I found one. Yes, indeed, I found one."

"May I hear you play?"

"Yes, with pleasure — but not now. My instruments are at home. Some day. Next time I see you."

"But I don't come to Vienna often. Who knows? I may not come again."

"Where do you live?"

"Jerusalem. I teach Yiddish at the University of Israel."

"I do travel on occasion. Perhaps I will come to Jerusalem."

"You will be most welcome. At my home. Just tell me what arrangements must be made, what your needs are."

"Next time I see you I will play for you. That is a promise. And a Mozart, unlike Archbishop Colloredo or Prince Esterhazy, a Mozart keeps his word."

(to be continued)

Yes, Gafni had to admit, there were parallels between him and Ezra Shultish.

But —
how
who
when
where
and why
would someone write about him, if that would-be author didn't know Gafni's secret thoughts, the hidden vibrations of his mind, the dreams and wishes he had in those butterfly-colored, fleeting moments before he drifted off to sleep?

Wait! The parallels continued. He remembered how Batsheva had gone to Tel Aviv to tend to her sick, widowed sister, Nechama, just as Zera Tishler's wife (based on Mrs. Shultish) had done in Agnon's masterwork, *The Yemenite Girl*. And then, recalling that Batsheva, like Mrs. Tishler, fell ill herself, a frisson of de ja vu went through Gafni, its tingle running down his back from the nape of his neck. Sometimes Shmulik felt there was a deviltry in the air with Shultish, casting a spell, throwing an invisible little net over Gafni that created these uncanny parallels. The *ayin ha-ra*, pronounced *ayin ho-reh* in Yiddish. The evil eye, which to ward off one had to spit — "tfu tfu tfu" — three times. Maybe that thrice "tfu" (or "poo poo poo" if you use Brooklyn or Bronx pronunciation [less fricative, less spittlelishly plosive]) is what saved him when Shultish almost sabotaged a famous feud, which you have a way to go to read about (and can even skip when you get to it).

AFTERCHAPTER 3

Shmulik Gafni has already had experience advising one three-initial president, as we (that is, you and I) already know: JFK. Eisenhower didn't have the privilege of a three-letter initial, for who would say DDE, which sounded more like an insect spray than the initials for Dwight David Eisenhower. But at least he still had a three-letter monicker: Ike. (A later president, Bill Clinton, also had a monicker.) Truman's HST had a brief fling in press headlines, but it couldn't work because of the overpowering FDR, which immediately conjured up the face and personality of the war-time president. The only other president to earn his three varsity letters was LBJ, with whom Gafni had a fruitful relationship.

For Johnson Gafni wrote speeches, even though he can't write English. Cognizant of Johnson's Vietnam problem, Gafni suggested an American attack on Malta to divert attention. Malta, traditionally pro-Arab, provoked no tears in Gafni, but he did recall its last Yiddish speaker. (See Addendum to Chapter 1.) Gafni's suggestion was rejected — but years later, when Gafni had amassed lots of foreign affairs experience, it was used by another president who had no foreign affairs but plenty of domestic ones and who diverted himself from his diversion. You know who I mean, the one with the non-three-letter monicker, who to divert attention didn't bomb Malta but another small country in the region.

4

HE LOVES BOOKS SO MUCH HE CAN'T TEAR
HIMSELF AWAY FROM THEM

SHMULIK Gafni had lots of talents. One was displayed at the University of Israel library.

Please note that he loved books. He loved the thrum of pages as he riffed through them, feeling, especially in old books, the velvety texture of page edges on his fingers. So much genius compressed into such a tiny format. Where else can you have someone talking to you from two-thousand, three-thousand years ago?

Gafni read books from cover to cover, just like he stayed to the end of a film to read every last credit. In indices, he couldn't help looking for his name, and when he found it, his estimation of both the book and its sagacious and generous author rose. Even his own books fascinated him. Looking at three or four copies of one of his books made him marvel. He couldn't believe that one was like the other. He knew books were like his daughters, identical twins, replicated; but yet each should have a personality of its own. He thought of writing a novel that would have a different ending according to geographic locale. In English translation it would have one ending east of the Mississippi and another west of.

His father, Yosef, loved books too. He would spend his last zloty on a book and his son caught the fever, holding a newly acquired book in his hand as if it were a newborn baby. It was Jews after all who, one thousand years ago in the famous Yom Kippur prayer, created the image of the book that reads itself, an image more suitable for magic realism than liturgy. Not only did the Jews read books, but the very books they read, when the eyes that read them weren't looking, exchanged culture by reading themselves.

But no matter how much he played with a book, it was what it was, and other copies of it were exactly the same. Like Socrates said: You can't converse with a book. It says only what it says, over and over, like a broken record. Like the tape of the Yemenite girl in Agnon's aforementioned masterpiece, *Ha-na'ara ha-temanit,* * who keeps repeating the only lines she knows, again and again.

---

*English version, *The Yemenite Girl,* by a novice translator, C. Urtl Eviant, of whom the reviewer in the *Times Literary Supplement* said: "The translator, a recent refugee

Shmulik Gafni tried hard to penetrate the mystery of a book but could never succeed.

Gafni could understand the genius of writing. But music? That he couldn't fathom. Music had only seven notes and five half-notes, and yet that sufficed for thousands of melodies. How did the composers do it? They were the supreme geniuses of this world, creating an endless vocabulary with a miniaturized alphabet. He began humming the first movement of the Mozart Piano Concerto #22 and let his thoughts flow with the music, until they became wordless and more like music. Words are miracles; music makes them.

A Delightful Little Man (continued)

"And Herr Mozart," I asked him, "do you also compose?"

"Of course. Composition is in our blood. But it is still something I cannot understand. How, in the *Requiem*, for instance, my beloved ancestor had all this music in his head, hundreds of voices, a full orchestra, four soloists, all working together, and harmonically and contrapuntally against each other. To listen to it is hard enough, divine stress, but to have created it, that's a miracle of God."

"So you have composed?" I asked again.

"Yes, but given my size, I am limited. Do you expect me, like Gulliver among the Brobdignags, to jump from key to key on a piano, as I compose my tunes? No no, do not answer. I like rhetorical questions. But, you might say, I compose on the viola or the cello, But then there's the problem of notation, which for me is difficult too. My size limits me. Physicality influences esthetics and so by nature I am a minimalist.

"If not for music," he continued, "I could not live. To quote the Psalms, 'It restoreth the soul.'"

"I too believe in the magical, restorative power of music," I said. "I am sure my wife, Batsheva, has survived with her illness as long as she has because of music. Especially Mozart."

The little man nodded.

---

from the Isle of Man, of mixed Icelandic and Alsatian ancestory, brings eclectic, foreign-tinged English to the translation, but yet he was able to miraculously negotiate his way through Agnon's densely Jewish language,"

"Would you like sit on my hand? This is not a rhetorical question."

We both laughed.

I stretched my hand out to the rim of the cup and he jumped into my palm.

"I heard you speaking Yiddish to someone as you came in," Mozart said.

"Yes, a colleague. He had to go off to an appointment. Why, do you know Yiddish?"

"Well, I can make it out from the German ... Will you please call the waiter? I have to leave for a few minutes."

I called the waiter who, understanding the signal by the tiny figure, lifted Mozart to his ear and then brought him to the back of the café. The waiter returned to clear the table.

"Has Herr Mozart been telling you all kinds of tales?"

"Indeed he has."

The waiter raised his chin and gave a conspiratorial smile.

"Don't believe half the things he says. Then I would discount by half the other half as well ... Herr Mozart is a notorious liar ... "

"How does he make a living?"

The waiter closed his eyes for a moment and lifted his forefinger.

(to be continued)

THIS was Gafni's talent: his autographing skill. Every man has his secret and this — don't breathe a word of it! — was his.

BEFORE Gafni actually signed a book, he rehearsed in his mind the strokes of the letters, the shape and angle of the ligatures, with such verisimilitude that he clearly saw the signature materializing as if of its own accord in a perfectly calligraphed script. His first signing was done in the third floor stacks of the University of Israel's vast library, where he went when he was bored — and lately, what with his sb (scholar's block, remember?), he was bored more and more often. Ah, that virgin-breaking debut. There's nothing like the first time of anything (except for the second, third and fourth times), and he felt a secret little thrill that paralleled an erotic impulse.

For a book by the mid-19th century English travel writer, Donald

Carey Murchison, he used the long, slanted lines he recalled seeing in copies of 1840's letters. And while inditing the author's name Gafni sensed not only a kinship with the man but felt he had become for a moment the writer himself, transported back to 1848, when Murchison's *Travels in the Fertile Crescent*** with its depiction of the rare, mind-altering, golden hamsin in the Sinai desert, was published. At the same time, Gafni also imagined the joy the next reader would have at opening the book and seeing the author's autograph on the title page.

At first Gafni passed autographing off as an amusing little pastime, his secret compact between himself and the books. Then he realized that his little secret talent might be an obsession. He shrugged. Even gave a little smile as he remembered Juvenal's wry remark: *"instane cacoethes scribendi"* — an incurable itch for writing, and extended it by adding: "a signature in other people's books." If it was an obsession it could not be helped. (You have to get help, he heard someone advising him. He gets help. Goes to a psychiatrist. Sits in his book-laden study. The doctor excuses himself to go to the bathroom. Gafni quickly takes pen, dips it into his ink bottle, plucks a volume of Freud from the psychiatrist's bookshelf and signs it … No, he doesn't need help, and the doctor doesn't need any more autographed books.)

Over a period of months he autographed scores of books, giving hundreds of readers the surprise and special delight of holding in their hands a book that the author himself had once held and signed. Gafni smiled as he read the headline:

THE UNIVERSITY OF ISRAEL'S LIBRARY — THE ONLY LIBRARY IN THE WORLD WHERE EVERY BOOK HAS BEEN PERSONALLY SIGNED BY ITS AUTHOR

As a professor Gafni had access to the library's normally closed stacks. Free to wander in the maze of books, he would pluck out Darwin's *Origin of Species* and, with his practiced mid-nineteenth century scrawl, inscribe the book with a flourish, "To my dear friend Wilkins, Yours Chas. Darwin." At first he favored Sholom Aleichem volumes and was proud of his ability to sign the humorist's name exactly as Sholom Aleichem himself had done, joining one letter to another until Sholom Aleichem was one calligraphic entity surrounded by his signature (no pun intended; or maybe yes) oval

---

* Very few copies of this rare, mid-19th century book, privately printed in London, are extant. However, extensive passages appear in the opening pages of the novel, *Passion in the Desert.*

enclosure. Don't think that knowledge wasn't needed for all this ersatz signing. He had to be professional; he had to know when writers died so as not to autograph a posthumous book.

But lately it wasn't all joy. The last few times he wrote someone else's name, Gafni felt his soul dividing in two. One said: Stop this, enough! You're a grown man, a professor, shame on you! And for a moment he felt abashed, like when his mother caught him slipping a cookie into his pocket when he was seven.

"Did you take a cookie?" his mother asked.

"No."

"You're lying, Shmulik. It's not nice to lie. You're already in the second grade. Didn't they teach you about lying?"

"No. Lying is a third grade subject."

Then came the other part of his soul, which said: Just one more, just one more book and then I'll stop.

Once Gafni walked into the stacks, began browsing around the foreign language section and sensed a feminine presence, a perfume, a scent, a fragrance of hair, a whiff of cosmetics, the smell of a woman's body. Malina? Could she have come here looking for him? Suddenly, a shock of panic, a red wave, like a blush, beginning with his face and descending to his knees, ran through him. My God, what if Malina learned of this? Signing library books! He stopped, turned left and right. No one. Only his footfalls echoed on the empty floor.

But the inevitable showdown had to come and it prompted Gafni to swear — never again.

How did it come? As usual, a total surprise.

"Professor Gafni!" came the disembodied voice. "What are you doing here?"

Stunned and shaken that he was called by name, frightened, flustered and nervous, he actually felt the blood rushing from his face. In the perfect stillness of the library (the damned interloper must have worn sneakers), Gafni heard only, What are you doing? His heart beat wildly. His cheeks, first white, now turned crimson. The blood rose from his feet to his head, defying gravity. Again and again he heard, "What are you doing?" His legs felt wobbly. For a moment he went deaf; his vision faded. He was about to press the button on the *Chaver* monitor but decided against it. But even in misfortune there is occasional good fortune. Fortunately, the man had not come up the same aisle, but peeked at Gafni over the rim of books at eye level from another aisle just as Gafni was putting the last swirl of letters on the title page of a first edition of the classic Italian memoir of the Duke of Mantua, Guido Veneziano-Tedesco's *Diary of an Adulterous Man* (1892).

Gafni searched for the face, saw only the two eyes of his unknown interlocutor. The man, for he was sure it was a man's voice, unless it was a woman who had been smoking for decades, the man couldn't see Gafni's pen or the Italian book he had in his hands, or the little bottle of ink on the edge of the shelf, for all were out of sight. Oh my God, he thought, what if it's Malina disguising her voice.

"I'm taking notes," Gafni explained with a tremor in the vowels. He dropped his pen. The book he had just autographed slid with a slight bump off the shelf. A forward thrust of Gafni's belly blocked the book's descent. Holding the memoir in one hand, Gafni bent to pick up his pen with the other, saw a man's garb in a quick blur through the empty spaces between the shelves: a white shirt, loosely knotted blue polka dot tie, blue jacket and matching trousers. Thank God, at least it's not Malina.

The two men still stood on opposite sides of the stack, their view of each other blocked stacks of books, most of them not by Gafni.

Who could it be? Gafni wondered. It could only be a faculty member, a graduate student or a visiting scholar, for no one else was allowed up here. Oh, no! Could it be his colleague, Chaim Shimen Meichl-Rukzak? That's all he needed was to have the man everyone considered his bitterest rival catch him signing books. Wait. Vaguely familiar was the voice. The man's Hebrew had a slight patina of Polish — in other words, an accent like his. But as Gafni repeated the man's question in his mind a bit of American drizzled in between the vowels. Well, at least it wasn't Meichl-Rukzak, unless he was purposely changing his accent. Again Gafni heard the echo of "What are you doing?," an echo curiously louder than its original voice. The fright still pulsed in Gafni. His chest and throat still constricted, the feeling a wildebeest must have, he imagined, just before the lion snaps his jaw into its jugular vein.

Suppose the man had seen me writing in the book? Just watched from afar, hands folded over his chest, an ironical smile on his lips, while I was committing the worst sin a lover of books could do? How quickly the word would be spread. A man of the book defacing books. His career would be ruined. Why did that sneak have to come now and interrupt this intimate moment, like someone telephoning, or knocking on the door, or worse, barging in during intercourse with one's own or someone else's wife?

"Are you all right? I don't hear you speaking, Professor Gafni."

Now Gafni realized that it was an older man speaking to him.

"I'm fine. You startled me. There's rarely anyone up here in this part of the third floor."

"Professor Gafni," the man sounded apologetic. "I sense you still don't know who is talking to you. And in any case, what kind of conversation is this when two people throw words like arrows above and below book shelves and hear, alas, only orphaned voices without seeing the esteemed visage of one's interlocutor?"

Those Biblical cadences, that elegant, slightly bookish Hebrew of which the early 20th century lexicographer, Eliezer Ben-Yehuda, would have been so proud! Who was it? So familiar. It definitely wasn't Meichl-Rukzak. The man's name was on the tip of Gafni's tongue. At any moment he could say … that it was …

"Shall I part the books here … " the man continued, "like Moses did the sea and then you'll see me, or shall I rather come … "

Now his voice trailed off. The man was obviously walking around the stack and, no longer thinking of repeating Moses's miracle, approaching Gafni.

" … and introduce myself as your old acquaintance … "

5

STILL IN THE STACKS WITH GUESS WHO

" … AND introduce myself as your old acquaintance … "

Now he revealed himself, the man behind the stack, a little smile of triumph on his lips, melding voice and person, now slipping the glove of a recognizable being onto the voice. Oh, the dramatic epiphany of his appearance!

"Ezra Shultish!" they both said at the same time.

"Amazing! And I was just thinking of you the other day. For a moment I thought it was Professor Meichl-Rukzak, but then I remembered, what does he have to do with research? And then I had a hunch it was you, given the unique turn of phrases. Are you doing Slavic research?" Gafni said quickly, seizing the initiative before Shultish questioned him again.

Shultish shook hands vigorously with Gafni.

"I'm looking for some possible early Polish antecedents to one of Agnon's stories set in Poland."

"How wonderful that after all these years you're still devoted to Agnon," Gafni said happily, delighted that the focus had shifted away from him. What he really wanted to say was: What? After all these years still on Agnon? How about something new? But at the last minute Gafni toned down his acerbity. "And what in general brings you to Israel?"

"Should I not reverse the question and say: What doesn't bring me to Israel? The Land draws one to come to the Land, more by the power of the Land than by one's own will."

"Well said, Shultish, well said, in your own inimitable manner, even if you've borrowed, I'm sure unwittingly, a line from one of Agnon's classic stories, stories that you know far better than I."

"I beg your pardon, Professor Gafni, the lines I just said may sound like Agnon, and I thank you for the backhanded compliment, but they are, I assure you, of my own formulation."

"Well, then, a thousand pardons, Professor Shultish, it's just that I was overwhelmed by the beauty of the lines. In any case, spoken like a true Zionist who lives in America. Yes, it's true, a Jew needs no reason to visit Israel."

Gafni saw that Shultish was about to speak, to rebut his Zionist-in-America jibe, but he held back.

For a while they didn't say anything to each other. Had he insulted Shultish with that double-pronged assault — the quote from Agnon and the Zionist jab?

To break the silence, Gafni said:

"So what is new, dear Shultish, since I last saw you?"

Gafni looked at the shelf. His heart leaped. A nervous tremor went through him. Oh, my God! That little bottle of ink. How to make it vanish? Don't look at it, Shultish. Please don't notice it.

"Well, since you ask, I'll answer. Three things, to be precise, three things are new. Can you imagine, my *Style and Word Usage in the Fiction of S.Y. Agnon* has been translated into three more languages."

"Three? Let me guess. French, English and German."

"No no, never German. I forbade it."

"Then Swahili, Turkomenic and Crypto-Mayan."

"No no, surely you jest."

"Wait, I remember reading that your first translation of an Agnon story was into German."

"Ah, yes, you have a good memory, Gafni. But those were different times, long long ago, when I was young. When I did graduate work at the University of Vienna before the murderers came in. Wait a minute! Did I hear you say English before? Are you being ironical? I wrote it in English."

"Oh my!"

Gafni brought the palm of his hand to his head, pretending surprise and taking a quick look at that little bottle of ink which, despite his fervent wishes, was still on the shelf. He knew Shultish had written the book in English. "I thought you wrote it in Hebrew."

How to get rid of that blasted ink bottle? A bottle that wouldn't violate Newton's law that objects at rest remain at rest.

"No no. I wrote it in English for an American audience. Let's see, it came out in Swedish and most recently in French, Spanish and Italian."

"Well, then, viva la France!" Gafni said for lack of anything more encouraging.

He saw the flicker of disappointment in the older man's eyes. Why am I blowing darts into his balloon? Why not clasp his shoulders and say: That's wonderful! *Mazel tov!* Just because Shultish appeared when you were signing a book is no reason to blame him for that inscribus interruptus.

"That's wonderful!" Gafni shook Shultish's hand. "Your book in Swedish no doubt helped the Swedish Academy in its decision to give the Nobel Prize to Agnon."

"I've been told that," Shultish said proudly.

"And into French! The French are always slow. What took them so long to discover your fine study, which if I'm not mistaken came out some twenty years ago? You know, when a scholarly book appears in French it already has an international imprimatur. It may even help get your book into Hebrew."

"Or maybe out of it," Shultish retorted. A little smile quivered on his lips. "You see, it is already in Hebrew. Pardes Press. Of course, I myself supervised the translation." Words accompanied by an ever so slight satisfied tick of his head.

Gafni stared at that impudent ink bottle as though answers would be found on its shiny, crystal-like surface. If he looked at it it might attract Shultish's attention and then the focus would be on him again.

"Wonderful. Again *mazel tov!* When?"

"Three years ago."

"I didn't know."

As Shultish was about to say something, Gafni saw that obtrusive and compromising bottle of ink becoming bigger each time he looked at it. Violating which of Newton's laws? He had an idea. Finally.

"Shultish," Gafni pointed to the window. "Look at that sky, that fantastic view, those mauve and beige hills surrounding Jerusalem."

As Shultish turned to look, Gafni swooped the bottle into his pocket.

"Did you get it?" Shultish asked as he turned back.

"Yes. It's in my pocket," Gafni blurted and then, realizing his gaffe, coughed.

"My book is in your pocket?"

"No no," Gafni laughed. "I was thinking of something else, sorry."

"Then you didn't get the Hebrew copy I sent you? I even inscribed it personally for you."

Gafni shook his head, pressed his lips in complaint. "So you autograph books too? No, sorry, I don't recall seeing your book. I get so many books," he said, "I need, how do you call it in your English language, a large We-Haul — "

"U-Haul ... "

"Yes, thank you, a large I-Haul to cart them away. My shelves are sagging like a beerdrinker's belly from the masses of unwanted books, not that yours is one of them, God forbid. One of my graduate student assistants must have taken it home and never returned it. Come, let's sit down here on the window ledge. You're looking good, Shultish, so nice to see you again. Look, half of Jerusalem is spread out before us. One is tempted to just sit here in the October sunshine, looking over the illusory tranquility of Jerusalem and do no work. Ah, what a delicious temptation ... "

And saying that word, Malina at once came to mind and blocked out everything: books, Shultish, even Gafni. How lovely she looked in that bikini last year. Note, Malina, the difference between the printed *daled* and the *resh*. I'll show you now the written form. And as she watches him indite the letters, she moves closer and her large, firm breast presses into his elbow and forearm as he slowly writes and never wants to stop. He takes a deep breath, careful not to move his arm, and the letters *resh* and *daled* sprout wings like helicopters and fly and swirl above the desk. And then, blinking, he sees Shultish standing before him.

Shultish smiled at him as if to say — it will never happen. You will never sit here in the sunshine with nothing to do. When you juggle thirteen projects, you have to keep juggling. Otherwise, everything comes crashing down.

"Well, I hope your graduate assistant will return the book some day. In pristine condition. There is nothing worse than a person returning a book with more than when he originally borrowed it."

"What does that mean?" A nervous shiver ran through Gafni hearing Shultish's words.

Shultish grinned mischievously. It was a wide, even grin, a smile too large for his mouth. Gafni wondered if all the teeth were false.

"By more," Shultish continued, "I mean handwritten comments. The chutzpa of it, putting your pen onto the paper of a book that doesn't belong to you. Absolute desecration, not so, Professor Gafni?"

"Absolutely, Professor Shultish," Gafni tried to keep his voice calm.

For a moment Gafni's thoughts stopped. Saw only misty haze and a distant blue sky made entirely of autographic ink.

"How is your family?" Shultish's voice cut through the mist.

"My children are fine. Batsheva isn't too well; she has diabetes, you know. And kidney problems. And how is your dear wife?"

"Alas, in *oylam ha-emess.*" Shultish used the Yiddish pronunciation of the Hebrew phrase: in the true world.

"Ah, I'm so sorry to hear that. When?"

"Two years ago, in Miami. I just observed the yorzeit for her a week ago."

"Is it that long I haven't seen you?"

"We last met three years ago here for the Agnon conference."

Gafni knew that Shultish had no children, so he could not inquire after their well being. So the only other thing was his work.

"And how is your research coming?"

"Fine," Shultish said rather too quickly. "And yours?"

"I've come to the conclusion," Gafni said, "that research is a fraud. All information is somewhere. Like the flesh of the banana, it just has to be peeled away."

Shultish nodded.

"Basic research is peeling the banana. Complicated research is peeling the banana and several other fruits and making a fruit salad. So, then, there is no such thing as original research, because everything is already there, even underground in archeological digs. The only original research is *creatio ex nihilo*, fiction. Ipso facto, to be original, facts have to be invented, something never there before has to be introduced." Like the signatures he introduced into the books he signed.

Shultish, polite as always, waited for the zigzags of Gafni's fecund mind to cease their convoluted, provoluted and involuted peregrinations before he said:

"Do you know, I've retired from the Manhattan Hebrew Teachers College?"

"Really?" Gafni knew that too. "I didn't know you were of that age."

"Professor Gafni! I ... "

"Why don't you call me Shmulik? Remember, I told you this years ago. Why all this formality between colleagues and friends?"

"Thank you. And you can call me Ezra ... Shmulik, don't you know I'm seventy-nine?"

"Incredible! You don't look a day over eighty." But seeing the hurt look coming over Shultish's face like a drear wave, Gafni added, "No no, I'm just joking ... I thought you were sixty," Gafni lied.

"But I'm much older than you, Shmulik."

"Not by that much."

"I thought you were sixty," Shultish lied too.

"Ezra, *yedidi*, I'm a great-grandfather. That seems to interest people more than the fact that I've discovered the source, the etymology, the everything, for the word *davenen*."

Gafni couldn't help it. Since he was already in the shvung of lying, he couldn't resist this one.

Shultish clapped his hands. His mouth dropped open. Gafni could have sworn he gave a little hop of joy.

"No! I don't believe it! You have? The source of the word to pray? My God, in the field of Yiddish that's the equivalent of squaring the circle or solving Fermat's Last Theorem in mathematics. Mazel tov! *Davenen* is one of the handful of words in Yiddish that have eluded etymologification." The last word, uttered in English, impressed Gafni.

"Eight syllables? My, my. I never heard that word before."

"Neither have I," Shultish said shyly, eyes glowing. "Because I just made it up. You are present … you have just witnessed the birth of a new word."

"I didn't know you were a neologist, Ezra."

"Your rival, Professor Sh. Meichl-Rukzak, if I may quote him, has called me a neologizing philologist … So let's hear it. *Davenen* is one of my favorite words."

"I can't, Ezra, *motek*. My hands are tied. My publisher has forbidden me to speak of it until the official day of publication."

"Which is when?"

"We don't know yet … And also, you know, copyright provisions."

"But you know I won't violate your copyright."

"And how I know it! If anyone won't violate my copyright, it's you. Among non-violators of copyright, you head the list. I know you won't, but it's the others out there. That's why I've been bidden to keep it a secret." What if he asks me where it will appear, a sudden fear ran through Gafni — what will I tell him? I won't answer. I'll just put a finger to my lips.

"But it's not a medical discovery," Shultish pressed on. "I know the *New England Journal of Medicine* has a policy like that before official date of publication, but this is not a medical discovery. It's just a word."

Gafni stared, rather glowered, at Shultish.

"What do you mean?" he said slowly, crisply, "it's just a word. It's not just a word, *motek*, it's the word."

"I'm sorry. Of course. Not only the word but the the the word. My absolutely most favorite word. *Daven, davenen.* I can go on all day conjugating that poetic word in all its permutations. It rings like scared music in my ear."

"Scared?"

"Did I say scared? I mean sacred. I metathesized. Sometimes I'm also known as the metathesizing neologizing philologist." Shultish laughed, hoping that Gafni's stubbornness would melt.

But Gafni only smiled.

"Come, Shmulik, tell me. Please. I won't tell a soul. I'm an old man. I don't have time to wait till your article appears. You can trust me."

Oy, what did I get myself into, thought Gafni. One lie leads to another and there's no way out.

"I know that," Gafni said sympathetically. "But as I told you, my hands are tied."

"Then I'll unbind you, if you wish. Let no one say that I came across a man with tied hands and did nothing to set him free."

"Very kind of you to metaphorically unbind me. But — "

"Actually, *davenen* is not only one of my favorite words — it's my most favorite word, not only in Yiddish but in English where it too has earned a respectable place, even being included in the English dictionary, even though, truth to say, I myself don't *daven* every day."

"You don't? I always thought of you, Ezra, as a traditional Jew."

"More semi-traditional. I'm more of what my good friend, Sammy Brussell, also called Shmulik, said about himself — that he's non-practising orthodox. But look — "

"It's no use, Ezra, much as I would love to share it with you, I cannot. But when the article comes out, you'll be the first to know … What are you doing now?"

"Talking to you. Trying to find … "

Gafni laughed. "No, I mean in general, I mean, do you have any big projects?"

"Well, I live in Miami Beach now and I'm … " Shultish paused. A self-deprecating tone crept into his voice. "I'm studying the use of Yiddish among the elderly. European-born, ex-New Yorkers in Miami Beach."

"Well well well," was the only thing Gafni could say.

"I hope you don't mind."

"No no, of course not. Do you think I have a monopoly on Yiddish research?"

"Well, that's what they say," Shultish muttered.

"Again that amorphous they. You mean in the ya-ta-ta blah-blah crowd who sits in the coffee houses with nothing better to do than spread gossip about Yiddish professors?"

"The very same," Shultish said bluntly.

"Well, never mind, I'm delighted you're doing something with Yiddish. Welcome! Still, it's amazing. You, the Hebraist par excellence, moving into Yiddish," Gafni said, thinking: He's become absolutely sclerotic. Some challenge, making a list of words uttered by the old, the feeble, the demented and the decrepit.

"Yiddish and Hebrew," Shultish exculpated himself, "as you well know, were always bound together, especially in Eastern Europe, brother and sister, *mame-loshn* and *tate-loshn*, mother tongue and father tongue. Related."

"Cousins, like the Arabs and the Jews," Gafni couldn't resist a tweak.

There they stood, facing each other on the third floor of the stacks of the University of Israel library, each wondering who the other would next tweak.

But one must rescue politesse (or call it critique) from the cellar of mutual pique, reset the see-saw of tit for tat for a modicum of balance to see where everything is at.

"And what are you working on?" Shultish asked Gafni so innocently, so without guile, it caught him by surprise.

"Something new," said Gafni with more enthusiasm than he felt. "A cultural map of the streets of old Jewish Warsaw."

Aha! thought Shultish, pitying the detumescent scholar. Alzheimer's setting in. And so young too, ran through Shultish's mind. He's barely seventy or seventy-two. Maps! The project of the demented. What's next? A survey of barber poles in Boro Park?

And so they fell still for a while. Shultish pondered where the center of gravity was now, on his side or Gafni's. He sensed it was on his — but, not wanting to take a chance, added:

"Street signs?" he couldn't help tweaking. "Lists of streets?"

"This project has had meticulous peer review," Gafni said with carefully modulated hauteur, once more lying through his recently brushed teeth. And since the Talmud states that one lie drags another in its wake, he couldn't help but succumb to Talmudic wisdom. "And I've been given a Guggenheim for it," he popped another fib, which was unusual for Gafni, for he never lied twice in one sentence, except when the occasion demanded it.

Shultish knew that Gafni was lying, and Gafni knew that Shultish knew. How magnificent is silent communication, slower than gossip but quicker than speech.

"Your Miami Beach project sounds wonderful. I didn't know you were fluent in Yiddish," Gafni said. "Remarkable ... "

Shultish pretended to be insulted. He continued in Yiddish. "What do you mean? You think I was born in Kansas?" Then he gave a little smile, small but happily boastful.

"Remarkable," Gafni continued, "how your accent is off. Is it your native language?"

The pretense melted; insult remained.

"What do you mean is it my native language? Of course, it's my native language ... That's where I was born. But of course because of Polish anti-Semitism I studied in Germany and Vienna, where I got my doctorate — that's why I was able to translate Agnon into German so easily."

"Ah, German. Now I see how your accent is compromised."

"Oy," said Shultish. "No matter what language I speak, there's an accent. My Yiddish has German. My German has Polish. My Polish has Yiddish. My Hebrew has English. My English has everything."

"And what does your Filipino have?"

"The keys to my apartment."

"Remarkable," said Gafni, admiring the old man's sense of humor.

Shultish decided to continue in English.

"I don't speak English that well," said Shmulik.

"What?" crowed Shultish. "Everyone in Israel speaks English."

"Except me. I read it but I don't speak it felicitously." Only to Malina, he thought, do I speak English.

"You really don't speak English?" Shultish said in Yiddish. "I thought you spent a year at Yale on a fellowship."

"True, but the English they speak at Yale is totally useless anywhere else. Anyway, that was years ago and I haven't been back."

"Remarkable. I thought every professor in Israel teaches in America every few years."

"Except me. I go to, have gone to, will go to, Poland."

"Even more remarkable. How do you explain that?"

Gafni wasn't in the mood to explain, so he said instead:

"Let me give you a parable. Like Shakespeare said, as my research in Elizabethan Yiddish has shown, when Dr. Roderigo Lopez, the court physician to Queen Elizabeth, began speaking to Willy in Ladino, Shakespeare gave his famous reply 'I have small Hebrew and less Ladino.' So Yiddish, as you probably know, if you read my article in the *Quarterly for Elizabethan Studies*, Yiddish was their only common tongue, for Dr. Lopez too did not yet know English well, having just gotten off a boat from Amsterdam several months earlier. But when Lopez made fun of Shakespeare's Yiddish, the enraged Bard betrayed Lopez to the police as a Jew — Jews were forbidden to reside in England at that time, as you know — and he was executed in, I believe, 1594, an event that inspired both Shakespeare's *Merchant of Venice* and his *Comedy of Terrors*."

"Remarkable," said Shultish.

"What's remarkable?"

"Remarkable how you can fantasize."

"I told you, Ezra, fiction is the last avenue now left for original research. Now pure inventiveness must take over, for in traditional scholarship everything is based on everything else … *Ex nihilo* must now become modus operandi."

"But professors are not supposed to have imagination, Shmulik. Look at me, a true professor, without a shred of imagination. But my ear, thank God, is perfect. After that Elizabethan monologue and flight of fantasy of yours, I begin to detect a Byelorussian accent in your Hebrew."

"You do have an excellent ear, Shultish. I have been looking at Byelorussian lately and it's no doubt spilling over into my speech. And in your speech I hear some glottal stops and double clicks. Is it your teeth or your stammer? Someone told me you are studying some African language."

Shultish looked ill at ease, as if he'd been caught writing in library books.

"Yes ... who told you?"

"I don't recall. I may have read it in *Olam ha-zeh*, our equivalent of your *National Enquirer*."

"It's true. Your gossip reporters have no equal. I'm working on Swahili, and I assure you the double clicks are not my teeth. But I didn't want to tell anyone about it yet. I find some affinities to Hebrew — see, I'm not holding back from sharing some exciting discoveries from you — from the old Semitic roots of Swahili, especially in the absolute infinity mode. I'm also writing an article on words that have disappeared from Hebrew, words not even mentioned in the Torah."

"Can you give me an example?"

Shultish searched his pockets. "Oh my, I must have left them at home ... And I also know that you're studying other languages too besides Sub-Carpathian Ruthenian."

"Who told you?" Gafni said, his emotions rocking between astonishment and outrage.

"Same blabbermouth who told you about my Swahili. I see we're both engaged in exotic languages. How is your Chinese?"

"Tortured. And your Korean?" Gafni said.

"Superb. He now does windows ... Your Italian?"

"Sotto voce. To understand the Jews in the ghetto I had to master the Venetian dialect."

"Then how is your Venetian?" said Shultish.

"Blind. Poor thing, she now has a seeing-eye dog ... Your Finnish?"

"Yes."

"So am I."

AND with that the encounter was done. It was somewhat nerve-jangling, but it still had its chess-like pleasures, peppered with occasional checker-like onslaughts and merciless jumps.

"Why are we sitting here?" Shultish jumped up with the agility of a man half his age. "I'd like to invite you to lunch."

Gafni rose too from the window ledge. He looked at his watch.

"Dear God, I'm late for an appointment." He hoped Malina wouldn't be angry. "I can't today."

"What about tomorrow?" Shultish looked at his watch as though it told tomorrow's time.

"You have the menu there, writ small perhaps?" Gafni teased.

"No no, I'm just checking the bus timetable."

The old man looked serious. But Gafni wasn't fooled this time. That the old Agnon scholar could joke with a straight face impressed him. But he still couldn't forgive him for interrupting his inscriptions. On the other hand, maybe he should thank Shultish for curing him. After the experience, Gafni swore he wouldn't autograph again. Until next time, if not sooner.

"All right," Shultish said, "let's see, today is Sunday. How about Wednesday?"

"No, Wednesday is no good. I already made plans for Tuesday and Wednesday. So how about last night?" Gafni couldn't resist saying. "That's always a good date, I find, for getting together."

"You expect me to eat leftovers?" Shultish replied. "You must be joking. Last night?" Gafni is sclerotic, Shultish thought. Like a true plagiarist, Gafni has everybody else's diseases — Alzheimer's, Parkinson's, Tourette's, Down's, Jakob-Kreuzfeld's, Tay-Sachs's and Crohn's — except his own.

"Why not?" Gafni continued. "A day or two in the past always works."

Shultish consulted his watch again. "Not for me. I'm busy last night. I have concert tickets."

"Ezra, your continuing good humor surprises me. Let's meet Thursday at the University cafeteria. At 5 pm. That's right after my class. I'll invite you to supper. I presume you'll still be in Jerusalem on Thursday night."

"Of course, and if not I'll send in a pinch-eater."

But Gafni, not being a thoroughbred American like Shutish, did not get the baseball pun.

6

WHAT'S FOR SUPPER? A DISTRACTION

ON Thursday at 5 pm, as Gafni set out to meet Shultish, he bumped into his sometime assistant, Nussen Koifman, near the bus stop opposite the university cafeteria.

Nussen, a tall, thin, nineteen-year-old with long black curly *payess*, stood with another similarly dressed fellow who, it seemed to Gafni, could have been Nussen's twin. Nussen came from a pious family near Me'ah She'arim, the ultra-Orthodox quarter of Jerusalem. His pale face, as if he'd never seen the sun, was made even paler by his long black coat, open collar white shirt and round-brimmed black hat. He was a part-time yeshiva *bokher* and did research for Gafni in commentaries to old sacred Hebrew texts, looking for Yiddish glosses and handwritten marginalia. (Gafni considered the latter a kind of exculpation for his own secretive semi-marginalia.) Knowing the poor circumstances of the large Koifman family, Gafni paid Nussen generously. Even though they opposed each other's way of life — the religious and the political aspects were just two of the polarities — a kind of symbiotic truce settled between them.

"I'm so glad I met you, Professor Gafni ... " the boy said in Yiddish.

"Nussen, what brings you here on a Thursday evening? And why so excited?"

"I'm excited?"

Just then one of the Egged buses passed and emitted a foul-smelling thick plume of black diesel smoke. Both men jumped back.

"Yes, the excitation is vibrating on your face and in your voice."

"Well, then, yes ... I purposely came ... in the hope of seeing you ... I'm so glad ... I ... was about to go to your office." Nussen's fingers opened and closed nervously, as if clasping something. But he only clasped air. "I know you have evening classes — "

"In the spring, not the fall."

"But you see, it's God's will that we meet anyway."

"So indeed it must be ... And what is it that's so important? You look highly charged. You still haven't told me why you're here.."

"I'm here because" — Nussen took a deep breath — "because there's a ninety-nine-year-old Jew from Warsaw visiting. He's in my parents' apartment now and he's flying back tomorrow ... but if you're busy … "

"From Warsaw? How did he get here? How did he survive? A ninety-nine-year-old survivor from Warsaw? Incredible! I must talk to him."

"I don't know details, Professor. I just know he has a perfect memory. He's a phenomenon."

Yes, Gafni thought. They all are. He too must be one of the special ones. Where has he been keeping himself? I thought I knew all the old Jews in Warsaw. And maybe this visitor knows — and just then the name of the Warsaw man Gafni wanted to say slipped out of his mind. The *shamesh* … what's his name?

"He knows Warsaw backwards and forwards," Nussen continued. "The stories he tells."

"What's his name?"

Nussen hesitated a moment

"He's in your parents' house and you don't know his name?"

"I think it's Moishe … But what's the difference? If you're interested, come, let's go."

"But I have a supper appointment now. I'm waiting for someone."

"The old man won't wait."

Nussen began gesturing, but somehow his finger motions were off-rhythm to the phrases he was saying. "He knows all the lanes, the side streets, all the back alleys, all the shops and who was in them. Perfect for your current project. He's an encyclopedia from 1900. He's like a movie film," said Nussen, even though he had never seen a movie film. "It's like having a television camera from seventy, eighty, ninety years ago," even though Nussen didn't have a television, which his rebbi and teachers and family forbade as lascivious and seducing one's thoughts from Torah and Torah study to all the *shmootz* and depravity in Israel, except when Nussen stopped in front of an appliance store window on Jaffa Street which showed excerpts from videos and he stood there openmouthed, fascinated, riveted, enchanted, with no thoughts of Torah in his mind. In fact, as he watched the videos, he consciously divested himself of Torah thoughts and verses from the Psalms so he could curse the nakedness of those *koorves*, those whores who modelled bathing suits which were made just with two fringes like those on tzitzis, tfu, God forgive the comparison; or when those young sluts, may they burn in Gehenna, gyrated their hips and thrust their breasts toward his face to music he couldn't hear because of the thick window, he stood there amazed, unable to tear himself away, so angry was he at the State of Israel, which he did not recognize, except for its paper currency, for allowing such seduction of the innocent.

Hearing the word "video," immediately a split screen appeared in Gafni's mind. On the right (in color, no less) he saw Shultish, and on the left, slightly larger, and much to Gafni's discomfit, the ninety-nine-year-old man. There were some questions he wanted to ask Moishe, if indeed that was his name — Gafni rather doubted it; Nussen just pulled that one out of his sleeve for some reason — questions not about Warsaw streets either, questions he couldn't ask Malina. Yes, it's strange he hadn't heard of Moishe or met him in Warsaw. Could he have been too feeble to come to shul? Evidently not, if he could travel to Israel.

"How long has he been here?"

"About two weeks."

That's about right, Gafni mused. They dare not stay away more than two weeks.

"And tomorrow he flies back to Warsaw."

"Why didn't you tell me about him sooner? My God, almost two weeks here and now you first tell me, the night before he flies back home."

"I just found out, Professor Gafni. That's why I rushed to see you. Please excuse me. I was at the yeshiva. He came to a neighbor and now they brought him to say hello to my parents. What's the difference? It's done. Come, let's go."

"Give me the address, Nussen. Or would you like me to give you a lift?"

"No, thank you. My brother, Peysakh, is waiting with his car. Come. It's quicker than one car following another, and maybe getting lost in the maze of the small streets of Me'ah She'arim and, even worse, trying to find a parking space."

"What? I don't believe I'm hearing what I think I heard. A car? Did you say 'his'?"

"Yes."

"I thought you come from a family of modest means."

Nussen stood there abashed, looking like someone caught stealing.

"You once told me, Nussen, that your mother has several little ones at home and a few others in school. Your father is a *shamesh* in a shul. And your brother can afford a car? How come a yeshiva *bokher* can afford a car? Did you win the lottery?"

"No."

"I've been teaching almost fifty years and I could never afford a car till last year."

Nussen's abashed expression turned into a sly smile which he immediately surpressed with a frown.

"We support the political party, Shas," he explained in a musical singsong. "And they support their supporters."

A Delightful Little Man (continued)

"How does Herr Mozart make a living?" I asked. The waiter smiled.

"The Café Mozart has been in his family for generations ... Wait, I'll bring him back now."

Little Mozart now sat on a dollhouse chair on the table.

"I hope you haven't been listening to Fritz," he said. "Ever since he was rehabilitated he badmouths everyone, but at least he doesn't smash dishes anymore."

I began speaking Yiddish to him, a homey Polish Yiddish with lots of folk expressions. Mozart nodded, but I'm not sure he really understood.

"You're not here for *gemutlichkeit*," he said. "I sense that. You're not here to enjoy Vienna. You have a story."

"You're right. But how do you know?"

"Every man has a story. You're only passing through. This is just a point to go elsewhere."

I pondered if I should share my secret with a man who might be no more than a fairy tale, a figment of my imagination prompted by exhaustion, someone who might vanish when I woke from my dream. But then he asked another question and I had to respond.

"Who, what, are you looking for?"

Without thinking, without muzzling the words and thoughts I had always censored before, I blurted out, as if after a dose of truth serum:

"I'm looking for a murderer."

"An Austrian?"

"No. A Pole."

"Because the Austrians were adept at this too. After all, it's the Austrians who invented Nazism. Hitler and most of his henchmen were Austrians. And I, like the Jews, was also in extreme danger, even though I was a youngster."

"You? A scion of Mozart? In danger? I know

that during the Nazi period the Germans used a tune from Mozart, I think the *Magic Flute* motif, on Radio Berlin as a sign-on or sign-off."

"True, but you must remember, along with the Jews, the deformed, the crippled, the outcasts were also undesirables, hence also marked men."

"So did you run away?"

"Where could I, who depends totally on others, run? A good man hid me in his house." Mozart laughed. "Of course, it isn't too hard to hide me ... When they came looking for me here, the *pattisseur* hid me inside his chef's hat ... Another time, I was in a cup of chocolate shavings — not a bad place to hide." He giggled. "Then they stopped looking for me ... And my parents, who were also in danger, hid a Jewish couple who had been provided with false papers in their country home. They pretended to be deaf mutes ... But wait, we're off the subject. You said you were looking for a murderer."

"Yes."

"Where? Here?"

"No. In Poland. But I don't know how to proceed."

Mozart brought one hand to the edge of his chin.

"Let me think ... Will you be here tomorrow?"

"No. My plane leaves for Warsaw tonight."

"What time?"

"10:15."

"Can you come back at 6? ... Good. I will think. Put out your hand please and I will jump into it."

I did as he requested. Then I brought him close to my face. I saw that Mozart had fine black lashes.

"You are a good man," he said.

"Thank you for saying so, Herr Mozart."

"Please call me Amadeus. Or better yet, Wolfgang."

"Then you must call me Shmulik."

Mozart bent forward to kiss the palm of my hand. A surge of warmth and tenderness unlike anything I had felt before, perhaps akin to the feeling I had when my father came to me in a dream, coursed through every limb. Perhaps the kiss of an angel. It seemed to me that a tear was clouding my eyes.

"Now please bring me to the cashier along with my chair."

I carefully brought Mozart back. The cash register was an old-fashioned one, silvered cast iron, where the numbers appeared on an elongated rectangular glass panel.

"This bill is on the house, Hanschen," Mozart told the tall, thin bald man. By the flicker of annoyance on the man's stolid face, I knew that this wasn't the first time that Mozart had done this.

"Until six," he said.

(to be continued)

"WAIT a minute," Gafni said, astounded. "Shas? The Shas party is for Sephardic families. And you're Ashkenazic ... You've become a Sephardi?"

Nussen laughed. "We've all become Sephardim. Can't you hear the Moroccan accent in my Yiddish? Do you think it's so hard to start a blessing with 'barukh ata' instead of 'boorikh ato'?"

"For a new Toyota," Gafni said, "I'd change my pronunciation too."

"I mean, they didn't ask me to eat pork, for goodness sake!"

"And for a new three-bedroom apartment, would you switch to pork?"

"Completely furnished, with air-conditioning? And a new refrigerator? On wheels?" Nussen asked.

"Yes."

"That's half a million dollars, professor ... Well, I might just take a teeny tiny bite, but I wouldn't enjoy it."

"I can't believe they gave you a new car."

"To every family that supports Shas they promised a new car. That was part of the coalition agreement with Netanyahu."

"And my taxes are paying for your car. Very nice."

"What do you care? The Americans are paying for it. Foreign aid. The UJA. Keeps the economy going. No unemployment for America, more foreign aid, and more UJA dollars for us. You see, no one loses."

"And I always thought that the deal was that for Shas's support the government would give twenty million, or is it one hundred million dollars, for the Shas yeshivas."

"Nu? So? So what? You're one hundred percent right. So it goes to the yeshivas, true — and then the yeshivas buy cars for us. To keep us enrolled. To keep us happy. To keep us out of the army.

To keep us voting. This way, with our cars, we don't have to ride in those *traif* buses with those whores, those *koorves*, in miniskirts and bare arms and long naked legs up to the thighs and have them shamelessly pressing against us as they move like Liliths to the back of the bus or sit opposite us enticing us away from *Tehillim*, from reciting Psalms and prayers."

In which you pray, Gafni thought, that one of those sluts who rubs up against you will stay there for a while and not move to the back of the bus.

"No wonder there are traffic jams downtown since the elections," Gafni quipped. "Wait a minute, I have to stop by the cafeteria for a moment. I must tell my colleague that I won't be able to stay."

"No time for that. Come. The old man is in a rush. You may miss him," Nussen turned to Yonah, who had been silent till now, and said in Yiddish: "Yoina, run to my brother and tell him we're coming."

Just then Gafni saw Shultish approaching the cafeteria entrance.

"Ezra, Ezra!" Gafni called. "Over here."

Shultish, all smiles, drew near. He looked questioningly at the yeshiva bokhers with Gafni.

"*Makhst a minyan*," he joked. You're helping to make a minyan? "I didn't know that …"

"No no no, I'm not going to *daven* with them. An emergency came up … Sorry for the change of plans … I can't join you for supper now. Please excuse me, *yedidi*. Nussen here, my assistant, tells me there's a ninety-nine-year-old Jew from Warsaw in his house who's flying back to Poland tomorrow. I must speak to him."

Gafni saw Shultish's face falling. He felt sorry for the old man. Knew it was not a nice thing to do. But in all his trips to Poland Gafni had never met a person that old.

"I'm sorry, Ezra. I can't give this up. Please understand. He may have answers to questions I haven't been able to get answered. So, please, Ezra." He clasped Shultish's shoulders. "Call me tomorrow morning at home. We'll reschedule."

A horn honked. Nussen waved. "Come. Let's go."

Shultish didn't respond and Gafni didn't wait. He entered the car, a rather comfortable five-seater, with the three young men and the car sped off with a roar.

Shultish didn't like the haste with which Gafni was rushed off. He had a vague feeling that he must do something. Scenes from the few adventure films he had seen flashed. But what to do? A cab. Yes, that's just what he needed, a cab. He looked around. A cab, sent by God, was waiting near the bus stop. Perfect. Shultish jumped in, yelled instructions, the first of which was, "Follow that cab, I mean, that car."

A ninety-nine-year-old Jew from Warsaw, Shultish thinks as he seats himself uncomfortably in the taxi, the way Shultish usually sat in cabs, *toosh* at the edge of the seat, during the rare times he used taxis, on pins and needles, watching the quick ticking of the merciless meter. What a *bobbe-mayse*! Ninety-nine-year-old man, my foot. Shultish often wondered about that silly expression. Why should "my foot" mean "baloney"? In fact, why should "baloney" mean "baloney"? What a queer language English was! Why was he thinking of baloney when there were more important things to think of, like suspicion? Because as soon as he approached Gafni and Gafni mentioned Nussen's name, the two boys, in a seemingly rehearsed gesture, pulled down the brim of their hats, as if they didn't want to be recognized. Very suspicious. And since when do yeshiva *bokhers* have cars? Suspicious even more, feeling a high of Sherlock Holmes adventure, Shultish tries to get more comfortable. When was the last time he hailed a cab? When do Jews hail cabs? Like the old Jewish joke: When do poor Jews eat chicken? When one of them is sick. Draw your own conclusions on the cab.

"Is that the car?" the driver said.

"Yes. Good. That's the one. But don't be too obvious. You understand, right? That's it, terrific," Shultish said, pressed to the side of the car as the cabbie made a sharp left turn. "And step on it. But slowly. Don't let them notice." His Hebrew in this instance was somewhat convoluted. American murder mystery cinematic dialogue does not trippingly on the tongue convert to modern spoken Hebrew. Still, the cabbie got the point. Yes, very suspicious. That pulled-down brim. Just like Al Capone.

In the Geula section, behind the old Jerusalem bus station, Shultish sees that the new Toyota has stopped and Gafni and two young men enter a doorway. The car pulls up another twenty or so feet and the driver goes into another house. That too was suspicious. Shultish, a short distance away, pays and leaves the taxi. By now dusk has become dark. He walks up to the doorway. In a second floor apartment the lights go on. The white shades, probably plastic, are already drawn. Occasionally, Shultish sees the shadow of a wide hat, occasionally the shape of Gafni's head.

A moment later, Shultish will look down and pick something up. But in so doing, the linguist can't help thinking: How come you don't hail a car, a train, a bus, a tram, a bike, a rickshaw, a plane, a ship? Only a cab.

7

GAFNI IN THE APARTMENT

NUSSEN and Yonah brought Gafni upstairs to an empty apartment. Not chair, nor table, only white plastic window shades drawn to the paint-chipped sills. Nussen locked the door.

"What's this?" Gafni looked around at the bare walls.

"What's what?"

"Why did you lock the door?"

"So no one disturbs us."

Gafni didn't like that answer. He felt his eyes narrowing. The two boys with the black hats looked different now. Taller, lips compressed, faces constricted. Unpleasant. Yes, that's the word, Gafni had to admit. Unpleasant. A little rill of shivers ran through his left arm. Strange how his body did things totally out of his control. What's next? he wondered. My hand shaking?

"What kind of apartment is this?"

"For one of our boys."

"Where's the furniture?" Gafni noticed for the first time the tremor in his voice. Fear is like a viral infection, he thinks. It overtakes you bit by bit.

"Not delivered yet."

"Where's your brother?"

"He went to *daven*."

And you're exempt from going to shul? Gafni thought.

"And where's the old man?" Asking questions staved off the feeling of unease in his heart.

"What old man?" Nussen said innocently.

Yonah laughed.

"Don't play the fool. The old man you told me about." Now Gafni felt he was walking the wrong way on an airport moving walkway. He felt he'd been placed into a black-and-white mystery film but didn't know which role to fulfill.

"Oh, him."

"I can't imagine you don't know his name. Think." They said Moishe before, Gafni remembered.

"It's Yidl or Yosl. Maybe Yankl."

"Yankl?... That's the name I'm looking for ... " Suddenly Gafni's discomfort melted. "From Warsaw ... and for the life of me I couldn't remember his name." Then it came to him, the name of the old man in the shul on Paderewski Street. "Yankl Shtroy? Is it he?"

"Yes."

"Then why did you say Moishe before?"

"I must have forgotten. Yes, it is Yankl Shtroy. In fact, I'm sure of it."

"Wait a minute. I saw Yankl Shtroy a few years ago in Warsaw and he was in his late sixties, maybe early seventies. So how could he be ninety-nine now?"

"So maybe he's only seventy-five now," Nussen said. "How can I tell? Old is old."

Gafni turned to Nussen's friend. "Yankl Shtroy? Here? I must speak to him."

But the friend was silent.

It was the morose silence that affected Gafni and removed at once the joy of discovering that Yankl Shtroy was in Jerusalem. The unease of before returned, edged with a vague wave of fear.

"And how come your friend doesn't talk?"

"He's shy. Why so many questions?"

Gafni imagined taking the step forward before he took a threatening step toward Nussen. He felt he had to take control. After all, he was one and they were only two.

"Don't play with me!" Gafni said sharply. Nussen retreated. "Tell me what's going on here," knowing exactly what was going on. He could have scripted what was going on and what would happen next. He just didn't know why.

Suddenly Yonah found his tongue.

"You tell us. A man, a professor like you, running around with a *Poilishe shikse*."

Gafni saw a blue wave rising before his eyes, little stars exploding.

"Where do you get your chutzpa?" he said in his loudest baritone as he moved to the door. Both boys blocked him.

A surge of anger rippled from Gafni's hands into his fists, clenched, ready to punch the chutzpanik in the face.

"What business is it of yours?"

"We like to keep morality among Jews."

"And kidnapping is morality? There is a prohibition against stealing in the Ten Commandments."

"Look who's teaching us Torah," said Yonah. He pronounced it "Toireh" in the Yiddish fashion.

"Aha," Nussen said sarcastically. "So you know that 'Thou Shalt Not Steal' refers to stealing human beings. So how come you can't follow the commandment just above it?"

"Let me out."

"Don't resist. There's more of our *chevra* outside and they may be more hotheads than us. It'll be better for you if you listen to us. We're doing this for your own good."

Gafni decided to take a different approach.

"What's gotten into you, Nussen? Are you out of your mind? And you assume no one saw me getting into your car?" Gafni said, thinking of Shultish.

"Nothing out of the ordinary. Dozens of cars and taxis line up near the bus stop … You got into the car of your own free will. We didn't throw you in. So why should anyone be suspicious? No screams or shouts were heard …"

"I see you planned this out very cleverly. Like terrorists. So what do you plan to do with me?"

"You'll stay here until you give up the *shikse*. The world will assume you ran off to Poland …"

"Good riddance, *tfui*." Yonah spat.

"And how happy your rival, Professor Meichel-Rukzak will be. He'll dance for joy!"

"I'm going to tell you two things. One, I have a bad heart. If something happens to me, you'll not only be in court for kidnapping but you'll have murder on your record as well."

The two boys exchanged glances.

"And what's the second?" Nussen asked.

Gafni waived a finger at them. "That I'm not telling you. And what's more, no judge will have mercy on you. This is the thanks I get, Nussen, for providing you with an easy job, excellent pay, more than you deserve, because I wanted to help you and your poor family. And then you stab me in the back."

"I know what you did for me," Nussen said, "and I'm grateful to you for that. I didn't want to do this, but I felt it would go against everything I believed in if I didn't take matters into my own hands."

"But who says your assumption is correct?"

"Everyone says so."

"And if everyone says that Jews are parasites, need blood for matzas, and killed Jesus does that make it true?"

The three historical referents and canards went over Nussen's head.

"It's all for you own good, professor," he said lamely.

"I'll be the judge of what's for my own good. I don't have to explain my private affairs to you or anyone else. But if it will make you feel better — " and at once regretted stooping to their level to explain himself — "she's not my girl friend. I'm a happily married man with a very sick wife."

Nussen began to speak but stopped midway in his first word.

Gafni couldn't read their minds, couldn't tell if his threats made any impression. But thinking of the stupidity of their move and how it couldn't possibly succeed made him feel a little better.

"One last warning before you get into serious trouble with the police. I'm wearing an electronic monitor." Then he strode to one of the windows. The boys did not stop him. Perhaps the windows did not open. Perhaps the shades do not work. But instead of trying to pull up the shade, he lifted his hands over his head and spread them wide so that anyone looking would have seen a man with upraised hands as though in surrender.

"Now step aside and give me the courtesy of a ride back to the university. I will not press charges against you if you let me go now, peacefully."

The two youths stood adamant, hands folded over their chests. Now Gafni first noticed a pitcher of water and a plastic cup on the floor. Aha, those bandits had made preparations in advance.

"Where's your electric monitor?" Yonah asked.

"Not electric. Electronic. And do you think I'm going to tell you? And once pressed it cannot be cancelled. It's electronically digitalized and yahoo encrypted via satellite remote control on a laserised synapse." Gafni shook his index finger at them and added loudly, "And to the third power."

But instead of pressing the pendant on his chest, which he couldn't find now — perhaps it had somehow slipped off — Gafni slowly and ostentatiously twisted the tip of each finger with the thumb and forefinger of the opposite hand while moving his lips in non-existent Kabbalistic spells. Or maybe he had forgotten to put the *Chaver* on after all. It had happened before. Perhaps it was better that he didn't have it, because if he pressed the button the ambulance would have gone to his house and frightened Batsheva. On the other hand, perhaps it signalled his location. He didn't really know; he had never read the instruction booklet.

"And when the police bang on the door, please open up, because if they have to break in the punishment is even more severe. You just have a few minutes to decide."

"We don't care ... "

"You don't care, huh? You don't care about the legal costs your parents will have to bear? You don't care about the shame of having their names in every newspaper? Now unlock the door."

The boys didn't move.

"There is a higher law, which few in this God-less State of Israel follow."

"Who set you up as the guardians of morality?"

Yonah bent to Nussen. "I can't take this anymore. Why are you going so easy on him?"

"Because he's a friend of mine and he's an old man."

That hurt, Gafni thought. He had never been called an old man before.

"Are you crazy?" Yonah shouted. "First you asked me to help you and now you stand up for him. I won't let him talk like this — you'll end up getting it from me too."

"Then leave if you don't like it. No force, I said. We can show him we're not like them."

"But we are 'them', you idiot. Whose side are you on?"

"It's not a matter of sides," Nussen said. "It's a matter of doing it the right way. It's a matter of stopping him from being with that *Poilishe* and making a laughingstock of his wife. It's against morality and modesty and against *halakha*."

"It's against *halakha* to kidnap," Gafni added.

"Here it's a mitzva."

"The trouble with you people is that you always cloak nasty behavior with mitzva deeds."

"See? See?" Yonah broke in. "Listen to that 'you people.' Doesn't he deserve to be smacked?"

"What do you mean 'you people'?" Nussen asked. "We're one people."

"Ideally, yes," said Gafni. "But it's you who are making divisions, separations, exclusions. So: the trouble with you people is that you let *halakha* over-ride all your behavior. *Halakha* gives you the right to kidnap me and threaten me, huh?"

"No speeches," Yonah screamed, pressing his fists to his temples. "Why do you let him talk?"

"Let him talk. It doesn't bother me." Nussen looked up at the ceiling with theatric disdain, his eyes blinking rapidly.

"You see," Gafni continued. "I hold dear, even sacred, the concept of *rachmonim bnei rachmonim*, Jews as a compassionate people. And that's why I wouldn't break anyone's bones who watches television. You know what I'm talking about, don't you?"

"No." This time Nussen looked at Gafni.

"You really don't know or are you just pretending? Didn't you read about it in the papers, or doesn't your newspaper print that kind of news? About what a few yeshiva *bokhers* did to an old, disabled Holocaust survivor, a seventy-eight-year-old man for having a television set in his house? No, of course not. Your paper would never report that."

"Whoever published that is a liar," Yonah shouted. His eyes grew wide and the tendons on his neck stood out. "The secular papers always besmirch us. There's a smear campaign against us Torah-true religious Jews. They never say anything nice about us."

"I suppose the stones the youngsters throw on Shabbat at the cars that drive by," Gafni said with a sweet, controlled rage, "are paper stones — "

8

WHAT SHULTISH PICKED UP

A moment later Shultish did look down and did pick something up.

At this point there are contradictory versions — not regarding what happened to Gafni (that we'll get into in a moment) but what happened with Shultish outside the apartment. Since Cicero — only the truth — is one of our epigraphic heroes, and his apothegm our little Bible, we'll offer both versions A and B. But in any case, it is agreed that what Shultish picked up was very small and black and had at least one button and a concavity into which he spoke.

VERSION A:

The very small black thing was a cell phone and the ensuing scene went like this:

All alone on the sidewalk now, no one else in sight, everything in chiaroscuro like in a dim black-and-white movie, Shultish is about to cross the street, the cameraman (he used to work for Hitchcock) lies there, the cobblestones highlighted from that angle, their graininess in prime focus, they take up a good one-third of the composition. Shot from below, Shultish casts a long shadow. At the edge of the street one of his feet, probably the left, touches something dropped perhaps by Gafni, perhaps by Nussen or Yonah, maybe by someone else. (In alternative versions of events there are lots of "maybes,"* one or two "perhapses," and at least one "probably," just like in good biographies.) Shultish bends down and picks up the little black thing, about the size of a packet of cigarettes (menthol), only longer and a bit narrower.

It's cool now. The evening air of Jerusalem, dormant during dusk, takes wing with the onset of darkness. A chill wind now blows from the sea over the hills that surround Jerusalem. Shultish steps into a doorway across the street. He is alone, cold (as is the cameraman still lying on the cobblestones about fifty feet away) in the late October air; it's about 6 pm. Everyone is eating supper indoors. Except him.

---

*These "maybes" (unlike June bugs) don't sting; on the other hand, they don't give honey either.

He could have been eating supper indoors too. If not for Gafni.

Shultish looks up again to the window across the street. He sees Gafni's shadow, his two arms upraised as though in surrender. His suspicion peaks. It even supresses his hunger.

Ezra Shultish regards the little black box. Yes, he had seen things like that pressed to people's ears. It wasn't shaped like a classic telephone but it sure acted like one. He had seen people in Israel, many of them, most of them — in fact, all of them — except infants and the hand-less talking into one of those flat boxes. One summer he even saw some people walking around with two of them pressed to their ears. At first he thought they were earmuffs, but then again, why wear earmuffs in July? Another time he passed a couple. Both strolled along together speaking into the tiny boxes pressed to mouth and ear. Yes, darling. Of course, honey. One would think they were conducting an illicit affair with others while walking next to each other. But no — it was the man and woman talking, evidently more comfortable using the box than conversing directly.

Shultish often wondered what differentiates a *meshuggener* from a sane person. It was that little box. Imagine a man without a phone going around talking to himself, gesticulating, talking as he walked, shouting as he ran. A confirmed and certified madman. But once you had that little black box or any other tiny thing pressed to your ear with your hand, you could be as looney as you wished and no one would say a word.

Shultish was waiting for Gafni and Gafni wasn't being obliging. Shultish was getting suspicious. Wait. He wasn't getting. He already got. Otherwise, he wouldn't have jumped into a taxi. And what made him more suspicious was the way those yeshiva *bokhers* walked in with Gafni. That he didn't like at all.

Shultish dialed 911.

Then thought quickly. If he told them someone was being kidnapped, they would ask questions, he would stumble, they would laugh at him and hang up. So he said:

"I'm having a heart attack."

"How do you know? Are you a doctor?"

"Yes. In fact, this is Doctor Shultish calling."

"What kind of doctor are you?"

"A neologizing philologist."

"A specialist, huh?"

"Yes, I'm a linguist with the City University of New York. CUNY."

"So you're a CUNY linguist."

"What difference does it make where I work? Will you please hurry? What kind of 9-1-1 is this anyway?"

"Sorry, mister. This isn't 9-1-1. This is 7-11, your neighborhood convenience store."

"I don't believe this."

"Neither do I ... Just joking ... But we want to be sure. You see, we have so many false alarms here at the First Aid Squad. Last year we had twenty-two expensive false calls. Can you describe the symptoms?"

"Please hurry. If you wait any longer you'll have a dead man."

"Then there's surely no need for the rescue squad."

Something in the man's voice, smugness, unwilling to help, as if he'd been disturbed during his eight-hour tea break — sounded familiar. Yes, Sherlock Shultish was suspicious again.

"Wait a minute. I think I recognize your voice. Did you once work for the fire department?"

"Once? Many times. For years, in fact, before I retired. I was at the emergency fire center. Now I volunteer here and help keep the ambulance where it's supposed to be. In the garage."

"Some years back I called you to report a fire on a hill, but I sensed you didn't want to go out and fight it. You said Jews are a peaceful people. We don't like fights."

"Yes, it was me. For a man who's having an alleged heart attack your memory is quite astounding. We only go and fight real fires, authentic hot and true, not imaginary ones, with the one shiny red fire engine the UJA sent us."

"And when you asked me if I can actually see the fire, I said: Of course not. There's too much smoke in the way."

"Aha! So you can't actually see the flames, but yet you want us to wake up our three firefighters."

"What do you mean wake up? It's the middle of the day. Why are they sleeping?"

"They play chess all night and it knocks them out. Not cards, mind you, but chess. These are Jewish firemen. And anyway, we don't make housecalls any more. Just like doctors. You have a fire, bring it to us."

"Tell me, do the firemen here like to slide down the poles of the firehouse right into the fire truck?"

"Yes, of course. That's an international tradition. It's all in the training videos. But — "

The man stopped. There seemed to be a plaintive tone in that "but."

"But what?" Shultish asked.

"Unfortunately, we don't have poles, so a lot of the boys get hurt."

Shultish couldn't help himself. He laughed.

"Seems to me you're feeling better, right? Laughter is the best medicine, said Sholom Aleichem. I've been running the emergency First Aid Squad for six years now, and I'm proud to say we've never sent out our ambulance. Not even once So stay well and be healthy and keep laughing *biz hundert un tsvantzig* and don't call us. We'll call you. Shalom."

Now Shultish thought he'd really have apoplexy. He dialed information, since, alas, there is no O for Operator in the Israel telephone system, and told the woman to quickly send the police to such and such an address.

OR PERHAPS HE PICKED THIS UP

Version B:

The black slightly rectangular little object Shultish retrieved from the street was not a cell phone but Gafni's little *Chaver*, the emergency pendant that got loose and fell to the pavement.

Shultish assumed it was a cell phone. Yes, it's time to call the police. Apparently, Gafni didn't go up to that apartment voluntarily. Shultish pressed a button and asked for the operator. But he knew that with the Israel phone system it was in vain, so he put the phone in his pocket in frustration. This stupid phone didn't even have a dial pad.

Before Shultish could take a breath the First Aid Squad arrived. Two men jumped out of the ambulance.

"I'm Dani, he's Avi. Who has the locket?"

Shultish thought they were asking: What's in your pocket?

So he said: "This."

"Lie down," said Avi, as Dani wheeled out the stretcher.

"What for? I feel fine."

"That's what they all say."

Shultish barely had time to utter, "What do you mean?" when the two men lunged at him. Shultish struggled, elbowed left and right at the rib cages of his rescuers. He wasn't going to let them throw him down on the stretcher and bind him with elastic cords as thick as suspenders. Dani had the oxygen out, ready to put the mask over Shultish's face.

"Why are you giving us a hard time? You pressed the button on your little *Chaver* — so you must be sick."

"I have a big *chaver* and he doesn't have buttons. But I did press a button on this — see it? — little cell phone. The man who lost this is my *chaver*, my friend, and he's upstairs, rushed up there under suspicious circumstances by two black hats. He needs our — "

9

GAFNI STILL IN THE APARTMENT

"I suppose the stones the youngsters throw on Shabbat at the cars that drive by," Gafni said with a sweet, controlled rage, "are paper stones, thrown by make-believe hands ... This, this," he shook a finger at them, "this is where fanatical thinking takes you."

Gafni stopped to take a breath. Things were moving too quickly for him. He felt as if the film of his life were being speeded up. His head hurt and a dull, grey feeling floated through him like a miserable ghost seeking exit. A chill tippled his right leg.

"Lecture to your students, not to us," said one of the boys, Gafni couldn't tell who.

Now an odd pain at the nape of his neck. He had never before had a headache in the back of his head. Maybe his heart would collapse with all this excitement. He sensed a tremor in his voice even when he was silent. Suddenly, the words to a prayer he hadn't recited since he was a Bar Mitzva boy came back to him: "Oh my God, the soul You have given me is pure. You will take it from me, but will restore it to me in time to come. So long as this soul is within me, I will give thanks to You." As soon as he said the word "soul" he thought: Why wait till then? I have a soul now and a body too. Now, with a rush of optimism that ran like a beneficent elixir through him, he moved toward the boys before he had even completed his thought.

They will not defeat me, flashed in his mind. He ran up to Nussen, grabbed him by both shoulders — Nussen at once went slack as though made of straw — and spoke into his face. When he saw Nussen's pink lips quiver and the red capillaries snaking in the whites of his eyes, Gafni knew he would emerge victorious.

"For a while I thought of going easy on you when the police come, but I won't. You get away with too much. But not with me."

"The police won't come."

"It's because of this delusion that you did this stupid act. They will come. They are on their way."

Two veins thrummed on his forehead, pulsing pain into his head.

"Tell me, who ordered you to lure me here with your fake ninety-nine-year-old Jew from Warsaw?"

"No one gave us any orders. It was all our decision," Nussen replied.

"Congratulations on your independence," Gafni said bitterly.

Yonah went into another room and brought out a chair. Gafni thought he would sit down on it and was surprised when Nussen took it from his friend and offered it to Gafni.

Only when he sat down did he realize how tired he was, exhausted physically and spiritually, and angry at being fooled and betrayed.

"The police will be here any minute." Gafni sighed, took a deep breath. "With this stupid, senseless, fanatic act, you've lost your job and my friendship. No apologies or entreaties will help. Is this how you repay me for all my generosity?"

Before Nussen could answer there was a tapping on the door.

"They're here," Gafni said. "Better open it or you're finished."

He slumped forward in the chair, but his heart surged. Someone was coming to rescue him, his abracadabra bearing good kabbalisitc fruit after all. He was about to say, "See?" when Nussen opened the door and another yeshiva *bokher*, dressed like the others, black hat, black jacket, black trousers, white shirt, came in with a young woman. She wore a long-sleeved blouse and a long skirt down to her shoes. What was most surprising was that her face was totally covered, like an Iranian woman under Khomeini, except for a slight opening for the right eye.

"We've brought your girlfriend," he said and left at once.

Gafni opened his mouth to say something, then decided to hold back. The woman was all in dark blue, except for a cerulean blue head scarf. The eye that looked at him registered no recognition, no affection, no fear. It was a blue eye, a dark blue, not Malina's green eyes. Those fools, Gafni laughed to himself. At least they could have padded her.

"How did they bring you here?" Gafni purposely did not say her name. Why give them more information?

She didn't say.

"Are you all right? The children? How are your husband's conversion lessons going?"

Gafni caught the look of astonishment and confusion on the boys' faces.

"She's been instructed not to talk. Of course she's all right."

He said something in Polish to her. She did not react.

The woman's eye, if indeed it was a woman under all that cloaking, was neutral. It might have been made of glass. And perhaps it was a large doll that stood before him. But it moved like a human being. He knew it was not Malina and wondered if they knew that he knew. Not only because of the flat chest and the wrong eye color, but because Malina's mobile eyes could express joy, tenderness, fire, and this one's eye seemed dormant, even moribund. Yes, it might be glass after all.

But Gafni played along.

"Why did you bring her here?"

Suddenly the woman breathed quickly, quicker and quicker; she made insucking noises with her nose and burst out with a sneeze. But it wasn't Malina's little daisy sneeze, but rather a Brunhildish overgrown sunflower blast that shook the room with decibels more on the male than on the distaff side. And what's more, no little post-orgasmic giggle followed.

"What are you doing to her? She's not even one of us."

"That's our business."

"I beg you, say something," Gafni said in English.

"I told you," Nussen said. "She's been instructed. She won't talk. But she too will stay here as long as necessary."

"Do you know what you're doing? Do you have any idea what you want to accomplish with all this?"

"Yes. Very easy. You'll stay here until you promise not to marry her."*

"But I am already married, you fools."

"And in writing. In front of a bes din, a rabbinic court, which we will convene."

"I told you. I'm married."

"For the future, may your wife live in good health to one-hundred-twenty."

"And what about the woman?"

"She has already agreed. She sees the situation much clearer than you do."

"Show me her signature."

"After you sign we'll show you."

Gafni aimed to delay as long as he could. He was sure the police, the ambulance, would come any minute. And if by some slim chance it was Malina, he didn't want to insult her, even though he had no intention of marrying her anyway. But in the depths of his skin he sensed that if he got to know Malina better, certain knotted secrets from Poland would gradually become unraveled.

"I'm going to count to five. If I'm not released by then, I will use Kabbalistic phrases to put a spell on you. Your eyes will pop and

---

*At that moment, a fuzzy, inarticulated reaction, like a countervailing force that hasn't yet been unleashed, surged through Gafni. He hadn't the words; the ideas were not expressed. Still, a movement, a something that at one point was here and at another there inched or sped along. At any rate (yes, pun), he couldn't at that moment categorize what it was, but it was a reaction, like antibodies to germs, yet still inchoate, in chaos.

your ears will ring. Phlegm will choke you and bonds will fetter you so tightly you won't have the breath to utter the prayer to God who unbinds the bound. Your stomach will rumble and wrench. Your knees will buckle and your hands will quake." Then Gafni whispered a phrase in Aramaic and repeated it three times.

Nussen and Yonah, standing in the middle of the room, were thrust back to the wall, pinned by an invisible wave of force. The young woman did not move.

"I have nothing against you personally, Professor Gafni," Nussen said, but his voice was weaker now. "It just hurts us that you, a Jew, a dear Jew, are doing this ... "

"I'm still counting. One ... two ... three. You cannot take God's law into your own hands, and certainly not the way you've done it ... Four."

There was no response. The two boys, pretending ennui, gazed at the floor and at the ceiling.

"I think I told you I once had a heart attack ... Do you want to be responsible for my death?"

"We brought you a chair, Professor Gafni."

"That's it. Five."

At that moment a dozen feet rumbled up the steps, quick, a-rhythmic muffled thuds. Someone twisted the knob, then knocked loudly on the door.

"Police. Open up."

"I wasn't joking, Nussen. You had your chance."

"Open up or we break down the door."

Gafni leaned back on the chair. He couldn't understand what kind of magic caused the police to come just when he predicted it. He closed his eyes for a moment, mouth open, as if having difficulty breathing.

One more sharp rap on the door, like the onset of a battering ram.

"Move," Gafni commanded, but the boys stood there as if frozen, unable to budge.

"Police. Open up."

The young woman ran to the door, unlocked it, swung it open, and hid behind it.

Four policemen rushed in.

"They kidnapped me," Gafni said weakly.

"Are you all right?" one policeman ran up to Gafni, while two others handcuffed the boys.

"You're under arrest. Down to the van."

"What happened, professor?"

"You know who I am?"

"Of course ... we were told ... Did they hurt you?"

"No ... Wait. I want to tell them something."

The policeman stopped Nussen and Yonah in the middle of the landing. Both looked down at their shoes.

"I can forgive you for your religious zealousness," Gafni said from the doorway. "But do you know for what I can't forgive you?"

The two still averted their glance.

"I can't forgive you for stealing from me that ninety-nine-year-old Warsaw Jew ... "

"If you expose me, my father will disown me for working for an *apikoyres*, a non-believer like you ... Please, professor, have *rakhmoness*."

Gafni hesitated, pulled by the word for compassion, then said:

"No. You always want people to extend niceness to you — but you'll never extend it to anyone who doesn't think and act like you ... Now get out of my sight."

Gafni followed the policemen out to the street. But for some reason they forgot about "Malina" behind the door.

And there, standing next to the police van, was a beaming Shultish. How does that man manage to materialize everywhere? Conferences. Library. Police van.

"It's all thanks to him," said one of the officers. "Even though he can't tell a cell phone from a *Chaver*." He smiled and threw his arm around Shultish's shoulders.

Gafni asked the expected question. "What are you doing here?"

"I'll tell you later, Shmulik," said Shultish. "It's too complicated." But he held up a little pendant.

"Officers," Gafni said, "please look behind the door upstairs." He beckoned them to follow him. "One mouse is missing from the trap."

An officer pulled the door forward. The young woman stood there as if part of the wall. As Gafni watched, she tore the headgear and veil off her head and face to reveal a young man.

Now Gafni felt a little spurt of joy running through him and he quoted to the young man the Torah injunction against cross-dressing.

"This chap didn't do anything," Gafni said. "In fact, he didn't even say a word. It's the other two who dressed him as a girl ... Please don't charge him with anything — but he might be able to tell you a thing or two about the fellows who worked with him."

Then Gafni beckoned to the officer who seemed to be in charge and said softly,

"Listen, please. I've already had one heart attack and don't want another. My wife is seriously ill. Please, if you can, keep this from the papers."

"We'll do our best, professor."

When Gafni was outside again, Shultish approached.

"I'm still hungry, Shmulik. How about supper now?"

Gafni knew Shultish was joking. But then again, maybe he wasn't.

Yankl Shtroy, he thought. At least one good thing has come from this. The two boys prompted me to recall the name of the *shamesh* of the Warsaw shul, a name I won't forget any more.

10

DINING WITH SHULTISH, FINALLY

BUT they did meet a few days later.

Gafni hugged Shultish, which was something he had never done before.

"I can't thank you enough for rescuing me, my Jewish Sherlock Holmes. If not for you, God knows how long they would have kept me, and if anyone would have found me."

During the meal at the student cafeteria Gafni tried to concentrate, but his thoughts wandered off and he had to fetch them with a butterfly net of his own concoction, swoosh, get back here. The net seemed to work a good part of the time, but his right hand grew weary of the movement.

For a few minutes they ate in silence. Shultish noticed the morose expression on Gafni's face and wondered what he could do to amuse him. He looked out the cafeteria window at students going and coming, and then, out of the blue, without moving his hand, he pulled the following gem out of his sleeve:

"Did you know that Manet and Monet were the same person?"

"Really?"

"Yes, a typographical error in a 19th century art magazine, *L'Art Francais*, created another persona."

Gafni smiled. "How remarkable! Then how do you account for their different first names?"

"I'm not an art historian," Shultish said. "But I'd say scribal error."

"What about Menet?" Gafni tried.

"Oh yes," Shultish said at once. "The ancient Persian wall artist who always signed his name twice."

How absurd, Gafni thought. Menet. He looked around the cafeteria. Everything was still in a haze. Yes, there seemed to be wall paintings all over the place. And then Gafni slapped his forehead. What an ass I am! That double *mene* was straight out of the Bible.

"*Mene, mene, tekel upharsin*; from the Book of Daniel." Gafni laughed. "Ezra, you're a clever old owl. The famous writing on the wall. Well done."

Shultish smiled, pleased.

"Tell me, Shmulik, after the events of the other night, do you trust me enough now to share that discovery about the etymology of *davenen* with me?"

Gafni felt as if he'd been slammed in the solar plexus. Shultish's request took his breath away. It also depressed him, reminding him of a remark he should not have made. What a blow, absorbing a one-two punch with a physical and metaphysical set of gloves.

"Ezra, *yedidi*, there's no doubt in my mind, I can trust you. But you wouldn't want me to break my word, would you? I cannot break my promise. I know you can understand and accept that."

Shultish moved his head left and right, like a scale trying to find its balance.

Then Gafni flashed a smile. "I saw a Viennese chocolate cake on display. How about dessert?"

A Delightful Little Man (continued)

"Ah, nice to see you again, Professor Gafni," Mozart said at the counter when I returned at 6 pm. "Choose any table you want, indoor or out. I have saved a special Viennese chocolate cake for you."

"Thank you so much. But it's Shmulik, remember?"

"A thousand pardons, Shmulik ... I'll be with you in a moment."

I chose a table outside. I wondered if Mozart's promised advice would be as magical as he. Could he really help me, or was I at the point of groping for straws like a drowning man?

When Fritz brought Mozart to my table on a little tray along with the cake, he was sitting on a tiny plush red settee, the sort I had once seen in a doll house in a children's museum.

"I have thought through what you told me this morning ..." and then Mozart continued in Yiddish. A slightly Germanized Yiddish, true, but Yiddish nevertheless.

"What?" I blurted, thoroughly astonished.

"I see you're surprised, Shmulik ... but first of all, medieval German is not that far removed from Yiddish. Second, the couple my family saved in our country house — guess what language we spoke when no one else was around? But let's get back to your matter. I have a prediction."

"What is it?"

"You will succeed."

This is what I returned to the café for? I thought.

"You don't like that remark."

"Frankly, no. I was ..."

"You were expecting ... magic? A solution pulled from a hat? Abracadabra?"

"I don't know what I was expecting."

"All right. Let me be more specific. You have to go back to the town where the murder took place."

"I did."

"But not as yourself."

"How can I not be myself?"

"By assuming a disguise ... You know Polish?"

"Perfectly," I said.

"Without an accent that can betray you as a Yiddish speaker?"

"Yes. That to a degree saved my life when I was with the Resistance."

"Go back not as yourself but as someone else. Someone from the regime, let's say a right-wing organization. In some of these communist lands there are token parties whose anti-Semitism is disguised by names like Patriotic Party, which the anti-Semitic communist regime tolerates. Make believe you are a historian of such a patriotic party, or some kind of official in it, and you'll see that doors will open up for you."

"That's a brilliant idea."

"Do you know the murderer's name?" Mozart asked.

"No. But his face is etched into my memory."

"My goodness! I haven't even asked the most important question. Whom did this man murder?"

"My father. And my uncle."

"Oh my God! I'm so sorry. When?"

"After the war, in the notorious pogrom in Kielce, Poland, in July 1946, more than a year after liberation, when the Poles killed dozens of Jews."

Mozart shook his head, commiserating.

"Go back. One thing will lead to another and you'll find him when you least expect to. And when you find him, what will you do? Do you know?"

"Of course I know! And how I know! I've rehearsed it often enough."

"What will you do?"

"I'll kill him."

And Mozart, as if blessing me, bent forward and kissed the palm of my hand once more.

Deep into the cake — each of us noticed smears of chocolate on the face of the other — Shultish asked: "How is your colleague, Meichl-Rukzak? I tried phoning him but got no answer."

"It would be odd if he did answer, especially since he's in Los Angeles for a month."

"How nice! And ... and ... is everything all right ... you know."

"Of course. It's still the same. We're still public enemies."

Shultish pondered the last phrase but said nothing.

"So what else is new, Ezra?"

Shultish brightened. "Did you know that Agnon included me in one of his fictions?"

"You don't say!" Of course Gafni knew. Who didn't? But he wanted to please the old man.

"I do. In his posthumously published novel, *Ha-na'ara ha-temanit*. In English they called it" — here Shultish grimaced — *The Yemenite Girl*."

"Then you're immortalized, Ezra ... You're in a Nobel laureate's work. You've achieved something I'm striving for — immortality."

"But your works have done that for you already, Shmulik."

"That's so kind of you, Ezra."

Gafni glanced quickly at Shultish's wrist to see the time, but Shultish was quicker. He had already withdrawn his hands to his lap.

"In the novel he called me Zera Tishler. I'm wondering if I

should take action."

"What kind? A strike? Picketing? A hue, a cry? A shout, a raising of hands?"

"I mean a suit."

"Single- or double-breasted?"

"I see you're in good humor, Shmulik."

"Just let me say, Ezra, that there are at least ninety-nine people all over the world who are envious of you that you're in one of Agnon's novels. And, anyway, who says that Zera Tishler is you?" Gafni again tweaked the old Hebraist.

"Zera is an anagram of Ezra," Shultish said. "And Tishler is pretty obvious, no?"

"Don't look so gloomy," Gafni said. "Some ten people have told me, 'Why couldn't the old man write about me? I knew Agnon better than Shultish?' But I didn't hesitate to tell them, 'That may be true, but perhaps you're not as interesting.' So, whether you like it or not, be pleased with the attention. You're in the master's masterwork. Sing hallelujah!"

"I can't carry a tune," Shultish said. "Like Agnon, I'm not a music maven."

Gafni waited.

Shultish still looked meditative, as if deciding what he must do.

"So I shouldn't sue?"

"You must be joking. You can't sue a dead man."

Gafni looked at the walls of the cafeteria. How come there was no clock here? He itched to look at his watch, restrained himself, but knew he would have to know the time sooner or later.

"I'd like to tell you something, Shmulik. I hope you're not in a rush."

Truth is, I am in a rush, Gafni didn't say. I have a student coming, and he tried to take a peek at his watch. But that would hurt the old scholar's feelings. Gafni had abruptly cancelled their supper the other evening and then Shultish rescued him. And Gafni had twice pushed off Shultish's request about Gafni's non-existent article about his concocted discovery of the etymology of *davenen*. So he had to be polite.

Gafni's wrist literally tingled, longing to be turned.

11

SHULTISH, TRANSLATOR MANQUE

"I think you know the story of me translating Agnon's book into English," Shultish said.

"No, I don't. Mazel tov. Now that's really remarkable. Let's hear."

Gafni knew the book had already appeared in English as *The Yemenite Girl*. Was it being redone?

"But I don't want to give you the wrong impression, Shmulik. The fact is, I did not end up translating it — and I wanted to translate it so badly."

"And I'm sure you would have," Gafni couldn't resist saying. But Shultish, in an elegaic mood, mourning what was not and could never be, heard only words, not subtext.

"But to my regret I did not ... While Agnon was writing it — and I didn't know the subject — he told me he was considering me to be the translator, and then he died, poor man, and the next thing I know is that young shneck from Iceland and Alsace, C. Urtl Eviant, who called the work, *The Yemenite Girl*, was appointed the translator. Imagine a ridiculous title like that! My title, *The Maiden From Yemen*, captures so perfectly the Agnonian cadence and flavor, a touch of the elusive Old World, the romantic, the lost. Now isn't *The Maiden From Yemen* a better title? Why are you trying to glance furtively at your watch? Are you late for something?"

"I have a student coming at one."

"Still time ... Since I interrupted myself, I'll repeat the question. Isn't *The Maiden From Yemen* a better title?"

"Indeed," Gafni said quickly. "A much more mature choice. So how did the reviews go?"

"I don't know. I don't read reviews. But I understand the Oshkosh Sentinel gave Eviant's translation the review it deserved."

Shultish stopped to take a labored breath. His face became redder. Gafni was afraid that the old man might be working himself into a stroke.

"Ezra, calm down. Why flirt with apoplexy? No translation is worth compromising your health ... Take a few deep breaths and relax."

Shultish obeyed.

"How C. Urtl Eviant came to translate the old man's novel I'll never know. How does he know Hebrew, he's not even Jewish?"

"How do you know?"

"Did you ever meet a Jew from Iceland?"

"Yes, in fact. Itsik Iceberg, who caused the Titanic catastrophe."

"Please, I'm not in the mood for jokes."

For an eyeblink, even less than that, Gafni looked down at his lap where his hands were. He saw nothing. His jacket sleeve hid his watch. But Shultish saw. He peered distrustfully at Gafni's hands, now up on the table. He's wondering, Gafni thought, when I'm going to look at my watch. Because eventually I will have to.

Shultish growled. He made little incomprehensible muttering sounds in the back of his throat, the middle of his mouth, and the tip of his tongue. Perhaps gibberish, perhaps one of the dozen minor languages that Eviant's, poo-poo-poo, away with you, evil eye, original translation would be rendered into.

"What's the matter, Ezra? You're not speaking in tongues, are you? Or is that an Albanian dialect I'm hearing? ... I see you're sad, but consider, the old man couldn't possibly have asked you, for then you would have discovered yourself in the manuscript and sued, thereby halting the production of the book and ipso facto terminating your own contract as translator, which is the very thing you wanted to do, translate his book. Don't you see?"

"You're too logical, Shmulik."

Gafni looked at him for a while, tempted, oh so tempted — like the temptation to autograph a Chekhov work in the library — to look at his watch. But he still resisted.

"So you're still planning to sue?"

"My lawyers are still consulting."

The sunnier delivery of that line showed Gafni that Shultish was being self-mocking.

"You look distracted, Shmulik, staring out the cafeteria window."

"Oh," Gafni said. His voice seemed to come from somewhere else.

"And your face, Shmulik, I didn't want to tell you before, your face looked pale, like it did the other night when the police freed you. But now, all of a sudden, the color has come back into it."

"Has it?" Gafni said, touching his face with his fingers to see if his cheeks felt as warm as they looked. He didn't tell Shultish he had just seen Malina on her way to his office. She was wearing a pale yellow jacket with matching short skirt and a saffron silk scarf whose edges were fluttering in the wind. How beautiful she looked.

Well, at least Shultish didn't know about Malina, probably one of the few scholars who didn't read gossip columns.

At the moment when Malina's saffron scarf fluttered, Gafni made the decision that some sensors in his body had made four days ago when Nussen told him he would have to sign a paper promising not to marry Malina, sensors that his body did not translate into words. Sometimes we make decisions regarding the rest of our lives not because of action but reaction. The little bastard wanted him to sign. What kind of crazy power did that young fool think he had over him? But Gafni would show Nussen who controlled whose life. When and if the time came, Gafni would do what he wanted to do. The religious police would not, could not, stop him, from doing anything. And he would visit Nussen in jail. With her. And holding her hand too.

Now that Gafni had made up his mind, the tension in him dissolved.

Gafni rose, thanked Shultish, said he hoped he would see him again soon and gave him another hug. Under no circumstances did Gafni fantasize that he was hugging Malina. And the thought made him smile.

Malina was coming. Malina was coming for a lesson.

Up the stairs to his office Gafni runs. He laughed at the words he used about his colleague, Meichl-Rukzak. Public enemies. And he remembered, as though it had happened yesterday, the scene where an attempt was made to end the long-standing feud.

12

SKIP THIS CHAPTER (IF YOU WANT TO SEE WHAT
HAPPENS NEXT) UNLESS YOU WANT A BOX SEAT
WATCHING SOMEONE YOU KNOW UNDO
THE GREAT YIDDISH FEUD

THEY were two and yet known as three, yes, a mystery, but not as mysterious (in the theological sense) or incredible as the one-is-three and three-is-one credo foisted upon naïve believers, a mystery that up soon will be cleared (taught were we, remember?, years ago, not to end a sentence with a proposition, to wit: Me would you like to go to bed with?), and since truth and nothing but is what we promised, we might as well tell you now that Gafni wasn't alone in the universe of global Yiddish studies, no loner he, but helped (and hindered), as some would say, quoting Genesis, where it is written: "Eve was a helpmeet against her husband," by Chaim Shimen Meichl-Rukzak, an autodidact (no, not one who teaches cars) who had not gone beyond the tenth grade but who had a formidable command of Hebrew, Yiddish, German, and all Slavic languages. A slave to Slavic am I, he might have said, a) had he mastered English, and b) had he had a sense of humor in the tongue he had no mastery of.

Meichl, you should know, means a "tasty dish" in Yiddish, and since he signed his articles Chaim Sh. Meichl-Rukzak (rukzak means "knapsack")*, people read his name as "Shmeichl," which means "smile." And since wags in Jerusalem, of which there are no lack, already had a *meichl* and a *shmeichl*, all they lacked for a culinary apothegm was a *beichl*, or little belly, which moniker they soon appended to Meichl-Rukzak's colleague, Gafni, although as has already been noted, had no paunch whatsoever. But since the name was given to him and widely used, and since, as is well known from Biblical times, a man's name forges his persona, shapes the bone and marrow of his essence (for instance, Gafni/Weingarten did not hate wine, raisins or grape juice), and since he was already jocularly called "Beichl," he began walking with a little outward midriff thrust like a woman in her third month who doesn't yet show but would like to put on a show of showing. And so, folks, the two of them,

---

*Knapsack, created from a portmanteau of two separate sentences with a similar idea. I'm tired, I'm going to take a knap — I'm tired, I'm going to hit the sack.

Gafni and Meichl-Rukzak became three, Shmeichl, Meichl, and Beichl, there you have demystified your mystery of how two is three, no theological Christian conundrums as you can see, thus creating the well-known Jerusalem folk-saying, *"A gutn meichl in beichl macht a shmeichl"* (a tasty dish in one's belly makes one smile).

It was no secret that Chaim Shimen Meichl-Rukzak, Gafni's elder by three years, whom Gafni had hired two years after establishing the Yiddish Research Institute and Teaching Center at the University of Israel (before the name change to Global Yiddish Studies) had married a Russian gentile woman. But wait, she wasn't a goy, or, to be more grammatically accurate, a goya, when he married her (and even a goya isn't always a female, especially if he paints portraits of noblemen or sells cellophane-wrapped packages of garbanzos or other beans and legumes), for Meichl-Rukzak, in sacred memory of his beloved, martyred parents, murdered by the German Einsatzgruppen and their willing Ukrainian henchmen in 1942, would never marry a goya.

But his goya, Katya, and her mother had saved and hidden Chaim Shimen for three years in their home at great risk to themselves (one of the few Ukrainians who had saved Jews), and it was for him that Katya converted to Judaism before marrying him, then took on the new name of Sara. And what a conversion it was, with a vengeance. First Sara wore a hat, okay, not so bad, lots of pious Jewish women wear hats, and then a kerchief (not atop the hat, instead of), and then a *sheytl*, a marriage wig — we compress a long millinery span of time here into brief phases — over her own hair, and then she had her head shaved like the ultra-Orthodox women of Jerusalem and donned the *sheytl* over her bald pate, and finally, after discarding the sheytl she moved up to the top-of-the-line holiness and tied a kerchief, called a *tikhl*, over her naked head, like a nun. Then came the crowning blow. Sara refused to sleep with Chaim Shimen, her own husband, in his bed, even on the days she was permitted to, and, to the chagrin of other Yiddish scholars, with anyone else's husband, because, she said, it wasn't modest.

So they began calling her "the Jewish nun," but Katya-Sara never-minded this sarcasm for she had always averred that there must be Jewish blood in her, for only Jewish women were so hot (she, however, was able to contain it nunnishly) — it should be noted that everyone, men and women alike, agreed that Sara was a shapely, pretty, tasty morsel, *"a meichl far Meichl"* as the Jerusalem wags put it. But, Jewish as she claimed to be, Sara wasn't averse to crossing herself when she got excited, and this drove poor Chaim Shimen Meichl-Rukzak crazy when she flew into a tizzy of Jewish ecstasy, like when reciting Psalms in Hebrew for a sick friend while swaying back and forth, not a word of which she understood, and muttering through clenched teeth the heretical "dear Jesus!" in Ukrainian between breath stops at the end of a Psalm, which lapse she shrugged off by her passionate belief, faith, devotion, piety and commitment to the one and only God of Israel, the Eternal One, blessed be He — and if I lie, she swore, you can take my life, sweet Jesus, Amen! Yes, poor secular-minded Meichl-Rukzak had, in his old age, religious problems, none of his own making, all of them hers.

Oh, how small is the world of Jerusalem. One man gives out a yawn in Yaffo Street in the center of town — and across the span of neighborhoods, some five or six miles away to the west, up in the hills of Bayit Ve-Gan, three superstitious women, hearing the yawn, spit three times, *tfu tfu tfu*, then added three poo poo poos for good luck and good measure, for any extra spiritual armor that pious Jews who believe in one indivisible God have in the never-ending struggle against demons who gleefully rush into a person's innards when he opens wide his mouth, that is, his inmost vulnerable self, and yawns is welcome and efficacious. A countervailing thrice-uttered pagan poo can never hurt.

Everyone said that Gafni was trying to imitate Meichl-Rukzak in running after a *shikse*, the pretty, amazingly well-built Malina — remember her? — who still hasn't shown up for her next Yiddish lesson, delayed as it were by this intrusive chapter. But, actually, it was the older Meichl-Rukzak who was competing with his slightly younger colleague, Gafni, who always outstripped his rival with more books and articles per year.

About Meichl-Rukzak there never was the slightest whiff of scandal; the only scandal was the way he tried to catch up to Gafni in publications but never quite succeeded. Everyone in the academic world kept score: 105-86, or 111-98, the latest numbers. You'd think, yay team, a basketball game, the NBA finals — but no, it was the sum total of monographs and books by Gafni vs. Meichl-Rukzak. (Why he had a double name we haven't figured out yet, but will probably come up with a plausible answer soon enough. Maybe he was Mexican. Why? All Mexicans have double names.)

But, Meichl-Rukzak in private, if you caught his ear, which wasn't hard to do because both his ears were rather large and lopey, would tell you that in the world of scholarship quality counts. Enough said. And if indeed you lower yourself to sports statistics (the word "stats" he wasn't quite familiar with), you have to count accurately; namely, Gafni likes division, he — Meichl-Rukzak — likes addition. To wit: Gafni would take one article and divide it in five installments in let's say, the daily newspaper Ha-aretz and count it as five articles. If he did this shtick conservatively four times, that's 20 articles out of 4, his score is already down to 95 (just minus 16 on your calculator, those of you whose brain has already become calcified to manual subtraction). So, yay team, who's the winner now, coach, with the numbers now at 99-95? And moreover (and what follows are Meichl-Rukzak's words), one must admire Gafni, a supporter of recycling. (I said "recycling," which does not mean: Ma, can I use the bike again?) He would take one article and send it, after it was published in Jerusalem, to the New Zealand Yiddish Quarterly and to the South African Yiddish Bulletin, and God knows where else. No wonder his score is 111. How do the chicken pluckers describe, in their inimitable lingo, an unfair move? They cry: Fowl! I won't say, says Meichl-Rukzak, that the 111 is all one article. But only in Lower Math does 111=111.

Rumor had it, ask anyone in Jerusalem, that Gafni and Meichl-Rukzak were bitter rivals, such mortal enemies that if perchance, once in a blue Tammuz, they were seen entering together the building where they had their offices, Chaim Sh. Meichl-Rukzak would race to the stairs and Gafni would take the elevator, even though generally Gafni, bent forward, would take the steps two at a time. Once, a Tel Aviv magazine reported, Gafni was so flustered seeing his foe that he too raced up the steps with Meichl-Rukzak, and even — just shows you how gafnified he was — he even greeted him.

Beichl and Sh. Meichl were different not only in education (Gafni a Phd, Meichl-Rukzak not even a high school diploma), stature (Gafni middling height, robust; Meichl, slight and small), but also in garb. Except at conferences abroad, Gafni never wore ties, while Meichl-Rukzak always wore jacket, shirt and tie (both always wore pants) during the long Israeli spring and summer, and when it was cold during the fall and winter rainy season, Sh. Meichl wore long-sleeved sweaters that sagged at the elbows, like Einstein's famous sweaters. The word was out that Gafni probably didn't even own a tie.

All this competitiveness, disdain and disparagement, mind you, took place only in public for the delectation of gossip columnists in the Friday magazine supplements who covered the university world with as much energy as American gossip columnists covered the movie and tv stars. Good planners they, both men knew that public relations stunts were important even in a world as narrow as Academe. It was important for the public to know of your existence and it permitted double fundraising too, one from Gafni's loyal supporters and one from Chaim Shimen Meichl-Rukzak's, all deposited in the Global Yiddish Studies Fund, aka Yiddish Research Institute, aka Mame-Loshn Ltd. But if no one was around (please don't tell anyone; the following is just For Your Eyes Alone), they both entered the elevator together and enjoyed each other's company and even helped each other with the research projects they undertook. They even, Shh!, visited each other, which they told no one about.

There was one famous incident that took place in the University of Israel swimming pool early one morning, which proved they got along swimmingly — until two other meddling profs entered for their bi-monthly swim and to their shock and consternation saw the two of them, Sh. Meichl and Beichl, swimming laps, whereupon one professor approached Gafni and said:

"Don't you know you are swimming here with him?"

At which Gafni constricted his face; his lips compressed as if he'd just bitten into an *esrog*, or been bitten by one; his eyes narrowed as if a policeman had shined a beam of light into his eyes; his nostrils pinched as if his olfactory nerves had suddenly been insulted by an unbearable stench. So distorted was his face it looked like he'd just been ambushed by angina pectoris.

"Oh, my God," Gafni gasped, holding on to the edge of the pool. "He must have entered when my face was down, otherwise I would have spun around and left. You see, I do the Australian crawl and don't see anyone when I swim with my face in the water."

And at once Gafni swooshed the hair from his face to rid himself of the polluted water he had just been immersed in and walked, yes, you read it right, walked across the water of the pool, the shortest way to the dressing room, while the second professor passed the bad news on to Chaim Shimen Meichl-Rukzak and gave him the same glad tidings.

Meichl-Rukzak's reaction was a series of pained facial tics, after the partial subsiding of which he explained:

"God in Heaven! I can't believe it. Him? Here? In the same water? Oh, pollution! You see I do the Kovno crawl, which is half Australian crawl, half sideways schnauzer or German shepherd dog paddle. It was developed by the Lithuanians in honor of Hitler in preparation for the 1936 Berlin Olympics, which the ever-corrupt International Olympic Committee decided to hold in Germany despite four full years of oppressive Nazi racial rule. Are you following?"

The bamboozled professor, locked into a crouch as Meichl-Rukzak held on to the edge of the pool, nodded dully.

"But this delighted the Lithuanians, who wanted to out-Teutonize the Teutons and did in fact begin murdering the Jews of Kovno after a sermon by the Bishop of the Kovno Catholic Church, long before the Germans even set foot in Kovno, to the delirious delight and wild appreciation of the Lithuanian folk."

"But what does this have to do with you being in the pool with Beichl?"

"Wait, I'm coming to it. Back to the Olympic swimming competition with their Kovno crawl, which I was doing when he, unbeknownst to me, was with me here. In that 1936 competition, the Lithuanians with their Kovno crawl came in last, 89th out of 89, with their combo Australian crawl, which symbolized for me their crawling to the Germans and their German Shepherd dog paddle, which signified for me the damned dogs that they are, and so doing this stroke was perfect reason for me not seeing my bitter enemy, for I swam half on my side, facing the other way, and didn't know anyone else was in the pool."

And Meichl, without another word, turned and dove back into the water deeply and took an underwater exit to the locker room.

For years people tried to end the feud. Ezra Shultish tried too. Yes, the dean of American Hebraists, whom you've just eaten supper with and whom you'll no doubt meet again, the very same whose first language was Yiddish (whose wasn't?), knew both of them. The very same Shultish whose book on the Israel Nobel Laureate, S.Y. Agnon, so won the esteem of the old writer (who couldn't read a word of Shultish's English book) that when he was asked the meaning of a certain story, Agnon tossed off his oft-quoted remark: "Ask Professor Ezra Shultish! He knows what my stories mean better than I!"

One day, about three years ago, when Shultish was in Jerusalem, in the little apartment that he had bought for himself in Bet Ha-Kerem, he tried his hand at mediation. He took the initiative he thought no one had taken before and, unbeknownst to the other, invited both Gafni and Meichl-Rukzak to his home for an evening tea. Shultish was then still teaching, and was probably in his late seventies — maybe early eighties — no none knew for sure. Shultish wasn't in the habit of showing his passport and, like a recalcitrant horse, he didn't let anyone count his teeth either.

Since Shultish was older and often came out with rare Yiddish sayings from his Polish childhood,* which both Gafni and Meichl-Rukzak treasured, both men accepted Shultish's invitation.

Obviously, they did not come at the same time. One came first and, as logic and the time-space continuum would dictate, the other came later. Shultish, wise old owl that he was, told both to come at 7:30, knowing full well that only one would come on time. Oh, when the two would be there, he could begin his masterful reconciliation of two men he liked. Sh. Meichl-Rukzak came first and, seeing three

---

*"You inspire me," Shultish would say modestly, when they complimented him on another saying. "Eighty years fly by like a dream and I hear my mother and father speaking." Then, realizing that he had given away his age, he added: "Of course, I mean this metaphorically, like the Biblical number forty, meaning a long time."

plates on the coffee table, asked: "Who's the third plate for?"

Shultish smiled beatifically and said, "Where there's two there's three," which should have tipped off Meichl-Rukzak, given the earlier two-is-three nexus between him and Gafni.

When Shmulik came (late), completing the threesome, a number of astonished looks were exchanged. Shultish and Meichl-Rukzak gawked at Gafni. Gafni and Meichl-Rukzak glared at Shultish. Gafni glommed at Meichl-Rukzak. The latter glowered at Gafni. Then, to Shultish's shame and astonishment, both professors began berating the meddling American for attempting to break up the great fun they had had over the years as supposed enemies and rivals; moreover, they took the old man to task — and in a juicy, vituperative Yiddish too — for attempting to harm the financial welfare of Yiddish studies at the University of Israel.

"And we forswear you to silence, since we both like you and know you meant well. You're the only one in the world who knows this, Shultish. Do you swear?"

"As I once stated in a New York night traffic court, which was a total surprise to me, since I don't drive ... I said: I don't swear, I affirm."

"Then what were you doing in court?"

"I was standing on the corner of Fifth Avenue and West 57th Street, minding my own business, when a red light passed me. So a cop gave me a ticket ..."

Neither Gafni nor Meichl-Rukzak understood the arcane New York City traffic laws. But that didn't interest them now.

"Can we trust you with this, our secret? Do you affirm?"

"Yes."

"Who won't you tell it to? Give us names."

"I'll name no names. I'll list no lists. And I'll make sure that the two or three friends I'll tell this to will also keep their mouths shut."

And all three broke out in laughter.

"Seriously, Ezra," Meichl-Rukzak said. "You're the only one who knows. Others may suspect. But you know."

"You've told others about this tea," Gafni probed.

"No," Shultish lied, badly.

"Okay," Meichl-Rukzak said. "We can permit you one lie today. This one. But no more."

"When you tell your two or three so-called friends — I can't imagine you having any more," Gafni ordered, "you will tell them that your attempted reconciliation was a disaster. Better yet, you won't tell, you won't volunteer — but if, IF, *if* you're asked, then you'll hesitatingly say ... struggling to find words ... that it was a disaster ... You can embellish it any way you like ... After all, you're a master of style ... Say Gafni had a tantrum fit ... Meichl-Rukzak got up in a huff, knocking over his cup of tea which spilled on your good carpet, the only good one you own, and stalked out, bumping into the wrong door and bruising his nose."

"Your nose. Leave mine out of it," Meichl-Rukzak said, then added. "And say that Gafni was so enraged he forgot his coat, which you've been wearing ever since."

Then without missing a beat, Gafni said: "I can't believe you did this, Ezra. What kind of anti-Semite are you?"

"I've never been called an anti-Semitt before, so how can I know what kind I am?" Shultish replied. "But I'll look into it and let you know." He gazed at the two men. "So you're really friends? I'm astonished. Surprised. Pleased. Absolutely delighted." Shultish's eyes shone. He was so happy he was on the verge of tears.

"As soon as I got your invitation I phoned Shimele to tell him," Gafni said, "and I immediately ... "

" ... told Shmulik," Shimen Meich-Rukzak continued, "that you invited me too."

"Why did you invite him first? I know you longer," said Gafni.

"Probably because you reviewed his Agnon book," said Meichl-Rukzak

"The truth is," said Shultish, "I invited both of you first, at the same time, but your line was busy," he turned to both. "So naturally there was a delay."

"Never mind," Meichl-Rukzak said. "Let's get to the point. Don't dream of breaking up a good feud, you hear? If you tell anyone about us not another one of your Agnon translations will be published anywhere ... "

"I told you, I affirmed ... "

"And what's more," Gafni continued. "We'll engage the Icelandic Alsatian, C. Urtl Eviant to do those translations."

At which Shultish turned white. Poor man, all his facial blood sank down to his feet. A little surge of static electricity made his white mane bristle vertically in terror.

"No no no, you have my word. I promise to operate, copoperate with you," the shaken Shultish stammered. "Have regard, if not for me, then for the master's oeuvre."

"So may we count on you?" Gafni said gently.

"Yes. I'll even swear if you twist my hand. But the left one, please. I write with my right."

"You see, dear Ezra, this is all a game. A charade. A public relations stunt. It's all for the public which loves feuds, enmities, backbiting, rumors, gossip ... Chaim Shimen Meichl-Rukzak, whom I call Shimele, is actually my best friend."

At which Meichl-Rukzak threw his arm around Beichl's shoulder, uniting the legendary Sh.Meichl, Meichl and Beichl trio, and said, "Amen to that. Now let's have tea."

"It's ready," Shultish said. "The tea is prepared, the biscuits are in the tin. Here let me have your jackets. I don't know why they heat these rooms so much, it's not winter any more. They overheat this place something awful." And Shultish took Gafni's and Meichl-Rukzak's jackets and swung them around the highbacked chairs. In doing so, two cigarette-pack-sized black machines flew out of the jacket pockets and landed. At once, they began emitting Yiddish sentences. But when Shultish bent down to scoop up the tiny cassette recorders, a third one joined them, thereby recreating once more the mystery of where there's two there's three. It fell out of Ezra Shultish's deep shirt pocket and landed on the play button. Now all three little black gadgets lay on the floor expostulating in Yiddish in unison, reprising all the conversations of the previous thirty forty minutes and affirming the truth of the old maxim that history does repeat itself. Meanwhile, the three profs sipped tea and munched cookies, so pleased with how devoted to Yiddish and Yiddish folklore were they that they would even compromise their own egos and record themselves — so each of them explained to the others' satisfaction, and if you think they were embarrassed at seeing their duplicity on the floor, you're dead wrong.

First they listened to their entire conversations with smiles on their faces and then each commenced exegesis on text. Shultish, the elder, began:

"I always record my conversations, for I like to keep a record of the folk sayings that pop out of me and, by the way, I'll have you know my recorder is so sophisticated, listen ... "

And he fast forwarded it to a remark, a Russian Yiddish folk expression that neither of the other two remembered Shultish uttering.

"You see," Shultish explained, "it even records things I didn't say."

Then Gafni explained his recorder.

"I too wanted to preserve Ezra's bon mots, but I'm also writing a book about Shimele and didn't want to lose one gem of my friend's remarks."

To which Meichl-Rukzak responded:

"I guess I'll have to lie like the rest of you and say I wanted to preserve every one of your remarks for posterity, for at what other occasion can three of the world's senior linguists be under one roof and insult one another in private without anyone knowing about it? It's a pity the world wasn't listening — but you know what? It was

... it was."

As Gafni and Meichl-Rukzak left Shultish's apartment they didn't say a word. They just pressed an index finger to their lips (each to his own). What Meichl-Rukzak was thinking of when he did this is hard to say. But when Gafni put a finger to his lips, for a moment he thought of Malina's lips.

He turned to Shultish.

"And can I have my coat back, Ezra?"

AFTERCHAPTER 12

Gafni couldn't remember rightly how he helped Nixon, who was beyond help, but he didn't hinder him either — the latter fact he now withdraws, for Gafni did tape-record Nixon's private anti-Semitic remarks.

They can be heard on a thirty-minute cassette (Best of Richard M. Nixon's Anti-Jewish Epithets, Gafni Productions, Jerusalem), delivered in Nixon's radio-flavored, vowel-rounded and polished Pacific Coast all-American accent.

II

HERE AND THERE

1

SHIVA

SHIVA.

Even dialysis could no longer help. When Batsheva had recovered from her last crisis, Shmulik felt so euphoric, he thought she would live forever. But then death took her, and Shmulik, by surprise. There was no postponing it. With our first cry we begin to die. During shiva, the seven days of mourning, Gafni, his son, Yosef, and his twin daughters, Rivka and Rachel, sat on low stools, acknowledging the many people who came to fulfill the mitzva of comforting the bereaved. Visitors would enter, nod, never saying hello as was the custom in a house of mourning, stand awkwardly before Gafni, he felt sorry for their unease, and utter some words of consolation. At night, with more people present, the room was abuzz with conversation. Occasionally, at the far end of the room, a note of laughter would rise, but Gafni didn't mind. Laughter was good. The passport away from death was laughter. When, if, his time came, he wanted to die laughing, to expire with a smile. What better way to go? But now, even if he wanted to, he could not. Then, in the jumpy, jaggedy circuits of his brain, the words "live forever" ran like a fluttering banner. It haunted him, that two-word phrase — a high pitched sound, pleasantly painful — and would not go away.

Talking made the hours pass. Nights were more difficult. His children helped, Yosef especially. Gafni realized that his son, who had flown in from Seattle for the funeral, was very wise, truly his father's son. While sitting next to Gafni, Yosef asked him to speak about Batsheva's early days, about their young years together before the children were born — precisely the sort of questions Gafni would ask when he made shiva calls, hoping to ease the mourners' pain by memories. He nodded slowly. Remembering is consolation. Recalling the dead is one way of bringing a person to life. But then he twisted his lips, recoiling at the banality, the unreality of the thought. At least one deludes oneself, if only for a moment, into believing this. Illusions also console. While they last the feeling is good — but then, with a blow to the head, reality returns.

Yosef asked, Gafni answered, remembering. Rachel and Rivka asked. Their father replied, recalling. Strange, he thought, they were the real twins, but they didn't finish each other's sentences, as did their daughters, Zehava and Penina, the first cousins who were born at exactly the same time, whom everyone called "the twins."

Then he remembered the nightmare that occasionally came during the years they were married: he was single, alone, unmarried, half himself. He ached with loneliness. In his dreams he wondered, worried, pitied himself, why was he still alone. And then woke up to find Batsheva next to him and he was whole again.

DURING the shiva, Gafni didn't think of her. He willfully extirpated her from his thoughts. There was a time when the image of Malina was so large it filled the screen of his imagination; it overflowed its frame, and parts of her were cut off like a picture too large for a frame. But now he daydreamed only of his beloved Batsheva. Ran the film of their life together inside his closed eyes, scene by scene, from the time he met her in a history class at the Hebrew University to her last days. Poorly edited, that film, but so it goes with memory.

Between visitors, Gafni stared at the Persian carpet before him, seeing for the first time the hinds chasing one another into the tendrils and rosettes and, as he entered the world of roosting and flying birds, his thoughts went off on a journey of their own.

Memories came unbidden. Why he remembered the little dog puzzled him.

Holding hands, he and Batsheva were returning one evening from a concert at the Jerusalem Theater. They made their way past the old former Arab mansions of Rehavia, past the Prime Minister's house, then cut through a narrow lane. Then, from out of nowhere, a little white dog appeared, stopped, and looked at them. The dog gave a little dance of joy, raised his tail, spun around once, and followed them.

Gafni didn't like dogs. The Germans had dogs, loved them more than people, used them to hunt down and attack Jews. In the shtetl, Jews rarely kept dogs. Dogs were invariably in the Polish houses, trained to bark at Jews who passed by. In his mind dogs were German, dogs were goyish, dogs were Polish, dogs were bad. During the Nazi era, in public parks in Austria and Germany there were signs, Dogs and Jews Forbidden. But this white little dog, Gafni bent down to look at him, this one didn't have sly eyes like some dogs. This one had gentle eyes, Jewish eyes. This one, Gafni could have sworn, this one gave him a smile. The little white dog followed, bounding like a new-born lamb, as if it belonged to them. It trailed them innocently, naively, without fear, as though it had already arrogated them as its master.

By the time they approached their house, Gafni already had fantasies that they would take the dog in. He didn't say a word, but

Batsheva, sensing his thoughts, said:

"First of all, you don't like dogs. Second, you don't like dogs. Third, who will take care of him, walk him once or twice a day, feed him, tend to him if we go away?"

The dog had a familiar face. Maybe that's why Gafni took to it. He knew that the kabbalists believed in reincarnation. The dog could very well have been a colleague or an old family member. He didn't want to think it was his murdered father. The God who possibly did not exist would not play a trick like that on him.

Then Batsheva smiled. "Remember those two dogs from years ago in the Galil? ... You don't think, do you? ... "

"No," he said. "Impossible."

The little dog scampered up to the door with them as if already knowing that its fate had been decided. It would be taken in, find a family. It wagged its little white tail and smiled again.

"No, no." Gafni bent down to the dog. For a moment he considered speaking to it in Yiddish, but changed his mind at the last minute and spoke in Polish. In Eastern Europe one would speak Yiddish only to cats because cats were lovable, dogs were not, cats were friendly, dogs the enemy. On the rare occasion that a Jewish farmer had a dog, he would speak goyish, the language of the land, to the dog, because of the nature of dogs. Cats, Jewish; dogs, goyish. But this one, no doubt about it, this one was a Jewish dog, with Jewish eyes.

Nevertheless, Gafni said, "Shoo, go home ... sorry," as an apologetic afterthought. The sad look on the dog's face would always remain with him, as would the ameliorative thought that the dog belonged to someone, that it would find its way home, for stories abounded about dogs lost for months who found their way back to their masters.

"It looks familiar," Gafni told Batsheva, "but some poor soul is already missing it."

The dog didn't move.

"*Gey aheim*," Gafni said finally, but with an upbeat tone. Hearing the Yiddish, the dog spun around and ran off.

But this incident in no way matched the one that Batsheva hinted at, when years ago Gafni walked in the fields north of Safed with Batsheva and the "twins," the grand-daughters. Suddenly, seemingly out of nowhere, two dogs appeared. They too were small and white, like the Jerusalem dog.

"Are you good little dogs?" he asked in Yiddish, forgetting that he would only speak goyish to dogs. But since he'd been talking to the little girls in Yiddish, he continued in *mame-loshn*.

"I am," answered one, "but my brother is a bad little dog."

"But I can be good too," said the second, "if you give me a couple of pieces of paper and a pen."

"*Sabba, sabba*, talking dogs," Penina and Zehava, then five or six, shrieked merrily and clapped their hands.

Batsheva opened her pocketbook and gave Gafni a pen.

"I don't have paper," he said.

"Then I must be a bad little dog," said the second dog. It screwed up its brown eyes, twisted its mouth, yawned, showed its teeth, and raised its tail, stiff as a flagpole.

Gafni pulled out his pocket calendar. Searched for a blank page at the end. "These are marked pages."

The dog shrugged.

Gafni tore out two pages and gave them to the dog.

"And the pen, please."

Gafni gave the dog the pen. "Are you a lefty or a righty?"

"Don't get political," the dog said.

"Now I'll get older quicker. Two days from my calendar gone," said Gafni.

"We want pages too," Penina said. "Otherwise, we too … "

And her cousin, Zehava, concluded "… are also going to be bad little dogs, woof woof."

Reluctantly, Gafni tore out two more pages and gave them to the children.

"No, you'll get younger quicker," the second dog said. "You'll go back in time. We call it life-saving time … You've lost pages from your calendar but you've gained days, maybe weeks, even years, of life."

Again "live forever" flashed on the screen of Gafni's closed eyes.

Then the dog wrote something, so did its friend, then they barked gaily at each other and ran away.

One dog wrote in Hebrew: "Be happy and have a good life."

The other wrote in Yiddish: "*Zy gezunt!*" Be well.

Gafni recalled the radiant, beneficent look on Batsheva's face as she read the little notes. There was no one he knew who had such an angelic countenance. His father had a folk-saying that would have applied perfectly to Batsheva. When he wanted to describe a *mentch*, a kindly soul, whose facial mien matched his heart, he would say: "*Di gootskite ligt im afn ponim.*" The literal translation: the goodness lies on his face. Meaning: his kindness shines from his face. Or: one look at his face and you can see his beautiful soul. That one line encapsulated Batsheva. Yes, that is, was, is, my lovely wife. Gafni didn't know if he would use those words as an epitaph on her tombstone. But they were surely engraved in the tombstone of his heart.

And his, what about his epitaph? Let's see. Like the famous Yiddish poet (he forgot who) said: My lungs thrive on Yiddish. But I'll expand on that. Inspired, Gafni elaborated on the ground theme, adding: For me Yiddish is oxygen. Give me gills and I'll swim in the ocean of Yiddish and will breathe pure air.

JUST as we cannot control memories, we cannot control thoughts sparked by a previous flash of words.

Tombstone/Batsheva elided into tombstone/father. Did his father have one? He couldn't remember. He thought and thought until his head ached. He was buried in the old cemetery in Warsaw next to his grandfather and Gafni's mother. But did he have a stone? That's where he would like to lie too, when his time came. But as soon as he saw the image of his father, at once his father's doppelgänger, the other, appeared. Gafni wanted to banish him. He wanted to forget him but could not — could not allow himself to forget until justice was done. But Gafni didn't want to think of that beast now, so he forced himself to shift thoughts away, away, until he thought of his father's father, who lived in a shtetl about an hour from Warsaw.

Yes, one can will memory, but then memory's own engine takes hold and it's out of your hands. Next thing Gafni saw was the cherry tree in his grandfather's yard. Why that, out of all the memories compressed into that vast granary of memories?

One June, the usually fruit-laden tree did not yield any fruit. His grandfather, Moshe, in order to make the children happy, in order not to disappoint them when they came to spend the summer, bought pounds of cherries at the market. Then he climbed a ladder and tied the stems of the cherries to the tree with thin white string. When the children arrived they saw before them the familiar tree brimming with ripe fruit.

Shmulik could still taste the tart, sweet juice, the firm flesh of the cherry, its crackle when his teeth bit into the fruit. He swallowed. A sudden feeling of childish joy overwhelmed him.

But then Batsheva slid in with the ease of a gliding door and in came an empty feeling, a tweak in his heart. She was gone. His father was gone, murdered. His mother. His uncles and aunts and cousins, killed. His *zeyde*. The cherries, their juice sweet and tart. Only the bitter tang of unripe cherries remained. Of time that yielded bitter fruit.

The ashen apples of Sodom.

DURING the shiva Malina didn't come to the house. He had not expected her to. It was wise of her not to come. It would have upset the

entire shiva. Only in some absurdist novel, a soap opera or a sadistic
fiction could Malina have been able to pay a shiva call at Gafni's
house. He wondered if conflicting thoughts had run through her mind.
Should I go or shouldn't I? She dropped him a polite, almost formal
note, in Polish. Its impersonal tone disappointed him; yes, hurt him
too. He read it again and again, trying to squeeze a different meaning
out of it. But the few words did not open themselves to any other
interpretation. Malina's letter was among the hundreds he received.
He was surprised and touched. He hadn't realized he was worthy of
the attention of so many people. And scores of people came to pay a
shiva call. The President of Israel came, the Prime Minister, cabinet
ministers, members of Knesset, writers, scholars, even people from
the rival Hebrew University. The known and the unknown. Only in
Israel could a famous intellectual elicit the personal attention of so
many famous public figures.

And Sh. Meichl-Rukzak, of course, from his own department at
the University of Israel. Seeing him entering, Gafni stood up from his
low stool, waited for him to approach. They embraced, for the first
time in public, and wept on each other's shoulders. Onlookers were
shocked. Skeptics viewed this as a one-time spectacle and did not
trust their embrace. Everyone regretted there were no photographers
around to record this incredible event.

SHMULIK remembered Meichl-Rukzak once telling him, his head
shaking in disbelief, that he came home from school one morning
and saw his wife, Sara, baking bread stark naked. She claimed it
was a return to nature. In Eden, she said, Eve didn't get dressed
up to prepare food. So this was one way for her to achieve a state
of primordiality, to unite in spirit with her first mother. But please
don't tell anyone, Meichl-Rukzak pleaded. I won't, said Gafni, and
he kept his word. But who knows how many other people Meichl-
Rukzak had asked not to tell a soul? For soon enough it was all over
campus, all over town. Once the word spread — e-mail, fe-mail, he-
mail, rooftop shouts, kaffee-klatsch innuendo — Sara had so many
invitations to give private baking lessons, she could have opened
a school. Gafni too was tempted to learn back-to-nature challah
baking, but rejected the idea for religious reasons. If something
went wrong with the baking — the yeast doesn't rise, the crust is
burnt — the ex-goy Sara might cry out "*Sh'ma Yisroel*" and "Sweet
Jesus" in one breath, and Gafni wasn't prepared for such sacrilege.

THAT night, when all the visitors were gone, in his dreams
reappeared his beautiful, devoted Batsheva, and he enfolded himself
into her as in the old days. But holding on to dreams is like holding

water. No, not water. With water at least your hands get wet. It was more like holding air. Dreams give nothing. No, not nothing. One thing.

Heartache.

THEN the shiva over, the house empty. Yosef back to teaching in Seattle; the twins, Rivka and Rachel, back to their families. And Gafni too returned to his classes and tried to smile, so as not to make his students and colleagues uncomfortable or miserable. But whereas the outside puts on a mighty good show, the inside has nowhere to hide, *and* nowhere to go.

During the *shloshim*, the thirty-day period of mourning, Gafni, as was to be expected, was still in loss. He couldn't find his place. He walked into the kitchen or the bedroom and didn't know why. He started reading a book, got to the bottom of the page, and realized he hadn't absorbed a word. At night, the bed was seemingly larger than usual, endless in fact during the long long nights. In his sleep, just before dreams brought Batsheva back, he moved closer and closer to the middle of the bed, longing to touch her, to press close to her, mold his limbs into hers. But now he found only emptiness, wishes, air. He heard himself groaning, didn't know he moaned until he heard the sounds and tried to untie the knots in his stomach.

Oh, the various sleep positions they had, original, unheard of, unique. Always in some kind of embrace. One would have to be a gymnast or an acrobat for the close sleep positions they invented. With Batsheva he slept so much as one, slithered, slipped, knotted, curled into and around her, *kknoyled* was a word he liked to use, slipping one leg between hers and the other around her and one hand around her chest and the other godknowswhere here and there until he didn't know, couldn't tell, whose limbs belonged to whom and he was lucky to wake up with his own arms and legs, which happened most of the time. And when they clasped hands before they fell asleep, they shared the same dreams.

BUT after *shloshim* thoughts of Malina surfaced, hard to stop. Like stopping the waves, damming the tides. Once, as he slept pressed close to Batsheva, she began crying. Why did this woman, still pretty in her late sixties, with hardly a wrinkle on her face, begin to cry? Her sobs seemed wordless, but he thought he heard her saying "*Di Poilishe*" — that Polish woman.

"What? What? What's the matter? Why are you crying?"

But she either would not answer or he could not fathom what she was saying in her sleep.

I wasn't thinking of her, he thought, I was thinking of your lovely face.

Perhaps Batsheva did not say that after all. But what if she had? And who told, who would tell her about Malina? Yes, rumors fly. Yes, rumors are all over the place, like pigeons in Venice, but they are not necessarily messenger pigeons who carry the rumors straight to the wife.

Malina again. If something were to happen between them, no, it couldn't, it was just a passing thought, a fleeting dream, shadow of a quickly moving cloud. But if for some reason, for the sake of argument, let's admit for the moment the possibility, if it were destined that they be — There, that was the first time that sentence was fully formulated in his mind, even if it was incomplete. His jagged thoughts alternated between loyalty to Batsheva and a magnetic pull towards Malina. He saw the "if" in capital letters. A huge neon sign atop a building. If the "if" became real, it could only happen a year later, at the end of the traditional one-year period of mourning. Thinking this, Gafni's heart constricted. The next thought came of its own accord — as did many of his memories during the last few weeks. He had nothing to do with it. Somewhere, someone pressed a button and there it was. The biggest problem, if the "if" came true: would she, and how would she, convert? His heart beat rapidly, palpitations they were called. A light sweat on his forehead. From under his armpits rose a foul, stale smell. He felt frightened, as if he were hiding from the Germans and someone was coming. How swiftly the thoughts were propelling him forward. Malina loved Yiddish, had started learning Hebrew — what was her goal, he wondered, when she finished her studies? To open an institute in Poland? Yes, she loved Yiddish but had never given the slightest indication she wanted to become a Jew. Now that he thought of it, even in studying Yiddish, if he didn't offer them first on his own, she never asked him about the religious or liturgical links inherent in words or phrases. And even then, the usual bright light of interest in her eyes dimmed a bit, unsuccessful in her attempt to hide her boredom.

Although in the past, Yiddish and *Yiddishkeyt*, the Yiddish word for Judaism, were as inseparable as *Sh'ma* and *Yisroel*, in the classic Jewish prayer, nowadays you could find a wild assortment of individuals with an interest just in Yiddish, like the Japanese man who had been a student for a year at the University of Israel. Or the professional scholars of Old Yiddish, guess wherefrom? Gafni still shook his head in bemusement, remembering that lately many Old Yiddish scholars were not only not Jewish — they were Germans. *Germans*. Germany and Yiddish. Now there's a matching jacket and pants, as the ironic Yiddish expression had it, a Yiddish idiom

Gafni's mother loved to quote, smiling, when she wanted to accent something totally mismatched: *a sheyne por kleyder*. So Gafni never deluded himself into thinking that just because Malina had fallen in love with Yiddish she had necessarily fallen in love with *Yiddishkeyt*, or that Yiddish was a path toward that goal.

If, IF, *if*. But suppose it did happen? Suppose they did get together. He could imagine his family's and his friends' shock at learning that Gafni was considering marrying or had already married a *shikse*.

Oh, he knew what they would say. That awful mindless *they* that milled all rumors. It's the old story. The classic comedies of which he was now the hero, from the Latin comedies of Plautus, through the *commedia del arte*, through the Restoration comedies, through Rossini and Donizetti and beyond. The old husband, the young wife — perfect setup for laughter and derision.

What makes one old anyway? he wondered. Was it a look in the mirror mirror on the wall whose polished surface had been lying to him for years then suddenly repented, the glass seemingly staring into the mirror of its own soul? Yes, it reflects, now I will tell the whole truth.

Or was it the child saying: Look at the old man?

Or was it remembering songs and personalities from ages ago, which no one knew or remembered today? Or was it the telltale pallor of one's shins and ankles that showed old white legs, poor circulation, a slowing gait? Or does old age come when one day you want to sign a check and the letters of your name become edged, jagged, and a straight line that you attempt to make looks like a stretch of barbed wire? No amount of will power can stop the sign of aging, and you realize that your will and your body can go in two different directions without even kissing you goodbye. No wonder, Gafni thought, Hebrew has the remarkable idiom, *kavtza alav ha-zikna*, old age jumped on him. One minute it ain't there, the next, like a rider leaping onto a horse — there it is.

Then he had an answer. Unexpected. Out of nowhere. It was his frayed, decades-old little address book with the faded and peeling-at-the-edges faux red leather covers, in which he had been jotting names, addresses and phone numbers since he had come to Israel. Once, months ago, he had taken the little book out of his briefcase to write down Ezra Shultish's phone number. As he turned the tiny pages to find a blank spot, a little pinch of pain, as if sadness were a brief pincer, ran like an electric charge through him. He knew why. Just by glancing briefly at the two-page list open before him where a line was empty on the bottom right. Now I know what old age means, Gafni thought. Not that I'm part of it, God forbid. Not that I'm succumbing to it. But on the page where he listed Shultish, everyone was dead. Later, he riffed through other pages. More and more deceased. In fact, more people in the address book were dead than alive. In his palm-sized book Gafni had a list of the dead, like a shul's memorial plaque. Friends and acquaintances, relatives and colleagues, all of them in *yenne velt*. If, for a *Yizkor* service, he would list them all by name, it would take him more than half an hour of recitation. Why did he make friends with so many old people? he wondered. Or so many who had died?

Yes, Gafni concluded, that was it. His address book proved it.

Gafni was officially an old man.

Maybe.

But only, he laughed, and it was a proud laugh, a happy laugh, a laugh in his manly baritone that expressed his full vigor and life force — only from the waist up.

Old age made the attempt to leap on him — but he shook the rascal off.

During the year of mourning, he shared his thoughts with no one. But when the year was over, he knew what he would do, had to do, was driven to do.

Destined to do.

2

THE TRAIN RIDE FROM WARSAW TO LODZ: FIRST RETURN

THE train ride from Warsaw to Lodz (Gafni loved the liquid Polish pronunciation: Wawdzh) was normally a two-and-a-half hour ride. But somehow, in the special world he was in, it either felt like six minutes, or six hours.

As the train rounded a bend, Gafni saw the engineer, an old man with a lined face. He remembered that face when years later he saw the film *Shoah* and the wizened, impassive, even cruel face of the engineer guiding the cars right into the maw of Auschwitz. And when he recently saw the same face, wrinkled and creased, smiling now, in the *New York Times* ads peddling Polish vodka, he was again reminded of the engineer's face.

From his window, he saw an express train passing him on another track. Flames enveloped the cars as they sped by, one after another, a comet of fire, one and then another.

Although Gafni didn't want to speak to any Pole, he couldn't help addressing the only other person in the compartment, a tall, thin man with slicked down hair and an arrogant mien.

"Did you see that?" Gafni said in Polish.

"What?"

"That train. Those cars. On fire." He jumped up and pointed, but the train had gone by. Only a trail of flames remained, shaped like a railway car.

"Look! As if a halo of fire. As if given a hoop of flames. As if fire is accompanying the cars. Flames out of every pore of their metal skin."

"Fire? What fire? I don't see any train on fire." The man looked suspiciously at Gafni.

"There. Look! Those flames. First I saw it out of the corner of my eye. Then when I looked at the cars I saw a ball of flames, as if a meteor were coming at me, a flying star. And then I heard the roar of the train and put two and two together. But every train I see passing, look, there's another —— "

"I don't see a fire. I just see a train."

" — every passing train — can't you see? — looks like it's flying with fire, wrapped with a bonnet of light."

The Pole, mumbling under his breath, stood, took his leather suitcase from the overhead rack and left.

A few minutes later, dazed by the experience and lonely in the compartment, Gafni also got up and went into another car with row seating. Here too he was alone. Chug-a-chug, chug-a-chug, goes the old train, who knows how may Jews had one-way rides on this one?, telephone poles strut by, erect as danseurs, and fields roll past, green and gold and beige fields where Jews may have tried to hide, or gather grain at night, fields not purified by the ashes of the saintly martyred ones whose bits of ash still float in the air above the land.

Why couldn't he see what he saw without history, and people without the past? How he wanted to wish it away. He wished, oh how he wished, that the Holocaust deniers were right — that Jews emigrated, exaggerated, died of typhus, not millions but maybe, just maybe some 80,000. But then where were all his relatives? Where had the Jews of his street gone? To Nome, Alaska? Kuala Lampur? Or Timbuktu?

3

WHAT WAS IT THAT MADE HIM MEET MALINA
THAT DAY?

WHAT was it that made him meet Malina that day — was it
two-three years ago already? — in Nice? Was it just hormones
(read "just" as "merely," not "just" as "equitable" or "righteous"),
or was there a greater purpose? I.e., in some way fated? Ordained
by God. Gafni wasn't a particularly observant Jew. In fact, people
in the field of Yiddish were generally seen as socialist-leaning,
non- or even anti-religious. Gafni, like many Jews in Israel who
did not regularly attend Sabbath services, went to *daven* in his
neighborhood shul on the High Holidays and other festivals, more
in memory of his parents than for himself, more to inculcate a chain
of tradition in his children than for himself. Why is it, he wondered,
that we always do things up and down — for the former and the
future generations — but we skip ourselves? And, of course, for
his father's and mother's *yorzeit* he went to shul to say Kaddish in
their memory.

So if there was a greater purpose in his meeting Malina, it
eluded him. At least up till now. Why did a Polish Jew whose family
suffered under the Poles even more than under the Germans, why
did he end up with a *Polishe shikse* (a redundant phrase if ever
there was one, for "*Polishe*" already meant a non-Jewish girl). Was
he ashamed? Yes, briefly. Very briefly. Even less than that. Then
he swallowed his shame. He swooped it into a side pocket quickly,
like a shoplifter in a store, while sensing the shame and outrage of
his family and friends.

Outwardly, however, he shrugged it off. He shared his feelings
with no one, which increased Gafni's reputation as a Jew who
betrayed history — the worst insult that could be hurled his way.
Because for a Jew to betray history was akin to apostasy. There
was no greater execration. Yes, he knew he had to suffer some
punishment for his deed. It was inevitable. Whether he deserved
it God only knew. And God not only knew, He would ultimately
judge. But despite the theological fibrillations, little up and down
bumps on a nervous graph, deep down Gafni felt there was a reason
for his doing what he did. Tolstoy wrote, God sees the truth but

waits. Gafni too would have to wait.

In time, he too would be able to say loud and clear to his children and to everyone, See, that was why I married her. There was a reason after all. He felt it, sensed it, knew it. It fluttered in him like an inner banner.

4

GAFNI IN A WARSAW SHUL

WHAT made him search out a little synagogue in Warsaw on that Sabbath morning he did not know. But he did know that all of men's steps are pre-set. And only after he arrived at the old shul did Gafni realize how right he was. With his grandfather's tallis around his shoulders — the prayer shawl he had carried with him during the war years — he enjoyed the age-old words and the melodies wedded to them.

Here in Warsaw, the city of his birth, he found himself in shul without even planning it, as if he were the subject in an experiment in automatic movement, a mannikin programmed to proceed in a certain path.

Shmulik usually disliked the rigor of repeated ritual. Hours upon hours in the synagogue saying the same thing a hundred different ways. He imagined God clapping His hands over His ears and saying: Enough! Leave me alone!

But here it was different. Once he left his hotel, he followed a predetermined course, not prompted by an exterior force or someone else's plan. He just followed his feet, for one's feet take one where one is destined to go, says the Talmud. Soon he stood before the shul on Paderewski Street, near the demolished former ghetto. A small stone building, with no markings. But the arched windows gave Gafni the sign.

By the end of the service he knew why he had been bidden to come to this synogogue. He was witness to an extraordinary numinous experience, which the older people in the shul, survivors all, considered a normal phenomenon.

"*Yungerman*, young man, what you have just seen you will say is amazing, but for us Jews the abnormal is normal," one of the oldest davenners later told Gafni in Yiddish. "If a ladder would descend from the sky and angels dressed like *klezmorim* — fiddle, clarinet, bass and cembelum — would be playing a *freylakh* for us, it would not surprise."

In retrospect, it should not have been surprising to him either, given the astonishing events he had seen — the train of fire, he thought, the train of fire — and, as we shall soon see, would

see. There were things that Gafni sensed just below the level of
perception, a vague sense of cognition that would slip away from
him like a small piece of soap in a tub. He knew it was there, but he
could not securely grasp it.

The phenomenon was this:

He had come in to the shul early. The old-timers, men in their
seventies and eighties made up the congregation. Pensioners, they
were called, for Saturday was a working day in the communist society
and no one dared take off from work for counter-revolutionary
worship. The prayer leader used the shabbes melodies and style
of prayer that Shmulik remembered from his youth. Was someone
rescripting his boyhood? We get one chance to die, he knew, but
he never thought that a daydream could live twice. Real life does
not turn back the clock, but dreams, imagination and fantasies bring
back the past; But now, today, this shabbes, it was as though he had
stepped into his father's shul of the late 1920's and 30's, the same
melodies and Warsaw pronunciation one no longer heard, except on
records.

No prologue or advance notice could have prepared him for
what he saw. When the *chazzen* chanted the "Hear O Israel," the
Sh'ma Yisroel, the Jews' classic affirmation of faith, Gafni could
have sworn he saw the Hebrew letters floating up from the *chazzen*'s
mouth to the top of the Holy Ark, in a draft as though the letters were
migratory birds soaring to the area between the two lions atop the
Holy Ark. First the *shin*, then the *mem*, then the *ayin*, then all three
join to form the word *sh'ma* on a gauzy, airy substance that wasn't
paper, parchment, cloth.

Gafni looked at the other worshippers. They didn't react. Did
they see? Was it only he, the guest, who saw, or was it a trick of his
stirred-up imagination, his joy in hearing familiar melodies in the
city of his birth, his fathers' fathers' land, even though the Poles, the
others, had never considered the Jews native sons?

Gafni tilted his head back to follow the letters' flight. Was he
witness to a magic act that, once explained, would solve the mystery?

Now the letters of *Yisroel* came out of the prayer leader's mouth
and swirled up, black on the white of that airy gauze that wasn't
paper, wasn't parchment, wasn't cloth, but lay on a milky, flimsy
white mist that looked like hand-loomed muslin — rather more a
tiny cloud heading up up up until it faded away behind the lions on
the Holy Ark, the lions with the little red bulbs in their mouths. And
then, when the *chazzen* recited the name of God, the four letters of
God's name — *yud, hey, vav, hey* — did not look like little printed
letters black on white; they emerged as tongues of fire, like the train
he had seen the other day, the chariot of fire, a fireball charging along

the tracks.

Again Gafni turned to the congregants. They said nothing. Exchanged no glances with him. Should he speak? he wondered.

Yes, he should.

When someone experiences a numinous event, one should not remain silent. Didn't Moses make an utterance when he saw God's voice in the burning bush?

Since speaking is forbidden during the recitation of the *Sh'ma* and the Silent Devotion that follows, Gafni held back. Still, he felt the men were looking at him with a suppressed ironic gleam, as if saying: We can't wait to hear what he has to say —— letters emanating from the *chazzen*'s mouth, the name of God graphed in fire, and the entire line of the "Hear O Israel, the Lord our God, the Lord is One," joining in a banner near the top of the ceiling until it fades like a slowly ebbing light, an unforgettable sunset.

"Did you see that?" Gafni finally ventured, realizing that he was partaking in a dialogue rehearsed long ago.

5

IT WAS EVENING AND IT WAS MORNING

IT was evening and it was morning, the words sound familiar, don't they?, and so the days passed for Shmulik Gafni and his new wife, one good, the other better, and others plain as straw, for what Gafni sensed was predestined had come to pass, much to the chagrin, disappointment and rage of others. But his two daughters (his son, Yosef, was in America, remember?) could not, would not, adjust to the new woman in their father's life, who was so much younger than they. Gafni knew that his twin daughters, Rivka and Rachel, resented the woman, the *shikse*, who had replaced their mother. Gafni knew they felt betrayed — betrayed by his running off to Warsaw to get married in city hall. Betrayed by the fact of the marriage. Betrayed by his choice. Betrayed by the haste. The man known as the King of Yiddish — with a *shikse*. And a *Poilishe* too. Who knows who her father, mother, grandparents were, are? But Gafni defended himself in his thoughts saying, I can feel Batsheva's chagrin, her pain too. So what kept him going? His classes, his work, and his desire to get back to Poland to fulfill his mission.

His enjoyment of everyday was tempered — here's something new for Gafni — by watching the clock, being aware of time passing. Previously, he would enjoy a concert and never look at his wrist. Now he constantly did, saying to himself, Only one-and-a-half hours to go. He wanted to enjoy the concert, but at the same time sought to compress time, to rush it along. And do what with the time?

Gafni knew that theoretical physicists, exploring the relativity of time, found that not only do clocks slow down in outer space, but that even here on earth clocks run on their own speed. For instance, digital watches run slower than regular clocks, although on the face of it they show the same time, a mystery cosmologists are assiduously trying to solve. One practical aspect: a swimmer can stay underwater much longer if he wears a digital watch than one using a regular timepiece. Which means, Gafni concluded, his body clock was digital. That's why he felt so young.

But life doesn't imitate art, and art doesn't imitate life. Both go their separate paths and only occasionally, just before infinity, do they intersect. If we were to chronicle what Gafni did every day in Jerusalem, we'd have to tape record every sound he made from morning to night, from night to morning, and photograph and film his every movement.

But by focusing on truth (art) and Smulik Gafni (life), we bring art closer to life. So, then, we're at, or near, infinity after all.

6

"SO?" SAID ONE OF THE MEN IN SHUL

"So?" said one of the ten old men in shul.

That impolitic monosyllable, hurtful for a moment, actually made Gafni feel better, for it confirmed what he thought he had seen. It added to the puzzle, yes, but made the seeming private aberration a public phenomenon.

"But ... look ... this ... " Gafni stumbled as he spoke, as if he were walking his words across a field strewn with stones he could not see. "This is ... " — he hesitated to use the word *miracle* — "curious, isn't it? I've never ... "

"We're used to this," said a smooth-shaven man with rose-red cheeks sitting next to him. Gafni could tell that this man with the dusky yellow hair had once had blazing red hair.

"What's your name?" Gafni asked.

"Yankl Shtroy."

"I'm Shmulik Gafni ... Weingarten."

Yankl Shtroy shook his hand.

"You mean this happens all the time?"

"Even more than that."

Now the scholar/researcher in Gafni was prodded awake and questions tumbled like circus clowns one after the other. Hardly articulated was one when followed another.

"Is it only that *chazzen* or any prayer leader?"

"Anyone."

"Did it happen to you?"

"Me? Yes."

"All the time?"

"Every time I lead."

"In shul or at home too?"

"Only in shul."

"Shabbes or weekdays?"

"You ask a lot of questions."

"I want a lot of answers. Weekdays too?"

"Every day."

"The other day in a train to Lodz I looked out the window and saw an entire train sheathed in flames."

The men shrugged, not impressed.

"When did it begin?" Gafni asked.

Now, as in a play, the supporting actors rose and stood behind the lead actor.

"When we had our first minyan after the war. When we came from the camps. From the cellars. From the sewers."

"The attics," said another.

"The forests," said another.

"From under the earth," said another. It was Yankl Shtroy again.

"From the graves," said another.

"From the dead," said another, until the entire minyan had spoken.

"Does it happen in other shuls?"

"We don't know."

"Don't you ask?"

"No."

"Why?" Gafni asked.

"I want to show you something." Yankl Shtroy walked slowly to the bookcase in back of the shul. He returned with an old Siddur. Gafni could tell by the binding that the prayerbook was more than one-hundred-fifty years old.

"Look. Open."

The pages were blank, but the paper, Gafni could see, the fine old paper of the early 1800's that would last forever, the paper was authentic.

"Interesting, right?" Yankl Shtroy looked up at him.

Gafni was puzzled. "What are you trying to show me?"

"Think. Think of your first question. Think. You're a smart man. Connect."

Gafni burst out with, "The flying letters."

"That's right. This Siddur was touched by the *reshoyim*, the evil ones." Yankl Shtroy made a spitting motion without actually spitting. "The evil ones, the murderers. And so the letters fled from the pages. You see?"

"Incredible."

"We're used to miracles. Once we survived them, that, those … " Yankl Shtroy pointed vaguely out there, "then everything is a miracle and nothing is a miracle. Nothing surprises us any more."

"I would think that something so amazing like letters of fire, coming out of a *chazzen*'s mouth, you would want to spread the word."

"You sound like an American," Yankl Shtroy said. "Main thing is publicity. Get it in the papers. Then think later. Very American."

"I'm from Israel."

"From Israel?"

"Yes. Israel."

"Ah," they all said, an exhalation that was a sigh and wonder. "Israel. *Yisrael*. The Land of Israel. *Eretz Yisroel*."

"All right," Yankl Shtroy said, realizing his sarcasm may have offended his guest. "I should say, I told you we're used to unusual happenings. This one is nothing."

"Then what is?"

"You're really from Israel?"

"Yes. Really. From Jerusalem. *Yerushalayim*."

"Ah, *Yerushalayim*." Now their exhalation was wonder and awe. They put their hands to their hearts.

"Would you like to go there?" Gafni asked.

"Oh, yes."

"Yes yes yes," they all said.

"Well?"

"But we can't," said Yankl Shtroy.

"Why?"

"We cannot. Don't ask."

"We must not," said a second.

"We dare not," said a third.

"Impossible," said another voice.

"Because of the political situation?" Gafni asked.

"No. Not political," said Yankl Shtroy.

"Theological?" Gafni knew that some Jews would not visit Israel if they could not stay there.

"No. Not that. Don't ask," said Yankl Shtroy. "So if you're from *Yerushalayim*, then *sholom aleichem*." And he stretched out his hand to welcome Shmulik Gafni.

"*Aleichem sholom*," Gafni responded. But he didn't want to relent. He didn't want to be diverted, distracted; i.e., nudged from the track of his thoughts. "Then what's more unusual?"

THEN men exchanged glances. They all fell silent as if the Silent Devotion had begun again. Talkative before, eyes wide open, ears pricked up, surrounding Gafni, now they spoke even though they didn't say a word. Talkative before, finishing one another's sentences, they now were still, in a conspiracy of silence.

Finally, one of them, not Yankl Shtroy, said, "We don't talk about it."

At another time such words would have prompted more questions, but Gafni's mind was clouded by the vision of the flying letters, letters that at times were black and white and at times trailed fire like a tiny comet. How did they come out of the *chazzen*'s mouth and why? How high did the letters fly? What were they made of?

And of what was made that cloudy screen that held the letters? And was there any sense in analyzing something so surreal in the first place? It was as absurd as subjecting angels' wings or cherubs' tears to chemical analysis. What was it about this cursed land that made the uncommon seem so commonplace? Was God's grace shining — years too late — as if to make up for His absence in the 1940's?

Gafni knew the kabbalistic concept of *tzimtzum* — God contracting His essence to make room for the rest of the world — so there was precedent for God changing His ways. But how did that play out in holy Hebrew letters flying from a man's mouth and fiery trains hurtling along the rails? Or was this any different from meeting a miniature Mozart or seeing talking dogs years ago? Wait. What an interesting affinity. God becoming smaller, so to speak — and Mozart, his essence also contracted.

He was glad he had spoken with the Jews in shul and not remained silent, not keeping to himself what might have been a trick of the imagination, because when one is exhausted or spiritually exalted, drunk or delirious, one sees things no one else can see. So it was good that other people confirmed what he saw. But that compounded the problem, for a trick of the imagination is more readily explicable than a miraculous phenomenon publicly seen.

The next Sabbath Gafni did not go to the synagogue again, although during the week he dreamt twice of the rising letters. But his inner turmoil, a scale tipping in his equilibrium, stopped him from seeing again the tongues of fire that formed the letters of God's name. Perhaps one such vision sufficed for any man.

And what was the unusual phenomenon the old men didn't want to talk about? And why do they dare not leave Warsaw to visit Jerusalem?

7

AFTER THEIR WEDDING

AFTER their wedding in Warsaw, a civil ceremony of course (one wonders if there are any psycholinguistic, if not totemic powers and affinities, between ceremony and cerements — a ceremony ce(re) ments a relationship, you might say, if you stutter), for Shmulik Gafni could not have married in Israel, where no rabbi would have married him to his unconverted *shikse*, and where in any case no civil marriages were possible (weddings may be civil, quipped George Bernard Shaw, but divorces are not), so Warsaw it had to be.

It could also have been Cyprus, a popular civil ceremony destination for Israelis who detested rabbinic intervention in marriage, but Gafni thought Cyprus was too close, and since both partners were born in Poland, Warsaw it had to be, for it was conveniently far away from the bubbling cauldron of antagonism and indignation of family and friends.

And of course there was another reason, which Gafni told no one about, certainly not Malina. He thought that by marrying in Poland, it would officially strengthen his Polishness, so to speak — remember his wish expressed to the old Jewish survivors in the shul: "*Ikh vil zine eyner fun eyekh*," I want to be one of you?

Meanwhile, in hundreds of outdoor cafes across Israel the imminent wedding, the actual wedding, and the post-wedding were A Number One topic of discussion, ya-ta-ta and tra-la-la.

They said Gafni was crazy — remember that "they," that amorphous, ineluctable "they," the masses, them asses? They called him mad. Labeled him *meshugge*. They tried to create all kinds of synonyms that would express not so much their rage — for after all, what should they be angry about, he did them absolutely no harm — but their impotence at expressing their consternation at the lunacy of Gafni's outrageous deed. I just can't believe it. Can you believe what he did? And the heads shook, tsk tsk tsk, from right to left and left to right. First of all, his age. That indeed was crazy. Cuckoo. Absurd. An old man with a young woman. My God, did you know he's already a great-grandfather? What? Yes, you heard me right. I did not say grandfather. I said great-grandfather! And secondly, with a *shikse*. That's where the real rage was directed. Oh, the ecstasy of the I-told-you-so's, who were the first to criticize Gafni for consorting with her (remember what was known/"known" in Jerusalem?), which others poo-poohed as a lot of rumor and gossip. Oh, how those I-told-you-so's crowed, standing up on their hind legs and craning their necks and crowing their prescience at daybreak, which Shakespeare calls cockcrow. And so, they aimed their rage at his marrying a *shikse*, if what frothed on their lips could be called rage. Not that they were religious. They weren't. He wasn't. None of them was/were.

Let's call their rage more cultural than theological. How could a man who was universally regarded as the world's greatest expert not only of the Yiddish language, folklore and literature, but Yiddish everything, marry a *Poilishe*, a Polish gentile Christian Catholic goyishe *shikse* from a land where the ashes of three million Jews still hovered in the air tinged with a brackish oily smoke that would not go away?

Shmulik Gafni was by common consent, but sans scepter or ermine collar, called the King of Yiddish. How could a man like that, a Jewish icon, a Jewish culture hero like Marc Chagall (oh, if they only knew, those innocent theys, how their hero Chagall too had betrayed them, well, it was actually his wife's decision, by being buried in the Catholic churchyard cemetery of St. Paul de Vence) betray them like that?

But Shmulik Gafni did not think of it that way. He had his life, his choices, and he didn't care what others thought. He could imagine their laughter, or as Yiddish writers, reflecting Russian peasant custom, would say, "They laughed into their fists" (see Chekhov). A man lived only once in this world and if he didn't now do as he wished, he would never do it. Life was short. The older one got, the longer the shadows, the shorter the light. Opportunities came once. The fateful knock on the door was one short rap, not two. You don't answer pronto, the knock don't come again. Phate doesn't phone or phax.

Gafni was proud to have a *khatikha* — that marvelously evocative Hebrew slang word which meant "piece" — like Malina. In a room all eyes were on her. They can't help it, they're seduced, drunk, drugged, drawn not only to her but to her chest, as if little neon lights were flashing, Look at me, and they did. Those neon lights pulled, reined in your eyes, blocking out all else. A million 3-D multihued tv's could have been on and no one, boom boom boom, would have paid attention when Malina was in the room.

And that dusky voice of hers, one thing we haven't yet mentioned, with its timbre like seductive twilight, a calm spring day just after sunset, stars about to appear. It was a low tenebrous voice — low in pitch, low in volume. Her melodious contralto and her body, a happy coupling. And her pretty face, despite the thin lips, completed the picture, nicely framed, which glided on smoothly oiled wheels right at you.

THEIR wedding photo was recorded for posterity in the full technicolor rotogravure, on page one of all the Israeli Friday magazine supplements (yes, Israeli newspapers had already converted to polychrome). This gave everyone the modicum of an impression that they had participated or at least been partial witness to, even if they hadn't been invited to that desecration, that humiliation, that *shandeh*, that execrable civil ceremony in Warsaw.

In case you already recycled that Friday morning edition of *Ma'ariv* or *Yedi'ot*, here's what you missed, plus some extra details for those of you with photo — (no pun intended) — graphic memories.

In the picture both are smiling. In what you might call a wedding portrait, Shmulik Gafni looked like Yitzchak Rabin from a middle distance, more in photos than in real life, a noble rectangular face, iron-grey flecked hair, grey eyes that had an ironic gleam, laughing at someone — but whom? nobody knew. He looked thinner than usual. He wore a dark grey suit and a blue tie speckled with lavender fleurs-de-lys, a pink carnation in his lapel (a first for him), looking unusually formal and bourgeois — for his university classes he always dressed casually — gazing straight at the lens with his serene, eye-smiling, manly wise look. He held a pen, as if he were president and it's an important bill he's about to sign, unseen attendants hovering behind him at this great photo op, waiting to be presented with the pen(s). Malina, green eyes lowered demurely, pretty in her mid thirties, either ruddy-faced or with highly rouged cheeks, busty, blowsy, wore a flouncy mauve hat, peaked and high, rhomboid in shape, as though copied from a seventeenth century Dutch master portrait that hinted at a touch of eccentricity, and an off-white, wide-lapelled linen suit whose shoulders poofed up, accenting her own broad shoulders. She was also signing another document, as if she's vice-president or something. The what-would-come-later of her ever-expanding physiognomadic destiny was obvious in that wedding portrait. Not only do cameras not lie, they predict the future.

In the inside page photos, we have another view of the new couple, black and white this time. He looks at her as she, a feline smile hovering in her eyes, as if she's got the present and the future all figured out, knowing that the camera's attention is on her, signs the marriage document.

Glad was Gafni that none of his friends and relatives were present. And how could they have been? It's hard to come to a wedding you haven't been invited to in a foreign and little loved land and wouldn't come to even if invited. The reasons?

Too far.

I don't attend mixed marriages. That is, I do — if one partner is male, the other female.

I wanted to come but couldn't get plane tickets.

I bought plane tickets but the plane got lost.

I lost my credit card.

I found my credit card and the plane but lost the tickets.

I had a headache.

I didn't have a headache but wishing I had one gave me a headache.

I lost my headache.

Me too, but the time I found it, you won't believe this, it was right on the night table where I left it, but by then it was too late to catch the plane.

Even Malina's relatives didn't show. She had an only sister, she said, who lived in East Germany, or eastern Poland, and she would/ could not come. Malina had told Shmulik that her father had died in a construction accident in Lodz years before. Her mother she didn't mention. It was on the tip of his tongue to ask, And your mother? — but he withdrew the words further back into his throat and pressed his lips shut. If she didn't mention her, certainly he would not. He felt uncomfortable about the older generation. The fewer questions the better. The father was dead. Finished. Good. Who knows how many Jews the father and mother, grandfather and grandmother had turned away from their farm, or turned in to the Germans?

With Jews Gafni asked lots, loads, of questions, wasn't ashamed to ask where they came from, where they were born, where their parents came from, what sort of schooling they had. For they were family, brothers. With Jews he wanted to know everything. Yet as close as he felt to Malina, her he asked almost nothing. Certainly not about family. And she never protested, like women are wont to do: How come you don't want to know about my parents, my family, my childhood, isn't it important to you? She kept quiet too, and he was glad of that, except for bare facts, revealed en passant.

So don't think Gafni entered this liaison with naiveté or without trepidation. As proof, even as he was signing the marriage document, if one looked closely at the capital "G" of "Gafni" and the "el" of "Shmuel" (for that was Shmulik's formal first name), the "el," meaning "God" in Hebrew, if one looked carefully, one could see the tremor in the letters. The heave in Gafni's soul as he mused who Malina's relatives might have been expressed itself in the tremor of his hand, especially when he had to write the "el" of Shmuel, as if God Himself had a pang of conscience and a sudden quake that caused Gafni's hand to shake.

If Malina's family had done something good, don't you think she would have been the first to share the news? She would have told him right away, for every Pole usually had a story of how many Jews he had saved at great risk to himself and his family. Or perhaps her silence was a manifestation of great self-control, not wishing to brag and risk a sarcastic or prickly response.

Yes, the fewer questions the better. No wonder Shmulik's children wanted to have nothing to do with her or with their wedding. Gafni's two daughters were too upset to talk to him, so they sent their daughters, Zehava and Penina, whom everyone called "the twins," the ones with whom he had seen the talking dogs, to speak to their grandfather before his wedding trip to Poland. As they were growing up, they learned from Shmulik and his friends about the Poles' endemic Jew hatred. Now in their mid-twenties and one already a mother, they remonstrated with their old grandpere as to what he was doing with a *Poilishe*. Gafni responded with a banal: she's different.

"Yes," said the twins in unison, for they often spoke together as if declaiming from a script, "but how do you know who her parents and grandparents were?" The very words he would have used had his son Yosef brought home a *Poilishe* — even if he had brought home this very one Gafni himself had fished out of a linguistics conference pond. Our grandfather has gone mad, both Zehava and Penina thought in their hearts, did not say it aloud, and then exchanged glances and nodded, each hearing the other's unsaid words.

Gafni's response was a morose and angry silence, the sort of abrasive silence he was master of, for even silence has a pitch, a tone, a metaphysical weight. Only his now labored breathing was heard in the room. And in between breaths the slow ticking of the clock, which was strange because there was no clock in the room. Or perhaps it was the ticking of the clock, the inevitable ticktock of precious time slipping away until its final gasp.

"You know how much Grandma loved you. She once told us," Zehava said, "oh, months before she died, with a little dreamy smile on her face: I love your grandfather's smile ... "

"... and his tan in the summer, the blond hair on his arms," Penina continued.

Gafni looked down. He wasn't used to praise like that. And he certainly wasn't used to hearing his wife's praise filtered through his granddaughters' lips. If he hadn't known that Batsheva had indeed said remarks like that he would have thought that the granddaughters' made them up to make him appreciate his late wife all the more.

Again, only the ticking of the clock that wasn't there was heard in the room.

Or perhaps it was the beating of Malina's heart in the next room, contemplating if now was the time to make a dramatic entrance and once and for all foil this stupid cat and mouse game.

Whose anger was louder, the girls' silent rage or his stubborn muteness? Gafni stared at his granddaughters, stared right into their eyes. A little mocking gleam danced in his eyes and, as usual, they could not meet his gaze with theirs. His trick, of course, learned ages ago, was not to stare right into one's eyes but to look at the area above the nose, between the eyes. They're no longer babies, he thought later as they walked out. One of them is a mother too. And I'm a great-grandfather. And my daughters are middle-aged. Approaching old age. The only one who's young is me.

Zehava and Penina left knowing they couldn't make their grandfather change his mind. They would have to live with this *shandeh*, this shame. Defeated, they said only one word at the door: Father. But each granddaughter said it in a different way, remembering how their mothers addressed their father. Zehava said, "*Tateh*" in Yiddish, while Penina said, "*Abba*" in Hebrew, as if to signal Gafni that they were speaking for their mothers too.

SHMULIK purposely did not talk of the past, but don't think that that restraint did not cost him. It cost him. It cost him plenty. Dammed up water seeks exit. Ditto dammed up thoughts. If they don't leave the mouth, they burrow, worm, drill into the brain, heart, kishkes, doing their subtle invidious work, inexorable as cancer cells, but having no name.

Malina too did not talk of the past. After their wedding in Warsaw, he brought Malina into this apartment in Jerusalem where Batsheva had died. His daughters opposed this too and didn't talk to their father for weeks, until he bumped into Rivka one day at the Supersol. She was in front of him in an aisle, her back to him. He wondered for a moment if he should greet her, then tapped her on the shoulder, startling her. For a second he had a vision of Sholom Aleichem's Tevye turning away from his daughter Chava, who met him on the road, Chava, who had betrayed her father and mother and her people by marrying a Russian peasant. He wondered if Rivka too would flee from him as Tevye on his horse-drawn wagon had fled from Chava. But as his daughter turned, a momentary angst and anger flashed in Rivka's eyes and then, seeing the anguish in her father's face, fell — restraining her tears — into his embrace in the canned fish aisle, steps away from the bagel and bialy stand and the fresh fish counter.

But it wasn't all violins and roses. The Yiddishe Mama scene had an acidy bite.

"Abba, Abba, what have you done?" Rivka said, "Why did you spoil the harmony of our little family?"

Gafni didn't, couldn't, respond. But a strange thought, morbid at worst, realistic at best, flitted in his mind as he saw his daughter suddenly burst into tears as she spoke about how her father had not done justice to her mother's memory, nor to the Jewish people, his ancestry, everything he stood for, when he married Malina. And seeing those tears, those tears that touched his heart but could not change his mind, the odd thought flashed; when I'm dead that's how she and her sister will shed tears for me, mourning the man they'd known all their life who was now gone forever.

They moved down the aisle, away from the oncoming customers. He too felt his eyes brimming with tears, thinking how shoppers would react seeing this older man with more white in his hair than black and the middle-aged woman in a tearful embrace within sight of the live carp and dead salmon. And wouldn't you know it — remember the small pebble in the lake? — soon a rumor flew that the newly-married Shmulik Gafni, Professor of Intergalactic Yiddish Studies at the University of Israel, had had his first spat with his bride who, by the way, isn't as goodlooking as her pictures or as the word-of-mouth rumors would have it, much older in fact, why do people insist she's a gorgeous and curvaceous thirty or thirty-two, when she looks more like a chunky fifty? Their argument was so nasty, folks swore, they brought each other to tears. And the contretemps reached its height right by the herring barrel. It began by the bagel, bialy and baguette stand and then moved slowly past the long appetizing counter to the fresh fish, where — so the blah blah blah reported — the fighting continued over which fish to buy for Shabbat, what a scandal, even though it was only Monday, and everyone knows fresh fish doesn't come in till Thursday.

Gafni let his daughter do the talking. Let her get it off her chest. He knew it was a mistake to bring Malina into the apartment. But he didn't tell this to Rivka. She and Gafni parted a little closer than they had been before the wedding, but neither invited the other to visit or to call.

Yes, he admitted to himself, and admitting a wrong to oneself was a giant stride, as Kierkegaard avers. He should have sold the apartment and started anew. The only change Malina insisted on was the bed.

But more on that later.

8

GAFNI RETURNS TO PADEREWSKI STREET

THE next time Gafni was in Warsaw, it was five or six years later, he returned to the little shul on Paderewski Street. Now he didn't follow his feet. Now he followed his will. He entered and, as if waiting for him, let's be precise, as if expecting him, was Yankl Shtroy.

"Remember me? Gafni from Israel?"

"Of course. Why so long away?"

"I can't come so often to Warsaw. I think I told you. I'm a teacher."

"You didn't, but that's all right. And I'm a *shamesh*. Yankl Shtroy."

Like last time, he was dressed in an old blue serge suit, shiny in spots, a white shirt and a darkish blue tie, carelessly knotted. He wore a black yarmulke. Gafni could tell at once by the way he was dressed that Yankl Shtroy had no wife, but lived alone. He couldn't tell how old he was, but noted that the old man with the yellow hair did not look much older than last time. The only one who looked older was Shmulik Gafni.

Then, as if in answer to Gafni's unvoiced question, Yankl Shtroy added:

"And I'm also the head of the *Chevra Kadisha*, so to speak."

"So to speak?" Gafni caught the nuanced mystery of the ask-me-more remark.

"Yes." And Yankl Shtroy repeated; "So to speak."

Gafni looked at him, lifted his chin as if to say, Nu? Tell me more.

But the man's face was as mute as his tongue, maybe muter.

"Why do you attach a 'so to speak' to the activities of the Jewish Burial Society? Are you hinting it's not a *Chevra Kadisha*? Can you explain, please, the 'so to speak'?"

What Yankl Shtroy said next he uttered with barely moving his lips, as if he were a ventriloquist. His eyes betrayed nothing.

"I say no more. I cannot speak. I want to speak but my mouth and tongue are tied."

For a moment there was silence — thick and weighty, like Egyptian darkness. Once again, like the last time, Gafni felt he was in a theater watching a drama unfold. Then, as though slowly entering a dimming stage, a group of elderly Jews — Gafni recognized many of them from his last visit — elderly by face but not by movement, had gathered. Gafni did not see them coming, could not tell from which doors or stage doors they had come. They slipped in like actors in the dark. Stage lights on — and there they are.

Yankl Shtroy looked at his friends as if waiting for instructions. In chorus they shook their heads. From left to right and right to left without stopping, as if a mechanism had been switched on in their necks, and smoothly and slowly they moved their heads, left to right and right to left, creating a little warm wind in the shadow-filled old shul that looked like the shuls of Gafni's childhood, all wood, where shadows were one with wood in the old shul which like the men had survived the terror but still contained its umber glow from Then.

The darkened walls huddled close as though in need of comfort. The room started a slow spin, and the black yarmulkes the men wore were little hovering tops above their white hair or bald heads.

As the old men — Gafni didn't count them at first — looked at and past him, surveying their shul while shaking their heads from side to side in one motion without stopping at the edge of their "no," the shadows sharpened, as they took in the old dark oaken *Aron Kodesh*, on top of which were the two sad-faced, brown-painted little porcelain lions holding tiny red bulbs in their open mouths — that's where the Hebrew letters from the *chazzen*'s mouth had flown last time — near the time-stained, hand-carved wooden bimah with twisted poles. It didn't look real, this shul; it looked more like a stage set for a play, like the makebelieve shul in the Habimah Theater's production of Isaac Babel's *Sunset*. The ur-shul of Eastern Europe.

Shmulik too felt he was on a stage, an unwitting actor in a play directed by unseen hands. Despite the age of the shul, it didn't smell old. Its aroma was a pine grove. Neither did an odor of old age exude from the men. They too smelled as fresh as pines.

"He cannot speak," the men said in a chorus, perfect in their timing.

"He must not speak."

"He dare not speak."

Eight — now he counted them — eight old men were they, with nearly wizened faces, but amazingly robust and radiant. Nine with Yankl Shtroy. And ten, a minyan, with Gafni.

"*Ikh bin eyner fun eyekh*," he said. "I am one of you. I'm from here."

"We're from There," said the minyan minus one.

They were hiding something from him, Gafni knew, teasing him openly. He saw the secret in the purple velvet folds of the *Aron*

Kodesh curtain, in the fluid shadows that skitted around the room. He sensed a silence he could not fathom.

"I'm from There too. I fought them in Russia, in some Polish units, while my entire family was murdered here. In Treblinka. In Auschwitz. My father and uncle survived. My uncle lived in Kielce." Gafni's throat tightened. He looked at the men. As soon as he said Kielce their heads dropped a notch. He nodded. They understood. They came closer, formed a semi-circle around him.

"I was coming back from Russia, in 1946. Repatriated. A young man of twenty-six. I heard that my father had survived and made his way back here to Warsaw. I wrote to him. He wrote back that his brother too had survived and was back in Kielce. It wasn't a pleasant place for Jews, but where else could they go? They were tired of running, spiritually and physically broken. And everyone kept hoping that some family members would return. From Russia. From hiding. From the DP camps. And some did. And that gave hope to the rest; it vindicated their decision to stay in Kielce and wait. In June that year, in 1946, an eighteen-year-old girl returned. She'd been a housemaid in a remote hilltop farm and the farmer didn't tell her the war was over. Why should he? Free labor. But once he sent her to town to do some shopping and she learned the truth and ran away ... Where were we? Yes, my uncle back in Kielce. And I — a move I bear within me like an open wound that never heals — I write to my father in Warsaw, Meet me in Kielce, because that way, coming back from Southern Ukraine, I could see him sooner and see my uncle too ... I try to salve my conscience by saying to myself that it was my father who suggested that we meet in Kielce. But it isn't so. It was my doing. The month was July, 1946. *Oy li, ve-mar li.* Ah, woe is me. Oh, bitterness in me. I came into town that evening ... July 4 ... and ... you ... know ... the rest."

Shmulik Weingarten sat, covered his face with his hands, and began to weep.

9

HOW HUSBAND AND WIFE TALK, LIKE BOXERS, WARY, SPARRING IN A RING — BUT WITHOUT THE GLOVES, WITHOUT THE RING

WE know Gafni didn't want to talk about Malina's parents; wanted to know nothing about them. If she volunteered information he would not clasp his ears; perhaps a shutter in his heart would close. If you happened to visit a Pole in any little town and told him you once lived there, in fact your parents lived in the very house these Poles were now living in, the Pole wouldn't feel the slightest regret, guilt or discomfort. In fact, he'd point to the leaky roof and ask you to pay for a new one; after all, it's your house, a house, he said, looking you straight in the eye while lying through his teeth, a house that secretly sheltered a Jewish family during the war. And his neighbor, who had stolen his house from another deported Jew who never returned, would put in a similar request. He too, said the neighbor, had also saved a Jewish family, and who would pay for his new roof? Would you mind, Pani, doing my roof too? Now either they all shared the same Jew, or if every Polish family had saved a Jewish one — where did all the Jews go? The Holocaust deniers were right, Gafni thought. All the Polish Jews were now living on an island in the Baltic Sea. All three million of them. It was crowded, like a subway, like a cattle car, but thank God they managed.

In his office one day, Malina told him that despite coming from a workingclass family, she'd gotten a university education. When she was growing up, the communist regime encouraged youngsters from lower income homes to get a higher education. But Gafni wasn't paying attention.

He looked up at the photograph of Sholom Aleichem above his desk.

Then she mentioned Kielce.

He bristled. As if woken up. Slapped in the face.

"Yes, yes, I know." She lowered her head, ashamed, as if personally responsible for the tragedy.

"Kielce?" he wanted to know. What connection was there between her and Kielce? And his heart started pounding, a sour pounding, a sad, somber taste in his mouth.

Either she hadn't replied or was hesitating. Or perhaps he hadn't heard.

So he said again, "Kielce," flatly, with no reverberation of history, no tremolo in the letters.

"Yes, Kielce," she said. This time he heard her.

In the balance scale of his mind, he weighed how she sounded the word, When a Jew says Jerusalem, the melody is different than when a goy says it. Was there an awareness in the music of her voice to what Kielce meant to a Jew? To him? Did the threnody of Kaddish thread its way between the "K" and the "i," its mournful melody the warp through the woof of the letters?

"Kielce?" he asked again.

"Yes, yes, I know what happened there." She lowered her head again.

"Kielce?" he said once more.

"Why are you repeating the name so often?"

She didn't know its link to him, he concluded. Or didn't care. Or perhaps did know and didn't care. In the human heart a palette of infinities.

"Never mind," he said.

"Oh," she said. It was a strange "oh." He couldn't figure out the music of that "oh."

"Kielce?" he asked again.

"It was terrible," she said. "One year after the war."

"Fourteen months," he said. "July, 1946."

"Terrible," she said.

"What were you doing there?"

"Visiting a cousin of my mother's," she said. "She wasn't a native. She moved there in the 60's. And you, you have personal ... " Malina hesitated, choosing the word carefully ... "personal resonances in Kielce?"

Then really she doesn't know, Gafni decided. He was about to tell her, then changed his mind.

"I've been there," she said softly. "I know. I'm sorry."

"It's not your fault."

"Still."

"Where's your family from?" he asked.

"All over."

He didn't like that answer. "What does that mean?" he asked rather sharply.

"That they moved around. My mother from Warsaw — my father, Lublin. They met God knows where."

You don't talk of them, he thought. Ever. You never talk of them, he didn't say.

Still, his heart pounded as it did the first time Malina uttered

Kielce. Why was he drawn to her? he asked himself. Was it the magnetism of opposites? Or the simpatico of like souls, a wavelength that both hummed on, despite differences in religion, culture, even age, yet linked by their roots in Poland and their love of words?

He wanted to ask her if her parents were alive; he wanted to and didn't want to. Then remembered. She had once said that her father had died. She saved him the trouble by saying, "I presume your parents are no longer alive."

"Yes," he said, but he didn't ask about hers.

"Only one of mine is alive."

Again he didn't ask. His thoughts, his hearing, moved away.

"My mother," she said, "but there was a strained relationship."

Or she might have said, "My father."

He wasn't sure. Didn't know. Didn't ask. Didn't care.

She held her head in her hands and again said, "Kielce. What happened there. Terrible. The Poles."

Gafni looked up. That sad look on Sholom Aleichem's face, as if he knew what the tuberculosis was doing to him; what the Germans and their helpers would do to his people a generation after his untimely death in 1916.

With closed eyes, as if chanting, Malina said:

"We are rotten folk. We haven't learned to help others. We don't enjoy another person's success or happiness. I go back to my home town and when we hear stories about someone who did well, we quickly get jealous, wish that person ill, and pray that misfortune beset him. We don't have self-help and we're not charitable. Here I once heard one Jew saying to another, 'I see you're not feeling well, so I'll be over to help you with your *sukka*.' He doesn't even say, Should I come over? He phrases it at once in the positive. That never happens with us. Instead of extending a helping hand, we turn our backs on one another. There's no free-loan society like you have here. None at all. When we bake, we close our windows lest some poor man smell the bread and knock on the window to ask for a piece. Oh, how happy we are when someone is down on his luck, and oh, what a thrill of joy we get at someone else's misfortune."

"*Schadenfreude*. Of course only the Germans have a word for this. They may even have made it up as a sarcastic gibe against Doctor Sigmund."

Gafni gauged Malina's reaction. Does she know I'm joking? He winked at Sholom Aleichem.

With his mournful eyes, Sholom Aleichem winked back.

He couldn't believe what he was hearing. It was the first time Malina had let her guard down and spoke openly about her kinsmen. Nevertheless, as soon as he heard her remarks his scholarly combativeness rose like a balloon. He loved to refute, even if it was a struggle to find facts. Although he knew she was right, he wanted to tell her that no other people in Eastern Europe had saved so many Jews. Yes, it was only a tiny fraction of the population — but still. And so there were more Poles honored as Righteous Gentiles in Jerusalem's Yad Va-Shem Institute than any other national group. And no Poles ever served as guards in the German concentration or death camps, only Ukrainians, Latvians, and Lithuanians. True, the German's didn't trust Poles, considered them *untermenschen* just one notch above the Jews. On the other hand, they were the only people who killed Jews long after the war, something not even the Germans did. Because the Germans were an obedient folk. When the regime said, Kill — they killed. When no orders came, they desisted. But the Poles followed only their inner promptings.

This thought pricked Gafni's balloon. Still ringing in Gafni's ears was that mocking "What? You're still alive?" said by Poles when Polish Jews returned to their hometowns in May and June 1945 to look for surviving family members.

A chill rolled down Gafni's back. He was trapped in his memory, vision that wasn't sight.

How quickly the mind works. How swift is the flow of the soul's energy. With what speed it can change direction. What weights the soul can bear and how easily it shifts a mountain of ideas.

Gafni did not rebut Malina's remarks.

But he did say, "After your portrait of the Poles, maybe it's better that Jews weren't accepted as Poles and that after five hundred years of residence in Poland they still were considered Jews, not Poles."

"But, but," she sputtered, "what does acceptance have to do with it? It is impossible for a person to be a Jew and a Pole. It's either or."

"My God!" Gafni slapped his forehead in exasperation. "That's exactly what Eichmann said: 'One is either a German or a Jew.'"

"But there is some truth in that formulation," Malina continued, "even though said by an evil man. Even the Polish Jews, after centuries of living in the land, still considered themselves Jews, not Poles. They never even bothered to learn the language."

"You're reversing it, Malina. It was the Poles who never considered the Jews Polish, and with the exception of the first welcoming years in the fifteenth century, persecuted them continually."

"Look," Malina said in her most reasonable debating timbre, "I think you should understand that the relationship between Jews and Poles was always problematic. It's not all black and white."

"I see," Gafni said. "We have to balance it out. Take the other side into consideration. Be fair. Like we forgot to put into the mix the

severe anti-Polish laws the Jews have passed over the centuries, the
pogroms against the Poles organized by the Jews and their rabbis,
and the centuries of anti-Polish agitation by Jews, the beatings
and murders of Poles, not letting them into our schools, or if we
let one or two percent in, we made them stand in the back of the
classroom, while Jews mocked and cursed them. And let's not forget
how the Poles fed the poor Jews when they were hungry and how
they clothed them when they were ragged and then how miserably
we Jews treated the Poles during the Holocaust, when the Poles
were rounded up and killed by the Germans and we stood there and
cheered and looted the Poles' houses as soon as, even while, they
were loaded into waiting trucks and watched as the Polish children,
babies, the feeble and the old were thrown, yes, thrown into the trucks
like garbage ... Problematic!" Gafni spat out. "What a despicable
word." He looked at her, hatred in his heart, and walked away.

GAFNI could have gone on and on, but his spirit was drained. His
own wife. Like an enemy. Coolly taking the intellectual anti-Semites'
mode of reasoning. The chill, arrogant disdain of the classic upper-
tier Pole, coupled with the beastly fury of the vox populi. Like in
Germany, a murderous coupling. That's what made German Nazism
successful. That nefarious fusion of thinkers and thugs.
    Gafni closed his eyes, tried to think pleasant thoughts. But he
couldn't. As soon as he thinks of the children-oriented, children-
loving schools in Israel, he can't help but contrast that love with the
hatred of Jewish children in the Polish schools of his childhood. First,
the teachers beat all the children, Jewish or not — but they especially
singled out the Jews. Once, when a math teacher hit Shmulik for
not knowing an answer, he told his father. We'll see about that, said
his father. One day he waited until all the children were dismissed
and the math teacher came out of school. Without greeting him,
Shmulik's father went up to him, stood close and stared straight into
his eyes. "If you dare lift a hand against my boy once more," he
hissed, "I'm going to break every bone in your body." The teacher,
who had the sly, pointy features of a dog, looked once at Pani Gafni,
then turned away. He never touched Shmulik again but kept giving
him low grades. One teacher made Shmulik stand with his hands
over his head holding up a Latin text; another insulted him and other
Jewish pupils. And another, a Ukranian, called the Jewish children
"kikes." Things are changing, he said. You Yids, just remember,
things are changing.
    And the man was right. Anti-Semitism increased in the high
schools and in the colleges too, where Jewish students were forced
to stand in the back of the classroom. Gafni still remembered that

humiliation in high school and in his first year at the university. In the early 1930's, in tandem with the rise of the Nazis in Germany, in Poland the National Democratic Union voted to exclude Jews from all professions. And all academic organizations — the cream of the intellectual elite in Poland — voted to abridge Jewish rights and reduce the number of Jews in professional schools. They even voted to create ghettos, years before the Germans invaded. And all the while, newspapers were clamoring for the removal of citizenship of Polish Jews — and of Jewish children from Polish public schools. Thugs and thinkers.

No wonder many Jewish families had begun taking their kids out of the public schools and sending them to Jewish ones. But Shmulik's father, though deeply Jewish, sought to accent his place in Polish society. But it wasn't working. Shmulik was miserable. He wanted to get out. He was fourteen at the time and already reading Virgil. And like Virgil, Shmulik too wished he could have the magical ability to sail away in a boat he drew on the wall of his prison cell.

Gafni looked up for a moment at the photo of Sholom Aleichem. Like his own, the Yiddish writer's eyes were sadder too.

10

SHMULIK WEINGARTEN WEPT

SHMULIK Weingarten wept. The cries loud and uncontrolled. The sobbing propelled his body forward and backward, and he swayed as if in prayer, in mourning. His hands were wet. Moving back and forth, remembering what he had witnessed, what he would never forget, what he could not will from his memory, what he has never stopped seeing on his open and closed eyelids.

The men drew closer.

"*Yisgadal ve-yiskadash sh'mey rabo*," they began the Kaddish. Magnified and sanctified be His great name.

Gafni stood and with eyes closed recited with them.

"Amen," he said when they were done.

"Amen," they echoed.

For a moment he could not distinguish between the sharpened shadows and the men. He wiped the mist from his eyes.

"I'm one of you. Trust me. Don't hide anything from me."

The men nodded slowly; they were listening.

"I don't usually pray, but here in Warsaw," Gafni said *Varshe* in Yiddish. "Here in *Varshe* I love to daven with you. I feel in every fibre of my body that I am one of you. *Ikh bin eyner fun eyekh*."

"What are you doing in Poland?" Yankl Shtroy said with an uncommon sharpness. "Why should a Jew set foot on this cursed soil?"

"If you tell me what you're hiding from me, I'll share my secret with you, and perhaps you can help me."

Now it was Yankl Shtroy's turn to lift his chin and signal Gafni to speak.

"I'm a professor of Yiddish at the University of Israel in *Yerushalayim*."

"*Yerushalayim*!" they all said at once, singing the word, rolling it like a melody in their mouths, reveling in the surprise of it. "*Yerushalayim*." The word they said daily a dozen times in their prayers.

"Remember, I told you last time that I come from Jerusalem. I come here to do research on Yiddish. But it's just an excuse for the real reason. Which is: to look for him. The murderer. To hunt down my father's killer. I know him. I saw his face," Gafni keened. "I see him always before me. I can photograph him for you from my mind's eye. Perhaps you can help me look for him … Will you trust me?"

Yankl Shtroy stepped toward Gafni. The men sat down in the pews as if preparing for a service.

"Kielce, 1946, was the turning point," said Yankl Shtroy. "That was the last time they killed us. That's when we began to notice it. It's not something you notice right away. You notice it slowly. But little by little it seeps in."

"What? You're teasing me again."

"I won't any longer," Yankl Shtroy said. "What is your full Hebrew name? Your name and your father's?"

"Shmuel. My father was called Yosef. Shmuel ben Yosef is how I am called to the Torah."

Yankl Shtroy ran forward to the rows where the other men were sitting.

"*Eyda kedoysha*! Holy congregation! Do I have your permission to speak to Shmuel ben Yosef?"

The eight old men stood and said as one:

"Yes. Yes. Yes. You have our permission to speak to Shmuel ben Yosef, who is one of us, who was born here and with his family was There. You have our permission to speak. To speak and to reveal. To reveal and to swear our brother Shmuel ben Yosef to eternal secrecy," they said as one.

One of the old men, he too had wispy white hair, walked up to the bimah, opened a door to the reader's table and took out a tallis. He put it on and recited the blessing. He went to the Aron Kodesh, kissed the curtain, and opened the ark. He took a Torah, reverently kissed it. He seemed to hover in the air as he brought it and placed it on the reader's desk.

"Do you wear *tzitzis*?" asked Yankl Shtroy.

"No," said Gafni.

"Then put on a tallis. With a *brokhe*."

Gafni wrapped himself in the tallis, made the proper blessing, and held the fringes with one hand. He knew what Shtroy would ask him to do.

"Kiss the *tzitzis*, hold it to the Torah, and say after me: What I am about to hear … "

"What I am about to hear … "

"I swear by the holy Torah … "

"I swear by the holy Torah … " Shmulik repeated.

"I will never reveal … "

"I will never reveal … "

"… to any other human being, any other human being, ever."

"… to any other human being, any other human being, ever."

"Amen."

"Amen."

"Now kiss the Torah with your lips to seal the sacred oath you have just taken."

Gafni kissed the Torah with eyes closed. He saw his father, his mother, his uncles and aunts, he saw his entire family, while he stood alone, the only member of his family alive, kissing the Torah and swearing silently not to reveal what he was about to hear and having no idea what secret they would share with him, as tears he was unaware of streamed from his cheeks once more and fell on the wine-red velvet Torah coverlet, swearing too that he would not rest until he had found the murderer of his father and his uncle.

"Would you like to return the Torah to the *Aron Kodesh*?"

"Very much," Shmulik said. Once more he kissed the Torah, shut the two doors of the Holy Ark, and drew the curtain. The little metallic zing of the brass rings on the horizontal pole as the curtain moved reminded Gafni of a similar sound in the shul of his childhood.

"Sit down," said Yankl Shtroy. "Now you are one of us. There are so few who are one of us."

"One of us," the chorus said.

"Here we all know what you are about to know," Yankl Shtroy said in a low voice, "but we have never told anyone from the outside."

"Never," the old men said, their lips barely moving.

"But we will tell you now," Yankl Shtroy said. "Because you are not from the outside any longer. Now you are one of us."

11

WHERE MALINA DID NOT WANT TO SLEEP

BACK to the bed, as promised.

Malina did not want to sleep in the same bed as her late, lamented predecessor, all of whose pictures she immediately removed from the various rooms and placed face down in a bottom drawer somewhere, for if the photos were placed face up who knows how far up and out the former wife's malevolent gaze could go. Malina didn't even want to utter her name. Not that she couldn't pronounce Batsheva. That was easy enough. She just couldn't bring herself to voice the letters, a classic case of tongue and willpower in tandem. She kept calling Batsheva "her" and "she," suddenly an expert in all pronounal variations and permutations, and when she ran out of pronouns and verbal substitutions in Polish and English, she used her eyebrows, hands and fingers, especially her thumb — indicating that one, over there, gesturing thumbly to *yenne velt*, the world beyond. It annoyed Gafni (the bed business, not the pronouns; that just peeved him), but he didn't say a word. The bed he and Batsheva had slept in was an old, massive oak bed with a curved wooden foot- and headboard, an English antique acquired in Tel Aviv decades ago.

It turned out that from Malina's point of view it was neither ethics nor discretion; it wasn't sensitivity or insensitivity to Shmulik's former life partner, now dead, alas. It wasn't sentiment or jealousy.

You know what it was?

Fear.

Plain and simple old-fashioned fright. Terror may be more on the mark.

Malina, drenched in a guilt she couldn't articulate, dreaded Batsheva's spirit. Negative vibes of replacement. To the point of shivers and shakes, quivers and quakes. It was primitive, Shmulik knew, a Polish primitiveness that not even two PhD's could dislodge. But who says a doctorate expunges stupidity? It doesn't. Nothing can budge bedrock moroninnity. The PhD is just a cosmetic coating. And two doctorates are as efficacious as a double layer of talc on a third degree burn. Her irrationality was something out of Haitian voodoo, but Shmulik indulged her. She was superstitious, one of the few things super about her now, atremble that the demon of her deceased predecessor had settled into the bed. That her ghost had somehow infiltrated the old oak and would leach therefrom like polyurethane. That the soulstuff of the she that had remained behind had seeped and would continue to seep into the mattress. That the very space of the bed shook with her vibrations which had invisible little stingers aimed at Malina, to haunt her, choke her, take her breath away, shorten her days, the potent revenge of that now dead Jewish version of the Polish witch Yadwiga. One had to be careful of former wives, Malina maintained, lapsing now into a crystalline, hard-edged Polish from the polite, well-thought out English she most always used with Shmulik. One had to be more careful of dead wives than of living, divorced ones because the latters' power was limited — she said to his face that was now blotched with incredulity — but once they passed on, Malina maintained, these dead wives called upon all the resources of the netherworld to battle the usurper.

"Just where is this netherworld?" Gafni asked, enjoying the sarcasm. "Tell me precisely."

And without even stopping to think, Malina said, "Just below the Netherlands."

"Below meaning south, like Belgium? Or below meaning under, like beneath the ground?"

"Obviously, under the ground. That's where the netherworld is. What has Belgium to do with it?"

"Is Belgium lacking demons?" Gafni said. "For your information, Bruge is co-capital of the netherworld, along with Rotterdam in the Netherlands."

Gafni was amazed that a woman as educated and modern as Malina had such a storehouse of neanderthalian ignorance and downright dumb folk beliefs. But then again, he knew that love of literature was no shield against folly or even evil. Neither was an advanced degree — remember Hitler's propaganda minister, Josef Goebbels, PhD in Literature, burner of books, burner of Jews? — a guarantor of rational or even decent behavior.

Then Malina said: "Your wife is in … "

"… the room?" he finished for her.

"Your wife is in … "

"the bed?"

"Your wife is in … "

"In you?" Gafni couldn't help joking.

"Let me finish, will you? Your wife is intruding."

He realized for the first time that Malina might be mad.

Thought a moment. Then changed his mind.

Not might be, he concluded.

Is.

Reluctantly, he sold the old bed and bought a new one.

12

SHARING THE SECRET

Y<small>ANKL</small> Shtroy adjusted his yarmulke and closed his eyes.

"We began to notice it after the 1946 Kielce pogrom," he continued. His lids were whiter than his face, as if they had not absorbed enough sunlight over the years. Just above his left eyelid stood a pink little mole. His yellowish hair was thinning. Like the other Jews in shul, he was smoothly shaven. As Yankl Shtroy spoke, a few tiny red blotches appeared on his face and neck.

"After Kielce they stopped killing us, but to this very day they haven't changed. Anti-Semitism here is nurtured like a flame. It possesses an energy of its own. But they don't kill us ... They can't ... "

So they don't kill us, Gafni thought. They're not killing us in Germany or Russia now either. Gafni spread his hands, questioning. Was it for this that he had participated in such a sacred ceremony?

"Because ... " Yankl Shtroy dropped his voice to a whisper, then suddenly asked, "Do you believe in miracles?"

I don't know, Gafni thought. It didn't happen in Kielce, in July 1946. The Jews were miraculously saved from the Germans until the anti-miracle of the Kielce pogrom. His head swirled, clouded. And then, suddenly, appeared little Mozart sitting atop a wafer in the Cafe Mozart in Vienna, pecan-sized and chatting with him. Am I not a miracle? tiny Wolfgang urged.

"Yes, I do," said Gafni.

"Then listen," said Yankl Shtroy. "They can't kill us, because ... Because we don't die ... That's why the 'so to speak' when I mentioned the *Chevra Kadisha* ... We don't die any more. It's as simple as that. Unbelievable as that. But it's only we Polish Jews who have stopped dying ... Not the Jews who come from other lands to visit. That's why we have a *Chevra Kadisha*. For them. But our Polish Jews, the few thousand who remained here, we don't die."

The other eight men stood and recited formally:

"We don't die ... We have stopped dying ... No matter how old we are, we do not die."

Gafni spoke slowly. He felt a chill spiraling down his back. The talking dogs, he remembered, the dogs he'd met north of Safed years ago. Their good wishes. You've gained years of life, said one dog.

Can it be?

"Have you perhaps considered good health, luck, good genes?"

"I don't know, my friend," said Yankl Shtroy. "We haven't had a funeral since 1946 … God played a cruel trick on us in the 1940's and then decided to reverse Himself."

"Doesn't anyone notice? Haven't the newspapers written about this phenomenon?"

"*Aleph*, they don't pay much attention to us. You think the Poles care if we live or die? Makes no difference to them. We're so small, almost invisible. *Aleph* prime. We discussed this years ago, remember? You and me? Publicity is not our goal or our desire. *Beys*, maybe some goyim do sense it, but are afraid to utter the words." Yankl Shtroy looked toward the window, rubbed his chin. "You know what's interesting? From time to time some Poles come and say they want to become Jews. But we don't let them. We tell them that according to Jewish law they have to be told to come back next year and the year after that, and then if they come back the third year, we tell them there is no rabbi here and that's the truth. And who needs them? And that's the truth too. They think if they become Jews they too will never die, a plague on all their bones."

"You've found the Philosopher's Stone," Gafni said.

"What's that? A *shtayn*? I didn't find a stone," Yankl Shtroy said, then turned to his friends. "Did any of you find a stone?"

Gafni smiled. "It's from the Middle Ages. People believed the stone gave immortality."

Yankl Shtroy shrugged. He wasn't impressed.

13

RE BATSHEVA'S POSITION IN BED

THE first time they were about to use the new bed Malina asked: "On which side did she sleep?"

Gafni took notice, he weighed the word, how Malina still said "she," not "your late wife," and certainly not "Batsheva." Never Batsheva. God forbid she should utter Batsheva's name. Even now that their old oaken bed was gone.

Gafni saw at once what Malina had in mind. Clickety-click and lickety-split the dominoes, transparent as glass, transparent as Malina's thoughts, lined up in Shmulik's mind.

Just as Malina had rejected his bed, Batsheva's bed, their bed, she was now on her way to rejecting Batsheva's place on the bed, the very spot vis-à-vis Gafni where his wife had lain. Oh, how he saw through Malina's glass dominoes. Oh, how he would shatter them.

"So tell me, on which side?"

The only way to answer her, he decided, was to outfox her.

"My side," he played for time.

She gave him a skeptical look. Her thin eyebrows, eyebrows that matched her lips in pencil-line thinness, her eyebrows arched. Are you joking? her look seemed to say. But as the light in her green eyes changed color; it also said, Give me a straight answer.

"But which?" she persisted.

"You mean direction?" he played with her.

"Yes. To your left or your right."

"You mean politically?" he played the fool.

She sniffed, snorted, turned her head sharply away from him, as if he weren't there, as if denying his existence. What drove her? he wondered. First she had been afraid of their old bed, and now, with a new bed, she was afraid of sleeping on the same side that Batsheva had occupied. She still feared Batsheva would invade her, dybbuk her, spook her.

"What difference does it make?" he asked.

"It does."

"But what's the difference? I just got you a new bed because you didn't want the one Batsheva and I slept in. What difference should the side make now? It's a new bed, for goodness sake!"

The color rose on Malina's face. "I just don't want to be in the same position she was. I just want a fresh start. So tell me."

For a moment he thought of an evasive reply. For a moment he thought of not answering at all. For a moment he didn't know what to say.

"You still haven't told me why."

Malina drew a breath, exhaled. Said it with just the slightest tinge of self-consciousness:

"It's bad luck."

Gafni couldn't believe what he was hearing.

"That too? I thought it was just the bed."

"No. Not just that. But yes, it's bad luck. That's what it is. Bad luck." Her accent made it apropos: bed luck.

"Bad luck? Superstition? Enough!" he shouted. "I can't stand superstition. You have one-and-a-half, maybe two, PhD's and you believe in bad luck?"

But he felt a little twinge saying this, for he wasn't entirely free of such ideas himself. When it comes to superstitions we are adamant about others' stupidity, he confessed to himself, an attitude that may cloak our own superstitions. We are outraged and impatient when others display the same flaws we possess — and not only for superstitions. Put another way: the nasty traits we abhor in others we tolerate in ourselves.

Why did these insights suddenly bubble up in Gafni? Because at the civil wedding ceremony in Warsaw he had fully expected Batsheva to make an appearance of some kind, either directly or in some ghostly fashion. Or at the very least, to hear her admonishing voice.

So how different was this from Malina's obsession with the bed? Easy. It was his obsession, not hers.

Another thing. Right after returning from Warsaw with Malina as his new bride and sharing the news of their wedding with no one, he bumped into (of course, it leaked out all the same. All the newspapers, even photographs. How? The Warsaw photographer whom Gafni had privately engaged to record the administrative ceremony went and secretly sold the prints to all the Israeli newspapers, the bastard; and even before the photos appeared, the café klatsch crowd knew, and the shout-it-from-the-rooftops syndrome went into high gear), he bumped into the rabbi of the shul he occasionally attended. As they stood on Keren Ha-Yesod Street (the newspaper story plus photos had not yet appeared), the younger man gave him a friendly hello and said:

"I haven't seen you in a long while. You look suntanned."

"Yes, I was in Eilat a while back. So you noticed my face is darker."

The rabbi looked him in the eye and said in Yiddish:

"*Abi nisht keyn innerdikke finsternish.*" As long as it isn't an inner darkness.

What did he mean by that? What did the rabbi know? Had he some inner vision, an ability to look into Gafni's soul? Did the rabbi realize that Gafni wanted to get away from him as quickly as possible lest unwanted questions be asked? Had the rabbi heard something through the malicious grapevine? Had he found out about their old bed — seeing the bedstore deliverymen bringing in the new one and carting out the massive old one? — and put two and two together?

"Bad luck is no respecter of education," Malina came back. "Just like cancer or diabetes doesn't care if you're rich or poor, big or small, smart or stupid."

"What does cancer or diabetes have to do with it?" Gafni wondered if the diabetes was a jibe.

"Then you don't understand my analogy," Malina said.

"Analogies are usually logical. And you're reversing my question and being illogical as well."

"Luck and illness defy logic."

"But illness is beyond our control, while superstition is within it," Gafni said impatiently, shaking his head.

Malina just stared at him.

"So you really believe in bad luck." Not a question, you notice. Just an affirmation.

But Malina wouldn't budge.

"Whether or not I believe in it is irrelevant. Do you believe in cancer, diabetes or heart disease? Makes no difference if you do or don't. It's still out there. Same with bad luck. No matter if I believe in it or not. It believes in me, whether I like it or not, and I have to do my best to avoid it."

Gafni rolled his eyes.

"I find it hard to believe that your brain has two compartments: the smart and the absurd."

"Then I guess," she said with a triumphant little smile, "my brain, like your bed, has two sides … So which side did she sleep on?" she said softly, almost seductively.

"She slept to my right."

"But that's still relative. Left and right are relative. East and west are stable, permanent."

"She slept to the east of me … actually, northeast."

"Very funny. But at least we're getting there. But which way to your right? If you're on your belly or on your back."

He was about to shout in his booming baritone: Enough! In decibels that would put her in her place. But just then his will collapsed. He figured he had had enough trouble with the new bed. No use wasting any more energy and arguing about Batsheva's position. He didn't want hard feelings, bad vibes in the air. Bad vibe. What a pun! *Vibe* in Yiddish meant "wife." A bad *vibe*. Then he remembered he had once switched positions with Batsheva, sleeping to her right. It didn't work. That night everything went wrong. It took Gafni a long time to fall asleep. And once asleep, his dreams were reversed, inside out, left to right. He couldn't read signs. Newspapers were printed upside down. His sleep was edged, bumpy like a washboard. He woke up completely disorientated, thinking he was Batsheva. Wake up, Shmulik, he told his wife, his voice higher pitched. Exhausted up woke he.

For a moment he considered sleeping on the wrong side of the bed, on Batsheva's, for the sake of peace. But he rejected it at once. He couldn't go through with it. To sleep on her side would be permanent misery. Yes, he would have to outfox Malina.

"So you definitely don't want to be in Batsheva's position in the bed."

"Right. Definitely. Like I told you. It's bad luck."

"I suppose you've had lots of experience being a second wife."

She didn't answer.

"All right," Gafni said with mock resignation. "I'll agree. It's absurd, but I'll agree." And he sighed dramatically, as if making a huge sacrifice.

"On my belly," he said, clinching his normal bed position.

"Then I want the other side," Malina said.

As the months passed he noticed a change in himself — and in her. In people around him too. Invitations to social gatherings diminished, but Malina didn't seem to mind. When he invited guests (heart in mouth, his speech aflutter, not sure he wanted to do what he was doing, not sure that their acceptance was sincere), they came, but the conversation was strained, forcedly merry, like two people who have just been introduced and don't know what to say to each other, or perhaps want to remain mute. Or better, like mourners riding in the limo behind the hearse strain to joke and laugh to suppress the fear of riding alone one day in the long black motorcar just in front of them. After a burst of conversation, rat-a-tat like a spurt of gunfire, in no predictable rhythm silences would fall and land with a thud. The uncomfortable silence not of strangers but of the estranged. Not the pleasant Haydn silences between lovely musical passages that highlight the melodies at either end, but unpleasant vacuums, full of ignominy, heavy as shame.

At times, two people, facing each other in uneasy chairs, would begin to speak at once and stop. Then another two would attempt to fill the embarrassing gap, only to widen it. This made Shmulik so angry he wanted to take the cup of now cold tea he was holding, smash it to the tile floor, and shout: Go home! Leave me alone! Don't sit here in my house and pass silent judgment on me and exchange those obvious glances of collusion and resentment. Why did I invite you in the first place? To show you how normal my life is? Vexed by his shaking and rattling the teacup against the saucer, Gafni placed his forearm on the armrest of the chair, which silently absorbed the trembling. He couldn't wait for the guests to leave so he could remove the smile pasted on his face and put it back in the drawer for the next time — if there were a next time. One evening, after two couples who were visiting had left, Malina was about to say something, then stopped. He knew. It was emblazoned on her forehead like operatic supertitles:

Perhaps we made a mistake.

THEY DID NOT SAY A WORD,
THE MEN IN THE BACKGROUND

ALTHOUGH the men in the background did not say a word during Yankl Shtroy's monologue, one could sense their kinship, not only because they were Jews and had undergone the same pain and torture, the same losses, but because over the years a special bond had formed between them. Gafni could feel the silent assent of the men in shul to Yankl Shtroy's words.

"Never die!" said Gafni in wonder.

"Never die," the eight men, the nine, said from their seats.

And they continued: "We have eaten from the Tree of Life."

Then the chorus added: "Blessed are you, Lord our God, King of the Universe, who has given us the fruit from the Tree of Life."

"Amen," said Yankl Shtroy, the head of the Warsaw *Chevra Kadisha*, so to speak.

Gafni too said, "Amen."

"Now I'd like your help," Gafni continued. " I have sworn this by the Torah that I will not rest until I have found the murderer. I see him before me and I will describe him to you." Gafni stopped, took a deep breath, a long breath, a breath as long as the Jewish exile, and he drew into his lungs the clear air of the Polish meadows, the pine-tinged air of the mountains mixed with the ashes from the chimneys and the ovens that still hovered like a maledicted cloud over Poland. He described for the minyan what the killer of his father and his uncle looked like, where he came from, the timbre of his voice, what work he did. Gafni asked for their help, but urged discretion, for one false move could ruin his and their quest. They promised to keep eyes and ears open, to ask the right questions.

GAFNI THINKS HE'S INVINCIBLE

SHMULIK Gafni thought he was invincible. Here he was in his early seventies, with a wife in her thirties, second wife to be precise — as a scholar he had to be precise* — and he feeling like a young man. All his signs were vital, as was he. His blood pressure like a twenty-year-old. No problems of any kind. Not since his minor heart attack fifteen years back. The *Chaver* (remember, his electronic monitor?) certainly had helped him when he was kidnapped, with special thanks too to Shultish. But Gafni chucked it just before he was married. How would it look to be the husband of a pretty young woman and wear that thing around his neck? It would be like walking with a crutch or a white cane. Healthy (no knocking on wood; that was for woodpeckers and the stupidly superstitious) and no diminution of desire. Au contraire. Sounded like a good title for a novel, *No Diminution of Desire*, a novel by Shmuel Gafni. Cholesterol, at last check, okay. And seminars and lectures abroad to keep him busy for years to come. He remembered reading that when Stokowski was 96, he had conducting engagements well into his 100th year. And sabbaticals. Gafni had so many sabbaticals accrued, he would have to live forever to use them up. Even seven years past forever. He remembered seeing Casals at ninety-five. He had read about George Burns who at 98 also had bookings into his 100th year. Or was that Casals? One of them was a comedian, he knew, but wasn't sure which one. But of this he was sure: Joseph Green, the legendary director of the classic Yiddish films of the late 1930's was showing his Molly Picon films in the 1970's and '80s when he was in his mid-nineties. And Toscanini and George Bernard Shaw. He could go on and on. Chagall and Miro and Picasso. The list was endless. If Sholom Aleichem hadn't died at fifty-seven and Chekhov at forty-four, they too could have lived to a ripe old age like he would. There was only one problem. He had no successor. No secular native Yiddish speaker from Poland went into linguistics or Yiddish. The black-hat observant Jews here, who had generations of Yiddish, didn't go into secular studies. Like that *bandeet* Nussen, who did simple research for Gafni only for the money. He wouldn't

---

*Me too. See Epigraph. Again.

dream of devoting his life to Yiddish.

So poor Gafni, he worked in a vacuum. Yes, there were students, born in Israel, and their Yiddish was acquired, whether at home or in the classroom, but not on the street. You have to roll on the unscrubbed street (*m'darf zikh valgern afn gahss*), Gafni felt, to inhale a language.

He took stairs, never elevators, bounded up the former two at a time, felt strong as a horse. He had a lovely young bride. He liked that title, *No Diminution of Desire.*

But the "they" out there thought that the new "she" would finish him off. An overabundance, call it plethora, a nice word, or in plain English, too much *shtoop-shtoop*. The old chap, folks said, was exerting himself too much. What else can you expect from a thirty-something wife (although his sixty-eight-year-old wife, even in her last year, was no slouch in that department either)? The new *shikse* had her expectations, so went the blah-blah, and poor Gafni was expected to fulfill them. Or maybe her expectations and his desire coincided. Because, they said, he had been in practice all these years. There were persistent rumors, some of which we've already heard, that this vigorous, good-looking man with the shock of grey-black hair and the powerful bass-baritone rumble in his voice had always had some liaisons with the many girl students who came to study with him — rumors that in fact were dead wrong.

16

WHO WANTS TO BE WITH WHOM

"*Ikh vill zine eyner fun eyekh,*" Gafni said passionately. It was a forthright remark, not subject to ambiguous interpretations, although isolated phrases falling into wrong (or right) hands can always be stretched like truth, especially if recalled years later. After learning their secret, he said:

"I want to be one of you."

Shmulik didn't think his words were ambiguous at all. But with words, like with radio, there is a speaker and a receiver, and hence they could have been heard from a different perspective than was intended. "I want to be one of you" could also have meant that Gafni wanted to be with, to remain with, these Polish Jews, either now or in the future.

And if the men in the little shul heard the *vill* as *vell*, as is quite possible when words are uttered quickly and heard in haste, or heard by listeners slightly hard of hearing, the sentence becomes more insistently declarative: "I will be one of you," a remark that excises the wishful pleading.

Which is why when Yankl Shtroy replied, "*Du vest zine eyner fun unz,*" a smile crossed Shmulik's lips. He was pleased. He heard the words, "You will be one of us," uttered with utmost seriousness by Yankl Shtroy, as an antiphonal response in a synagogue. He took them as a promise, even though these words, as indeed his own initial remark, were as full of ambiguities and multilayers as a puzzling Biblical verse.

"*Ikh vill* [or: *vell*] *zine eyner fun eyekh.*"

"*Du vest zine eyner fun unz.*"

The prayer leader banged on the table to signal that the Evening Service would begin.

Listening to the cantor's chants, Gafni was witness to the suspension of time. He imagined it like a bridge, bridges the kind you never see in Israel, rather a bridge like the bridge he once saw in New York, stretching across the East River from Manhattan to Brooklyn, the bridge they call the Brooklyn Bridge, and he was suspended in that Warsaw shul in time, just like a bridge, but he wasn't a bridge between here and there, it was more like here and then, and he neither moved backward nor forward in time, feeling he was the suspension and he stood there dangling in time and time moved around him, like the cars moved around him as he was suspended in that bridge called time. The advantage was that he did not have to move among the *chazzen*'s melodies; they rushed, they washed over him, and now as the suspension began to fade, he felt he was in two places at once, and he was able to walk slowly backward in the no-time zone that held up both ends of the bridge.

And then, when the cantor chanted the *Sh'ma Yisroel*, again the letters flew up and out toward the area above the Holy Ark where the little lions with the red bulbs in their mouths rested, and God's name, when uttered, was a scroll of fire.

17

TWO BITS OF NEWS

ONE day Shmulik got two bits of news, one good, one bad.

The good news — Malina was pregnant. She always did like to draw attention to herself. Now she had one more reason.

The bad — tingling in the fingers of his right hand and the tips felt numb. Bees and mosquitoes buzzing around his fingertips, like the bzz-bzzing of a Bartok quartet. Yet he had no pain in his heart or anywhere else. At the same time a wave of fear and gloom slid over him like a hood, but he couldn't tell if that came as a partner to the numbness or an aftereffect. Suddenly he was afraid. Without realizing it, he put his hand on the *Chaver* pendant he wore around his neck. (Lately, he had begun wearing it during the day, removing it and hiding it before he went to sleep.) He didn't tell Malina; didn't want to spoil her moment of joy. He was afraid to share his mortality with her — and he did not see a doctor.

As if exercise could drive the numbness away, he kept opening and closing his fingers. In a day or two the numbness faded. But it prompted a decision: it was absolutely imperative to spend more time in Poland. Perhaps the magic of Polish Jews would finally rub off on him. After all, he was a native son. And the men in the shul had promised that he would be one of them.

Back to the good news.

As her pregnancy proceeded, Gafni noticed changes that came so quickly they tumbled over one another. Malina was going to pieces. To pieces of cake, to pieces of bread. Put another way, pieces of everything fell onto her and stuck. During pregnancy women gain weight, a given. But Malina harvested this given with a vengeance. Her appetite was Brontosauran. After breakfast she lusted for ten o'clock tea and cakes, which led to lunch, a pregnant woman's wishes must scrupulously be granted. One meal segued into another and she gained three pounds for every pound of food she ate, living proof of the invalidity of Newtonian principles. Malina weighed one hundred twenty-five pounds when she met Gafni, one hundred seventy-five when she gave birth. Her hourglass figure became a grandfather clock, a solid rectangle, with added rounded ripples of fat.

She ate before meals, during meals, after meals, between meals. She ate what he left over, she ate what she left over, she ate what they left over. She would have eaten what the baby left over but it wasn't born yet. She wasn't prejudiced re direction — left over, right over. For instance, a friend (friend! let's better say acquaintance) called and said: I have leftovers; she said, I'll be right over.

After each meal she opened the top two buttons of the zipper of her slacks to let her growing belly and waist hang loose. Her little baby was growing all over her. Her cheeks puffed out; her neck thickened; her forearms gathered flesh. And her breasts grew in proportion, large and weighty.* She couldn't find brassieres to hold them.

The first time Gafni saw Malina's bra he jokingly asked her if it was made to order, for it looked so heavy and complex.

"Yes," she said. "I have a brassiere maker in Warsaw who does special ones for heavy-set women."

"But you're not heavy-set."

"For her I am. This seamstress doesn't measure my waist, my hips, my neck. Just my ... " and she drifted off, as if ashamed to utter the word.

But in bed, once her clothes were off, the bra was the last article of clothing to go — because it needed four, six, eight hands, an entire committee, to negotiate, defibrillate and undo. Sometimes he wondered how one person, could single-handedly open up such a complicated contraption, even with two hands, without an instruction booklet, with no rearview mirror or engineering degree to free herself — them — from their daytime incarceration?

And how she liked to draw attention to herself. As if her entire being were made up of little magnets that said: me, me, me, look at me. As she walked she looked left and right, as if hoping for the stare of others, men or women, it mattered not, for magnet women loved everyone's attention, including animals, plants, even pots and pans.

The items that those made-to-order bras contained drew attention to themselves, without ads, p.r., or business cards, just like they did in Nice, both on land and sea, and in the air too, when jets, jumbo and plain, and old propeller-driven planes, two balloons with their balloonists hanging upside down, tongues up, lingua franca out, with the sheer ecstasy of what they saw, and one Goodyear dirigible 3000 miles off course, plus a pirate frigate and two Malaysian subs, all congregated like at an air and sea show and zoomed down over the stretch of beach where Malina had put her twin pets on display to peek at the record-breaking bazoom-zooms that graced the fine

---

*During the next four years she lost not an ounce, but like a good corporation she solidified her gains. Like the perfect stock market, her chin had a 100% growth.

pebbled beach of Nice. And let's not forget the most phenomenal event of them all: those white storks carrying Eskimo babies on their way over the Alps to Morocco who swooped down, open-mouthed in awe, to stare and dropped their little moon-faced charges.

But magnets can't make you lose weight. All of Malina's magnetism didn't help her shed an ounce. She soon became what she was destined to become. All the cells in her body were slowly sending the subtle message: oh be, oh be obese. In brief, the former svelte body grew and grew as the baby developed within her. Men had always stared at her; couldn't take their eyes off her. Now they stared too — but for another reason. Even the lids under her eyes amassed flesh, rose like dough, flake pastry swelling in the oven heat. When she sternly pressed her face down to complain her double chin tripled.

And as her prettiness vanished (vanished? why mince words? she became more repulsive), she became more abrasive. The more repulsive, the more abrasive. With the decline of her charm, came the cline of her plaints. The light near the armchair was too bright. The shades didn't close properly. Windows open — too breezy, too cold. Windows closed — too hot, no air. Once she slammed the door of the refrigerator; it was too cold, she complained. The bed sheets were not pulled tight enough. The tea too hot. The toilet paper too rough. The roll was put in upside down. She liked to pull it from the bottom, not the top. That one Gafni had never heard before. The words almost bubbled out of his mouth, but he restrained himself: Where you grew up, you used old newspapers, if that! So why fuss with the position of the roll? But, as said, he pressed his lips shut. She couldn't help herself, he figured. It's hormones. The third- and fourth-month hormones.

18

A SON'S LOVE FOR HIS FATHER

ONE day, when he was eight or nine, Shmulik and his mother went to visit relatives in Lodz. He loved the train ride, the clatter of the wheels, the rhythm of the train, the conductor punching the tickets. And once, the conductor let Shmulik use the metallic hole puncher. With a shy smile on his face, he punched his own and his mother's ticket. Later, for a birthday, he got a conductor's uniform with a cap, a packet of tickets and his own hole puncher. His father couldn't come with them, couldn't leave his fur shop, was supposed to arrive a few days later, let's say on a Thursday night for supper but he was late. That night Shmulik lay in bed, in the Lodz apartment, waiting for his father. He felt his eyelids fluttering, but he wanted to be awake to see his Papa. He tried to push away the drowsiness, heavy as a laden barrel, but with a mighty surge of willpower he succeeded. He left his bed and walked into the brightly lit kitchen, his eyes squinting from the light, to ask if Papa had come, he knew he hadn't, the blue gloom around him, in him, Is Papa here? Why isn't he here yet? Don't worry, his mother said, he'll soon be here, go back to sleep, my sweetheart. The words no comfort, because back in the dark bed in the dark room, the blue became darker and with the door shut tight, the kitchen light extinguished, sensing something had happened to Papa, and he clutched his mother and began to cry, Is Papa all right?, and the deep blue gloom that swirled about his heart and between his eyes, like the cape of a magician he had once seen at a children's show, as he lay in bed in the dark room, sensing that something had happened to his father and that he would never see him again, and how many people in this world actually witness, helpless, something happening to their father whom they would never see again?

In the blue haze each hour was longer than the next and even the minutes suddenly lost their strict borders and began to stretch, until a minute stretched from one corner of Lodz to the other and the mood of dark blue gloom was a slippery path that led down down down and he couldn't hold on and stop himself, Oh God, dear God, let him come.

In his thoughts he ran down to the entrance of the apartment to wait for him. He ran to the tram stop to have Papa back all the sooner.

Maybe one of the trams got stuck. Or maybe he had to deliver a fur to a customer and had to catch a later train to Lodz. Maybe something, he didn't know what, had happened to his father. Perhaps just as he was shutting the lights in the shop and before locking the door, he fell and hurt himself and no one knows that he is lying there in pain, and that blue purple black haze attacked Shmulik's heart and spurted up like dark smoke inside him and he breathed in its malaise of spirit. Where is Papa?, he thinks now lying in bed, soon Papa will come, you have to go to bed now, he was eight or nine at the time, imagining that Papa had just gotten off the train and caught a tram, it's past ten o'clock, so late, and he was walking, Shmulik counted the steps, imagined one step after another, making him walk briskly, walking with his father from the tram stop, walking with him the first block, across the street, counting step by step, one two three four, then the second and third block, thirty-seven, thirty-eight, forty … sixty … two-hundred-three, now Papa enters the apartment building and makes his way up the staircase to the first floor, up the steps now, turning to the second landing, up up up to the third, he taps lightly on the door. Papa is here. Shmulik's heart sank again as he realized there was no knock on the door and he walked once more with his father from the tram, his throat dry, not even tears in his eyes, his heart rocking in his chest, how does one measure the love for one's father? By imagining step by step the steps he takes from the tram to the house until he arrives. The palms of his hands sweaty and the sheets by his cold feet damp with perspiration. The door opens. Was he awake now from a dream or was he still dreaming? He hears his mother give a cry, Where were you, Yosef? and Shmulik flew, yes, he flew, he did not run, he certainly did not walk, nor did he leap out of bed, but hearing his mother's cry, Where were you, Yosef? and the first words his father uttered, Shmulik flew from his bed to his father's arms and it took a while for the rocking of his heart, the blue and purple sadness, to decoalesce from his soul.

Didn't I tell you I was going to a Zionist rally tonight after work?

No, his mother said.

No? his father said, I'm so sorry, and Shmulik did not want to cry, for he wasn't a baby, but he began to cry and did not know if the tears were tears of joy or if he sobbed now because it was all the blue gloom spilling out now that his father had come back from the — he didn't want to utter the word, was afraid of the word, the emptiness in his heart was an anxiety so deep it could have been a mourning for the — But where else could he have been and was missing for how long? Go back to bed, Shmulik, it's after eleven, his mother said. His father hugged and kissed him. So you missed Papa, eh, and worried about him? Shmulik nodded. His father kissed

the tears running down his cheeks. I was walking with you from the
tram maybe ten times, Shmulik told his father, who at first did not
understand, but when Shmulik repeated these words and added, I did
it in my mind again and again until you came home, his father gave
a pleasant laugh and said, Tomorrow I'll bring you a new book and a
bar of chocolate. Bittersweet, was Shmulik's request and his parents
laughed and he didn't understand their laughter at his appropriate
word until he remembered it just now.

Tell me, Gafni said to no one, where in the world can you find
a father like my father?

THE experience was so vivid, he swore he could not tell if it
was dream or real. But after his father's death he once dreamt he
embraced his father and pressed his cheek to his own so tightly they
became one. In the next segment of the dream, Gafni was in his
father's shul on a Sabbath, where he floated like a figure in a Chagall
painting. He was rising with another congregant, their hands almost
touching. He didn't know the other man, but evidently they had the
same preternatural gifts. Floating up slowly, he tilted his head to
avoid the big brass chandelier. For a while he looked down at his
father, who sat holding a Siddur. He didn't know why he was up
there near the ceiling of the dimly lit shul, like a fish at the top of an
aquarium. Gafni did not recall what he did or if he spoke, but as he
descended he remembered thinking that one had to be more careful
going down, for more control was needed. But at that moment Gafni
knew that part of his father, maybe all of him, was in him now.
Levitating, he recalled thinking, was much easier when watching
someone else.

So real was the dream Gafni felt his father was resurrected. Even
more. As if he never died. He wanted the dream to last. When he
woke he at once closed his eyes, hoping he could sleep some more.
Ah, to sleep, perchance to dream again. But he knew it was futile;
the film was over. His father gone. In the dream, Shmulik was fifteen
or sixteen. He sat in shul with his father on shabbes. His right arm
was around his father's shoulder. On Sabbaths and holidays, when
he sat next to his father in shul, his father would point out unusual
words in the prayers, some rare grammatical inconsistencies, call
them errors, in the Psalms. His father would ask him the root of one
word, what another meant. These exercises, over the years, gradually
shaped for him his love of words, of phrases, of language. And at
home, Shmulik would write down folk expressions he heard his
parents and other relatives use. He looked at the fine black hairs on
Papa's fingers, the nicely rounded clipped fingernails, cut before the
onset of the Sabbath, the wave in the hair at the back of his head

where the fedora pressed it every day. *Taleisim* were everywhere. White, ivory, off-white, beige. *A yam fun taleisim*, as the Yiddish expression had it, a sea of prayer shawls. Only this sea was white, not ultramarine, and as the worshippers bowed and swayed, it undulated, that sea of white, in dry waves. He had his arm around his father's shoulder as the waves rose and fell, rose and fell. He felt his father's firm shoulder and — did he dream this too or was it a quick, vivid memory that flashed the moment he woke? — and recalled his Papa's strong, straight back when he went swimming with him, his straight spinal column, the backbone sheathed in its protective musculature, not like his own back where every spine bone protruded and one could, like on a xylophone, play a rhythmic line by rilling a little toy mallet from the nape of his neck down to the base of his spine, and a tiny berry-red birthmark on his father's back wobbled and wiggled when Shmulik played with it as a little boy, but he always resisted the temptation to tug at it, as Papa swam and puffed out his cheeks as if by making himself a balloon it would make him float, and then he turned on his back, something Shmulik could never do without sinking like a stone, were his bones made of lead? he wondered. Remembering his father breathing as he floated on the water, Shmulik recalled the breaths he took as he concentrated on a book; he would inhale two or three short breaths and then let them out in one long exhalation, like a sigh. Just like his father, his beloved Papa.

So real was his clasp of his father's shoulder, his fingers were still warm from the embrace when he woke, and the living presence of his father filled his being, and he still heard the echoes of the prayers. Shmulik knew that dreams rarely recur and hardly ever continue, but as a child some terrifying dreams did continue despite his forcing himself to wake by grasping the cold bedsprings before he fell asleep and pressing them tight if the dream became unbearable. But even though he woke and broke the dream, sometimes the nightmare, poo poo poo, spit three times like bobbe did to avert the *ayin ho-reh*, the evil eye, bad dreams, would continue. Then why can't good dreams return? Why can't good dreams stay? Why do we have nightmares when we sleep and witness living nightmares when we are awake? Why do good people have to die while the evil ones who murder live on? Why did my father and my uncle who survived one Them, have to be murdered by the other Them, who were the same Them but with different faces?

There was the hook. The living hook within him. The evil. The evil one had wedded himself into Gafni's thoughts about his father. He could not think of his father without thinking of him. Oh, how he longed for the days when he could think of his father, purely, without the dirt, the cancer that had invaded his thoughts, *yimakh sh'mo*, may that killer's name be blotted out forever.

SHMULIK'S hatred for that man was absolute; it filled him, it inhered in each of the liquids coursing through his body — blood, saliva, bile and urine. It did not lesson with the passing of the years. On the contrary, it hardened the rage, set it in stone. But the hatred did not blind him. There was no film of red rage misting his eyes. Gafni thought clearly, made his plans, carried them out with the precision of a military campaign. He knew his daily life and his research, his hatred and his desire for revenge, were two separate creatures, living parallel lives. One did not diminute the other; only rarely did they intersect or coalesce.

Could one picture his hate? Not imagine but picture it graphically? Turn emotion into a pictograph? Can one assume little hooked barbs flowing through Gafni that do not harm him but sharpen the edge of his hatred? He cannot see himself when he imagined his father's murderer as clearly as if had photographed him, and indeed he has photographed him, for the image of that beast floats like a miniature picture in his mind. Gafni never looked at a mirror when his hatred flashed, but his eyes narrowed, his brows arched, his lips became thinner, pink, no longer red, but not as thin as the narrow serpentine line of Malina's lips, and, thinking of the man he hopes is still alive, for the murderers are always blessed with long lives and die painlessly in their sleep, Gafni felt a little tic pulsing at the bottom of his right cheek, near the lips. Does hatred — note how many questions hatred elicits, few of them answerable — does hatred, desire for revenge, a gut wish to exact justice, oh how Gafni was dying to exact justice, does this hatred have a smell, a taste? Yes. It tastes of ash, it smells of blood. And when this hatred flashes, senses commingle, exchange places. He hears again, or maybe not again, but hears it still for the first time, the screams of the Jews, the Poles' bloody whoops of delight, feels he has his hands around the beast's thick throat and he smells blood and fire, tastes ash, hears blood, tastes fire, feels ash, Gafni pricks his finger on the barbs flowing through his veins and bleeds. But the bloodletting gives no satisfaction, does not vitiate the hatred; it only sharpens the barbs.

19

STILL, THOSE HORMONES, OH THOSE HORMONES

S<small>TILL</small>, those hormones, oh those hormones, were driving him crazy. A no became a yes. Yes gave birth to no. Malina was cantankerous, even though she didn't know what the word meant. Argumentive. Totally impossible. Whatever he cooked or prepared was no good. It was too sweet, though it lacked sugar. Too salty, though it had no salt. She narrowed her eyes when she complained; he saw two tiny bright green slits. She'd become a bitch. And not a little one either. So huge was she that people asked her if she was due next week. In the past, Gafni had a Malina to look forward to who would come to his office for Yiddish lessons, charging the air with her sub-, maybe even liminal sexuality. Now he had no one to look forward to.

When she was indisposed during her pregnancy, Shmulik took care of her — shopping, cooking, tending. But when he felt queasy, * who would take care of him? As she grew, ditto her staff. She had a personal attendant, a cleaning lady three times a week, a dietician, and a couple of physical therapists. Polish of varying dialects crowded the oxygen out of the air. The apartment suddenly had traffic jams. There went his savings.

Once, even though he had a headache, Shmulik went to the Jerusalem Theater, where the Jerusalem Symphony was giving an all-Bach concert. There he had a surfeit of oxygen. The third movement of the First Brandenburg — perpetual motion in music — was a lifesaver. It was like being in Paradise and grasping a branch of the Tree of Life. His headache vanished. If anything was a magic cure, a divine potion, it was Bach; music to undo the ills of the body and of the entire world. Walking home, the image of the little dog that had once followed him and Batsheva surfaced. Gafni held Batsheva's hand all the way back to the apartment. But the little dog was gone.

Once, in her fourth month, Malina, in a rage, overturned her plate. It was spaghetti with bits of aged cheddar. He had some job cleaning the mess from the tile floor (meanwhile wondering how to

---

*Flu, virus, dizziness, who knows? We're not doctors, so the fine points of medical diagnosis elude us (that is, me; despite the idiotic tradition of plural pronounal politesse in journalism,only one of us is indi(c)ting this narrative).

say "tile" in Yiddish), time he'd rather have spent with his research on the Warsaw Jewish quarter. But then she apologized with that phony high-pitched baby tone he didn't like, and with mixed feelings snuggled to her ample, now even ampler, breasts. He ascribed her actions to chemicals, not will. Out of shame and chagrin he told no one what was going on at home. (You're the first to know!)

It was her first child.

A first for Gafni too. His first goyish baby. The first in his entire family. The irony that his murdered father was the zayde of the coming non-Jewish child was not lost on him.

More: it gave him grief.

AFTER the baby was born there was a period of bliss for a while. About three days to be exact. Yes, bliss.

Ask not, but, about the circumcision, about the bris.

What happened before the bris, if bris it should be called, was this:

All along, soon as he learned he would be a father, Shmulik was hoping for a girl, even though out loud he kept uttering the old cliché with a sincere and even voice, I don't care what it is, as long as it's healthy, for as everyone knew, he already had a son and twin daughters, so the sex of the child should make no difference to him. (Even though normal people mouthed this cliché: I don't care what it is, as long as it's a boy.) But the truth was — and we've already repeated seven times seven times that truth and nothing but will be accented here; as indeed in life the truth is always hidden behind a mask of smiles and persuasive forked tongue sincerity — truth is, Gafni wanted a girl because a girl would pose no problems, a girl would not cause a rift between husband and wife, a girl would not create a triangular pull between the mother and the father, each in one corner of a never-before-seen three-cornered boxing ring.

A normal boy in Israel would have a brit or bris, no matter whether the child's family was secular or observant (only an extreme, anti-religious kibbutznik, himself duly circumcised, would proclaim that his baby boy would not be subjected to such a barbaric rite), and there would be an early morning party with l'chaims, wine, whiskey, liquors, food, not necessarily in that order, and unending shouts of mazel tov.

But this was not a normal baby boy and not because his father was seventy-two, or is he already seventy-three? This was a boy who was half his and half hers, but the half that was hers counted most. Since Malina was not Jewish, the baby, taking his mother's religion according to Jewish law, was not Jewish either, but thoroughly Christian. So how can you have a bris for a non-Jewish baby boy, a brit for a very Christian baby goy? On the other hand, for with Jewish dialectics, there are always three, sometimes even five or six hands, how could a son of Shmulik Gafni, a grandson of Yosi Weingarten not have a bris? Which, now you know why, is why Gafni longed for a girl.

But hopes and reality don't always — in fact, rarely — converge. Flash! Late-breaking news! He got the boy goy he didn't wish for and decided at once: no bris. For in any case, no mohel would do a circumcision on a baby known to be goyish.

And that's when Shmulik and Malina had their first fight.

As she held the baby to her breast for a feeding, Malina told him: "I don't want him to have that, you know, what you Jews call the snipping, it starts with a 'b' …?"

"The bris. Why?" Shmulik said, irritated that she had taken the initiative and probably for the wrong reason.

"Because a) no one in our family has it, and b) it also begins with a b … it's barbaric … It's cruel to put him through the pain, and c) I won't allow it."

That's when Gafni blew up. Witnessing her erratic behavior during the pregnancy he kept calm. But now, for the first time, he didn't restrain his fury.

"What?" he shouted, annoyed with her absurd and provocative reasons. "Here? In Israel? To a Jewish father? You are not going to allow a bris? Who are you here? Are you Titus or Antiochus?"

"I'm not anti anything. Except the bris, which everyone thinks is barbaric, even the religious, but they go through with this stupidity anyway. I won't allow it."

"Who are you to allow or not allow?" Gafni bellowed. "We're in Jerusalem, not Poland. Not Russia. Not Nazi Germany. In communist Russia they didn't allow a bris and Jews went secretly to the cemetery where there were no KGB spies and had themselves circumcised there. But we're here. In Israel. Jews have been doing brises for four thousand years and you, you are going to stop it now?"

His words seemed to glide through her.

"You forget one thing," Malina said with perfect equanimity. "According to your laws he's not Jewish. So what's the point?"

Gafni listened to the intonation. Was there a triumphant or even sarcastic tone in her voice? Yes, he'd been noticing things about her. Little things. A cold flicker in her eyes as he talked with her, as if she were a stranger; no, not a stranger — worse — but an enemy who radiated a cold, impersonal hatred.

"He's not Jewish," she repeated calmly. "Jewishness is determined by the mother."

At this the baby began to cry.

"Stop shouting," he said. "You're making him cry."

"You're the one who's shouting," she said with that unbearable calm in her low voice, a pirate guiding her ship with an icy implacable rage toward the helpless foe. "That's what's making him cry."

Maybe it's your goyish milk that's making him cry, he held back from saying.

"He's mine. I'm a Jew. I consider him Jewish."

"Your half-baked syllogism doesn't make any sense."

Suddenly vanished all his previous reasons for not having a bris. They turned sharply about face and, accompanied by klezmer music, marched toward Shmulik in a merry quickstep.

"I'm going to find a mohel," he said, "and there will be a bris. This isn't the Vatican. And you're not the Pope."

She snapped her face to the wall, closing him out of her thoughts.

"I won't be there," she said through closed eyes and pressed the infant closer to her breast.

He didn't tell her that mothers don't usually attend the bris anyway, but did mutter, "No great loss." when he really wanted to say, But the baby will. Then said it.

Now he could either call a mohel from the ultra-Orthodox quarter who didn't know him, but that would be deceiving the poor mohel, or engage one from the Reform camp. Since Reform had recently decided that Jewishness can also descend from the paternal line, their mohel wouldn't have to be fooled. Or maybe he would even have a doctor do it.

He needed advice. And at once he thought of little Mozart. The tiny man gave me good advice on how to look for my father's murderer in Kielce. Perhaps he can give me some objective thoughts about the bris. Gafni was about to call the Cafe Mozart in Vienna, but then realized that Mozart's high-pitched little voice would hardly be audible on the telephone from so far away.

THERE are varying versions of what happened at the bris. But on one thing all agreed. No family was present. At the ceremony the only people who were related were Gafni and the eight-day-old boy, and naturally, given the shout-it-from-the-rooftop shouts and the whispers that were whispered, there were those who doubted even that kinship. Which meant that no one at the bris was related. In order to fill up the room, a day before the ceremony Gafni went up to Gilo, Jerusalem's southernmost suburb, where a lot of new Russian immigrants lived, and engaged eight men to come form a minyan. He instructed them when to say Amen, when to say mazel tov, while Shmulik himself held the baby's legs, while the mohel did the job.

Of the stories describing what took place at the bris in Gafni's living room, two variants surfaced.

One went like this. The other is a product of Gafni's fecund imagination.

Or vice versa.

How can one circumcise a baby boy who is admittedly a little goy? Since no mohel who was worth his (kosher) salt would perform the ceremony, Shmulik finally got a doctor he knew to circumcise the child on the eighth day and bring him into the covenant of our Father Abraham. But the doctor, though not particularly observant, refused to say the blessings traditionally recited at a bris, claiming, "I'm a doctor, not a mohel." *Davke* because he was a Jew, the doc didn't feel comfortable reciting blessings for, let's face it (we don't mince words, remember?) an unkosher ceremony.

At which Shmulik patted down the yarmulke on his head and recited the blessings himself, but the words stuck, well, not exactly stuck, but sort of gargled in his throat as his father's voice, entering Gafni's larynx, shouted contrary dicta, and the words said simultaneously by the two of them, pa and grand-pere, came out not Yiddish nor Hebraish but a fusion of the two, a dialect known as Gibberish (the Swedes call it Yibberish), a northwest Semitic patois of Geebrew.

As Shmulik began the blessing, "*Borukh ato Adonaï*" (as if in rhyme with "my") — in honor of his late father, Gafni began the first two words with the Ashkenazic pronunciation rather than the Israeli-Sephardic one he was used to, but when it came to God's name, he slipped back to Sephardic — the elder Weingarten, grand-pa of the newly hatched little boy, cried out repeatedly from *yenne velt*, "But he's a goy!" Gafni tried to quell his *tateh*'s shout with a remonstrance, "Papa!," and so the blessing sounded like "Abrokh ato Papaguy"* — which anyone understanding both Hebrew and Yiddish would have understood to mean, "What a disaster you are, O Parrot." Gafni then tried to say "*Elohenu*" (our God), the next word in the classic incept of a Hebrew benediction, at which the elder Weingarten keened, "Oy vey, oy vey," which in double voice fusion Gibberish came out as "*oyveynu*," which in Hebrew meant, "our enemy." Throughout this botched *brokhe* Gafni pere kept shouting "A goy, a goy," until poor Gafni fils, continuing the mangled blessing, stutt-muttered "*melakh-ha-goylem*" (salt of the golem) instead of

---

* Even how people heard "Papaguy" there were two opinions. The other was that Gafni pronounced God's name in Ashkenazic too as "Adonoy." When combined with his father's "But he's a goy!" and Gafni's cry, "Papa!" it came out as "Abroch ato Papagoy," which meant: "What a disaster you are, O Father of a goy!"

"*melekh ha-oylem* (King of the universe). So as Shmulik's little *shey-getz* son was undergoing the totally meaningless and even deceptive rite, the first part of the blessing actually fit the occasion. For the few of you out there who are Kentucky hicks or live in the Alabama boondocks, let's recap the orison and perhaps even consign it to memory, for the next time you are in Jerusalem, you may hear it repeated as an in-joke among senior members of the University of Israel faculty (blame it on that blabbermouth doctor cum mohel who couldn't resist spreading the word the minute he stepped out of Gafni's house), where one half of an interlocuting team would begin by saying, "*Abrokh ato Papaguy*" and his partner, already stifling rising giggles, would conclude "*ovyvenu melakh ha-goylem.*" For our friends from the great state of Kentucky and the great state of Alabama we'll gladly English it again, but let's hear the original first. This is the way it was supposed to have sounded:

"*Borukh ato Adonai eloheynu melekh ha-oylem ... *"

Which meant: "Blessed are you, O Lord our God, King of the Universe ... "

But this is how poor Gafni mutt-stuttered it in double voce:

"*Abrokh ato Papaguy oyvenu melakh ha-goylem ... *"

Which meant: "What a disaster you are, O Parrot, our enemy, salt of the golem ... "

Luckily, the *shnit* around the corona was made before the abortive blessing, otherwise the muffled chuckles would surely have compromised the cut for, as everyone knows, a scalpel, a steady hand, and hysterical laughter are not a happy trio, especially at a bris.

A bris normally has family and friends, but for this one present only were the Russian hired hands (and feet) from Gilo, the baby, the doctor, Shmulik, and his father's complaintive voice. Malina, keeping her word, stayed in the next room wearing earphones and earmuffs, and loudly playing an Easter mass by the Polish Bach contemporary, Grzegorz Gorczycki.

THE truth of the matter is that among the entire company only Malina had the guts not to be present. The doctor didn't want to be there. Nor the Russians, who said Amen at the wrong spots and shouted Bravo instead of mazel tov. Some of them, understanding Yiddish, laughed when they heard familiar exclamations. Who else didn't want to be there? Shmulik.

No one asked the baby.

And some say a like event occurred, with a mixup of benedictions and Gafni ventriloquizing, but instead of a doctor it was a mohel, of some kind or other. Or maybe it's this version that Gafni imagined, or — as stated supra — the other way around.

But on one fact everyone agreed: for a period of time —
details below — Malina stopped speaking to him.

AFTER the bris, feeling an elation that wouldn't last too long, a
joy in a minor key overridden by sour feelings of futility in what he
had done and his father's voice still tickling his larynx and needling
his conscience, Gafni, feeling the temporary high of an alcoholic, a
high from which alcoholics plummet, brought the baby to Malina.

She removed the earphones and stopped listening to Gorczycki's
Missa Paschalis.

"Well, is the torture over?"

"It's not torture."

"Not only is it torture, it's bloody torture."

"And it's not bloody because it so happens that the coagulation
rate is highest on the eighth day."

"Primitive. Superstition. Barbaric." And then, "Why isn't he
crying? A baby is supposed to cry after the ... "

"You want him to cry?"

"Why are you being nasty? Isn't it enough I had to suffer through
his suffering?"

"We gave him a bottle. That quieted him."

Malina played with the earphones.

But Gafni was not going to be perturbed by her inattention.

"I named him Yonatan. After my uncle."

"I'll call him Janosz," she said.

"After?" he said, the blood pumping into his racing, trepidatious
heart.

"After all," Malina said.

Then she smiled.

That smile didn't please him. That smile had a glint. And not
of gold either. More like tinsel, pinchbeck, then Gafni remembered
an apropos French word, *clinquant*, which was strange, because he
didn't know French. Fool's gold. More like gilt, whose pun value,
negative tremor, flooded his brain. Gafni knew why he felt the way
he did, not only because of the faux bris, but because of what she
said next. He didn't actually know what she would say but sensed the
tenor of her coming words from the vibration of the unsaid remark
on her lips, much like thunder preceding lightning.

"For unto us a child is born, unto us a son is given," she sang the
melody of Handel's Messiah.

A sudden seethe of blue rage rose from Gafni's chest to his lips.

"You're equating him with a little Jesus?"

"Not Jesus. I'll call him Janosz."

"But you're singing the tune to the Messiah."

"Never mind the music," she said sweetly. "The words are from your Bible. From Isaiah … It's the words that count."

He couldn't argue with her. She had a way of twisting an argument, not so much twisting as subtly turning it, so that not she but he was in the wrong, and maybe less he wrong than she right.

She began nursing the baby.

"Janosz," she sang to him. This time Gafni couldn't detect the Handel melody. Maybe it was something from the Polish Mass. "That's what you'll be called. That's your name, sweetheart. Janosz."

And she snapped her face away from Gafni, a gesture he'd see repeated in the days and months to come, she shutting him out of her world. In punishment for what he had done to her little Janosz on the eighth day of his life, Malina didn't speak to Gafni for eight days.

THE full force of the child not being Jewish (half Jewish was as illusionary as tooth fairies, unicorns and stardust) didn't hit Gafni until after the sham *shnitting*, where the baby was supposedly brought into the covenant of Abraham by (as one version had it) a trained mohel from the Reform movement, or (according to another) by a doctor. But one thousand kosher mohelim snipping even one thousand mini-minuscule pieces from the little tyke's yoni could not have made the child Jewish. Covenant of Abraham, my foot! More like Covenant of Terah. The mama was a goya, neither a painting nor a can of garbanzos — a metaphor used many chapters ago, but as Diderot wisely observed: "Clever remarks should preferably be said twice, once for the listener's pleasure, a second time for the teller's delectation" — a plain *shikse* was the mommy. And Gafni's son was a goy. Period. End of argument. Until such time as he attained age of discernment, stood on his own two goyish feet, and elected of his own free will to become a Jew: study, convert, (re)join his father's faith.

MONTHS later, after her confinement, when he met casual acquaintances abroad at a conference, he would tell his story quickly. A typical colleague, let's say from California, whom he hadn't seen in several years, would hear it this way:

"*Sholom aleichem*, Mendl Fertlshtam (or Berl Eyzenboym or Itsik Mandelkern). It's been a while, right?"

"*Aleichem sholom*, Shmulik … Yes, about three years. How are things? What's new?"

"I don't know if you heard, but my beloved wife, Batsheva, has passed on," Gafni said with an appropriate regretful moué. "Two years ago."

"No, I didn't. I'm so sorry to hear that."

Mendl would look sad, avoid Shmulik's eyes, then look up and say: "Well, such is fate. May God grant you consolation."

"Thank you. He did. I remarried," Gafni would add quickly, voice merry now.

Mendl (or Berel or Itsik) would then have to turn on a dime, expunge the mourning mien, work up an enthusiastic smile, and exclaim: "Mazel tov!"

"Thank you." Surface then would the old Gafni glint and gleam and strong-toothed smile, which stretched from one end of the reception room to the other. "Thank you very much … But I have to tell you, you'll probably hear it soon enough anyway, she's not Jewish."

Again the morose look erased a moment earlier would be recalled.

"Sorry to hear that … "

"But she might convert."

Back to smile mode, Mendl. (And be quick about it.) "That's nice."

Gafni's shrug sent the tentative smile off to la-la-land. Then he turned serious for a moment, as if remembering something.

"But maybe not. It's up to her."

A neutral nod from Mendl, who shifted his weight from foot to foot.

"But you'll be glad to hear," Gafni stated cheerily, "that we now have a one-year old."

"Is that so?" said the now beaming Mendl. "A baby. Then double mazel tov."

Then he frowned, as if wondering if two mazel tovs were one, maybe two, too many.

"Thank you for your good wishes," declared an equally elated Gafni. "But, alas, the dear child is not Jewish."

Mendl couldn't take this emotional yo-yo, turning on and off joy and chagrin. He tried his best to look sad.

"So one would assume, but still sorry to hear that. But you still didn't tell me if it's a boy or a girl. Surely you know by now, right?"

Gafni laughed at Mendl's little joke. Or was it sarcasm? "Let's see, wait a minute, let me recall … yes, yes, it was a boy."

"And now?" came Mendl's tweaky riposte.

"What do you mean 'and now'?"

"You said it *was* a boy, Shmulik."

"It was, is, and will be a boy."

"God willing, later, if he wishes to, he can become a Jew."

"True, Mendl, true. That's what everyone says. But we, um, sort of helped it along. We had a bris."

"Glad to hear that," said Mendl mechanically, not glad to hear that at all — and not glad to say: Glad to hear that. By now Mendl no longer knew what he was glad to hear and what he wasn't glad to hear. What he did know was that he'd be glad to get away. But he did ask himself: What right does a goyish baby have to be circumcised?

By now both men felt uncomfortable and were anxious to move on to talk to other people. But at least Gafni was happy that he had gotten all his personal information off his chest. Rumors and gossip would be lessened with facts, or at least there would be solid facts on which to build gossip, rumors and downright lies.

But one thing Gafni would never confess to them, not even to colleagues from nine thousand miles away. Something about the baby. The first sign that matters were askew in the marriage was not the insufferable attitude of Malina. It was the baby, that little momzer. He was nice to his mother. But Gafni, every time he approached to goo-goo at the baby and brought his face close to his, the little testosterone-filled, genetically Polish little antisemitt would punch his *tateh* in the nose. His mama Janosz smiled to and nuzzled nestled into her generous bosom. But for Shmulik, all Shmulik got was an evil green glint in the baby's eyes as he stared at his father and snarled at him like an angry dog every time Papa drew near, the little Polish goy. Still, Gafni liked him; he was, after all, his.

Studying his harried face in the mirror, Gafni quoted to himself: Methinks I doth protest too much.

What have I done? he asked himself. Maybe Nussen and his friends were right to kidnap me.

DURING the next year Malina calmed down but remained fat. It was as if he'd acquired a new wife at the shuk. The folds of fat on her waist were now so thick he was able to poke his fingers into it and close the flabs around them. Once in a while, he longingly picked up a photograph of her in the old, pre-baby days when her body had that head-turning allure, or recalled how he had stood with her on the Nice beach years back, she wearing that slithery gauze jacket over her bikini which had half of Nice agape and the French Air Force jets flying special lowflight maneuvers just to get a glance at that gorgeous body. Who was getting even with whom he didn't know. Gafni didn't believe in sprites or spirits. Perhaps it was his father. Or hers.

Once, standing on a bus on his way back from the University (Malina was using the car that day), he overheard two men seated in front of him talking. Evidently he was, as the Yiddish expression had it, on everyone's tongue.

"Reuven, I tell you, she wouldn't have married him for the money."

It went without saying who the "she" was and who the "him."

There was only one "he" and one "she" in the plopl-patter in buses and cafés. And Gafni was proud that he was the first university professor to get into the gossip columns, which were normally reserved for pop and rock singers, movie stars, and international entertainment icons.

"Maybe so, Shimon, but then why did she marry him?"

"Remember, for every 'she' marrying a 'he' there is one 'he' marrying a 'her'."

Gafni disregarded the observation, and not just because the pronouns weren't quite parallel. For a while both men stared out the window, watching the white buildings of the Israel Museum float closer. The back of the bus was overcrowded. A woman with a full shopping bag pressed against Gafni. Grapefruits thumped against his leg. He noted that, like him, the two men had fringes of grey white hair. From their accent he surmised that both had come to Israel after World War II, in the fifties, and had spoken Yiddish most of their lives.

"Do you know why she married him?" Shimon asked his friend.

"For Yiddish?"

Shimon gave a disparaging flick of his hand. "What are you talking about, Reuven? Yiddish! How about love? Not every marriage is an act of expediency."

"Go enter the mind of a *Poilishe*."

"Then explain why he married her."

"Don't be naïve. Look at that picture of her in that trash weekly and you'll know why."

"I don't read that trash," said Shimon. "And certainly not trash like that rag."

"What rag?"

"You know. That shmatte that I don't read. That rag with all those half-naked pictures."

R: "Neither do I, Shimon. You know me better than that. Our maid showed it to me. I don't see how a country like this permits a scandal sheet like that to exist. And they call Israel a democracy. And they had the gall — tfu on then! — to publish that nearly naked photo of her in a bikini."

Sh: "Yes, I remember that!"

R: "You do?"

Sh: "I mean I remember hearing about it."

R: "And they published that bikini photo just to show how she looked a few years ago when he first met her."

Now Reuven leaned over to his friend and whispered into his ear, which made it all the easier for Shmulik to overhear. "But I hear she looks like a balloon now after the baby."

Sh: "What baby? Who baby? Where baby?"

R: "Didn't you hear they had a baby?"

Sh: (excited, almost jumping out of his seat) "No. Tell me. Tell tell tell. That old man? A baby?"

R: "Yes. A baby."

Sh: "Boy or girl?"

R: "Boy."

Sh: "Is it his?"

A twinge in Gafni's face; a turning in his gut.

R: "How should I know? I wasn't in bed with them."

Sh: "Well, even if you were in bed with them, it wouldn't be yours either."

R: "You're fifty per cent of a wit. I.e., a half wit."

Sh: "It's probably not his. A man in his seventies can't father a child."

R: "You mean you couldn't make a baby?"

Sh: "I'm not talking about myself. I mean others."

R: "In other words, hinting that I couldn't."

Sh: "Not you either. The rest of the others."

R: "Abraham fathered a baby when he was one hundred. And then, years later, when Sarah died, he even took another wife."

Sh: "People lived longer in the old days. And it's easier to make a baby when you're in a book … Did they have a bris?"

R: "A *shaygets* can't have a bris. Certainly not here in Israel. That's why I heard they took him to Cyprus to get snipped."

Sh: "Jews go to Cyprus to get married, not to get snipped. Where did you hear that nonsense about Cyprus?"

R: "From those rags they call magazines."

Sh: "Which you no doubt bought. Otherwise, where do you get all that information from? And don't offer me that salami that the maid showed it to you."

R: "I don't waste my money on junk magazines. It just so happens that dozens of copies of her face —" Reuven pointed vaguely out the bus window with his thumb — "and her body half-naked on that magazine cover were clipped to the news kiosk. It was the *shlagger* of the week. That photo of that slim woman with those big you should excuse me top heavy milk factories that stared you in the face along with that almost naked body of hers. And inside, that story about them in print so tiny you could go blind from trying to read, which the maid told me about. So if you saw that photo, I don't know how they got it, it was taken in Nice, that's in France, in case you don't know, do you think he sent it to the magazine — ?"

At this point Gafni bent forward, tempted to intervene, dying to shout, "I did not!" He knew what he was doing was stupid, but he couldn't help himself. This gossip was too much for him, so he blurted out, "No!" right into their ears.

The two men turned as one to look at him and said, "What do you mean, no?"

Gafni straightened up and tried to look composed. "I thought you asked if this bus makes the descent. Not this one. The number 44 goes down into the valley."

"No no," said Reuven. "Not descent. I said: 'he sent.' "

"Oh," said Gafni. "And I thought you said 'decent', which is why I heard 'descent'."

Said Shimon:

"Maybe you thought you heard Reuven say it slowly, 'de scent,' like in the phrase 'de scent of the roses was pretty.' "

"You thought you heard 'descend'," Rueven tried to explain, "because you assume we didn't say 'recent', like in the sentence, 'This is the most recent copy of the sex scandal magazine.' "

"That explains it," said Shimon. "No wonder you thought I misheard you saying 're-sent,' like in 'He re-sent the picture to them after they didn't acknowledge the first one he sent them.' "

Gafni straightened up, exhausted. By now the crowd had thinned out. He could look out the windows to the left and to the right. The area outside did not look familiar. He had missed his stop.

"So you think she could have sent it?" Reuven asked Shimon.

Shimon assumed a thinking pose. "Let me ... I'm thinking ... You are right. No doubt about it. Yes. She sent it. She loves the limelight."

SHMULIK moved to the front of the bus, afraid that the two men would recognize him. By missing his stop he now had one of the longest rides on the line back to his house. Gafni had always been shy of publicity; he let his books speak for themselves, rarely gave press interviews — and had not granted one since he had married Malina. Ever since then, he had to get an unlisted phone number in order to have some peace.

What thoughts ran through his mind now as he rode the long scenic ride down the hill to the Valley of the Cross? To the ground theme of regret at having missed his stop and the inconvenience of taking another bus back home came the treble variations of money and inheritance. She had never asked him about either, but his twin daughters did ask him directly if he would leave the apartment to her. (They too used pronouns instead of names.) Gafni assured them he would not.

Malina had an apartment in Warsaw, spare keys to which she kept in his desk. After his death, Gafni assumed, she would no doubt return to teach there. She would not continue living in Israel, a stranger among her peers.

20

TRAUMA AND SHAME

HE arrived in Kielce by train in the evening, his few possessions tucked into a rucksack. He was going to see his father, his uncle. Six years. Six years and a world away. He hired a wagon to take him to the edge of town where the Jews lived. A bonfire in the middle of the main street around which men were drinking blocked the wagon. The driver turned into a side street. From afar Shmulik heard screams of women and men.

"They're finishing off the Jews," the driver said, not with anger, not with joy. "Finally."

Shmulik's blood stopped flowing. His face, a red heat encompassed it. Then a chill brushed over him. He began trembling with cold, yet sweat was pouring out of him. He was afraid the man would kill him too.

"Here's where I get off." Shmulik paid the driver and watched him turn the wagon around. He hoped the man didn't notice his shaking hands.

Where should I go now? Whom could he ask directions to his uncle's house? He began running through the side streets toward the sounds. Shots rang out. Papa, he thought. Papa. He cut through back yards to the forest.

The sounds of screaming and whoops intensified. His skin was no longer his own. In his neck his heart pounded thickly. He stepped into the woods. Then, shielded by the trees, he moved closer to a clearing in back of some small houses. There he saw the slaughter. With pistols and rifles and knives and axes and clubs.

When he saw his father and uncle, an unearthly scream gagged his throat.

Because of the bonfires he sees the face of the murderer who is Shmulik's age, perhaps a year or two older. A blond man with hair that stood on end like brambles. He is inscribed in Shmulik's memory as if etched with an iron burr. He will wake up, Shmulik tells himself. Wake up from the nightmare, then leaps from his hiding place and clubs the man's head with a stick. He has a bent nose, high cheekbones and narrow, close-set light blue eyes. With one blow Shmulik brings the man down, then picks him up and swings him like a club until he has killed all the murderers. In the woods, Shmulik, who is dead, a life gone out of him, the life he has is no longer his own, Shmulik vows aloud that he will hunt down this man and kill him with his bare hands.

OTHER people are present at home or at the hospital when a parent's life ebbs. But Shmulik, from his hiding place at the edge of the wood, Shmulik saw his father being murdered and could do — did — nothing. Police! one wants to cry, but there is no police. The police are with the killers. Now Shmulik looks down at the memory tattooed on his skin. He jumps like Samson from his hiding place, standing between the pillars of the enemy's temple to bring it down upon the heads of the enemy with one last burst of strength. From his hiding place he leaps into the crowd, and with a swift sharp blow kicks one Pole into a ditch, and with one motion picks up and swings an axe, smashing the knives and staves and axes in the murderers' hands while swinging the axe round and round like a top, felling the hated Poles until all are dispatched and he saves his father and his father's brother and the other terrified Jews who had survived the war years in the death camps and the woods and come home — some home! — to their towns and shtetls to the taunts of the Poles, "What, you're still alive?" and when a young survivor came back into his parents' little house and saw nothing there but the bare walls and went next door to his Polish neighbor whom his father had helped with food and money before the war and saw his family's furniture, pictures, bed and bedding, the Polish neighbor, looking at the young Jew surveying his family's belongings, hissed: "If you value your life, get out of town in an hour or you'll be a dead man too," which was lucky because at least he escaped with his life, not like other Jews who were murdered when they came to ask for their belongings after the war.

Now Shmulik makes wish reality and his imagination restores the torn pages of the calendar and, like in fairy tales, films or dreams, fulfilling the fourth and fifth wish, he takes the brute whose face he will never forget with the blond hair that stood up on his head like brambles, close-set eyes, a short thick nose with a slight leftward twist as if broken in a fight, and the joy, yes the joy and thrill of murder quivering like sparks in his washed-out blue eyes, an ecstasy he had never felt before and would never feel again, how Shmulik wished he could have flown like an arrow and killed him on the spot and wiped the other murderers too from the face of the earth. And when he returned from his heroic sweep of the enemy, a daring leap from American films he had never seen and would not see until many years later, he knew the meaning of paralysis of will and body, a near death sensation, but in death you do not see what Shmulik saw, the dead are blessed that way, but what he saw was etched into his memory with acid, with gall and wormwood, the Biblical words for the terrors the Jews would face at some future time, but he, Shmulik, faced them now as he saw that man with the brute's face, the thrill of murder, never would he forget that savage, savagely lit by the grotesque, angled light of their campfire and the smells of vodka and the acrid smoke of burning wood sprayed with urine, and the terror-stricken faces of the Jews, his father, his uncle, the others from Kielce who sat on the ground under the point of guns and axes, acid and gall, until the cry, the signal, the call that lasted perhaps only a few seconds, oh the joy, the thrill of killing, but so penetrated Shmulik's being. In death you do not see, the dead are blessed that way, that it has hung there grating his nerves for centuries, a cry to action that he cannot mute and the more he wills it to vanish the louder it becomes, for all he saw was the swinging of one axe, gall and wormwood, and then another, and the rifle fired, led by the blond beast of Europe, and he saw what was done to his father who by miracle had escaped the poison gas of Auschwitz and returned to Kielce to visit his brother and him, per Shmulik's suggestion, and he either wished he could black out and die or did die, for his breath stopped, the dead are blessed that way, and his hearing stopped and his seeing stopped, but his shame and anger flamed and burned, one overwhelming the other so that it was hard to tell whether Shmulik was more ashamed or more enraged at his impotence, but impotence subsides but shame and trauma linger, soul wounds that never go away, for although he in one dreamsecond imagined himself leaping out to the rescue, for he wanted so badly to live and for his beloved father and uncle to live, the dead are blessed that way, his body was tied to the tree as if fused to the trunk.

But none of the ones he loved lived.

Only the murderers.

SHMULIK doesn't remember if it was hot or cold that day, humid or dry. He saw what he saw, could not wipe away — will never be able to wipe away — what his eyes beheld, like a blackboard eraser makes words disappear. Gafni occasionally kept notes in a diary, but this he could not write down. If he described what he had witnessed, copied down what was etched into his memory, his father would be murdered again. And diary aside, even if we were to imagine the horror or reconstruct it from eyewitness accounts, it would not please Shmulik. It would be an invasion of his private domain. During the Seder, just before we open the door for Elijah the Prophet, we offer a tribute, a memorial, to the Warsaw Ghetto fighters and to the Six Million, and include the following line;

"We do not dwell on the deeds of the killers lest we defame the image of God in which man is created."

So, in deference to Shmulik, his beloved father and uncle, and all the murdered Jews, we too, I too, will remain silent.

TREES were here that stood planted from the beginning of time, but Shmulik does not remember the overhang of birches or the scrub pines in the wood. The site near the little river is also a blank in his memory. Birds at night are quiet, but that night, excited, they chirped nonstop as if to drown out the agony of sounds and cries. That too is a zero, as if it did not exist. He doesn't even remember what day of the week it was, but does know it was July 4, 1946, because that's the date the history books record the infamous pogrom in Kielce, Poland, where survivors of forests, hiding, the death camps, were murdered once again. But the Hebrew date was more important. On that date Shmulik observed the yorzeit, said the Kaddish in memory of his father and his uncle and all the Jews killed that day by beasts who in a bizarre rite put on the masks of human faces. The Hebrew date he did not forget. It was the ninth day in the month of *Av*, when the Temple in Jerusalem was destroyed. And *av* also means "father" in Hebrew. He called the month Av *mar, mar* meaning "bitter" in Hebrew. For him it was mar, a bitter month, losing his *av, oy mar mar*, a bitter year, that stained his life with bitterness — a bitterness that to his surprise was in later years suppressed but not forgotten by the weight of his laughter, the mass of his smile.

The next day the police — the same police who looked the other way the night before — restored order. The Jews buried their dead. Shmulik, who was still Weingarten then, attended two funerals. But he promised himself, and kept the promise, to rebury his father in Warsaw. He said Kaddish, then went out to look for the murderer.

Shmulik looked in the shops, looked in the market, pretending to look for something else, trying to put on a naïve face but his glance sharp as a scimitar in his mind that he fantasized would with one swift stroke remove the murderer's head from the rest of his body.

Even years later, when he came from Israel as Gafni, in his mind and heart he came as Weingarten because it was as Weingarten that his father was killed, but of course he never told anyone his true last name lest they become suspicious, because murderers have long memories, even longer than those who seek revenge. No one knew him in town and he returned over the years under the guise — and in disguise — of doing research, surveys, some innocuous, scholarly chores. But during those trips he never found the man he sought with that pale cruel face, that savage with the blond hair that stood up like little nails and frightening washed-out blue eyes. Gafni never found him in Kielce.

Why?

Because during that year the killer never set foot outside the church grounds where he worked as a gardener although his profession was welder, ironmonger, the church he found refuge in after the pogrom, the church that turned away Jews during the war years when the Germans occupied the city. But the Germans had already been gone since December 1944, and from then on the Poles acted alone.

How he wanted to welcome his father back from the death camp. There were so many memories he wanted to share with him. How he wanted to thank him for teaching him. How he wanted to embrace and kiss him and hold him tight and never let him go.

Where in the world can you find a father like my father?

21

A LITTLE DISH OF MERCURY

WHEN Gafni saw a little dish of mercury in the medicine cabinet, he didn't pay much attention. A thermometer broke and she collected the mercury into the little dish, he thought. But when a few days later he saw a few mercury pellets neatly arranged on a gauze pad, a little question mark, razor thin and shaped like a miniature scythe, danced above his eyelids. The next time he counted them. Nine in all, three little rows of three each, like a tic tac toe board. A day later the middle one was gone. What's going on? he wondered. Then, one day, he saw Malina rubbing one pellet on little Yonatan's forehead. He didn't know whether to explode in rage, slam doors, or just laugh and tell her she's insane.

But he restrained himself. A day later, in the bathroom, he noticed that a corner pellet was now half the size. He walked into the bedroom. She was nursing the baby and — seeing this in midstride as he swung the door open — when she switched to the other breast, she rubbed a bit of something shiny and silvery on his lips.

Without even thinking, Gafni ran forward and seized his son.

"Are you crazy?" he shouted. "Mercury's poison. Like lead, even worse, it goes right into the brain ... Oh, my God. I don't believe it! What are you doing?"

"Give me the baby ... It won't hurt him. I learned about it in Warsaw ... "

"From whom? A witch doctor?"

"A Caribbean lady ... The wife of the Jamaican ambassador. Then I noticed the farm women doing it."

"Malina, you're mad. It's deadly."

"There's nothing wrong with it. Just stick to your books and leave the nursing to me."

She took the baby from him. For a moment he was so astonished — words, complaints, arguments swirled before him — he could not say a word.

"Even Paracelsus used mercury," she said.

"But he lived in the early 1500's."

"But he was the first to introduce the concept of disease, preaching against the imbalance of humors."

"Anyone who uses mercury today is imbalanced."

Gafni stopped, let his thoughts settle. Then looking straight at her, he said in a low even voice, snapping each word like a whip:

"This will not happen again. Not. Never. Not again. You hear? No primitive voodoo here. You can kill the child."

He felt the blood pounding in his temples, his throat constricting. If he said another word he would choke.

Paracelsus, he thought. Where does she get that combination of intellection and peasant stupidity?

Malina pressed her thin lips.

My God, he thought. I've uncovered a secret. It's like in a play, or in a novel, when the hero accidentally discovers something that shocks him to the core. "A secret, a secret," he murmured involuntarily.

But she heard him.

"Every person has a secret or two. Don't you have any?"

He didn't reply.

"Well?"

"At least mine," he said, "at least mine don't harm anyone."

"And I use it too. I survived a train wreck in Germany. I was the only one who survived. Because of the mercury."

"And everyone else was killed."

"Yes. Everyone. Except me."

"I suppose the mercury brought you good luck."

"Even more than that," Malina said, a bright smile on her face.

"But you know, it wasn't the mercury."

"Then what was it?"

"Ping-pong."

But she missed the bite of his remark.

"What are you talking about? What ping-pong?"

"I play ping-pong. That saved you. No, actually, my blue socks."

"Don't be absurd," she said.

My God, he thought. She's been using the mercury for ritual purposes, as a good luck charm. Poisoning the baby.

"Do you know you can be arrested? Put in jail? And I won't be able to save you. The jails are not pleasant here. Especially if you're in for child abuse ... And they'll take the baby away from us."

She paled, removed the baby from her breast, and pressed him closer. Little Janosz/Yonatan began to squeal.

"Didn't your people use garlic as a charm and mumble angels' names to ward off the evil eye to prevent Lilith from snatching the newborn?"

"I see you're mastering Jewish folklore. But none of these charms kills. Spitting three times harms no one. But mercury maims, mercury poisons, mercury kills."

She put the baby on the table and began changing his diaper.

"Mercury saves. It's the planet between us and the sun, and it absorbs the good rays and emanations from both. The sun gives us energy and life. So too the planet closest to it. Mercury measures our temperature. It is metal and liquid; it expands and contracts. It is the only element that is liquid; the only metal that is liquid. Its mystical qualities are many and enormous. It has a power. The power to save."

"It kills, you moron! And it's not going to be in this house again. If I see you using it once more, I'll call the police. Where's all your education, double doctor Malina?"

"It saves, you fool! Where's all your belief?"

Gafni closed his eyes, shook his head. "It's poison. Poison. Poison."

"Then why did doctors use it? To cure? To cure syphilis."

"What's the matter with you? If you're going to do research on mercury, do it right. The fact is that no one survived those treatments. They all died miserable deaths. I can't believe that a modern woman like you is slave to such a deadly superstition."

"And what about your superstition?" Malina said. "When you see a piece of dust on the floor, you won't even bend to pick it up. You won't even step across it. You walk around it."

Gafni couldn't tell if the laughter that burst out of him was hilarity or sarcasm.

"That's superstition? That's just laziness."

"And how about when you ask me to shut the armoire when you're in bed because you don't like all your ties staring at you? What's that? Superstition or just folklore?"

"Neither. It's just a joke."

But Gafni couldn't laugh. She's crazy, he thought. The river witch, Yadwiga, who so influenced generations of primitive Poles, has dybbuked into her, taken her over, bewitched her. And for a second time the thought flashed, as a little despondent shiver rilled over him: he had made a mistake.

A terrible mistake.

22

HOW MANY TIMES CAN A MAN BE BURIED?

"WHERE were you?" Gafni asked.

Yankl Shtroy knew what the question meant. It didn't mean where were you yesterday or where were you this morning. It meant only one thing. When a Jew asked a European Jew who stood — alive — before him after World War II, it meant only one thing: where — were — you?

"You don't want to know."

"I do want to know. If you're willing to answer."

"It's not important."

Gafni didn't persist but continued to look straight at Yankl Shtroy until the old man with the yellowish white hair and black yarmulke finally spoke.

"I was dead."

"Everyone was," said Gafni.

"Yes, but I was buried too. And I rose out of it. Maybe that's why I can't die anymore. A person can do lots of things many times in his lifetime. But buried he can be only once. Remember, in *The Odyssey*, Circe says, 'One death is enough for all men.' And not two, she meant."

Gafni was astonished, even shocked. How did this simple Jew, who probably never went beyond eighth grade, never read belles lettres, never even heard of Homer, know this line?

"Yes, I know, Professor Gafni, you're wondering, you're surprised. The lines of astonishment are running across your face as if they are having a race. But you should know this: when you've lived as long as me, anything is possible. Homer told me."

Now Gafni wanted to ask even more questions, but he remained silent. The urge to speak is greater than coyness; even greater than self-restraint. No mortal can keep a secret, said Freud. So very true. Mortals cannot keep secrets. But I can, Gafni told himself. What I've been told will never pass my lips. So perhaps, he laughed, pleased with his syllogism, that makes me a candidate for becoming immortal.

Yankl Shtroy looked down at his clasped hands. The skin there was dry and tight, the raised blue veins interlaced. Gafni knew he would talk. He waited for the old man to continue.

"Let me start by saying that our family went into hiding with a Polish farmer. For a price, of course. All went well for a few days. Then what happened next happened to a number of Jews, but only the ones that lived lived to tell about it. A neighboring farmer knocked on the door. I know about them, the farmer said, and I won't talk if they sign their possessions over to me. Our host farmer brought my father out. My father signed over his household goods to the other man. After he left our farmer said, and we believed him, What can I do? There is greed all around us. Better life than possessions. A week later the neighbor returned. He said the Germans were all around, it's very risky. Protecting Jews is risky. If we get caught, everyone, including both farmers will be shot. Now he wanted the house. So we signed over the house.

"The next day the farmer told us that the Germans were closing in. He would put all five of us, parents and three children under the hay and transport us to a safer place. Yes, safer. You know where they took us? They took us to German headquarters. But the Germans didn't shoot us. For their pleasure they created a better torture. They buried us, my father and mother and my two little sisters and me, up to our necks in the yard in back of their building and just left us there. Day and night within sight of each other. No water, no food. Please don't ask any more. We all died slow miserable deaths. One night there was a partisan raid. They surprised and killed the murderers without mercy, then went into the yard and found us. One of the partisans spotted me. He heard me whimpering, thought it was a cabbage head talking. He fainted. Then they dug me out. So I was buried once, but no more."

Again, immortality, thought Gafni. All ruminations return to that, like in the Spanish thinker Unamuno's famous phrase, the hunger for immortality.

"You've read Miguel de Unamuno?" Yankl Shtroy raised his eyebrows.

"I can't believe this. I'm just thinking of him. Do you read minds, Yankl Shtroy?"

"Minds? No, not minds. I just read the letters on your forehead."

23

HELICOPTERS DON'T MAKE NO DETOURS NO MORE

Now, with a two-year-old, she was beefy, mammothian, Brobdignagian. No helicopters would detour for her, not even southbound storks. Even those previously delectable breasts, which were truly big (compared to the rest of her) were now (compared to the rest of her) nothing to speak of, sing paeans to, or write home about. She'd lost it; lost her edge. Whatever she had was ensconced in memory or in old photos.[*]

Growing nicely. Like a baby. Israeli cooking. The hot weather. Constant snacking. No self-control. Hormones run amok. Who knows? Perhaps lassitude. Lack of will. The belly larger. The waistline thicker, like a man's. In conclusion: sex appeal gone. No mincing words; no euphemisms or circumlocutions. No personal ad terminology. No "full-sized" baloney. No "appealingly large-boned" verbal sleight-of-hand. Let's be frank, honest, direct.

A blob of blubber.

Is monosyllablism your desideratum?

Okay.

Fat.

Will two do?

Okay.

Obese.

Who would want her now?

Week to week she got fleshier. She had an edifice and built on it. Her cheeks (both northern and southern hemispheres) swelled, puffed up, they accreted mass in three dimensions, maybe four. One chin gave birth to another. Sexy was one chin and no more. On that, no compromise or negotiations. Added flesh her knees, thighs, belly, waist, calves — all her parts grew like a dreamworld investment. And if you prefer artistic metaphor, look at a Botero.

Bigger by golly got her belly. Boy oh boy did her belly bulge,

---

[*] Why, Gafni wondered, are memories limited in size, 4 x 6," 5 x 7," sometimes 8 x 10," as if the invention and development of photography ordained the packaging of memories? Could memories have been larger in the 19th century, before photography? Memories like his should be cosmic, unfettered and unframed, as large as his imagination. But back to big Malina.

her midriff burgeon. And not from beer or fatty sturgeon. Just plain eating. Beforetime, she would unbutton two top buttons of her slacks after dining, pop it went, the flesh protruding. Now, to baby the billowing bump, she unbuttoned the top buttons by her belly button before beginning gluttin. As Gafni watched her ingest and expand, he wanted to issue a fatwah against that fat mah. Malina had once said sadly that her father constantly belittled her. Maybe that's why she was now eating so much. In other words, according to pop psychology, pop's belittling her then made her pop and bebig now.

Strange, but the will power she had shown in intellection served her only from the forehead up. She couldn't quite muster enough of it to reign in her appetite. While she read the newspaper, she would absently dip into a bag of dried fruit or roasted pecans, devouring a pound of pecans and half a pound of dried dates as she imbibed the news. Pecans. Pecans reminded him of tiny Mozart, hardly bigger than a pecan. Maybe I should send Malina to the Cafe Mozart where little Wolfgang could give Malina instructions in size reduction.

But back to big Malina, that overbubbled berry.

The only exercise she got was mastication. But Gafni would not say a word lest he offend her. Maybe that negative side of her stemmed from the bad genes of her gentile makeup. In fact, it was Malina who brought it up, not he. He avoided all discussion of her parents. For if emotions were to prevail, he shouldn't have had any contacts with Poles. But he was a scholar and he knew that people should be judged on their own merits and not the actions of their ancestors. Judaism itself taught that, as far back as the prophet Jeremiah.

And then into this mix, this brew, this stew — all culinary terms as you can see — comes sexual allure, which takes emotional loyalty and scholarly objectivity and scatters it to the winds like seeds of a dandelion. Want another metaphor? It becomes as useful as a struck match.

It was Malina who said:

"I don't know why my mother married my father. Or maybe she didn't even marry him. Maybe they just moved in together. You see, my mother loved to read, she finished high school, and the few times I saw my father, I never saw him pick up a book."

A question bubbled on Gafni's lips but he held back. He had made up his mind and he was going to stick to it.

"I don't know how much schooling he had," she answered Gafni's unasked question. "Maybe none. Certainly culture none. Who do I take after? My mother, of course. Luckily, I didn't get too many genes from my father."

But maybe, Gafni thought, the body too came from her mother, no doubt a stout woman like so many of the Polish women, especially from the farm country. Which was why, perhaps, Malina was so hefty. Now she wore a particolored, dappled kimono, almost down to her ankles, not out of modesty, but to hide her width and girth.

Yes, she had been pretty; he was witness to that. But the explanation for her current size lay in an old photo. Among her pictures he found one, taken five years before he met her. Were one to believe psychics, tellers of fortune, tarot card readers, molten wax mavens, palm lines prognosticators, and other smooth-talking charlatans, that photo might have been a sneak preview. The picture was taken from down below, shooting up as if she were a high-rise. It showed a face that was not pretty — cheeks overfull, lips thin as angel hair pasta, and the eyes sardonic, aloof, smug, heavy-lidded. To uncoin a phrase, it wasn't a pretty picture.

But then again, how many of us get mug shots shot up from the tongue of our sneakers, as if the tongue were the camera's eye?

24

IKH VILL ZINE EYNER FUN EYEKH

HEARING Yankl Shtroy say that he had been buried once but no more, Gafni felt that now was the right time to make his request. He wanted to tell the men how comfortable he felt with them, how he sensed in the depth of his being that he was one of them.

"*Ikh vill zine eyner fun eyekh,*" Gafni said again — I want to be one of you — now with a more noticeable tone of pleading in his voice.

"I have nothing to do with it," Yankl Shtroy said, as if responding to a direct request.

That crisp, unemotional response coming from the gentle, mild-mannered *shamesh* sent an immediate wave of gloom through Gafni.

"It's beyond our control," Yankl Shtroy continued. "And it's not subject to a vote. No committee meets and nominates the next candidate … Do you understand?"

Gafni, the spirit sucked out of him, his heart blue and failing, said, "Yes." He had meant to say "No," but for some strange reason his tongue twisted it to "Yes."

"Good. Because I don't. I still don't understand it. No one sent me a letter: 'Dear Yankl Shtroy, you are hereby declared a candidate for … ' And you know what?" the *shamesh* shrugged and spread his hands. His voice was as passive as ever. "Maybe all this is just a coincidence."

"That's what I said sometime back and you disagreed with me."

"Because you said it. When I say it, it's different. Maybe it is coincidence."

"Meaning what?" Gafni asked, "What do you mean?" An edge of excitement now ran through him, a thin warm current through a cold stream. He felt that somehow he was approaching an explanation of the mystery, happy as a youngster going through an algebra problem, only one step away from an elegant solution.

"What I mean is, Who says that all men are mortal? Are we all born only to die? Is death built into our bodies? A special gene passed on from father to son? Just because some of us continue to live, does it mean we're going to live …?" But he didn't add the expected word.

"You're saying two contradictory things."

"I know. Because we are contradictions. Look, can we come to any scientific conclusion, just because the few of us here in Poland have not died? Who knows? Coincidence? Good genes?"

"Am I supposed to answer any of the questions you asked?"

"Not really," said Yankl Shtroy. He rubbed his red-lidded eyes. Suddenly, the mask of impassivity, even gloom on his face, broke. He gave Gafni a warm smile.

"Do you feel good?" Shmulik asked.

"Yes. Fine. Except for an occasional pain in my left knee."

"I see," said Gafni sullenly, wishing he could be blessed with what Yankl Shtroy was blessed — and have an occasional pain in his left knee.

Gafni was about to give up. Giving up is so easy. Putting down the pen is so easy. Doing nothing when something should be done is so easy. Keeping your mouth shut when it should cry out is so easy. But Gafni never let opportunities slide away. If I don't speak up now I'll never know. So he pressed on.

"But the phenomenon exists. It's been going on for years. And you've witnessed it. Surely you must have some thoughts about it. How did this happen?"

"God knows."

They looked at each other, did Shmulik Gafni and Yankl Shtroy, as if contemplating in each other's mystified faces one of the world's inexplicable phenomena.

"All right. Here's my theory. When Jews sin, they *klop al khet*, they beat their breasts in contrition during the Days of Awe. But who does God *klop al khet* to when He sins? For God did sin, and massively, during the war. So what did He do? He said, 'I've sinned, and since most of the murders occurred on Polish soil, I'm going to give a special bonus to the Polish Jews who survived and remained here.' He can't bring back all the Jews but us he gives special consideration." Yankl Shtroy stopped and added with a slight touch of irony: "I think ... That is, I'm still not sure. I told you. The few of us living on and on, that may be just a coincidence. Who knows, maybe tomorrow three or four of us will just keel over."

"God forbid!" said Shmulik Gafni.

25

FROM A FRIDAY AFTERNOON NAP

SHMULIK was waking up from a Friday afternoon nap. An Israeli custom, given the short working hours on Friday, usually till 1 pm, and the Sabbath day of rest that followed. He had fallen asleep with sunshine, but now as he looked out the apartment window it was nearing dusk. He went out to the balcony. It faced a courtyard full of trees and he sat at the top of the tree line and heard the birds singing. The streets were barren of cars; the usual noise of traffic abated and it was suddenly magnificently, even rigorously, quiet. The birds were singing because evening was approaching, and the streets were quiet because the Sabbath was approaching. The sun was about to set.

There is no light like the light in Jerusalem on a Friday before sunset. Sans noise the light intensifies; car traffic diminished; the roar of buses ceased. Gone the tumult of people rushing. With no noise, the focus is on light, the special pre-Shabbat light of a Jerusalem sunset, the sky a palette of mauves and reds and purple, the clouds fringed with a rainbow of hues, and a calm unlike any other breathes its repose into the city. That light, he felt, which touches the eyes and embraces the soul.

Gafni felt good from the top of his head to the tip of his toes. He wanted to compress time, squeeze it like a sponge to preserve this magical moment, when Jerusalem halted, the world stopped in honor of the coming Sabbath, and Shmulik felt good. He looked at the leaves, heard the circular sounds the birds were making in the trees in the narrow courtyard. Man is immortal, he thought, until he dies. And if he stretched the time of good feeling, he can live forever. But then how can he both compress time like a sponge and stretch it like strudel dough? Easy. He was mortal and mortal men can do anything with their minds. Until they become immortal.

Soon the sun would set. In Jerusalem, dusk falls swiftly into night. In Jerusalem there is no twilight,* unlike other parts of Israel where dusk becomes twilight and twilight slowly elides into night,

---

* As we have already learned from Agnon's description of Jerusalem in his novel, *Ha-Na'ara Ha-temanit* (*The Yemenite Girl*), for at times our knowledge of places stems from literature, not actual observation.

like a diver diving into a pool, filmed in slow motion. But in
Jerusalem the holy city night comes suddenly around the corner to
surprise you. That's why on Friday eves Sabbath comes sooner in
Jerusalem than in all the other cities in Israel.

Gafni had just finished dreaming about Shabbat. In his dream
he had been castigating a group of rabbis about lack of Sabbath
observance in Israel. Told them to be more unrestrained, more
vocal. Maybe it's a message to me, he thought. Usually, the dusk
of a Friday made him feel no different than the dusk, let's say, of
a Sunday or a Tuesday. But today the dusk had an overlay of his
dream. He tasted Shabbat in the back of his throat. The fragrances
of the coming Friday dinner, chicken soup, roast chicken, potato
kugel (all from the Supersol's specialty section, for Malina couldn't
make these traditional dishes), wafted in the air from all the open
windows. He tasted their smells and that enchanted ambience that
comes with late Friday afternoon. The bluing air was thick, filled
with Jewish vibrations. Sensing the Sabbath mood in his bones,
Gafni recalled hearing in his dream — probably prompted by
the actual sounds — the recorded shofar call that resounded over
Jerusalem eighteen minutes before sunset, indicating the time for
lighting Shabbat candles had come. He went out on the balcony,
breathed in the green of the leaves, the trill of the birds. He called
to Malina:

"Light the Shabbat candles."

"What?"

"I said, light the Shabbat candles."

"What are you talking about?"

"Can't you hear me? The Shabbat candles. It's Friday evening.
Light them."

"We never lit Shabbat candles before."

"So now is a good time to start. It's getting dark. It's darkening.
We're a Jewish family now. Light them."

"We don't have candles."

"Look for them. There must be some somewhere."

"I'm not even Jewish, for goodness sake, remember? What's
the matter with you? You married a *shikse*."

He came in from the balcony.

"Light them anyway."

"No," she said loudly. "My family are goyim. You're the only
Jew." But Malina didn't say "Jew." She said "zhid," which in Polish
meant "Jew." But in Russian, where Gafni had heard that word
countless times, in that same pronunciation it was a derogatory
term, like "kike" in English. That's the way Gafni heard it. In a fury
ran into the kitchen.

"Who are you calling '*zhid*,' you *Poilishe shikse*? I said light them. I want it. I need it. Now."

"Don't command me."

"I'm not commanding. I'm ordering you."

"No. *Parshiver zhid!*"

It was hard to say whether it was the remark that did it, or whether his condition brought it on anyway. But that instant, when she cursed him like a common anti-Semite, calling him a scurvy kike, was a core moment. He had called her a name, true, but it was not an insult. It was a designation. Descriptive. But she struck back with the most common Polish anti-Semitic epithet. Why did she marry me? he wondered. To have a Jewish baby? To have a child with smart Jewish genes? Yes, he concluded, that's why. At that moment he felt a rise in his throat, as if a fist were opening from within, the fingers spreading there, choking him, and his heart expanding and sailing up, letting all the blood rush down. With the path of blood rushing like a waterfall, his head imploded.

Then he saw a bright light. At first it did not hurt, but like thunder after lightning the pain came a few seconds later, as if a raw nerve in his tooth were touched and the electric shock was propelled in two directions. Up to his head, down to his ankles. He opened his mouth to respond to her vicious insult but could not say a word. He shut his eyes and saw himself going down a long corridor. He made left and right turns, he saw a shiny object on the floor, he saw it was a key, he picked up the key, but as soon as he had it firmly in his grasp, he stumbled and fell.

When he got up, Malina was next to him.

He sat down in an easy chair.

She brought him a glass of water.

"Drink," she said, but he was already sipping.

"I'm sorry for what I said," she said in Yiddish. "But I don't like to be ordered around. You reminded me of my father."

"Don't talk Yiddish to me," he snapped. "I can't believe you're like the rest of them."

"I said I was sorry."

You can be sorry from today till tomorrow — *fun haynt biz morgn*, went the Yiddish original — but your true nature came out in that phrase, he thought. He was too tired to argue with her.

"Did you light the candles?"

"Yes."

"Don't answer me in Yiddish."

She looked at him. He could not tell if it was a look of enmity or incredulity. But she held her peace.

But as we all know, peace doesn't last very long. It's just an interregenum between wars. For a couple of minutes later she asked, not plaintively, just asked:

"Why?"

26

THE FUZZY JEW

"WHO is that?" Gafni asked Yankl Shtroy. He indicated with his head to an older man, seemingly out of focus, sitting by himself at the back of the shul, reading a holy text. Gafni took off his glasses, breathed on the lenses, wiped them with a handkerchief. He looked again. The man was still hazy. He looked at the other congregants. Them he could see clearly. But the ninth of Yankl Shtroy's friends was a problem. If not for the *shamesh*, then at least for Shmulik Gafni. Gafni never saw that man whole. Want to blame it on some kind of temporary ocular aberration? If he did see the entire man, it was through a haze, slightly out of focus. If clear, he saw the top half, or only the left side of him.

Later, Yankl Shtroy explained:

"That's our reserve tenth man for the minyan. He comes if we need him."

"Is it me or is he always out of focus?" Gafni joked.

"It's not you," the *shamesh* said with neither sarcasm nor irony. "With you here we don't need him, so he's hazy. If you go, he'll be nice and sharp, in focus, all here."

"You mean," Gafni teased, "once I leave I'll be able to see him clearly."

"Exactly." But Yankl Shtroy did not smile. Yet he wasn't totally serious either, a conclusion drawn from the bright look on his face, like that of a child pleased with a clever response.

I'm blessed with seeing people who are beyond reality, Gafni thought, remembering his fascinating friend, the tiny Mozart.

"Who is he?" Gafni asked before he could stop the question. And in the futile attempt to suck back the query he had just exhaled, he realized with a chill that he knew precisely who the man was.

"He's one of us. A Yid," the *shamesh* allowed. A Jew.

As a child he had heard stories about how Elijah the Prophet appeared to help Jews in distress. At a certain point in the Passover Seder the door is opened and Elijah is invited in. Shmulik was always sent to open the door. He remembered the blast of cold air that came in from the apartment hallway, swathed in darkness, as he opened the door and rushed back out of breath, frightened, back to the Seder table, heart pounding, red in the face from fear and cold. Later, as an adult, Gafni studied and wrote about Elijah in Jewish folklore. He didn't want to think of the reserve tenth man as Elijah.

There were enough mysteries with the Jews of Poland.

27

BECAUSE IT'S *LOSHN KOYDESH*

"BECAUSE it's *loshn koydesh*," Gafni replied. "That's why I don't want you to talk Yiddish."

"I thought Hebrew is the holy tongue."

"Since what the Germans and their helpers have done, Yiddish has also become a *loshn koydesh*, a holy tongue, the language that rang out with the Jewish victims' last cries … But when you speak in Yiddish it's not holy."

Somehow, by saying this, he lost the edge of his anger against her. Still, he didn't want to hear her speaking his parents' language.

Sometime a stubborn silence is more efficacious than words. So he remained mute. Either she understood, pretended to, or didn't care.

Then it hit him again, the same pain, like a swing in a public park that hits a child in the head and the child, stunned, can't move, and the swing hits him a second time.

Malina, his wife, had called him a dirty Jew.

Back again to the Poland of the 1920's, the 30's, the 40's.

Gafni wanted to shout, Get out. Leave. I don't want you any more. Maybe he said it. Maybe not. And then, again, that bolt of electricity in his head. As if a pressing iron smashed against his skull.

"How could you? How? I thought you weren't like the others. Explain to me. How? With your love of Yiddish. Hebrew. Study in Israel."

Her voice was soft. She said what she said with a smile, as if mocking her words with that good-humored mien on her face.

"I never said I liked Jews. I said I loved Yiddish."

"How can you love one and not the other?"

"Don't you love Polish and not the Poles?"

There she goes again with that idiotic logic, like her defense of mercury.

"There's a difference. History."

She said nothing. Waited.

Then Gafni spoke.

"Yiddish is intertwined with the Jew. It's impossible to separate them. I'll ask you again. Think. How can you love one and not the other?"

"Easy. I'm a goy."

Gafni was stunned. But perhaps he should have expected it. Yes, she was a goy — actually, a goya — smart and primitive, educated and superstitious. It served him right. That's probably what his family and friends were saying to themselves but never to him: wait till her Polishness surfaces. The cat's claws beneath the pussycat purr.

Perhaps looking to be beaten, smitten, even more, his head still aching from the pressing iron's blow, Gafni added:

"But you liked me."

"One can like one Jew but not all Jews. Just as you liked this one Pole and not all Poles. You see, I once told you, Polish-Jewish relations are not black and white. They're problematic."

Was she doing this purposely? he asked himself, or were these words just being thoughtlessly scattered into the air?

"Tell me, what brought you to Yiddish? To Israel, to Hebrew, to get a degree."

"You. Fate."

Shmulik shook his head. A glass curtain had fallen between them and, in falling, smashed to thousands of pieces, like unbreakable glass shatters to smithereens.

"So I'm the beneficent exception ... Some of my best friends are Jews."

He didn't hear what she said in reply. Maybe she didn't even know the American expression, its sly bite. He didn't care what she said. She may even have muttered, "Maybe that's it."

It didn't matter. She wasn't his wife anymore.

28

WHAT DROVE GAFNI

Revenge drove him. It was masked as scholarship, nostalgia; disguised as tourism, remembrance. The crafted patina to the rage that burned in him like an underground fire, stronger than appetite, more relentless than sex, more overpowering than love of words that sent him from one dictionary to another, even in the middle of the night. Beneath all the controversial visits to Poland, under communist rule, when people in Israel, privately and in the press, criticized his "visits to a land drenched in Jewish blood," beneath all the trips cloaked with explanation about the necessity for research, the mitzva of contact with the few remaining Jews in Poland who shouldn't feel abandoned, the last of the elderly speakers of Yiddish, there lay Gafni's singleminded goal of finding his father's murderer.

And of course, something else. Let's not forget that something else: Gafni's hope that by visiting often and staying varying lengths of time the magic of Yankl Shtroy and his eight (nine) old friends would also rub off on him.

WHETHER OR NOT THE FIGHT

WHETHER or not the fight prompted her to announce she was going back home for a while was hard to say. It sure looked like that. Unmistakeable was the contiguity of the two events. One followed the other close as a shadow; hard to argue the two events were unrelated.

Actually, even before she left for Poland with the baby, he had known she'd go, don't ask him how. He just knew it, not in his bones, but somewhere in his psyche, which lacks the precise geography of bones. It can't be photographed nohow except by the soul of another and it floats freely between heart and head.

All right then, maybe better say his heart told him so; that's why he didn't put up such a fuss when she upped and left.

"Why are you going all of a sudden?" he said calmly, to which she replied, "My sister isn't well. I miss her. I must see her."

"Doesn't she have a husband to take care of her?" he said, his voice tremulous at her exaggerated, irritating softspeak.

"Her husband left her. I told you that." She walked in and out of the room as she spoke, opening and closing drawers, looking for something.

That he didn't remember. Had she told him he would have remembered a fact like that.

"She's all alone," Malina added, "and I need the air of my homeland for a while too."

"Did she write you?" Rhetorical, more or less, for he didn't recall seeing a letter from Poland.

"She called."

"How long you going for?"

"Two three weeks."

"No longer?"

"No longer ... Will you miss me?" she said, suddenly affectionate and coy, tilting her head. To deflect more questions, he knew.

A glimmer of the old beauty, beauty now long gone, surfaced on her moon face, puffed up like a balloon. But the air went right out of that balloon and, plunk, phhtt, down it went, both beauty and balloon. For Gafni quickly peeled sentiment and sentimentality, two distinctly disparate words as we all know, from her face, and saw her as she was. A *Poilishe antisemitt*.

"Yes, of course."

But Shmulik wasn't sure he meant it. What do you mean he wasn't sure? He was positively sure he didn't mean a word of what he had just said. Each word was a lie. He wondered if like eyes that radiate a different light when lies are said, if words uttered as lies have a different shape; perhaps they are not cut as smoothly as printed words but are ragged at the edges, for truth is whole and lies are flawed.

In his anger he wanted to tell her the truth: he wouldn't miss her at all. But a remark like that might prompt her to act independently in Poland, as if she were a single woman, and he didn't want that. It might strengthen in her a resolve already germinating in her. He wanted her back not so much because of her but because of the baby and because he didn't like her traveling away from him. She was his wife, if only in name now, and he really wasn't sure what she would do when away from him, what spell of attraction she would cast at men when alone and back in her home surroundings in the music of her native language, and what designs men, seeing her alone, would have on her. Saying he would miss her was just Mitteleuropa politesse. He wouldn't miss her at all. She had changed. She was no longer the old Malina.

Why is it that with the fattening of Malina, with her blowing up like in a trick-mirror in a circus side show, with her burgeoning, billowing, ballooning like a bellows from head to toe, not only had her prettiness been swallowed up, but sensitivity, niceness, and just plain likability also went out the window. Down the drain. Up into thin air. Out, down, up, the preps point correctly in all directions, except in. A strange inversion. As fat increased, sweetness decreased. The more pounds she put on, the more sharp-tongued and vituperative she became. Gone sex kitten, enter hex vixen. With plainness came the added baggage of a big mouth.

Still, there were some wonderful memories. First time Gafni made love to Malina, he thought he had left this earthly realm and gone to heaven, much like the hint of heaven the beach at Nice had offered, with Malina in a red bikini holding back the flowering melons that overflowed the snatch of stringy cloth that magnetized helicopters and southbound storks totally oblivious to the precious cargo of Eskimo babies in their bills. If he were a tiny Mozart he could spend months exploring the hills and dales, the aureoles embarrassingly large and mauve, the most amazing breasts he had ever seen.

In making love to Malina, he suddenly discovered the essence of a Torah phrase he had never fully understood before, where Isaac is "sporting" — actually, laughing — with his wife, Rebecca. And only when at the peak of his pleasure with Malina, when Gafni felt the gates about to open, in his ecstasy he began to laugh and cry out, the laughter overwhelming him, did he finally understand the laughter of love.

WHEN Malina left to visit her sister — Shmulik suddenly became aware of little spots of pain he hadn't noticed before. Yet, strangely, at the same time, a feeling of well-being, a sudden surge of joy. How to reconcile these opposites?

And Gafni had both sensations at the same time, as if he had become two. One Gafni was the Gafni of the night; the other, the Shmulik of the day. During daylight he felt fine — but at night little aches blinked like tiny bulbs.

Malina was gone. The baby was gone. Of course he loved the baby, but deep down, he didn't want to admit it, even to himself, he resented Malina putting her stamp on the child's face, her 50% of the little one's genetic makeup. Maybe he even resented the baby too. There was nothing of Gafni or his family's side in the little boy. He looked like Malina, same wide cheekbones and light-hued eyes. A *Poilisher*. Which member of her family the baby resembled he was afraid to imagine. Sometimes when Gafni held the baby and the little one was in a foul mood, he saw a mocking expression on his face, suddenly the face of a grownup that seemed to say: You wanted to make me a Jew, snip, snip, but I'm still a goy. What's from the waist up is what counts in this world.

Did he dream these thoughts or were they little electric shocks, fragments of semi-consciousness that flitted through him like subtitles in a foreign film whose language he could not decipher. It wasn't sleeping alone that bothered him; that he was used to from frequent trips abroad. It was waking in a dreamy doze, rolling over and not finding his young wife next to him. And maybe not so much that, for after a few days he got used to it. He realized it was something else: the thought of Malina waking up and finding someone else next to her.

When she left, Shmulik had to suddenly become a housewife again, like during the malaise days of her pregnancy. She didn't even bother to prepare a few meals for him in the freezer like other wives before a trip abroad to visit family. Gafni was on his own. Sometimes he forgot to eat. The same thing was said, he recalled, of Einstein. If he wasn't reminded to eat, the scientist would go without eating. Gafni took lunches at the university cafeteria or in a restaurant. He didn't want to frequent any one place lest people start, oh so innocently of course, asking him, And how is your wife?

Is she well? How come you're eating out so often? Oh, she left for a trip? Where? When? For how long? Did she go alone or with the little one? Both of them. Aha, I see. I see. That two-syllable phrase uttered with a faint whiff of disdain just barely susurrating through nearly clenched teeth. Gossip, tongue-wagging, the usual koffee-klatsch sport in Israel. He hated it. Wanted no part of it. Would rather starve. But he did, eventually, through trial and error, learn to make eggs and pasta. Not together.

Gafni missed a lot of things when Malina was away. He missed advising presidents. He missed signing books but was proud of himself for shaking off his obsession. He missed little Mozart who radiated confidence and that he would find his father's murderer.

Not once did Malina go to Poland with the baby but twice. Each time she left he thought she'd never come back, would somehow extort money from him in return for her return. But when he welcomed her back at Ben-Gurion airport, he had mixed feelings, which he did not suppress. Still, at night she pressed her body into his. Was it affection, or guilt and contrition? He didn't try to sort out the nuances of feeling. She has hexed me, Gafni thought, with her body.

The temporary return of her old sweetness made him forget his occasional half wish that she remain in Poland. Made him suppress her hateful remark.

Maybe the mercury was efficacious after all.

STRANGE THINGS HAPPENING

STRANGE things were happening. Like on a revolving stage, events turned before him. His image slid out of the mirror while he was shaving and then appeared on the wood panel of a mirrorless closet. At the Warsaw main terminal a train seemed to leave the station but actually did not move. A snakeskin of the train floated out along the tracks, leaving the real one there, an echo of the fiery Polish train he had seen years ago. At a movie theater he saw a Polish film. It told the story of a man obsessed with finding his father's killer. Gafni liked it so much, he wanted to learn, to copy the man's methods, to see again how he trapped the murderer and took his revenge. But when Gafni saw it a second time, it had a different ending and he knew it was his story screened from his imagination.

Shmulik felt fine — but these odd plays of his mind were shaking his equilibrium. He wondered, Am I drunk, or are my visits to Poland refracting my sense of everyday reality?

31

THE THOUGHT PECKING AWAY LIKE AN EVIL
WOODPECKER

GAFNI knew that the thought pecking away at his mind like an evil woodpecker, the sharp beak now rhythmically drilling, was absurd. Totally. Unequivocally. Unarguably.

Absurd.

The which was:

Gafni suspected that his son, Yosef, named after his murdered father, had his eye on his new wife. Which was admittedly strange since his son lived in Seattle. Unless Yosef had unusually eidetic (pun accidental, I swear; no, I don't swear: like Shultish, I affirm) penetrating long-distance vision, it would be extremely difficult to cast an eye across mountain ranges, the endless prairie, majestic rivers, around skyscratchers (a translation of the Hebrew term for these long, thin, elegant buildings, sixty stories [or two novellas and forty stories] or higher), across a vast ocean, a sea, nine time zones in all, all the way up to Jerusalem.

Maybe, just maybe, Yosef had cast not an eye — he'd never even met Malina, for goodness sake — but only an ear on the new wife, because Gafni remembered in the one conversation that Yossi had with Malina, when his son called to wish her and him mazel tov, and all three were on the phone, he in the kitchen, she in the bedroom, the still unmarried Yossi had a flirtatious tone in his voice. It was impolite to rebuke your son in the presence of his brand-new stepmother who was, conveniently for the son, just about the right age for them to be interested in each other, both of them now thirty-five, a novel could be written about that triangle alone, but not now while we're still struggling to shape this one, maybe Gafni would recommend that slightly dented triangle to his pal in Peru, Mario Vargas Llosa, a story about a stepson falling in love with his stepmama should make fascinating reading.

Gafni wasn't sure who had initiated that smilingly flirtatious tone, Malina or Yossi, but the vibes were flowing in both directions. And there was another thing Gafni wasn't sure of. He couldn't be one-hundred percent sure it was a flirtatious tone. Maybe it was just a bad connection? (But then how come a bad connection made it sound flirtatious? Why couldn't that allegedly bad connection make it sound familially polite or borderline contentious or, at least, let's say, neutrally felicitous?) And third, or maybe second, it wasn't nice to make a scene with your son while his new stepmama was on the line with him, or with your new wife, the boy's stepmother, leaning no doubt on a pillow in the bed and rubbing one naked leg over the other slowly and lasciviously, and let's add teasingly, during the nine-thousand mile conversation. And, who knows, she may even have unlatched her complex brassiere network too and freed those twin gazelles, gazelles more fraternal than identical, as are all such metaphoric gazelles.

Lucky for Gafni he was on the phone too, for had it just been Yossi and Malina, he not hearing what his son was saying, but present in the room with her, watching Malina's face light up, the roseate color rising on her fair skin, her eyes crinkling with a smile and a throaty laugh rippling, head thrown back in a consciously seductive pose, as if expecting a passionate kiss (no biting, please) on the throat, all this would have given Gafni an apoplectic fit, an instantaneous paralytic stroke, or the beneficent aspects of both, for which he would have had no time to activate his *Chaver* pendant. He remembered how Malina had thrown back her head that day in Nice when she took off her clothes on the beach and from an attendee at an international linguistics conference she turned within seconds into a berry-red bikini-clad bathing beauty. Yes, she threw her head back then too that sunny late May day and tinkled a warm and lascivious laugh whose music was in perfect rhythm to the waves coming in, coming in, waves that did not stop coming in, she laughing at a remark Gafni had made that wasn't particularly funny, but he did remember noting how remarkable and surprising was that transformation from someone who looked so professionally neutral (was it a suit or a dress she had worn that day?) at the conference, perhaps even fuddy-duddy and remote, to a sex queen — otherwise, how do you account for the seven police choppers hovering overhead when on a normal day you'd barely see one, probably snapping shots for the boys back at the precinct, and the low-flying storks carrying Eskimo babies to Marakesh and dropping them as they swooped down to look, he remembered them too, a languorous flap of wings, the dip and rise of their slack white wings, their sleek white wings.

Perhaps, thought Gafni, Malina might pick herself up and out of curiosity move to Seattle, an absurd thought, he knew. Stupid jealousy. He was becoming a figure out of an opera buffa, a foolish old man.

And who knows where Malina went when she went to "visit" her "sister"? He didn't know and that was the truth. For all he knew, she may have gone to Seattle to visit his son, and that's why when she came back home she was both in a heightened mood and nervous, in curious alternation. And could she travel to the USA? Yes, she could, on her new Israeli passport. Once, when she was out shopping, Gafni walked into their bedroom, opened the old chest of drawers, part of the set that Batsheva and he had bought, but the chest did not bother Malina — only the bed did — and opened up the drawer where she kept her passport. He saw it under her oversize bras. If she had gone to the USA, it would surely be stamped in her passport. Gafni actually picked up the blue document, then carefully set it down again between the bras. If she had gone to the USA, she wouldn't leave the evidence around for him to see. On the other hand, maybe she was stupid in that regard, naïve, a facet of her primitive, superstitious self. And if she had gone, he thought, he didn't want to know. To have seen the US Naturalization Service stamp in her passport would have broken his heart.

But.

But without looking he did see, under her passport, a little note in Polish, in her hand: "He makes me feel so sensual all over. We sit at a concert and he slips his hand into mine. His forefinger is between my thumb and forefinger and the blood races and pounds within me." Did I do that to her? Gafni wondered, or is she describing someone else? He pictured the placement of fingers in her description and nodded. Yes, it was probably me. And felt better — but not for long.

Marry an ugly woman, the Talmud counsels, and she'll be true to you. No, the wisdom of that remark lay not in its surface meaning, for there was no logical concomitant between the first part and the second. An ugly woman could betray you just as easily as a beautiful one. The subtext of that proverb was that if you married an ugly woman, there was slim chance that other men would be attracted to her, and you could sleep (with your mistress, perhaps) in peace.

THAT VOICE, THAT FACE, ANYWHERE

H<small>E</small> would know that voice, that face, anywhere. Even if he had
to use research as a guise for revenge, Gafni would do it. Luckily, he
spoke an unaccented Polish and could speak it with the twang and
slurred syllables of Warsaw, and if he had to, the farmers' dialect
of the surrounding countryside. He knew that with workers he
could mimic the singsong, the relaxed flat blasé sound of bluecollar
Polish, and of course with intellectuals he could shape the timbre of
his enunciation and mold his vocabulary like a violinist shapes the
tones of a musical line. And let's not forget the occasional inclusion
of a French or Latin phrase or two.

At times — thanks to little Mozart's wise advice — Gafni
pretended he was an official with the defense ministry. To his aid
came an old friend, a non-Jew named Vladek, an old forger who
had helped Jews during World War II by providing them with
documents when he was a young printer in Warsaw. He could forge
any signature, any official paper. From Vladek he got a pass from
the Ministry of Defense saying he was writing a history of World
War II Polish partisans, and a card from the Polish Patriotic Society.

But like a deer, a rabbit, nose twitching, sensing that prey is
on its way, the murderer was always one step ahead of Gafni. He
seemed to sense Gafni's presence. And when Gafni was told that
the welder, whom he knew by description but not by name, was
working in Lodz, by the time he got to the foundry in Lodz, Gafni
learned that his father's killer was no longer there.

A CHILD IS NEITHER SYMBOL NOR SYMBIOSIS*

A child is neither symbol nor symbiosis, Gafni concluded. Earlier, he thought differently. A child, half-Jewish, half-Polish/ Christian, would symbolize the symbiosis of their marriage. The half-Jewish was illusory, he knew, for according to Jewish law, the mother's religion determine's the child's. So, then, the boy was fully Christian, despite his bris, despite his Hebrew name. A man and woman bring not a symbol into the world but a child.

They (again that annoying "they" out there) were against my marriage. They were against my bringing a child into the world when I was seventy plus. And they were against — what else were they against? He forgot now, but whatever it was "they" were against it.

For two or three years Malina had been silent regarding the Poles' behavior during the war. Then she gave her famous confession, which she later subtly retracted. But now she was showing her true colors. He didn't like the way Malina excused the Poles' attitude to the Jews. Again she used the intellectually slippery word: problematic. And then she said something that brought out a hidden Malina, a Malina that surfaced from time to time. How many hidden Malinas could one big Malina house? He remembered every word of her thesis, heard the purposeful edge in her words, even though, as usual, she tried to disguise them with a bland, even innocent look.

"Perhaps," she said, "the death of the Jews is an offering, a kind of sacrifice, a gift..."

"The gift of the Jews, huh?" Gafni interrupted her.

"Yes."

"Whether you know it or not, you're probably referring to the compassionate remark made by Pope John Paul II; the great humanitarian," he said with vowel-dragging sarcasm, "that the death of the Jews during World War II was the 'gift of the Jews' to humanity."

"A kind of sacrifice to bring peace to the world, to allow others to die peacefully. Perhaps the death they suffered during the war was

---

*If you can figure out what this means, drop me a line. I wrote it and still don't know what it says.

meant for others." Malina stopped, looked thoughtful. "Maybe we even die for others."

"That's Christianity," Gafni exploded. "The stupidity, the unfeelingness of its theology. Absolute nonsense! And what kind of peace in the world? What peace? Where peace? And who, tell me, who did my father die for when a Pole brutally murdered him and his brother and scores of other Jews in July 1946, fourteen months after the end of the war, after they miraculously survived death camps and forests? Tell me. Who, who did he die for? Me? You? Your father?"

He had her. She didn't, couldn't, say a word. Perhaps some words flitted across her mind. But they didn't register. There was no hope for her. This supposedly sophisticated PhD in linguistics was a rooted Catholic, and like all deeply religious Polish Catholics, a superstitious one at that.

"If the situation had been reversed, how many Jews would have given up their lives for Polish Christians? Would you?... The Jews were always different," she said.

"So away with them!" he said. "Different should be killed."

She turned from him abruptly, as if shutting him from her thoughts. She didn't want to convert, claiming she favored no religion, was actually an agnostic, maybe even an atheist. And if Malina did convert, would it lessen her loyalty to the conjunction of the stars? Malina didn't believe in God, but in mercury she puts her trust. Organized religion, feh! Yet when it came to Christmas, she wanted to bring the child to Christmas services. And in Jerusalem too.

"Let him know what it's like," she said. As if a two-year-old could make sense of a church service. And she took him.

Symbiosis was going too far.

As it happened, on Christmas Day — it fell on a Sabbath that year — when she was in church too long, he pacing up and down the block outside, Shmulik finally went into the Dormition Abbey Church of Jerusalem to bring his son out. Enough was enough. But as he set foot outside, holding Yonatan's little hand, who should pass by but his colleague, Professor Moshe Andermann from the History Department, who saw Gafni and averted his face. As far as Andermann was concerned, Gafni had just attended Christmas mass at the church with his son. And on a Shabbat, no less. Finished. Done for. The story would circulate all over the university, all over Israel.

Soon the rumor spread through the cafés of Jerusalem and Tel Aviv. Gafni had married in a church on Yom Kippur in Warsaw; he celebrated it with a feast of roast pig whose lard dribbled over his shaven chin on the holiest day of the Jewish year. And now he celebrates Christmas in Jerusalem on the Sabbath.

34

IN KIELCE

H<small>E</small> arrived in Kielce by train at 2pm with just a briefcase in hand and headed for the hotel. Entering the small, rather dingy building near the station, he at once regretted his plan. He looked at the balding clerk and another burly man standing over, yes, over, not next to, him. Gafni imagined himself presenting his forged identity card with bravado, nonchalance, but wondered who was pounding on the wall behind the clerk's back, a rhythmic banging as if a workman within the wall was seeking exit — until he realized it was his heart. Better go, he thought. Heed the heart's signal. If he stayed they would have asked, And the gentleman has no luggage?, with bemusement and suspicion. They would have had his identity card with a false name and address. No sense risking a hotel stay; it might compromise the mission. Gafni would have to do his work without sleeping in Kielce.

To avoid calling attention to himself, he looked over the small lobby with its rough wooden coffee table and two scuffed easy chairs and regarded the long-unpainted walls as if assessing the hotel's suitability. Then Gafni asked about the rates. The clerk was animated but the man next to him was impassive. Perhaps the hotel was being inspected and the burly man was waiting for the usual bribe. Gafni nodded casually and left. It was a wise decision, he felt.

On the street Gafni stopped an older Polish policeman and without thinking too much — now his heart did not thump in warning — began talking to him, totally at ease. The first time in all these years speaking to a policeman. Maybe he was unconsciously following little Mozart's advice. Gafni showed him his card from the Polish Patriotic Society, which everyone knew was a code name for the ultra-nationalist organization. He took a chance doing that, for the man might have been a loyal communist and brought Gafni in for questioning. But sooner or later one had to take risks, and somehow sense when it was safe to be assertive, when perilous. It was a delicate task, like walking on a tightrope, no net beneath.

The policeman looked Gafni in the eye.

Gafni, unfazed, stared back. Here's where he arrests me, he thought.

"You're here for something special."

Gafni regarded the man's face. Typical Pole, he muses, narrow eyes, high cheekbones. A big man. Not the sort to have as an enemy.

"Yes, you got that right."

The other man looked down. Maybe he's afraid of me, Gafni thought.

"Do you have a bit of time? I'll buy you a beer."

The man looked at his watch. "Well, time for my break anyway ... Come, I'll show you where we can sit ... My name is Tadeusz." His big handclasp was like a vise.

"I'm Doctor Paderewski." If the man asked, Are you related to the great pianist and former president of Poland? Gafni promised himself he would give him ten dollars.

But the policeman merely nodded.

They walked down the main street away from the hotel and the train station. Nearby, Gafni remembered, stood the old synagogue. During the war the Germans had used it as a warehouse. After liberation, the Poles converted it to a public toilet and the large courtyard to a parking place for the peasants' horse-drawn carts. Gafni glanced quickly at the formerly grand building.

"A good beer around the corner," Tadeusz said.

As they turned off the main street Gafni saw a group of twelve-year-olds aiming rocks at the top windows of the synagogue. Every time a rock struck glass the boys whooped.

Gafni almost cried out, "Arrest those bandits!"

The policeman chuckled. Seeing him, the youngsters froze. One boy's hand was thrown back, ready to fling a stone. But the policeman passed them without saying a word. He just gave out another little laugh which the boys must have heard.

Gafni wondered if he could control the rage seething in him. He clenched his fist. Tadeusz talked, but Gafni wasn't hearing. The fathers or grandfathers of these boys dragged Jews out of their hiding places, handed them over to the Germans for sugar, or even without reward. During the war they dug up Jewish graves to take the gold teeth of those who had died natural deaths. And more than a year after the war ... A curse on their souls. May their bones rot.

"Here we are," Tadeusz said.

They sat at an outdoor table. It was a beautiful spring day. Life bubbled on the street. Shoppers, the tinkle of bicycle bells, car horns, the clomp of horses' hooves, laughter in the tavern. Inside, a radio was playing Polish songs. Life bubbled, but in Gafni death squatted with folded arms. An ashen taste in his mouth. He didn't want to recall the scene. Tried to suppress the perpetual film that ran in his mind. Not too far from here. At the edge of town, near which he would not set foot. He closed his eyes for a moment, that taste still in his mouth. Where in the world can you find a father like my father?

A young waitress came and took their order. Her voice pulled Gafni out of his bitter reverie. When she turned, Tadeusz looked admiringly at her legs.

"You must be a historian professor from the Society. Some kind of writer."

"Yes," Gafni said. "You're very smart. On the ball."

"I got to be. I'm a cop." He took a long swallow of beer.

"But today I'm here on a mission of another kind. The Society wants to give an award to those who were so helpful to the Polish cause during the war and after the war." Gafni accented the last four words.

Tadeusz sat up with pride. He raised his beer glass. "So you know about my father."

"Especially someone who did heroic acts after the war. To be specific — on July 4, 1946."

"Ah yes, I know the date. When we finally got rid of the Jews. Or most of them anyway. You people are amazing. So you know about my father."

Gafni looked into his briefcase. "Remind me his name."

"Like mine. Tadeusz."

"But his family name."

"Januwski."

"Of course. We have him on record."

"Yes, my father did his share. But ... " the policeman looked around and dropped his voice, "those bastard Soviets tagged him, put him on trial in one of those faked, rigged trials of theirs and had him shot. The ones who did more got away. And the Soviets were just as involved as the rest of us, those bastards."

"His share will come some other time. We know of him, of course ... But we have to be patient regarding that and them. " Gafni spoke softly too. "They can't hang in here forever, if you know what I mean."

"Right you are."

"You've shown me I can trust you." Gafni peered into his briefcase again for a moment as though to remind himself of a few facts. "We have reports about this wonderful Polish hero and patriot who excelled during the war and was so fearless that July 4, 1946. A tall, blond fellow who I think was a metalworker. But we neither know his name nor his whereabouts."

The policeman finished his beer. "Yes, I think I know who you mean ... "

HATING MUSIC

GAFNI woke up one morning hating music. How did he know? When he turned on Israel Radio's classical music program and heard Beethoven's *Eighth Symphony*, which he normally loved and could sing note for note, now it irritated him. Its exuberance was bombast, its melodies a pose. He knew he should turn it off but he did not, enjoying his irritation at the now ill-harmonious sounds.
And it was all Malina's fault. He went into Yonatan's room, saw a couple of photographs of the smiling little boy and turned away. The bed and changing table reminded him not so much of the child as of his mother's departure to Poland, again a negative image. What kind of impish mirror world was he living in, when music was grating and his baby's picture prompted miserable thoughts? Yes, it was all her fault. He realized he could have sentimentalized his approach, looked longingly at his blanket, raised it to his face, felt its soft fleecy texture. But Gafni did not do this. He stared coldly at the boy's bed and at his blanket and shut off the music. Did not wait for his favorite third movement with its syncopated dance rhythm that he never danced to but conducted superbly. He paced around the apartment, wondering how long this malaise would last. I'll try one other piece, he thought. He put on a record of the Bach *Suite #4* which he had mentally choreographed into a ballet years ago, with himself as premier danseur, making Nijinsky leaps into the air whenever the melodies soared — but this music too now soured him; he removed the record and slipped it back into its jacket. He preferred the silence that now hummed in the room.

No doubt about it, Malina had killed it for him. Now music irritated him, as if malicious children had picked up violins and were haphazardly drawing their bows across the strings.

VISIT TO KIELCE, continued

THE policeman finished his beer. "I think I know who you mean … Hey, you've barely sipped."

"When I'm excited I can't drink … But you can have it, if you want."

"You don't mind?"

"No. Help yourself."

Tadeusz took a long gulp.

"Yes, I know who you mean. Our Kielce hero … " The policeman closed his eyes. "His name is … Jan Gryszynski, the welder. A big blond guy with scraggly hair … "

"Yes, yes, that's what all the reports say. Is he around? Alive?"

"Sure he's alive. But he's not in these parts. I heard say he's in Lodz."

Gafni nodded calmly, almost absently. But his beating heart pumped blood into his constricted throat. It was a different pounding. Not like the rhythms of his heart when he stood in the lobby of the hotel. Surely his flushed face and the artery throbbing in his neck would give him away. He saw an untouched glass of water on the next table; he seized it and slowly drank.

"Yes, he might be the one," Gafni said in measured tones. He wiped his mouth, swallowed. "But our office must make sure. It will be a big honor and surprise for him, so if you happen to see him, please don't tell him … And we won't forget your father. We know of him."

Now Tadeusz smiled. He closed one eye, but after three or four beers, couldn't quite manage the wink.

"If any of you get further word as to where he is … " Gafni was about to say and hand Tadeusz a card he had imprinted, Please write to me. But then the warning coursed through him and he had a change of heart. As if a prescient wind blew over him, Gafni suddenly realized that if people became suspicious they would mislead or even trap him, and all his searching would be in vain. He had to know when to step forward and when to step aside. It was a chess game with invisible pieces on a three-dimensional board.

So he added, "Let me know next time … "

Tadeusz nodded.

Gafni looked at his watch. "Oh my goodness. My train is leaving soon. Well, thank you, Tadeusz." He stretched out his hand.

"And don't forget to tell them about my father. Remind them."

"I will. I tell you we have him on our list."

At the depot bathroom Gafni washed his hands again and again.

AND so, little by little, over the years, Gafni found out the name, the occupation, the places of residence of the man — but he could never locate him. He was always in the next town, or had just left this one.

But if it is destined for two people to meet, nothing will stand in the way. And Gafni kept little Mozart's advice in mind too. What is destined to happen will happen and nothing will change it, not time, not place of residence, not disguise, not error, not bewilderment. What is destined is written as if on film, and whether or not the film is seen, whether or not people shout or protest in the theater, the end will still be the same.

37

ALONE, HUNGRY, READY TO EAT

ALONE, hungry, ready to eat. He opened the refrigerator, shut it, opened the cupboard, where is she now?, wondering if the cartons and boxes, some with cellophane covering, saw him as clearly as he saw, was she with someone?, them. He mused what it felt like to spend a night alone in the cupboard, alone as he was alone, and if the boxes of cereal and pasta and salt and spices and tinned fish and sardines, oh, there's a jar of olives hiding in the back, was she taking care of the baby properly?, felt anything when the cupboard door was closed and they remained in the dark with what remained of his gaze, although there was no physical remnant to that look, nothing palpable, still something of his was left there, an imprint of his glance moving from one item to another, something of his was left there in the cupboad even when he shut the door and turned away.

When he went to sleep, alone, he felt sorry for the sardines and boxes of crackers that spent night after night in the dark and were only rescued from their, was she really with her sister?, loneliness when he opened the cupboard door and caressed them with the light of his eyes. Or was she in Seattle again with his son? He knew that that illogical "again" didn't come from him; it was that ludicrous opera buffa hero within him speaking again. (Yes, again that asinine "again.")

Alone in bed, the bed was huge. He turned and swam alone in the ocean of the sheets, floating until he, was she alone too?, fell asleep, floating on the lifesaver of his imagination.

It the morning he realized he hadn't eaten supper. He took stock of his food supply, making a conscious effort not to be seduced by metaphors, symbols, or the drama of dreams. To eat was his goal this morning, not to personify a box of crackers or humanize a tin of Telma *techina*. He cooked a medium-boiled egg. He removed it from the pot with a tablespoon, put it into a glass eggholder he had bought in Nice, same time he met Malina, funny how everything turned back to her, even when he was thinking of eggs, tapped the top, crick crack, a little circle, removed the little white hat of the egg, perfect albumen, just liquidy firm, not hard, and the yellow orange of the yolk, thick and viscous. Coarse salt on top added flavor, where was the bread?, in the bread drawer, too late to toast it now, he ate it as is, even dipping a corner into the yolk and sucking on it with childish delight. One spoon and then another and then nothing was left, even a last scrape brought just a quarter of a teaspoon of egg white. Making coffee was easy, just add a teaspoon of instant coffee into a cup of boiled water, and then a drop or two of milk, another piece of bread, this time he wasn't too lazy to toast it, he was proud of himself for making breakfast, who was making it for her?, for himself.

Then remembered: tomorrow evening would begin the *yorzeit* for his beloved father.

38

BUY A *YORZEIT* CANDLE

BUT first he had to buy a *yorzeit* candle and light it before he went to shul for the Evening Service. In the Supersol, down one aisle, he thought he saw his daughter Rivka. They had spoken a few times on the phone, he called her when the baby was born, but did not invite her or any other member of the family to the bris. Maybe it was a godsend, meeting her now, again, just before the *yorzeit* for his father began. Heart beating, he walked quickly down the aisle, about to tap her on the shoulder. He had already prepared a warm smile for her, then realized it wasn't Rivka. He had lost two women, his daughters, and gained one, maybe not even one — and he was losing her too, like a chunk of a planet that is torn away and slowly separates until it is gone.

Upstairs in his apartment he got dressed, suit and tie, as always when he went to shul, and then the problem surfaced. No joke, just like a woman, he had to decide what type of yarmulke to wear to shul. It wasn't a matter of style or fashion, oh no. Wearing a headcovering nowadays in shul was not a fashion statement — it was a political proclamation. If you wore a black yarmulke you belonged to one group; if it were knitted, you aligned yourself with another. Gafni didn't want this; didn't want that. Finally, he chose a simple workingman's cap with a peaked visor, the sort that the Jewish laborers had worn in prewar Poland.

As he said the Kaddish he wished it could last forever, so he could memorialize his father at every moment and not just on the day he was killed. Why did he have to die? He had lived through the terror, only to be killed by them, the murderers, those beasts, worse than beasts, for beasts do not get pleasure out of their kill, they work by instinct, but they, those, the Poles, they killed for the sheer brute joy of killing. Gafni found himself stretching the words of the Kaddish, saying them slowly, savoring them, thinking of his father, picturing his father at every word. The rest of the congregants were done, only he lingered over the words — they no doubt thinking he was some kind of ignoramus who could not chant the words with the proper speed and facility — as if by uttering them he were bringing his father back, returning him to life with the words of the Kaddish, which made no mention of death but just praised His great name.

Yitgadal ve-yitkadash sh'mey rabba. Magnified and sanctified be His great name.

The next afternoon, the twenty-four-hour yorzeit candle still flickering, Gafni went down to the mailbox. Perhaps, slight chance though, for Malina hadn't written except for one picture postcard, with no return address, postmarked Lodz, where her sister supposedly lived, but there was a sweet little squiggle on the bottom left of the card with Malina's tiny script, saying that little Janusz was sending regards, perhaps Malina had sent a letter.

There was a letter in the box.

From Poland.

But it wasn't from his wife.

39

POSTMARKED WARSAW

IT was postmarked Warsaw, and in the irritating European manner there was no return address on the envelope, no indication who had sent the letter. Gafni tore it open in haste, sensing something important, his psyche reading it before his eyes had even seen one word.

He quickly scanned the short Yiddish note, ran his eyes to the bottom and saw it was signed Yankl Shtroy. Then he read:

Esteemed Hoch-Professor:

Come to us. You will find what you want. What you are looking for.

Yours in friendship,
Yankl Shtroy

NOTHING more. No how are you? Not hope to see you soon. No regards. What could it mean? It could be one of two things, both important to him, which was more important he would not judge. One could not be weighed against the other. Either the *shamesh* had some news about the murderer or the group was inviting him to fulfill his dream to become one of them. Suddenly, as though he had taken a medication, a churning began in his soul, pulling him in several directions.

It pertained to his father, he was certain. Otherwise it would not have come on the day of his *yorzeit*. Yes, Gafni decided at once, at that moment. He would go, leave her a note. Malina hadn't called. Said her sister did not have a phone. She said she would call but only sent him one postcard. Yes, that's what he would do. It was August. He wasn't teaching now. It was a good time to go. Communism was crumbling. Things would be easier. He would go at once. Just like her. He would leave her a note on the kitchen table. She would call him from the airport but wouldn't find him home. Frustrated, angry, she would take a taxi, storm in, ready to burst out in recriminations — but her cries would echo in the empty apartment. Only then would she see the note: I've taken the other set of keys to your Warsaw apartment; that's where I am now; had to leave at once on urgent business. Could not contact you, then decided to add: as you well know.

Or perhaps, and he smiled, but it was a bitter smile, perhaps he would surprise her at her own apartment.

Then two more short notes. One to his daughter in Jerusalem, saying he had received an urgent letter to come to Warsaw. He would return in mid-October before classes began. He did not telephone, for his daughters always urged him not to travel to Poland. The second note was to Sh. Meichl-Rukzak, contents same as above.

IT will be good seeing Yankl Shtroy and his friends again. Being with them always expanded his hope. The pain in his head and chest he had experienced the day — a Friday night, no less, after she had lit candles per his order — Malina cursed him in Polish had not recurred. As his literary hero, Sholom Aleichem, said: A man may be likened to a carpenter. A carpenter lives and lives until he dies. Likewise, a man. Gafni didn't have overriding thoughts of dying. Not at all. But he did look forward to the trip to Poland. To — by just being there — get a new lease on life.

III

... AND THEN

1

IN HER APARTMENT ONE DAY

In her Warsaw apartment, a day or two after he arrived, a strange feeling overtook him, akin to a physical pull, tugged by cords around his waist and wrists, but another kind of pull as well, this one metaphysical. A kinetic surge in his muscles and a yearning too, a stirring in his gut and loins, and a shift in his soul. A magnet outside him drew him forward from the small living room. The feeling like the sweet ecstasy in the library stacks, the high splendor of using various inks and nuanced old calligraphy to autograph books he didn't write by authors he never met, where he got that skill from God only knew.

And now that indescribable pull again, not a hunger, not a thirst, not even libidinous, but perhaps a faint echo of that pull. Was it Yankl Shtroy's enigmatic letter that made Gafni rush off to Warsaw? He had gone to the shul but could not find the old man. His friends said he was visiting a nephew in Cracow, but did not know exactly where he was or when he would return. Yankl Shtroy knew that Gafni was looking for two things. Which one did his letter refer to?

Up and out of his chair, the *Warsaw Gazette* now on the floor, Gafni followed invisible ropes into the bedroom and stood before Malina's old pine dresser. A sudden flush of heat in his hands and forehead as he opened the bottom drawer told Gafni he was getting warm, as though in a children's game, close to the goal. Now you're getting warmer. Hot. Burning. Sizzling. On fire! Up came several neatly folded satin slips and camisoles which she'd no longer be able to get into, Gafni thinking: This is like going into our chest of drawers back in Jerusalem, mahogany that one, a finer wood, and finding Malina's passport. But then, when he found it that day — remember? — he didn't even look at it, because he wanted to drive away the stupid suspicion that Malina, instead of going back home to Poland, was secretly flying out to Seattle, carrying on an affair with his son, Yosef.

As we know, Gafni did not look at her passport, by no means wanted to even let the words cross his mind that she was a *Poilishe koorveh* who was sleeping with a father and son. But now no such reticence stayed his hand. Into the drawer went his hand and even through the padding of the lingerie his fingers sensed the cover of a

photo album. Why was she hiding it? flew through his mind. There
it was. He plucked it out, he did; lo, the right hand of Gafni raised
the album.

With heart beating, an arrhythmic thumping, loud too, Gafni
sank back in the easy chair and took in the gathering of black-and-
white photographs.

The first two pages, left and right, between almost thick-as-glass
old-fashioned plastic photo protectors, the plastic buckling with age,
some cracks in it, yes, it was annoying to look at, hard to turn, showed
pictures of Malina as a baby. Quite a pretty child, he thought, trying
to extrapolate from the innocent gaze the beguiling look she had in
Nice, seaside. Then some group photos with other children, maybe
one was her sister, he could not tell. No adults anywhere.

Gafni turned a page; a door opened and closed. Was it in his
mind, that closing door, or did Malina come in and slam the door,
or was the door in the picture he had seen, the door that closed, then
opened?

Gafni turned the page with the thick plastic hard as knotted,
aged veins. At once, no, not at once, sooner than that, two thin sharp
lines of pain, like needles, like razors, like lasers, ravaged his eyes.
Again slammed the door, again again. It slammed. Again. And again.
Like marauders, waves of pain assaulted him from all sides. From
his right big toe to his knee flowed a fiery current, an arc of pain,
intense at the terminal ends. Both temples clamped tight, a sudden
migraine. The ache pounded as if seeking exit. A strain in his right
hip, like after sitting too long, or walking too much. In his chest still
that offbeat thumping. His head hurt in more ways than one. Words
bobbing up and down on a carousel whirled in his head. He saw his
father riding on the word "Papa." He sat between the "p"s, pressed
down on the soft rounded lap of the "a." He fit into it and made
it concave. But how did his father hold on as the merry-go-round
moved round and round? By looping his hands through the hole of
the "P," that's how his father held on. And Gafni couldn't tell if the
"Papa" was large and his father lifesize, or if the "Papa" was small
and his father as tiny as Mozart. For he could not clearly see because
of the needles in his eyes and the pain in his head and the ache in his
legs and the strain in his hips and the hurt in his heart, oh the hurt in
his heart, hurt in his heart, in his heart, his heart, heart. And again the
door slamming in his mind and a bitter wind encompassing his soul.

Still spinning his head, the carousel turning this way, round and
round, the Papa that way, up and down, the blood the other way,
which way was which, which way was what, he could not say, could
not say, not say, and his hand a numbness in it, on it, out it, about it.

Shmulik tried to brush away the white curtain, maybe behind

the door, maybe not, the curtain made not of cloth but of thin strings of steel that stung him, once here, once there, held by an unseen, malevolent hand. But when he imagined his little Yonatan with hair that stood straight up like arrows in a quiver, arrows now aimed at him like the barbs of steel that stung him now, Gafni gave out an inner unearthly scream which, like Adam's voice in the Midrash, was heard from one end of the world to the other.

Suddenly Malina was there. He didn't hear the key turning in the lock. Didn't hear her shriek of astonishment at seeing him there.

"Get here when did you? Come you did why? Me tell you didn't why?"

His lips thinned; their color purple blue.

"Matter the what's?" Gafni heard.

"Papa," was all he said, seeing his father ride away around the infinite bend on the carousel, his hands looped tight around the curve of the "P." And then his hands let go and his father fell off, father fell off, fell off, off.

"Who — Papa — se?"

Gafni wanted to move his left hand, could not. Tried his right, Pointed at the album, then himself.

"Papa."

"Or Papa your mine?"

He said, "apaP."

"I don't under you stand under don't I."

"Pa," he said more softly than before, "pa." Nodded to the album faintly, then thumb to here and there, jabbing air, off the mark, finally to his heart.

"Matter the, Shmulik, what's? ... Wrong what's?"

"apaP," he said.

"You hear him saying Papa?" which Gafni heard through the white curtain as, "Saying apaP him you hear?"

He shook his head, no no no.

"You to brought baby the want you the baby brought to you you want?"

No no no.

Malina rang out a string of questions like a string of pearls breaking, rolling here and there: Is that your Papa? Want you Papa? Papa there? Who said Papa? Who's whose he's has my Papa. Want to see? I see, you see, we all see, want Papa apaP.

Gafni nodded.

Then his head rolled back.

Heard he afar from her call for an ambulance. In his mind the bris flashed. When he yelled "Papa" at his father for interrupting the bris by complaining that the baby wasn't

Jewish, that plaintive "Papa," the "Papa" he shouted to muffle
his father's cry, that plaintive "Papa" had a different timbre. This
"Papa" that became a camel, a horse, a beast of burden to take
his father away, father away, farther away, away, this Papa ...

2

WHEN GAFNI WOKE, HE KNEW WHERE HE WAS

W<small>HEN</small> Gafni woke — he knew he was in a hospital, a Polish one, he could tell by the old-fashioned white enamel rounded bed frame — first thing he saw as he opened his eyes were the Polish nurses speaking to him.

There to his left, Malina, her face coming out of a blur into sharper focus.

"Thank God you're better," she said. "I was so worried when you were speaking backwards."

"Backwards? I don't remember that."

"Yes, you said some words, some sentences backwards. It sounded like your thoughts were inside out."

"Wardsback?" he said. "Encessent?"

Malina leaned forward. Her brows narrowed. About to say —

Then Gafni laughed. "I'm joking. But I don't remember that at all. What happened to me? Last thing I remember is the world turning upside down."

"A stroke. Very minor. You'll be fine. You were looking at a photo album, which fell to the floor."

"How's the little one? Did you bring him?"

"He's fine. I'll tell you everything in a minute. When did you come? Why didn't you tell me?"

"How could I contact you? Did I know where you were?"

Malina stood. She was as fat as ever, he saw. She hadn't lost an ounce. Was it two or three weeks since he'd last seen her? And why did he suddenly fall ill when he was feeling so good? One thing Gafni did remember: Yankl Shtroy's letter, with its hint of good news to come.

"Guess what?" Malina said brightly, as if she were at a party making innocuous conversation and not in her husband's hospital room. "I've been offered a summer job at Lodz University. I'm teaching there Monday through Friday and found a woman to take care of Janusz."

"What day is today?"

Gafni could see the look of impatience cross her face. As if she were thinking: What's the matter with you? Don't you know what day it is?

Then she said:

"It's Sunday. Why don't you congratulate me on my job?"

"Congratulations."

"It's Lodz University. One of the best in Poland."

"I've been to Lodz," knots in his stomach, "a few times."

"And since you'll be going home in a couple of days, you wouldn't mind, would you, if I went back today. I'm teaching tomorrow."

Gafni nodded.

"So I'll see you Friday. I arranged for a woman to cook for you during the week."

"Bring the little boy."

"First you say, the little one. Now, the little boy. Don't you know his name?"

"Of course I do." He knew she would test him, so he summoned all his strength and thought of his son's name.

"Then what is it?"

"My son's name is Yosef."

"Right!" she said sarcastically. "That's your son. But I mean our son."

"Janusz, Yonatan," he said and knew now that he had said "Yosef" purposely. "Will you bring him?"

"Of course, but they may not let him into the hospital. Do you remember what happened to you yesterday?"

Gafni closed his eyes and thought. "I was sitting in the living room, making plans to go back to the Warsaw quarter I'm researching, when suddenly I felt as if someone had hit the back of my head with a brick and then I think I saw you as I was tumbling down a mountainside into a valley of pictures and then the world stopped."

Was it a dream? he thinks, then thinks some more and says, Was what a dream? And the word "suspicion" floats in unannounced, silent as a rubber dinghy in calm waters. Like his father, he loops his hand into the "p" for balance, for support. First time he met Malina he told her, "You look familiar." And it was true, not a come-on, not an opening for further conversation. If in the real world we can't figure out the truth, how can we find it in fiction, which is truer than the real world?

"You'll be fine," Malina said. She stood slowly, lifting her full weight, raising herself up lugubriously. "Get some rest … "

"But I still want … " he didn't finish because he didn't know what he wanted.

"I know," she said. "I said I would and I will." She kissed his forehead and then she was gone, and he saw once more the white enameled rounded frame of the cast iron hospital bed.

3

ABOUT FATE AND DESTINY

Was it months or years ago, Gafni could no longer remember, that he had thought about what made him meet Malina? Was there a greater purpose? Now he knew. He knew.

Everything was destined. God sets you in one place in this world and no matter what moves you make He brings you to your destined place. Now Gafni finally understood why he had met Malina, why he had to meet Malina. It was part of the larger jigsaw puzzle, the pieces of which only God with His bird's eye view, taking in three or four or five dimensions, was able to see. So all his trips to Poland, all his searches, even following little Mozart's advice, telling him how to slyly sniff out and search, all of that was in vain, all decoration. Froth.

Life was like a folktale. In folktales, people thought they had freedom of movement, but there was a power beyond them they weren't aware of. Like the promiscuous married woman in the Midrash who sought to avoid the Biblical bitter waters test of the suspected adulteress by having her virtuous twin sister drink the potent waters which would have made her thighs swell, her belly inflate, her soul expire. But since the twin sister was unblemished, she escaped the deleterious potency of the testing waters. In celebration, she came back to her sister, who hugged her, kissed her on the lips, upon which the adulterous wife at once fell to the floor dead.

4

THE YOUNG RUSSIAN NURSE

I<small>N</small> the hospital, Gafni met a young Russian nurse. Irena was blonde and slight, her superb figure noticeable even through her demure white uniform. The Polish nurses were efficient but stiff, but the Russian girl had a bouquet of warmth. Speaking to him once, she placed four fingers of her left hand on his cheek. Ill as he was, he was moved, even thrilled, by her touch. He gazed at Irena as she tended to him, a smile on her pretty face — and scenes from years ago encompassed him, memories he had long forgotten or suppressed, so clear he could have read them off her forehead the way Yankl Shtroy had once read Gafni's thoughts about Miguel de Unamuno.

He apologized to the sweet nurse in his thoughts. Why? Because her touch reminded him of an old girlfriend, Galit. He hadn't thought of her in decades, and now, one touch by Irena, and the past surged, inundated him like a gigantic wave, sending him and memories tumbling, like the flood of remembrances that overwhelmed Marcel as that madelaine softened in the warm milk tea. That's exactly what Galit would do, touch his face with four fingers. He had met her decades ago, when he was a student at the Hebrew University, long before he met Batsheva, and long before the University of Israel was founded.

Vivid memories of a past love — a first for Gafni. Most of his daydreams of the past were nightmares. When nightmares faded, his family appeared for a while in pleasant reveries, not old loves. But reveries inexorably led back to nightmares. There was no memory of his father without its obverse, the demonic shadow, the killer. But back to reverie, to love, to loss.

In an advanced Hebrew literature class, they were studying a midrash about Abraham's manservant, Eliezer, who was sent back to Abraham's homeland to find a bride for his son, Isaac. Shmulik, just out of the army, sat next to Galit. He was drawn to her. They walked to the library together, studied together, went for walks. One day, after a picnic that lasted hours, she presented Shmulik with a piece of parchment about eight-by-eleven inches that was a love letter, the first he had ever received, but it wasn't a letter and it lacked the word "love."

Even now, years later, he could recall it, as if photographed, saw clearly the beautifully calligraphed parchment:

REBECCA'S SEARCH FOR ISAAC

Eliezer, find the one who possesses the following:

A good nature, handsome features,
An ability to give as well as to receive,
The mind of a genius
heart of an angel,
body of an athlete,
and the soul of a poet.

When you have found the possessor of these traits,
Bring him forth —
He shall be mine
for all eternity.

WHEN Irena came back to the room he took her hand and held it for a moment.

"You remind me," he said, and didn't know if he squeezed her hand or just wanted to.

"Yes?" She smiled.

"Of someone I knew years ago."

"I hope she was nice."

"As lovely as you."

Irena blushed. He hadn't seen a woman blushing in years.

Galit loved sending him letters, even though they lived in the same city and saw each other in classes almost daily, Sunday through Friday. After once telling her there was going to be fireworks between them, she responded a few days later with a little card embossed with two goldfish looking at each other. Above one of the goldfish was a little comic strip bubble with the words: "Fireworks is an understatement."

He loved her, he knew. And she was not shy about writing it to him. "I love your smiling eyes," she said in a note. "They're laughing. Why? Because we saw each other today. No, that was a dream. I hope you had the same one. Did we dream the same dream? I love you."

Once, on a midweek school break for Purim, they hitchhiked to Beersheva and, looking for a place to sleep, happened upon the tiny house of a Romanian widow, a hefty, high-spirited woman with a healthy laugh and mischievous twinkle in her eye. For two days she became a mother to them. Although they paid only for lodging, the woman fed them and baked for them, was ecstatic for them over their love affair.

But then, the second night they were together in the little house — at the edge of the desert the weather in March was still mild and the full moon was the largest he had ever seen — he heard words he would rather have not heard.

Late that night in the rumpled little bedroom, Galit said to him, "I have to tell you something."

"I know," he said. "You love me."

"It's not that."

Although it was dark, he could see her looking down shamefacedly. Then her umber voice; the sad music of her words:

"Shmulik, I'm married."

The full moon, a black shutter passed over it. The dark room darkened.

"You're what?"

She said nothing. But she placed the four fingers of her right hand on his face.

Shmulik tried, could not bring a ray of light into the room.

"I don't believe it … You never told … "

"I know," she said. "I'm sorry."

But she need not have said, "I'm sorry." Even her "I know" was apologetic.

"And I thought we … "

He felt her removing her fingers from his face. Each finger a little loss, a minus, from his skin.

"So how can you leave for a couple of days?"

"He's in the United States for two weeks on a business trip."

"And he won't call?"

"I called him. I said I'm going to the theater with some friends the next couple of nights."

Theater of the absurd, he said to himself. He shook his head.

"I want a ruler."

"Why?"

"I want to measure the gap in my heart."

"I love you so much," Galit said.

"So that's why you could never see me on a Saturday night. It's not that you worked," he said.

Now Gafni looked at Irena, who could have been Galit's daughter. Oh, the love letters, the praise she showered on him. In class she would turn to him and mouth dreamily, "I love you," her eyes softening.

Did she love him so much because she disliked her husband, whom her parents had pressured her into marrying? The four in-laws were close friends, survivors, Galit told Shmulik, and their dream was having their children marry.

"I'm sorry," was all Shmulik could say that night. The darkness passed. Now the full moon showered beams of light onto their pillow.

"I'm sorry too," and she began to cry. "I didn't want to hurt my parents."

"Don't they realize how much they hurt you?"

"You should have seen how happy all four were at the wedding, dancing as a foursome and embracing."

"Then they should have moved in with each other and lived together. Why did they have to drag you into this mess?"

"How can we find happiness in this brief, sad life?"

"You have stolen my dreams."

When they returned to Jerusalem, she wrote him a card that said, "But I still dream of you. Every single day."

"Thank you, Galit," he told the nurse.

"Irena," she corrected him with a smile and put four fingers on his face, telling him with her touch that it was all right. As she was about to go, he lifted his finger, indicating he wanted something.

"What can I do for you?"

"Irena, sweetheart, I can't place a long-distance call from this phone and I must call a colleague in Jerusalem."

"What's his number? I'll call him from home."

Gafni smiled. "That's just what I was going to ask you. And I'll reimburse you for the cost."

"Please," she said. "It's my pleasure to help you. Give me the man's number and tell me what I should tell him."

Gafni wrote the information down on a little pad.

"Tell Professor Meichl-Rukzak that I don't know if I'll be back for my first class in mid-October. If not, ask him to start teaching my two seminars until I return."

"Fine," she said. "And I'll give him your number here and tell him when it's a good time to call, if he needs to."

"Thank you, Irena."

She didn't respond. She just took Gafni's hand and pressed it.

Little gestures, he thought, explode in the heart like beneficent angels.

5

HE WASN'T SORRY / PIX FROM PAST

HE wasn't sorry to learn the next day that he wouldn't go home as soon as Malina (and he) thought. What would he do at home anyway, an empty house that wasn't home? What was up with Shmulik Gafni? Odd rhythms in his heart, the doctor said. He should be monitored. Stay a while, Shmulik told himself, and make yourself at home.

From his sickbed — would this be his last place of repose? he wondered, then quickly chased the gloomy thought away — he hoped he would be able to slough off his illness like a snakeskin and crawl out hale and cured, a new man. But he knew — was that the realist suppressing the dreamer? — in his heart that hoping for a *refue shleyme*, a full and perfect cure, was as quixotic as assuming that someone would stick his head out of the old, unpredictable black-and-white tv screen up on a wall ledge opposite his bed, just like up there his own face was now doing, looking around, as if seeking the nearest exit from this room. Why Gafni, looking at the tv from his bed, why Gafni was also up on the screen, his face poking out as if sculpted, animated, three-dimensionalized, he did not know.

The two Gafnis regarded each other; their eyes widened, as if a spurt of recognition went through them. But do you need recognition when you look in the mirror?

Lately, there were lots of things he couldn't explain, more and more mysteries, questions without answers. How could he be both in his bed and up there on the screen? But he saw the cylindrical white poles of the bed, beds you only saw in black-and-white photos from the 1920's, the IV slowly dripping, and yet he also saw himself on the screen, not as if a tv monitor were filming him, like in a bank. The on-screen Gafni was completely independent of the Gafni in the hospital bed. Up there, Gafni was acting out a scene. He gets into a car, yes, now he remembers, he recognized the University of Israel buildings, the two boys who kidnapped him, took him to an apartment near Me'ah She'arim, Nussen was his name, a research assistant, a yeshiva *bokher* whom he overpaid generously, and then he stabs me in the back, but they only got a thirty-day suspended sentence, those bastards, the smirk on their faces when they heard the judge's decision he'll never forget, for they had no prior record, their lawyer argued, and no force was used to get Gafni into the car or into the apartment, and the judge agreed, but Nussen would never work for him or any other professor again, and they fooled him by concocting a ninety-nine-year-old Warsaw Jew.

Then, all of a sudden, Ezra Shultish's face came out of the screen like a *commedia dell'arte* puppet or a Pinocchio doll, as if looking for someone. Gafni waved to him from his bed, called to him, but Shultish couldn't hear, now Shultish's face receded into the screen and Gafni sees Shultish in a taxi, following the car Gafni is in, and then an odd scene he couldn't remember, where Shultish is talking to a dispatcher from the rescue squad, then the station switched to Polish news and the screen went blank.

But not his mind. He closed his eyes. Where was he in this world? Why was he here? Why do some people live and others die? He didn't want to die. He wanted to live, like Yankl Shtroy and his friends. He remembered telling Shultish a while back, "In one way or another we're all striving for immortality." Immortality. Immortalized. Immortal. Yes. It was a good word. He liked it. Longed for it. Not the metaphoric shading of the word, the immortality of, let's say, Sholom Aleichem, where your name is remembered forever because of your genius. No, not that. The immortality he longed for was the immortality of Genesis. The Tree of Life. But immortality was only one prong of his two-pronged longing. The other: revenge. Two things totally unrelated, except they both con(cern)(sum)ed him. Revenge for — we know what he wanted revenge for. That deed that shook the atoms of his soul. Decades later they were still trembling beneath his skin, between his eyes, moving haphazardly, in disarray.

When Gafni opened his eyes, the tv was playing scenes from his meeting Malina in Nice. Although it was black and white and somewhat grainy, he supplied the color: the hues of Malina's porcelain skin, the shades of red of her berry-red bikini. He sees her stretching out her hand and leading him to the water, while with his free hand he removes his tie and jacket. In his bed Gafni looked about. Were any of the nurses watching? No, he was alone. The nurses rarely came. He heard them chattering at the nurses' station. Then the cameraman must have lain down on the sand, for Gafni saw a full-length shot of Malina, from the legs up, what gorgeous legs she had then, he hadn't even noticed, and then up to her waist and the explosion of flesh by her breasts. And in the distance the storks and the helicopters doing aerial acrobatics to take a look at Malina's seductive body. She came closer and closer, was about to step out of the screen and into the room, then once again the scene blanked out for a moment. That's my life, he thought, seeing himself flirting with

Malina. No wonder the rumors flew, no wonder people thought what they thought.

And then he and Batsheva were walking in the countryside in the Galil and two little dogs come up to him. Now they speak, but now he cannot understand their language, for it is a mélange of Yiddish, Hebrew, Aramaic and Esperanto.

Then the screen showed a closeup of a cup of coffee, was it an advertisement? Gafni wondered. It focused even closer, on a wafer atop the whipped cream, where sat a neatly dressed tiny figure, little Mozart, at the Vienna café talking to Gafni. But before Gafni could react to the fleeting picture it too faded.

Now Gafni sees on the tv screen a blank photo, black and white, no face but a hazy outdoors behind the empty space. Fadeout and repeat. Again fadeout. And once more a photo of no one, someone without a face. Who could it be? Gafni wondered, feeling uncomfortable, ill at ease, prickles moving quickly up his arms and legs.

The camera, ah, his beloved university library, zooms in on a stack of books. A man takes out his beaten leather briefcase, an ink bottle and a pen and signs the author's name on the flyleaf. That's me, Gafni said, but not proudly. He felt his cheeks warming. He looked around, afraid someone else had seen, hoping Irena was not there. Why is that scene on? he wanted to know. To remind me that every man has a secret?

Gafni closed his eyes. In the university library one day, he had met Ezra Shultish who, without knowing it, shamed him, shocked him out of his nasty addiction of autographing books. And because he had met Shultish and made an appointment for supper, Shultish was able to help him when he was kidnapped. And because he was kidnapped, he recalled Yankl Shtroy's name. And because of Yiddish he had met Malina. But why he met her was still not resolved.

Then President John F. Kennedy came on. At a press conference he stops to thank Professor Shmuel Gafni for his excellent advice during the Cuban missile crisis, advice that helped reduce world tension and very likely prevented World War III. "So let's all give Professor Gafni a hand." And a smiling JFK leads the applause. Gafni is pleased, his smile as wide as his bed, then Kennedy's hand comes out of the screen; it moves now to the left of the screen, now to the right. This is the hand that JFK wants to give him.

Gafni pushed himself up on the bed. With his right hand he folded the pillow in half to prop up his head.

"Thank you, thank you," Gafni whispered to the fallen president, with tears in his eyes.

And before the applause died down, there, on the screen, Gafni's baby Yonatan was being circumcised. He saw himself, first holding the eight-day-old boy, then the ten Russian Jews he had hired (two extra in case one or two didn't show up), the *mohel*, and his father's admonishing voice. He did not see, but he imagined Malina, in the bedroom, sulking. And once again, as he had during the bris, an ambivalent feeling ran through Gafni. How can one circumcise a non-Jewish baby boy?

History does repeat itself, Gafni muttered. Fatigue overwhelmed him and he closed his eyes. Now that Gafni contemplated in repose what he had seen, he judged it not so extraordinary to see flashes of one's recent life on tv. Nothing should surprise him any more. Except, perhaps, the return of Batsheva, or his father. Still there will be surprises for him. Surprises and astonishments.

And for you too.

And then Gafni felt a presence, a person standing before him whom he recognized without even seeing. When Gafni opened his eyes, he saw

6

COME TO VISIT GAFNI, YANKL SHTROY

Yankl Shtroy approaching the bed.

"It's me, Yankl Shtroy, remember?"

Gafni smiled faintly. He wanted to ask him, In what capacity are you here? He wanted to tell him he missed him. He wanted to tell him, I haven't seen you in years but I've never forgotten you. He wanted to thank him for the letter, which prompted his trip to Poland. He wanted to tell him he looked exactly the same. Lately, there were so many wants on the tip of Gafni's tongue. The words floated within him like scattered feathers. He reached up to pluck one of them but the wind his hand created made the feathers fly away.

"I came to greet you, " Yankl Shtroy said slowly. "To wish you well."

"Thank you for your letter. That's why I came."

Yankl Shtroy nodded.

"I heard you were here."

"How?"

"From my friends in shul."

"But how did they, you, know I was in the hospital?"

Yankl Shtroy made a gesture like a Middle Eastern Jew who doesn't want to answer a question. He closed his eyes for a moment, eyebrows up, head tilted skyward, as if to say: No comment. Don't ask. It's a mystery. Who knows? It may come from God.

"You haven't changed," Gafni whispered.

Yankl Shtroy shrugged. "That's how it is."

"And how are your friends?"

"They are well, thank God. But how are you? That's why I came. Soon as I heard." He stretched out his hand. Gafni took it and held it. "Tell me how you're feeling."

As he held Yankl Shtroy's hand the words came back to him; energy coursing through Yankl Shtroy leaped into Gafni's palm. The feathers landed softly, all in a row.

"I cannot say good, but I cannot say bad either. That's the sad part. I don't feel consistently good or bad. Every time I feel good it seems it will stay that way, but then the ill feeling returns and it depresses me."

"A Jew has to have hope."

"I do," Gafni said, meaning more than he said, hoping that Yankl Shtroy would understand what he was trying to say, what he was pleading for with those two crisp words.

"*Du vest zine mit unz,*" Yankl Shtroy said. "Remember?" He removed his hand from Gafni's.

Yes, Shmulik remembered. Yankl Shtroy was saying, You will be with us.

"In your letter you told me I'll find what I want, what I'm looking for."

"Yes, yes."

"What did you mean?"

Yankl Shtroy licked his lips.

"Please tell me. Don't hold back. I made this long trip. It's very important to me. What do you mean?"

Yankly Shtroy spoke slowly. He bent over the bed and held both of Gafni's hands.

"It's not what I meant. It's what you mean. What are you looking for?"

Why is everything ping-pong? Gafni wanted to say. Why do words curve and bounce back like boomerangs?

"You know what I'm looking for. I told you what I'm looking for. Two things. One: my father's murderer. And two: to be one of you, to be with you."

"I already told you. You will be with us."

"Good. I feel better already. But what about item number one? That's even more important than the second."

"You'll be successful with this too."

"How do you know? Did you get any news? Any leads since last time I was here? Do you know where he is?"

"No. It's just a vibration in my wrist and elbows. A sixth, seventh, eighth sense. That's why I wrote you. You'll see how right I am."

"Good. I trust you. I have hope."

"Hope is the best word in the Yiddish language."

"Please come again. Next time bring all your friends."

"Fine. I'll try to do that."

Gafni smiled. He was happy.

"*Ikh vill zine eyner fun eyekh,*" Gafni sang out.

"Uh-huh."

But as is usual in language, what one means to say isn't what the other hears, and what the other hears isn't what the first man meant to say.

7

WHY GAFNI LAUGHED

GAFNI opened his eyes. Couldn't believe his eyes. Shut, then opened his eyes. No, I'm imagining. It's more of the tv he had seen the other day. Or was it today? No, it was not a dream. Not magical tv. It was them. They were here. Ezra Shultish and Chaim Sh. Meichl-Rukzak. Meichl, Shmeichl and Beichl together again. Both men approached and embraced him.

"You're here. I can't believe it." Gafni rubbed his eyes; perhaps the image would vanish. "Thank you. Thank you for coming. You don't know how glad I am to see you."

What a wonderful mitzva for his older friends to make such a long trip from Jerusalem. The Talmud says visiting the sick takes away one-sixtieth of a person's illness. So if two people come 60 times 2 is 120, or one-hundred-twentieth of a person's illness. No, that doesn't make sense, not double, half, one-thirtieth of one's illness, so if they stay one month I'll be completely cured.

Then something caught Gafni's eye.

He looked out the window, saw Hebrew letters flying into the room, inside out, from left to right, widely spaced, as in a mirror world, headline for a non-existent newspaper.

At first Gafni thought the letters were following a wrong path. Strange enough that letters were flying once again, but stranger that they were flying backwards. But then he realized that it was not for him, that display: it was for them, those opposite him, and for them the letters were sailing in correct fashion, from right to left, precisely the way Hebrew letters ought to fly — his words to Shultish and Meichl-Rukzak emblazoned in the air.

Shultish looked up. His head moved slowly, as if watching a propeller-driven plane trailing a long message over a beach.

"That's some welcome you prepared for us," the old Agnon scholar murmured.

Gafni nodded. "I saw this phenomenon years ago in the shul on Paderewski Street. The *gabbai*, Yankl Shtroy, was just here. Maybe it's because of him."

But when they looked up again, the letters were gone.

"SHMULIK, we have a surprise for you," he heard Ezra Shultish say, and a warm smile edged the old man's reddish blue lips. Shultish had gotten older. The thin lips had taken on a feminine cast, as old men's lips are wont to do at a certain age, when countervailing hormones begin to tip the fine balance.

And even before Gafni could say, What is it? he noticed. He turned to his night table. There, on a tiny wooden platform, on a tiny chair, sat Wolfgang Amadeus.

"I want to wish you a *refu'e shleyme*," said Mozart. May you have a speedy recovery.

"Another surprise? How wonderful to see you again, Herr Mozart! *A dank*, thank you so much."

"Wolfgang, remember?"

"Thank you, Wolfgang. How did you learn that?" Gafni looked at Shultish. "Did you teach this to him?"

"No no. Not me. It's a surprise to me too."

"Me too," said Meichl-Rukzak.

"I did it all on my own."

"How did you get here?"

"Our flight was routed to Vienna," said Shultish, "back to the city where I studied. And so we went — where else? — to the Café Mozart. When we met Herr Mozart, he asked us where we are from, and within minutes we established the connection, and at once ... "

"Even sooner," said Wolfgang.

" ... he wanted to join us."

"Of course. I don't need a passport. Just a pocket," and he gestured over to Shultish. "Just a pocket will do."

"And the café?"

"They can manage without me for a few days."

Now Meichl-Rukzak spoke. "If you can take another surprise, Shmulik, there is one coming right now. Close your eyes if you are ready."

Gafni closed his eyes. How relaxing it was to close one's eyes and see only the cobalt blue of one's eyelids and hear divine music from afar. Yes, over the hospital public address system they were playing Mozart's "Turkish" violin concerto. But there was something odd here. Something missing.

"You can open your eyes now," Wolfgang said.

Gafni saw Mozart, Gafni saw Mozart playing, Gafni saw Mozart playing a tiny violin. As tiny Mozart played the violin line of the concerto, Meichl-Rukzak and Shultish drew close. They stared with wonder at the descendant of Wolfgang Amadeus, who was coaxing his ancestor's melodies out of the tiny, perfect instrument, playing with eyes pressed tight.

When he finished, he opened his beautiful eyes with the silken black lashes. To the applause of the three men, he lowered his head and bowed ... "

"You see, Shmulik, I kept my promise to play for you next time I see you. *Ikh hob gehaltn vort.*"

Gafni shook his head in wonder at Mozart's perfect idiomatic expression. If so many incredible, even miraculous events were taking place, wasn't it a sign that something special would happen to him too? "It's the most beautiful music I have ever heard, Wolfgang. It rings of Paradise ... *Gan Eden* ... You have enriched my soul."

"Shmulik, may I kiss you on the forehead?"

"Please, please do ... Shimen, bring Wolfgang to me ... "

Mozart, standing on Meichl-Rukzak's palm, bent forward, one hand on the bridge of Gafni's nose and kissed him on the forehead above his left eye.

"Thank you, Wolfgang ... Your kiss is magic too."

Then back to the little platform on Gafni's night table. Mozart hopped off Meichl-Rukzak's palm. From his pocket Shultish removed a little case into which Mozart placed his violin.

"What a beautiful instrument," Gafni said.

"Wait ... " said Mozart. "And now for the next part of the concert."

This time Meichl-Rukzak went into his jacket and handed Mozart a larger case, one just a bit smaller than Mozart himself. Wolfgang removed a cello and a bow, played the four strings, tuned them, and then drew the bow again over all the strings until he was satisfied.

"This is for you, Shmulik."

Soon, the sound of the familiar, plaintive, age-old melody filled the room.

Gafni's eyes welled with tears.

"The Kol Nidrei ... " Gafni said.

"From Bruch's *Kol Nidrei for Cello and Orchestra* ... But I will begin again ... No talking, please, until I am done."

To himself, Gafni prayed along with the melody. For centuries Jews said one thing along with the chazzen, who sang the Aramaic words, the dry formula releasing Jews from vows made under duress, as the sun was setting and Yom Kippur, the holiest day of the year, began, while the haunting melody actually prompted them to think of themselves, their families, the welfare of Jews all over the world. They chanted the Aramaic, which few understood, along with the cantor, hoping for peace and health and cessation of persecution. It is amazing what a prayer can do, a prayer with a split personality, saying one thing and meaning another.

When Mozart finished there was silence. Gafni felt the air around him filled with holiness. Unreedemed sparks, like dots in a pointillist painting, hung in the room. The room was supersaturated with sparks and incandescent space.

"Thank you, Wolfgang," Gafini whispered. "Thank you from the bottom of my heart. How I deserved to have a Mozart give me a private, divine concert I'll never know. But I do know one thing."

"What is that?" Mozart asked.

"The worst part of dying is that one will never be able to hear music again."

Mozart waved his hand dismissively, while both Shultish and Meichl-Rukzak made protesting noises, meaningless plosive syllables like "bkh" and "peh" and "prr" which meant to say, don't talk nonsense.

"L'chaim!" Mozart sang out. To life!

"Mozart is right," said Meichl-Rukzak. "Jews don't talk of dying."

Gafni, laughing, said, "I'll sing Amen to that."

A good feeling came over Gafni. He had never felt so good before. A dream ambience of peace and good feeling, of eudemonia, that Greek word he had recently learned, overwhelmed him; happiness that would last forever.

"Shmulik ... " Shultish was speaking. "Shmulik, if you don't mind, I'd like to ask you a question."

Gafni, seeing Shultish's shy and uncomfortable demeanor, understood what was coming.

"Go ahead. Ask."

"Remember you told me about your discovery of the source of the word *davenen*? Is the article out yet?"

At once bliss vanished. A shadow crossed Gafni's face. So that's why Shultish came, flashed through his mind.

"Can you share it with me now?" Shultish persisted. He turned to Mozart. "The word means to pray."

Now Gafni was in a box. If he lied and said the article hadn't appeared yet, it would elicit Meichl-Rukzak's curiosity and the charade would have to be extended. He didn't have the energy to continue this game. A Yiddish proverb surfaced: *der emes is der bester lign*: the truth is the best lie.

"Ezra, my *chaver*, I will share something even better: the truth. Please forgive me, Ezra. Please excuse me." Gafni put both his hands on his chest as a sign of contrition. "But I was ... it was ... I don't know what got into me. *Der nar shtupt dikh*, like my mother would say. A spirit of foolishness. Idiocy overwhelmed me ... For that lie I was punished by being kidnapped." And for autographing books not of my own composition, he didn't say. "Please forgive me. I fabricated it. I'm so sorry, my dear friend … And I admire your patience in not saying anything all this time."

"Source of *davenen*, huh?" Meichl-Rukzak interjected, chuckling. "That would have been some linguistic feat."

But Shultish looked ashen. Was he about to cry? Gafni wondered.

"Come here, Ezra, *yedidi*. Come here and let me hold your hand. I'm sorry."

Shultish approached, gave Gafni his hand, and then spontaneously the old scholar bent forward and embraced and kissed Gafni again, showing that he accepted Gafni's apology.

"You don't know with what anticipation I've been looking forward to that article … But you know, maybe it's better that it's still a mystery. We need unknowns. They inspire us."

Shultish must feel, Gafni thought, the way I felt when Nussen fooled me with that ninety-nine-year-old Warsaw Jew, robbing me of the hope of meeting an old landsman … Sometimes, Gafni mused, God sends the punishment in tandem with the nasty deed.

Silence in the room again.

Then Meichl-Rukzak said to Shultish:

"Should we tell him now?"

Shultish nodded.

"Sure we should tell him now. If we don't tell him now, when will we tell him?"

Gafni looked at both men. "What should you tell me now?"

"What we should tell you now is this." And Meichl-Rukzak smiled a pleased smile. "Some staff members at the University of Israel Library discovered scores of rare books autographed … "

Gafni's heart began palpitating, then rocking, then pounding. He felt the blood rush to his face. His heart fell, stumbled, tried to rise. Suddenly, there was a sour, gut-tightening darkness in him. Another blow? I won't be able to take another blow.

"… by the authors," Shultish continued. "They say it's a magnificent collection, a rare find. No other library, not even our rival, the Hebrew University Jewish National Library, has such books."

"And so," Meichl-Rukzak said, "in honor of this discovery, they are going … "

Now his heart eased; the prickles on his skin faded.

"… to make a special collection of autographed books — in Yiddish, Hebrew and other languages—and they are going to call it the Shmuel Gafni Special Autograph Collection of Literature."

"Indeed! How nice!"

And Shmulik began to laugh. And the laughter made him feel

good. And feeling good eased the pathways of laughter and he laughed some more. The laughter just bubbled out of him. Seeing Gafni so pleased, Shultish and Meichl-Rukzak too began to laugh, then came a tiny bell-like tinkle, Mozart laughing along with them.

"I haven't ... " Shmulik sputtered, taking a glass of water to calm down, "I haven't laughed so much in years. You don't say? A special collection. Named for me?"

"Yes," said Meichl-Rukzak.

"What do I have to do with it?"

And Gafni laughed again.

Sometimes God sends a reward for nasty deeds. Well, maybe not nasty, but certainly not nice.

And Gafni laughed again.

8

LOOKING, SEEING, NOTICING,
THE DIFFERENCES BETWEEN

IRENA, the slim Russian nurse, was on duty. Just looking at her made Gafni feel good.

"Excuse me, professor," she said, stepping into the room, bringing light into the room, bringing an aureole of light into the room, like a Maria in a medieval painting, bringing in light like condensed sunshine.

Hearing Irena's voice, Wolfgang Amadeus hid behind the little flower vase on Gafni's night table.

"Please call me Shmulik," Gafni told her, then introduced Irena to his two friends.

"Yankl Shtroy is outside," she said.

"Again? Wonderful! Bring him in."

"But he has a minyan with him," Irena said.

"Minyan?"

"Surely you know what a minyan is."

"Surely," Gafni mimicked her. "But I didn't know that you … "

"Don't you know I'm Jewish?" Irena whispered.

Gafni shook his head.

"Of course I am. I thought you sensed that … But I don't … " and she shifted her glance to the hall, "let them know."

Suddenly, Irena became more precious to him. He wanted to ask who her parents were; how they survived the war. Were they in hiding with their parents?

"I hear you're a professor of Yiddish," she said.

Another Polish girl interested in Yiddish. Malina all over again.

"Why? Does it interest you?"

"*Ikh red Yiddish*," she said softly. "My parents taught it to me."

A smile of pure joy suffused Shmulik's face.

"I'm so happy to hear you speak Yiddish," he said in Yiddish. An angel sent by Elijah had come into his life. Why should he go home, if he could see her here every day? Talk of transformative vision. Where did she appear from, this Jewish beauty? Why couldn't he have met her and married her?

"Where are your parents from?"

"From here. They both escaped to Russia and were repatriated.

They had me late in life, after they had already given up hope. Imagine! My mother was fifty-two. They thought she had a tumor." Irena laughed happily. "But it was me."

Do all patients, Gafni wondered, fall in love with their nurses? Then he forgot why she had come in.

"So?" she said. "What's the answer?"

"What's the question?" Gafni laughed.

"Do you want Yankl Shtroy and all his friends in at the same time?"

"How many are there?"

"Nine or ten. Hard to tell."

Gafni understood.

"I tried to count them but I ... I'm so tired from working so many hours ... I get a different number each time."

Gafni nodded.

"We don't usually allow so many visitors, but Yankl Shtroy said it was for religious purposes, a ceremony."

"Yes, please, I would like to see them all."

Yankl Shtroy came first, followed by the others. Old men all, they smiled and chatted and wished Gafni well. Gafni introduced the visitors to Shultish and Meichl-Rukzak. So many hands were shaken — none crisscrossed, for four Jews do not shake hands over one another lest they form the shape of a cross — so many handshakes it looked like a shul at the end of Shabbes services. After the politesse of acquaintance came absolute silence. Thick, weighty, profound, accented by the distant machines humming softly somewhere in the hospital. Fourteen or fifteen men in the room and not a word heard, no sentence said.

Then, floating up from the stillness, a tiny voice asking Gafni:

"Do you think your friends would also like to hear the *Kol Nidrei?*"

Shultish drew the visitors' attention to Gafni's night table. The men stood on tiptoe and leaned forward, straining to see where the voice was coming from.

"A wonderful idea," said Gafni. "Wolfgang Amadeus Mozart, descendant of ... " he held back saying *the* ... "Wolfgang Amadeus Mozart, meet my friends ... You will now have the honor of hearing him play his cello."

Yankl Shtroy and the minyan nodded, bowed. Two or three of the old men even extended their hands to greet Mozart, then abashedly withdrew. Mozart's size did not amaze them. Their eyes did not pop; neither did their jaws slack at the incredulity. Given what they knew, nothing surprised them.

Meichl-Rukzak gave Mozart the cello case and a tiny chair. At once Mozart began to play. Small, intense sounds, like concentrated perfume, filled the room. Gafni looked at the minyan, saw tears rolling down every man's face. So rapt in attention were they to the melody each one knew by heart, no one attempted to wipe the tears away. What were they thinking? Gafni wondered. Whom were they now seeing? A foolish question, Gafni admitted. It was obvious whom they were seeing. They not only heard the music, Mozart's *Kol Nidrei* also made them see. Gafni recalled Yankl Shtroy's comment about not dying: "Believe me, Shmulik, what we have is not all mazel and blessing. I'd exchange it in an instant to have my family back. The trouble is we can't pick and choose miracles."

When Mozart finished, the men applauded. Mozart smiled.

Yankl Shtroy closed the door to Gafni's room, then bent close to Mozart and spoke to him in Yiddish, assuming he would understand.

"Thank you. I have never heard a *Kol Nidrei* like that. It's as though an angel from heaven played for us."

Then Yankl Shtroy looked at his friends. He didn't say a word; merely tilted his head toward Mozart. A moment of silence and an imperceptible nod linked all of them.

"Fine," said Yankl Shtroy. "Tell me, Herr Mozart, would you like to be bigger?"

Mozart didn't answer. Maybe he hadn't heard. But then again, maybe he had — for if a small face can register petulance, that is what Mozart expressed.

Yankl Shtroy repeated the question. "Is that something that would please you?"

"No one has ever asked me that before. I can't answer that. It's not a realistic choice. All my life I've been tiny. I have no basis for comparison."

The minyan gazed at Mozart with wide-eyed affection.

Yankl Shtroy was about to speak once more, but Gafni interrupted.

"I would like it to be known that Herr Mozart's parents, at great risk, hid Jews in their country home in Austria during the war. One of the few Viennese who saved Jews."

Mozart bowed his head. "I think I told you. With them we spoke a rudimentary Yiddish."

Yankl Shtroy said, "Herr Mozart, we have in unison a strength that each of us separately does not have. We have never done anything like this before, but we are willing to try. Certainly for a man like you, distinguished scion of a distinguished forebear, and of a family of righteous gentiles."

Again Mozart bowed his head.

"Are you willing to become bigger? To be like us — well, not exactly like us, we're old, very old — but perhaps to be able to do things on your own and not need outside help?"

Mozart turned to Gafni.

"Do you think I should?"

"What have you got to lose?"

"My uniqueness."

"True, but consider it. First of all, who knows if they can do it? Second, think of the advantages. Performing. Traveling on your own."

"So you think I should?"

"I think you should — and if you wish to have children, they will likely be of normal size. You did say that you get smaller and smaller with each generation and that you and your wife can't have children. And, remember, you once told me how difficult it is for you to notate music. By being bigger you could easily do that ... But you really have to make up your own mind."

Mozart looked to Shultish and Meichl-Rukzak.

"I think Shmulik is right," said Meichl-Rukzak.

"Me too," said Shultish.

"But what about my wife?"

"Where is she now?" Yankl Shtroy asked.

"Hannelore is with a joint Chinese-American entertainment venture, the Ling-Ling Brothers Babar and Bay Leaf Circus. Along with me she is the last of the really tiny people. Her parents and my parents were still able to have one child. We, my wife and I, as Shmulik just mentioned, were unable."

"We will have her in mind too," said Yankl Shtroy.

Nodded the minyan.

"Then all right," said Mozart. "Yes, I agree ... Thank you ... Just don't make me any smaller."

"Just close your eyes," said Yankl Shtroy.

Mozart closed his eyes.

All the men did the same.

Following Yankl Shtroy's lead, they began to chant in unison:

"*Zeh ha-kotn godl yee-yeh.*" They said these words three times and then three times more and three times more. Then they recited quicker and quicker these words from the bris ceremony where the father hopes that "this little one will become big," or, "May this little boy grow up to be an adult," and with eyes shut they stretched out their hands and with eyes shut but faces gleaming they took one another's hands and with eyes shut and faces gleaming and smiles on their lips they took one another's hands and entered the rhythm of the chant with a motionless dance, a dance of stasis.

Gafni and Shultish and Meichl-Rukzak looked at Mozart

standing on Gafni's white night table next to the old-fashioned black dial telephone. Without his hat Mozart could stand beneath the receiver and his thick black hair just grazed the mouthpiece. During the men's dance Mozart stepped forward, stood next to a half-filled water glass. At first Gafni and his friends could not discern anything. But imperceptibly, as the rhythmic chant grew louder and softer, sometimes accelerated, sometimes diminuendo, a change indeed was taking place.

Very slowly, Wolfgang Amadeus was growing.

Remember, Mozart's eyes were shut. His eyes absolutely still. The fine, tiny, silken black lashes, not a vibrato in them. At first, his closed eyes were obeisant to the instruction, a willful shutting, he aware that his eyes were closed, perhaps the thing to do when a possible magical event is about to unfold. But after a while his closed eyes remained shut of their own accord, no longer subject to will. Sleep, slumber, overcame his eyes, not the Hebrew *sheyna*, normal sleep, but *tardema*, heavy slumber, the same kind of anesthetic slumber that befell Adam when God removed a rib to fashion Eve. A beatific smile hovered on Mozart's face as he slept the sleep that sleep sleeps when sleep itself falls asleep and dreamt the paradisaic dreams that dreams dream when dreams themselves have dreams.

No one saw Mozart growing because he grew so imperceptibly that only by closing your eyes for a minute and then opening them would you have been able to notice a difference. But not Gafni, not Shultish, not Meichl-Rukzak closed his eyes. They didn't want to lose a moment of this phenomenon their eyes were privileged to see, but by keeping their eyes open, there's a conundrum, they really couldn't, didn't, see. That is, they saw, but they didn't notice; they looked but they didn't see. And the nine or ten others who chanted, "*Zeh ha-kotn godl yee-yeh*" without stop, also had their eyes closed, like the congregation when the *kohanim* chant the priestly blessing. So they neither looked nor saw, neither saw nor noticed.

As he grew, Mozart, an ecstatic smile made his face glow, like Moses' face when God spoke to him. As Wolfgang grew, he didn't realize, no one saw, even though three sets of eyes were open, no one noticed is the more accurate word, that as he got bigger, Mozart himself was not aware that he had hopped off the night table onto the pillowed easy chair, and there he remained, growing, getting bigger, like a flower in stop-frame photography. The smile on his face, the same beatific smile that graced his ancestor Wolfgang Amadeus when he composed the *Exultate Jubilate* or the *Clarinet Concerto.*

The nine or ten men chanted. I say nine or ten, because if you counted one minute there were absolutely ten; if you counted a minute later, and no one left the room or entered, there were nine. As the nine-ten men chanted, the three others stared, unblinking, Mozart was slowly transformed into a slim, forty-year-old man, five-foot-seven, weighing about one-hundred-forty-five pounds.

The miraculous was not his transformation from a pecan-sized man-kin into a normally proportioned adult, for men blessed with the miraculous can do almost anything. The miracle was that his clothes grew with him.

The minyan, their eyes still shut, sensed that their chant, their prediction, their prayer, their predigation had succeeded. They ceased their chant, their rhythms stopped, and Mozart grew no more.

For all of them, at once, as though a reverse blackout, eyes opened, sleep ended, dreams woke.

"*Mazel tov*," cried Yankl Shtroy.

Gafni, a smile of such radiance and bliss, as if he himself were cured, as if he had been given a choice by the men, in fact he imagined that this was the choice he had been given, either be cured or have Mozart become full size, his unselfish decision rendered, Gafni was so happy for Mozart, although one cannot deny that there was a tiny feeling of loss that such a unique human creature, who defied all biological laws, was no more.

What could Mozart say as he regarded himself, looked up at the ceiling, stared at his outstretched fingers, looked down at the floor that now was not so far away?

"I ... I ... I don't know what to say ... Thank you ... Thank you."

"How do you feel?"

"New. Born. Very new ... May I taste this water? I need to drink."

The phone rang. Gafni picked it up. Mozart carefully cradled the glass and drank slowly.

"It's for you, Wolfgang."

"For me? Who knows I'm here? Oh, it must be my wife ... Oh my, how am I going to explain ... ?"

Gafni imagined Mozart's wife perched on the rim of the receiver, clasping both round edges and shouting into the phone.

"Hello ... Yes, I know it's you, Hannelore ... What's the matter? Why are you shouting?"

Mozart held the phone away from his ear; now everyone could hear her say:

"I've been fired," and she burst into tears. "From the circus. After fifteen years ... What am I going to do now?"

"What happened?" He covered the receiver. "How am I going to tell her what happened to me?"

"Wolfgang, I just woke up, maybe fifteen minutes ago, and I was no longer in Herr Lenfel's thimble bed ... I was sprawled on the floor. Big as the rest of them." And she cried again. "What am I going to do now?"

"You will be a waitress at our café. We'll manage it together. But really manage it. Ourselves. You're not alone. If you know what I mean."

"No, I don't know what you mean."

"I'm bigger too."

"How did it happen?"

"It's too complicated … I'll tell you when I get back."

"You too? How wonderful. How tall are you?"

"I don't know. I'll ask … How tall am I?"

"About a meter and a half," said Gafni.

"About a meter and a half," Mozart repeated.

"That's about my size too," Hannelore said and giggled. "Papageno."

And she sang the famous little aria from Mozart's *Magic Flute.*

"Papagena … Pa … pa … pa … gena." Wolfgang sang and laughed. "We'll meet at home. In two days."

Then Mozart turned to the men. "So you succeeded making my wife bigger too."

Yankl Shtroy clapped his hands once in joy.

Then Mozart stretched, moved his shoulders and torso as if undoing a kink in his muscles. He bent over Gafni's bed and whispered into his ear:

"Did you find the man you're looking for?"

"I haven't seen him yet."

"I'm sure you will. You will." He took Gafni's hands and rubbed them. "I'm making these hands strong for you. Like David. Like Samson."

Gafni sensed an infusion of warmth rising from his fingers into his arms and chest.

"Yes," he said. "I feel it."

Yankl Shtroy and his minyan were set to leave. Again everyone shook everyone else's hands.

Shultish and Meichl-Rukzak shyly awaited their turn to say goodbye.

"Don't worry about your classes," said Meichl-Rukzak. "Just get well soon."

And Shultish said, warmly pressing Gafni's hand, "Imagine. I've been called out of retirement. The Overseas School of your university has asked me to lead a seminar on Agnon in translation — mostly for Americans — with an accent on his masterpiece, *The Maiden From Yemen.*"

"*The Yemenite Girl,*" Gafni corrected.

"*The Maiden From Yemen*," Shultish insisted. "I'm not using Eviant's, if you'll excuse the expression, pish-impoverished translation," he said in his best idiomatic English. "And can you imagine, this very same C. Urtl Eviant now works for the Foreign Service as a cultural attaché somewhere, probably as a spy for his native Iceland."

"How do you know all this, Ezra?"

"Easy. Research is my profession," then he paused and added, "which is a fancy synonym for nosiness."

Gafni smiled. He remembered looking up the review of *The Yemenite Girl* in the *Oshkosh Sentinel,* the bad review that Shultish happily, even gloatingly, cited. And, as Gafni suspected, guess who wrote it? Gafni resisted an impulse to tease Shultish now. No, it wouldn't be nice, especially after Shultish's long journey to Poland to wish him a *refu'e shleyme.*

9

EINSTEIN'S SAYING

GAFNI lay in his room — his visitors gone — savoring a momentary blessing of peace and well-being he knew would not last, for nothing lasts, except man's final act.

No one in the room. It was good to be alone for a while. He remembered Einstein saying, "God does not play dice with the universe," thereby assuring the public that the world is orderly, predictable, and under — if not divine then at least — cosmic control. Then, about a century later, along came Stephen Hawking who quips, "Not only does God play dice with the universe ... " pause for dramatic effect, " ... he throws away the dice." Replaying the line, Gafni realized that this was his own, perhaps better, formulation. What Hawking really said was, "Sometimes he throws them where we can't see them," which added enigma to the uncertainty, and perhaps a little hope that the dice will someday be found.

The impact of Hawking's remark was that not only was the universe disorderly (as proven by its inconsiderate and continuous expansion), but that the cosmic controller was an irresponsible clown. And if indeed clown, Gafni thought, what kind of costume did he wear? Moreover, like a good clown, he was inconsistent. He didn't put on the same show twice.

Which reminded Gafni to look up at the tv box for a moment, wondering if something magical would come on again. He looked, gazed, stared — but the screen was blank and grey.

What was he thinking? Yes, he didn't put on the same show twice. For instance, black holes would sometimes leak radiation, sometimes not. What's more, matter too could escape from them. Black holes undermined law and order in the universe. Hawking couldn't say how, Gafni recalled. He only asserted they did.

"The truth is in the mathematics," Hawking said with apt finality. A black hole, the physicist contended, was also mortal. A typical black hole would last trillions of years, which brought Gafni back again to the question of apparent immortality here in Warsaw. All this physics — and metaphysics — put Gafni's little world into doubt. If, as some postmodernist physicists argued, the universe was made of invisible strings in a six- (or was it nine-?) dimensional universe; if, theoretically, time could reverse itself; and if we could relive our past and change events — then all the order in the universe could be chucked out the window.

Such displacements meant that Gafni could participate in two different events simultaneously (you'll soon see how), and that a later event could precede an earlier one. This would confirm the midrashic comment regarding verses in the Torah that seem to defy chronological order: "There is no former or latter in the Torah" — meaning, Don't pay attention to apparent chronological illogicality. And, finally, it also meant that one event could have two different, even opposite, outcomes. There was no longer a choice between A or B. It was A and B. Your team could win and lose. Depends where you sat (and how much you paid for your ticket).

A possible explanation for Gafni why certain events in his life appeared to happen twice; others —not even once. And why there was a disarray in his personal life. If stars could disappear into inexplicable black holes; if astral bodies millions of light years away could swallow stars larger than the planet Jupiter — it was no surprise that Gafni himself, to the consternation of family and friends, was out of orbit; why Mozart and Yankl Shtroy and Yankl Shtroy's friends could defy laws that most of nature lived by. Immortality. Not to die. If Hawking could put gravity into his back pocket; if Einstein could bend time; if one atom could be in two places at the same time — then little glitches and pecadillos of a simple human being, like autographing books on the third floor of the University of Israel Library, or even marrying a *shikse*, could be explained and certainly excused.

So much for Einstein.

So much for dice.

The singular of which is die.

10

SOMETHING TO CHEER HIM UP

THE next Sunday Malina came, found him sitting in a chair. She gave him a perfunctory peck on the cheek, asked how we was, but paid no attention to his response.

"I have to be either fibrillated or defibrillated. One of the two." Then he added, "I thought you'd bring the boy."

That she heard.

"Again the boy? He has a name."

"You know how long I haven't seen him?"

"The him has a name."

"Don't test me."

My God, he thought. She gets bigger each time I see her. Maybe she ate the boy.

"You're looking at me with hatred in your eyes," she said.

"It's just the glasses," he said.

"You're not wearing glasses."

Gafni sighed. Why does she become so vehement so quickly?

"The boy. Him. He has a name, for goodness sake."

So did Batsheva, for goodness sake, he didn't say.

"I told you. Don't test me."

Malina noted his thinned, pale face and backed off.

"Janusz is with the babysitter. The hospital is afraid to let little ones in. You know, infections. The things that fly in the air in hospitals."

Give him mercury, he thought, for protection.

"But I brought you pictures instead." She placed an album on his lap.

Gafni regarded his wife. A glass wall, no, not a wall, a thick glass cube separated them. Everything about her had changed. Her size, personality, demeanor. A dybbuk, and not a Jewish one, had arrogated Malina.

He closed his eyes for a moment, then focused his gaze on the blank tv screen, the recent locus of so many strange images.

You should have seen her just two years ago, before the birth of our child, Gafni told an unseen interviewer. With that puffy face, all her allure is gone. But at least after I go, if I go, I can rest in peace, secure that no one will want her. Just take a peek at our marriage photos, where I'm watching her signing the document and she holds the eleven carnations that a priest friend of hers had given her.See her saying, Admire me. Me. Me. Me

But now she looks not like the wife of a renowned professor, but like a cheap washerwoman, an underprivileged, lowclass hausfrau who, instead of a proper diet, stuffs herself on pasta, spuds and Polish pierogies. All of which she soon resembles.

"Here. Look what I brought you. What you asked for. What I promised I'd bring you. What you were looking at the night I came home."

"I was?"

"Yes. My God, don't you remember anything?"

"No ... Well ... Maybe vaguely. A remembering that is not remembering."

"What is that supposed to mean?"

Gafni didn't answer.

"So I brought it to you to look at again."

"All right," he said, but he wasn't sure it was all right. His stomach tightened; he didn't know why. It felt the same as when she said "Lodz" last week and he replied, "I've been to Lodz a few times."

Gafni turns pages absently until he sees what he sees.

He has seen this before, but wind from another planet had sprinkled him with the stellar dust of forgetfulness.

Still, his mind may forget, but not his heart, the seat of memory.

We have seen, you have seen, what he has seen, but like a photographer making a portrait of an important subject takes the same shot over and over again, we shall do the same. This too is too important to shoot only once.

When Gafni's eyes slide across the picture, he sinks into the valley and, alone in the valley of the shadow of death, lets out a feral cry. We don't know if the cry is heard. Maybe yes; maybe no. But Gafni hears it. Like the man in the photo, this scene should be shot, again and again.

And again the sour, gut-tightening darkness in him, but now it is not fear of being discovered. It is the terror of discovery. A column of dark, firm as thick black smoke, the impenetrable Egyptian darkness, stands like a living creature in him. But unlike last time, in Malina's apartment, now he has the strength that Mozart and Yankl Shtroy have infused into him like a beneficent elixir, and he can, at least for now, battle the darkness, ascend from the valley.

"What's the matter?" he heard.

He couldn't, wouldn't, say, although "apaP, apaP" repeats and repeats in his ear.

From the swirl, the dark spin of meadow, now tinged with

roseate light, Gafni's head clears.

Oh, my God, went through his mind. Is this what Yankl Shtroy told me to come back to? And he re-read Yankl Shtroy's Yiddish message from the fiery letters that now trailed across the upper space of the room.

"Your face is flushed," Malina observed.

A nurse looked in.

At once Malina got him a glass of cold water. He drank slowly.

"Who is that?" He pointed. He sensed, he knew, but he wanted to be sure.

"My father."

"Where is he?"

"I told you he's dead."

"He's not."

"What do you mean he's not?"

"I can tell."

Malina gave a sarcastic laugh. "You can look at a photo and tell if a person is alive or dead?"

"Yes."

"How?"

"Hard to explain. But I'm never wrong. A dead man in a photo has a glaze in his eyes. Even if he's smiling. Your father is alive. Where is he?"

"I don't know."

Shmulik looked at her skeptically. She looked guilty, vulnerable. Guilt vibrated in her, like tiny springs in motion.

"That is, I can't tell. He's in hiding."

"So I am right, see? He's not dead."

"Shh." She looked around although there was no one in the room. "That's what everyone is supposed to think."

"Why?"

"Because the authorities, agents, the secret police, all are still after him. He's on their list. The communists have long memories. Even if they're not in power anymore. These communists shed their politics like a snake sheds its skin, but they remain communists with fangs deep within … He had a little shoe shop after the war … "

"You told me he was a railway inspector."

"That came later."

Gafni felt his heart pounding somewhere outside himself.

"The communists wanted to nationalize his store. He resisted. They accused him of hiding his stock. But could never prove it or find it. So he's on their list. For that and other things."

Shmulik thought for a while. Tried to calm his pumping heart, his racing thoughts where words barely had time to form sentences.

"Wait a minute. Now I remember. When we met, you told me that your father died. Something about a construction accident in Lodz."

"I was thinking of the man I called my father because he actually raised me. That was my uncle. I didn't want to talk about my real father. To protect him."

"But you said he was a railway inspector."

"He was. Both of them were. That's how they met."

"So first he's dead, then he's your uncle, then he's dead again, and then he's in hiding."

"Stop tormenting me," she screamed at him. That same tone in her voice he had heard before.

"And if he was your uncle, then your father is related to him. So how could have they met as railway inspectors?"

"I'm not going to answer that question. Did it ever dawn on you that it's an uncle on my mother's side? And what difference does it make to you if he's dead or alive and in hiding? Did you ever take an interest in my family before? Have you ever once, even once, asked about them? So what difference should it make now?"

"No difference at all." Gafni tried to control the edge of his voice. "But you should tell me the truth. You shouldn't keep anything from me ... Is his name Gryszinski?"

"How do you know?"

"I know everything."

Malina's face became smaller, contorted, lips pressed, nostrils straight, eyes constricted before she screamed again. "You're a spy. An informer. KGB. Secret police. That's why you know everything. They also know everything."

"Why did you take your mother's name?"

"None of your business. It was simpler ... "

"Yes, of course." Now it was his turn for sarcasm. "Przeskovska is much simpler than Gryszinski."

She stalked out of the room and slammed the door.

Only then did the full impact of his discovery penetrate his heart. He began shaking. He pressed one hand with the other to stop the quivering but it did not help. The chair shook, the room trembled, the entire city quaked.

Gafni didn't want to look at that repulsive face again, but he could not restrain himself.

Yes, it was he.

His wife's father. His father-in-law. He shuddered. He could not imagine the pain. Not his pain. His father's.

Shmulik Gafni thought of the two grandfathers his little boy had. He held his head in his hands and wanted to cry. He knew he should cry, but he could not. Gafni wanted to cry, to weep like a child, to pour out all his grief in tears and in self-pity.

He looked up. The fiery letters were gone.

Only the knot, double knotted, in his stomach remained.

And then she was back.

"Oh, and I wanted to tell you that in case you have to call me at the university, they don't know me as Malina. I'm using my given name, Christiana."

"Christiana?"

"Yes, Christiana, you heard me right. Christiana. My first name, my given name, my birth name, my primary name, my Christian name. Play with the symbolism if you like."

On one side of his brain the photo; on the other, Christiana. Each was taking baby steps to the little crossbridge where they would meet and fuse.

Oh, how he wanted to take a firebrand and hurl it at them both as they met, the cursed father and Christiana. But he had no strength.

"But I thought that … " he said feebly.

"That what?"

He tried to get up from the chair but fell back into it.

As if his finger on her pulse, he felt the thump thump of her impatience. Saw the cold flicker in her eye, an enemy who radiated a cold, impersonal hatred.

"That … that with your love of Yiddish you would distance yourself from your roots … Why did you do it? Raise Christiana. Bury Malina."

"Because I'm a goy. Goya. *Shikse.* Christian. Catholic. Polish. Primitive. Don't forget that. And so is Janusz, despite the snipping."

"What's happened to you, Malina? How you've changed … Why? Why?"

Gafni was replaying the film. He had had this conversation before. A man cannot be buried twice, as Yankl Shtroy said, but he can have the same conversation again and again.

"Because … because … " she exploded, moving to the door now. "Because I love Yiddish but I hate Jews."

"How can you love one without the other?"

"You asked me that once, but I'll tell you again … Easy: I'm a goy."

He stared at the empty doorway and closed his eyes.

With all his strength he shouted after her:

"The mercury has gone to your brain. This is not you, Malina."

But he knew it was.

The two marching images on his eyelids met, walked through each other, and exchanged places.

11

WHAT ONE DOES WHEN ONE DISCOVERS THE END OF THE WORLD HAS COME

What should I do now?

12

WHAT IS THAT DARKNESS?

WHAT is that darkness, that solid column of what seems like soot, thick and black, with a snakelike life of its own, rising from the hospital chimney?

It is umber overflowing from Shmulik Gafni's soul.

Back down two floors to Gafni's room.

First he dreamt he walked through Malina's photo album. Why that happened was a mystery. Worry causes dreams; wishes prompt them. He neither worried about nor wished for her pictures. Yet he dreamed about her album as if a virus from far away had infe(c)(s) ted him. In real life, pictures move as the hand turns the pages. In dream, Gafni moved. He was not as small as Mozart in his dream but his normal size. The album was huge and he walked through it, as if it were a museum with temporary walls. Instead of turning pages, he just walked through them. In dreams we sometimes see more clearly. But sometimes faces are unmarked, fuzzy, like an out-of-focus photograph, like the tenth man in the Warsaw shul. So why this peregrination through a photo album if the pictures were unclear? He was also amazed that the massive album had empty spaces; it meant snapshots had been removed, as if on temporary loan to another museum. That's why he dreamt what he dreamt: to be aware of negative space.

When Gafni awoke he had a desire, a hunger for seeing that album. He had never seen photographs of her family before, never wanted to. He had never asked. She had never offered.

Now the appetite was stirred.

But he didn't have a chance to ask. Malina came, a knapsack slung over her shoulder.

"Remember, you once said you'd like to see pictures of me and my family when I was younger? My sister finally found the album in a corner of the attic."

"That's nice," Gafni said flatly. He didn't remember asking for pictures. Had she seen his dream?

She opened her knapsack.

"Here it is," she said. "It has the pictures you asked about."

Was it cold in the room, or was the chill in her voice?

His face showed none of the enthusiasm he knew she'd be

assessing. When people turn pages in a photo album their eyes usually glow. But Gafni might as well have held a stick mask to his face; that's how much emotion he displayed. He looked abstractedly, lips pinched, turning the old black cardboard pages. He felt as if somewhere, somewhen, he had done this deed before and was now winding up a film that had once been screened. The small black-and-white photos were slipped into the black triangular paste-on corners he remembered from his childhood. As he turned the pages, he recalled his dream, walking through the life-size album. But here he had to turn the pages. He didn't even look up as a nurse came in to fluff up the pillows behind his back. But he knew it was Irena by the warmth she radiated, the erotic wavelength that connected her to him as her hand briefly touched his shoulder. "Thanks," he said softly. Seeing that he had a visitor, she did not put her fingers on his face. It took Gafni a moment or two to undo the effect of her presence. Then back to the snapshots. The photographs were old, men and women and children, mostly in stiff stern formal poses, occasionally a boy or girl outdoors, a house in the background. One showed a young boy, perhaps eight or nine, wearing a little cap, with thin lips like Malina's staring into the camera, his hand above his eyes, shielding them from the sun, but squinting nevertheless.

"Who's this?"

"My father. Probably age six or seven."

"He looks older here."

Malina shrugged.

"He looks like you."

"You mean I look like him."

"That's what I meant."

Gafni was tired, wanted to put the album away, didn't know why he was looking at it in the first place, all these goyishe faces, not his people. He didn't recall asking to see the album. But then why the dream and why did she bring the album, as if putting a coda to the dream? But something, the same willpower that had been his second soul for decades, drove him on and he turned the pages, looking for pictures of Malina. Bored and excited at the same time, he wondered what she looked like when she was ten or twelve.

Why do we do things? Either because we want to or are impelled to. Or driven to. Or bidden to. Or hypnotized to. Or as little Mozart said: destined to. With Gafni it was all of the above. A force beyond his control told him to turn the pages and he thought it was his own volition, blindly seeing the black-and-white images, and off in a corner of his vision he saw the tiny figure of Mozart. Then a stormwind came, stopped his hand, and Gafni at one and the same time wanted no more of these faded pictures with their impassive joyless detestable faces, and yet yearned, no, yearned is too strong, was curious to see more of these bland meaningless predictably posed snapshots of stiff people he didn't know, didn't care to know, a conglomeration of goyim who more than likely had a gut hatred of Jews —

Until.

Stop for a moment. Full stop.

Why was he in the hospital? Let's (not) mix up cause and effect. He was in the hospital not only because of his heart but because of the pictures he had seen in Malina's apartment. But now, in the hospital, he was reliving an event which had already taken place, proving right the theoretical physicists who study the cosmos and contend that, with string theory, opposing events, contradictory happenings, can take place once and twice, consecutively and simultaneously. But Gafni had already reviewed that a few days ago, when Malina was here last time. Two contradictory events, positive and negative forces, can occur at the same time.

Until.

He turned — walked through — the page.

"Who is this?"

It was rhetorical.

He didn't hear her answer. Thought she said, "My son," but that could not be. She had had no children before him.

It made no difference what she said. She could have remained silent. She could have said, Goliath. She could have spoken in silence. The blood that ceased flowing in his veins was response enough. Perhaps he heard her answer as a faint echo, a muted trumpet. But the heart hears better. The heart hears words not spoken. How right you are, Gafni thought, dear, tiny, incredible Mozart, perhaps a creature of my repeated dreams, my waking fantasy. But no, you are real. Now a full-sized man. I can still taste the *schlag* in the coffee at your Café Mozart in Vienna.

Then everything reversed. His blood unfroze; he could not hear. His heart beat rapidly; he saw Malina and the walls moving rapidly, as if still photos were changing quickly, like in the first moving pictures. Scenes were mixed up and a wave of fear, no, terror, overtook him. What was to stop him from expiring right now?

"What do you see?"

"See?"

"What have you seen? You are so agitated. Shall I call a nurse? You are not yourself."

"Who is? Who is oneself?"

"Tell me." For the first time in months he heard a tone of pity in her voice.

He thought of iron. He thought of steel. He thought of iron and steel and infused their essence into himself. Along with touch. Batsheva's embrace. Irena/Galit's four fingers on his face. The tender hug of Yankl Shtroy. The press of Mozart's hands. He looked at the white enameled iron of the old hospital bed.

"Who is that?" pointing to a picture of a man, his voice so calm it could only be called miraculous.

"My father."

"I thought he was dead," he said.

"But on the picture he's alive."

"Obviously ... "

She looked back over his head. Gafni continued:

"Remember, I once told you that your face looked familiar. First time I met you, I think."

"Yes."

"I see the resemblance ... Where is he?"

"In Lodz."

Iron and steel. Inhale, infuse their essence.

"Bring him here."

"Why?"

"I'd like to meet him. Finally, After all this time. He's my father-in-law, right? Janusz's grandfather."

"So you do know the little one's name."

"Of course. Will you bring him?"

"All right."

Her answer, her affirmative, surprised, astonished him.

Those two words were a bit of light for Gafni, even though a column of dark, firm as black soot, Egyptian darkness one could seize with one's hands, stood like a living creature within him.

Malina left.

Gafni winked to Yankl Shtroy.

Samson stands between the pillars, Shmulik imagined.

Yankl Shtroy winked back, not from the tv screen.

13

WHAT EMOTIONS RAN THROUGH GAFNI'S BLOOD

WHAT emotions ran through Gafni's blood, where feelings course, pumping oxygen and adrenaline, when he sees him. When he opens his eyes and sees him sitting there. A fusion of disbelief and rage, a mixed bag of sensations. When he sees him. When he sees him he could have leaped onto his throat with a bestial rage like a lion deprived of a cub and taken blood. But, surprisingly, the rage subsided and a strange calm, a muted nervous energy, came over Gafni when he sees him. Here is what he was waiting for all his life. No more hunting. No more Kielce. No more travels, disguise, pretense. No more Lodz. What he is waiting for all his life since ... since ... since ...

Then.

What should he do now? Certainly not reveal himself. Not show any agitation. But how control the twitching muscles, the quick, arrythmic heart, the black mist quavering like a toppling cylinder within? Not show any emotion. Not give, not give him, not give him cause to flee.

Had become old the murderer, but unmistakable was the grizzled, weather-worn face. Like the faces of homeless men Gafni had seen in New York. His now grey white hair still stood up like sharpened little knives, and the hateful look in his watery blue eyes still burned with an undying fire.

"I'm Christiana's father. Gryszinski, Janusz," he said in Polish in a low voice, looking at Gafni as his eyes opened from sleep. "She told me you were sick."

Christiana? Who is that? Gafni wondered. Maybe it was a mistake after all.

"She told me you wanted to meet me."

"Christiana?"

"Yes. Christiana."

Christiana? He wondered again. Who is she?

"Who is Christiana?" Gafni finally said.

"My daughter, Christiana. Don't you know her name?" the father said slowly, as if talking to a baby or a sick old man. "Who married Samuel Gafni," he added, with as much irony as he was capable of.

"I thought her name was Malina."

"That's her middle name. I named her after Christ."

So that's her name, he thought. Christiana.

The man looked around the room.

"You must be a pretty bigshot to get a private room here. People like us get put in a ward with twenty beds."

The best retort, Gafni knew, was silence. He bored his gaze into the space between Malina's father's eyes.

Then Gafni pounced.

"And how is welding?"

"Fine," the man said quickly, taken off guard.

For a moment they looked at each other. Something silent, immutable, passed between them. It did not start with one then pass to the other. It began midway between them, like a spark between two filaments, by the white enamel bend of the iron bed frame, and surged like an electric charge to both at once. That silence bound them. Time stood still, like on a photograph where two men are seen and no one can know their next move. It could have gone either way. Janusz could have left. Gafni could have sprung forward. Only the earth turns and a thick column of soot rises from the hospital chimney. A slow fire burned in Janusz's eyes, but one swift motion by Gafni tamped the flame for a second, like a deer blinded by light, and a flick of fear pulsed in the other man's eyes.

"How do you know about welding?"

"I know everything."

The man thrust his head back against the chair as though an unseen stormwind were pressing against his face, chin, neck. "Yes, Jews know everything."

"I also know Kielce."

Then kinesis overtook Gafni, his entire life a rehearsal for this moment. One could count the seconds it took him to get out of bed and do what he had to do, what he planned to do, what he dreamt to do, what his entire destiny destined him to do.

He pressed the buzzer.

Who would be on duty? he wondered. Let it be Irena, he hoped; Irena, he prayed.

Irena approached.

"What's the matter, Shmulik?"

"Nothing, Irena," he told her softly in Yiddish, "but please shut the door after you leave." He pressed her hand and half-closed his right eye in a wink.

Irena pressed back.

SHMULIK lies in the bed and the murderer sits in the chair, free as a bird, pretending concern for his daughter's Jew husband, that *parshiver zhid.* He wishes he could take the Jew's IV and wrap it around his throat. All Jews are the same. They belong underground. Burning in hell.

And Gafni, knowing who the other man is, for he is not blind, just weak, prays like the sightless Samson in the Philistines' temple, asks God for one last burst of energy to strike down the man he's spent more than half a lifetime pursuing.

God answers.

In one swirl of blurred arms and legs, Gafni leaps out of bed, unhooks his IV and wraps it around the murderer's neck, so surprised is he to see a figure in white suddenly rushing at him that now he is the one paralyzed, enfeebled and feckless, and Gafni, in one swift movement, pulls the plastic cord until he has   the murderer to death, "choked" or "strangled" is the missing verb in the empty space, done the deed slowly, so that the killer knew what was coming and could do nothing about it. And Gafni, in avenging his father and his uncle and all the Jews who were murdered, a surge of life comes into him, the life of Polish Jews after July 1946, the immortality that none could understand and none explain.

Then Gafni removed the IV, took off his gown, went to the closet, dressed and, with gossamer steps, walked away. He felt like the Hebrew letters he had seen ascending from the *chazzen*'s mouth to the top of the Holy Ark and the other letters he had seen in the upper space of this room. Gafni was an *aleph*, an *ayin*, a *yud*. He took a deep breath and entered.

It was not a tunnel of darkness. It was not a tunnel of light. You know what? It wasn't a tunnel at all. Little Mozart held his left hand and the now bigger Mozart his right. On the one hand he had his father; on the other, his mother. Hand in hand they walked. In the first hand he held his beloved Batsheva. There was no second hand. Forehand, his friends; backhand, his colleagues. Hands in hands as they walked. Autographs of Tolstoy, Chekhov, Dickens, Sholom Aleichem, Mark Twain, others and others, letters emblazoned in fire, like the flying Hebrew letters he had once seen in the Warsaw shul, lit his way. The praise that presidents had given him for his sound advice was background music. The talking dogs he had met years ago outside of Safed yipped merrily. Hand in hand, hands in hands, they marched forward into what wasn't a tunnel of darkness, a tunnel of light. It wasn't a tunnel at all. As they walked, Mozart, both this one and that one, said, "You will hear music again. You will never stop hearing music," which is another reason why there was a smile on Gafni's face. What Gafni entered, not a tunnel at all, was a ripe fragrant fig. The flesh of the fig was pink and buff, but the pink had subtle shades of garnet, mauve and rose blush. But what was most amazing was the perfume, the sweet scent of the fig, so heavenly, the deeper he breathed, the deeper he wanted to breathe the sweet perfume that Adam breathed when the entire earth and fullness thereof was bathed with the fragrance of the fig that ethereal Sixth Day, that fig that was on the celestial tree that Adam was forbidden to eat, that fig perfume from the Tree of Life that Gafni now breathed deeply, once and twice, as he entered once and twice again a shaft of light that wasn't a tunnel at all, but a fragrant path that was all fig perfume and sunrise.

14

WHY THE BIRD LAUGHS, THE CROW CROWS, THE RAVEN CAWS

At end revenge rises like a bird laughing, mocking, a crow cawing darkly, all the ravens of the world urging him to get up, Gafni up, up, now, now, up, caw, caw, up Gafni, up up up.

Shmulik knew that the mind often runs a preview of events to come, events that at times come true and at times are just wishful thoughts, the preview being the antithesis to memory. But here, now, he had not the luxury of planning or dreamwishing the event, of sorting it out, refining the details, and then acting.

Now he acted without mental blueprint, leaping out of bed with such grace, speed, will, that the nurses would talk of this for months to come until it became a legend in the hospital, and even now as he moved, was moving, moves the few feet to the easy chair where his visitor sat, he tore off his IV and sprang toward his father's murderer with a roar heard throughout Warsaw. Gafni's hands did not pause. They did not stop from the moment he unhooked himself from the IV and, plastic tubing in hand, saying only three words: "Kielce. July. 1946," as he wound the elastic cord around the man's throat until his eyes bulged, his face blue, then purple, and finally his black lifeless tongue hanging like a dead snake from his death-darkened black lips.

15

IRENA, I DID IT FOR YOU, TO BE PROUD OF ME

ONCE again, again and again, once more, the Pole — history repeats itself, almost like a film, same events but with different players, or same players different events — lifts his hand, fingers clutching the axe, all this Shmulik sees, a fusion of now and eidetic memory, and wants to split the skull of the Jew who quickly takes from under his pillow, we do not know, actually do not care, if the handle is studded with pearls, the prepared pistol, a Magnum, used but reliable, and fires it once, once is all it takes, no more than once, into the heart of the murderer, who had nothing there in the middle of his chest except some indeterminate glob of flesh, certainly nothing that any normal person would call a heart. The Pole's upraised arm drops at once, the axe still up in the air, which, obeying gravity, falls freely and lands on his skull, who said that just desserts are no longer served? When the nurses hear the noise, the commotion, the roar, the howl of wind that came from unseen corners, running they come from their hiding places. One covers her mouth and screams. Another, seeing blood, applies first aid, though last rites would be more appropriate. Another fixes, fiddles, with Shmulik's IV, although there is really nothing to adjust. She just does it to keep busy, to calm her nerves. But when Shmulik opens his eyes, nurses vanish, axe gone, no one in chair.

16

WHEN GAFNI SEES THE FACE HE KNEW SO WELL

JUST as a man has two hands, Gafni had two purposes in Poland: life and death. Like two trees in Eden, one for life, the other knowledge. But the trees were opposites. Sort of. Not like night and day. More like night and dawn. Not like black and white. More like black and grey. Life — good, great. Knowledge — iffy. Once man tasted from the Tree of Knowledge death ensued. Eternal life no more. Hence knowledge sometimes equals death. But Jews have made knowledge life.

When Gafni sees the face of his father's murderer, the face he knew so well from memories, the face whose every crevice he got to know from nightmares that creased his sleep; when he saw that evil man who represented every mistake that man and God had made; when he saw that face in the same room where he lay, sitting opposite him, so at ease in the easy chair, the living grandfather of his circumcised boy, Gafni's heart gave out.

But not his brain.

For his brain had capital thoughts and plans not easily snuffed out by such a mundane act as passing.

17

DEPARTING WHERE HE WANTED TO DEPART

Yes, Gafni died in Warsaw, which he wanted to do, but his daughters — while Malina was in Lodz teaching; that's right, she didn't call every day — with the quiet help of the Israel Embassy in Warsaw and El Al Airlines

18

IN HIS TINY *CHEVRA KADISHA* OFFICE

IN his tiny *Chevra Kadisha* office (to the guy reading over your shoulder, it's the Jewish Burial Society) in Warsaw, Yankl Shtroy sat and mused. That Shmulik Gafni, the only outsider to know Polish Jewry's magnificent secret and witness its little unknown miracles, was dead there was no doubt. One did not need a second opinion. The *problema* was what to do with him. To be precise, where to bury him, for few other options remained. That was one of the problems with Shmulik Gafni, poor man, he so wanted to live like us. The other — and there were many conflicting reports — was whether he had died in Warsaw and, as some say, after his twin daughters had flown in from Israel, was quickly shipped back to Tel Aviv with the quiet help of the Israel Embassy and El Al Airlines, without his missus knowing, for the only phone number they had for Malina was her Warsaw apartment where the phone rang rang, cawr cawr, rang rang; or whether Gafni had died in Israel after walking out of the hospital and flying straight home to Jerusalem, as some contrarians aver, subsequent to which his request to be buried in his beloved Warsaw was honored.

AFTER the pogrom in Kielce, in July 1946, the Polish army, under Soviet orders, had gathered the victims' bodies and brought them to a morgue in a local cemetery, where they were identified and buried. But then Gafni had his father reburied in Warsaw, next to his father — and that is where Gafni wanted to lie, in the old cemetery where the poor were buried. The guess was that Gafni had died in Israel, but since truth is what we are after — strange, but both Gafni and Yankl Shtroy knew Cicero's remark: the first rule of history is not to lie; the second is not to be afraid of the truth. And since that surely is not one of our fears — everything you read is the God's honest truth, which is a triple redundancy or pleonasm, for those of you who love words that few others know — for it is truth we disseminate and not, God forbid, fiction — we give the probability/possibility as well. But pleonastic or not, the God's honest truth was, and Yankl Shtroy didn't know this yet but soon will, was that Gafni had indeed died in Warsaw, was quickly trans-shipped for burial in Israel, but the coffin, oddly, bought a round trip.

So the problem, now that Gafni was definitely, finally and uncontrovertibly here, and absitively and posolutely gone, was where to bury him. Let's make that sentence shorter, without introductions and (r)(v)isible modifiers: where to bury Gafni.

MALINA woke up only after she finally called the hospital from Lodz to find out how Shmulik was doing.

She was told he wasn't.

"We've been calling your apartment for two days. Aren't you ever at home?" said the hospital administrator, a woman with a raspy smoker's voice.

"I'm in Lodz."

"Why didn't you tell us?" the woman scolded. "We didn't know you were there. You didn't leave us your number. What kind of business is this that a close relative or a wife doesn't leave an emergency contact number? Aren't you interested in knowing how your late husband is doing?"

"Mind your business! And don't lecture me!" Then she screamed, "Late? Did I hear you say late? The doctors said he was doing well."

"Well, now he isn't doing at all. Go listen to doctors. This is a hospital, lady. Doctors lie. To please the family. Everyone knows that in a Polish hospital you always check first with the business office … Yes, he's late. Very. Even later than that."

"They said he was in no immediate danger."

"And they're absolutely right. He's not in any danger at all. And don't don't apologize to me, lady."

Malina snorted. "I'm not apologizing and have no intention of doing so. So get that idiotic notion out of your head … When did it happen?"

"What?"

"What do you mean what? What are we talking about?"

"Your not calling. Or leaving an emergency contact number."

"What is your name, madame? I'm going to report you. When did my husband be … become late, you, you … ?"

"Two days ago."

"Where is he?" Malina screeched.

"Aha! So now you want to know, huh?"

"Yes. Where is he?"

"Don't you know?"

"No … I … Don't … Know … If I knew I wouldn't be asking you and be involved in this ridiculous, absurd, and stupid conversation."

"In Israel." Oh, the joy of malice in the woman's voice as she said, "Israel."

Malina shrieked so loudly the woman at the other end pulled the phone away from her ear.

"Who took him back?"

"Well, if you want to listen to me now, without shrieking your head off and without insulting me, I'll tell you. That's the problem. He may have gone on his own."

"What?"

"You're shrieking. I told you not to shriek. Not to scream. Not to shout. Otherwise, I hang up."

"He went on his own? My late husband?"

"When he went he wasn't late. And if he was, then his daughters took him back. It's still not clear — but it's under investigation."

"I don't believe this. His daughters? How did his daughters get involved?"

"Well, you weren't here, you know," the woman said sweetly. "They are relatives of some kind or other."

"Shut up, you bitch. He wanted to be buried in Poland."

Both women looked into the mouthpiece, waiting. The silence hummed pretty loudly too.

"Well, why don't you answer me?"

"You told me to shut up, remember, sweetie?"

Malina shrieked, groaned, raged into the telephone.

"It's out of our hands now," the administrator said.

And both hung up on each other at the same time.

FAT as she was, a demonic engine in her suddenly ignited, cranked up with a quick clockwise motion like the early model cars, or with a swift, sharp tug on the cord, like an old-fashioned motor.

Soon in Warsaw, driving like crazy, she called a press conference — an anti-Israel stance always attracted the media — accusing Israel and the family in Israel of "kidnapping my beloved husband from his rightful burial in Warsaw, as was the fondest wish of my late, lamented spouse."

Malina made sure to hold her child while she was on camera.

When she produced a copy of the will, which showed black-on-white that Gafni wanted to be buried in Warsaw, with an official Polish translation, she won the sympathy of all the media (they showed the relevant paragraph, enlarged, in all the papers) and the hearts of her countrymen.

THEN the will was shown on Israel television and printed on page one of all the Israeli dailies. When Malina filed suit in Jerusalem to have Gafni reimported to Warsaw, do you think the judge had much of a choice? The lawyer engaged by the Gafni family requested a stay, saying that Gafni must have been out of his mind, influenced by his Polish wife. How could a Jew, whose entire family was murdered in Poland, and whose father and uncle were brutally murdered by Poles after the war, possibly want to lie in Polish soil? But the Jerusalem judge reluctantly, even though he sympathized with the concerns of the Gafni children, ordered that the dead man's wishes be obeyed — for a man's will, properly witnessed and written of his own free, yes, here comes the word again, will, must be honored. It follows Jewish and civil law. There was no indication that Shmulik Gafni was in any way coerced, pressured or unduly influenced in his decision; nor was it shown that he was in any way (for the fancy-footed, tango-dancing intellectuals) cerebrally compromised, (for the middle-of-the-road, waltzing middlebrows) mentally unhinged, or (for the rocking, twisting hoi-polloi) had a screw or two loose.

So back he came.

THE simple pine box, shipped from Israel, came with a certificate of authenticity, authenticating its contents, authoritatively stamped by the authorities, and in three languages too: in English, for the international community, in Hebrew, since the "late, lamented" exported item originated in Israel, and in Yiddish, in honor of Yiddish culture's greatest son, popularly called the King of Yiddish, may he rest in peace, *olev ha-sholem*, the international luminary of Yiddish language and literature, the University of Israel's Distinguished University-Wide Overlyfull Professor of Intergalactic Yiddish Studies, Professor Shmulik Gafni, born Weingarten, an *emesser yiddisher nomen,* a true Jewish name, not that concocted Gafni, as fake as a three-zloty coin, as phony as a seven-star general.

Yankl Shtroy sighed. Yiddish, yes. Hebrew, yes. Even English, yes. But not a word of Polish. And this was Poland, the land, the country, the people, the state that was on the receiving end of the shipped goods, its final destination, so to speak — there came his favorite phrase again. And even the *Chevra Kadisha* of Warsaw was not going to bury anybody — no pun intended, stated simply as fact, with utmost respect, feeling and tact — even a Jew, if the sovereignty of Poland was compromised. Not that Yankl Shtroy gave a straw about the sovereignty of Poland, may it be plowed under like a despised and despicable ruin, tfu on it, but the law was the law. And administrative, bureaucratic ma(tt)(nn)ers had to be observed, otherwise the *Chevra Kadisha* would lose its license. The *Chevra Kadisha* could not bury anyone (note the discreet [discrete too] change of pronoun) without showing proof to the Polish authorities, in the language of the country, pure Polish, *po Polsku,* if you will,

Curt Leviant

that the corpse within was authentically, authoritatively and officially dead, in Polish. Patently Polishly popped. Otherwise — *problemas*. And the anti-Semites here, of them no lack, so went the thinking of Yankl Shtroy, would be delighted to cause problems. To be honest (see Cicero's remark, supra), the *Chevra Kadisha* wasn't exactly a busy place. The *Chevra Kadisha* hadn't buried a Polish Jew in years; they were quite out of practice. Thank God there were occasional tourists, visitors, businessman, dignitaries who died, let's say once in a while, that kept the *Chevra Kadisha* going, in practice, so to speak.

So few Jews were there in Poland — although people came out of the closet daily and admitted, or least claimed, they were Jews. So strong was the trend that even goyim, not Jews in hiding for two generations, were alleging they were Jewish. But Yankl Shtroy knew the real reason. Oh, he knew. They couldn't fool him with their "we always knew we were Jewish" song and dance "but were afraid of them, the goyim, so we hid it. Now we're proud," etc etc etc.

We know that Polish Jews have stopped dying. Read that last sentence again. Let it sink in. A seemingly innocuous bunch of letters strung together: Polish Jews have stopped dying. Period. The few thousand left, to spite their tormentors, did not die. Hunted down during the war, informed upon, sold for a bag of sugar and when sugar ran out, betrayed just like that, even by eight-year-olds, without reward, killed even after the war, now something had changed in the bodies of the survivors, a magic potion, an elixir from the Tree of Life, was infused into them and they just kept on living. It wasn't widely known, it didn't make headlines, but some people sniffed it out.

No wonder Poles were coming out and proclaiming they were Jews. L'chaim, they shouted ecstatically on the streets. To life! But no, friends, the boat was full, so to speak. Sorry, old chap, as the Brits would say, we can't take in any more. And to show you we mean business, a sharp *klop* to the clinging fingers at the rim of the lifeboat, not with the flat side of the oar, mind you, but with the sharp side, like an axe. "You tell me, l'chaim, I'll tell you, l'goyim," Yankl Shtroy muttered. If you can't figure out what that means, don't ask me. I don't know either. The Poles were going to extreme lengths, anything to outwit the Angel of Death, even saying they were Jews. To avoid extreme unction, pious Poles were even ready to say, to gargle, to choke on the words, "Aaghh, I'm a Jew."

But back to Gafni. As mentioned, there were rules and regulations, and the anti-Semites would be delighted to cause problems. We said it once before, now we say it a second time: Repeating a truth does not detract from its veracity.

From the coffin, no sounds. No talking, no whispers, no pleas, no scratching, banging, pounding, kicking. Not even an occasional polite tap-tap. On second thought, for Yankl Shtroy the lack of a document in Polish was not that problematic. He might, well, let's say it forthrightly, he would be able to get around it. What was more worrisome was who would be at the gravesite when Gafni was buried in the Jewish cemetery, where a Polish Jew hadn't been buried in ages. That the Germans did not destroy. They were too busy killing Poland's three million Jews, helped on occasion by the locals. The murdered Jews did not have cemeteries. The air of Poland, holding the windblown ashes of the Jews, was their cemetery, as were the roads paved with their burnt bones.

Too bad Shmulik Gafni did not stay in Warsaw. Yankl Shtroy remembered how Shmulik had burst into tears when he told how his father had been murdered in Kielce more than a year after the war, and that had prompted him, Yankl Shtroy, and his eight or nine old men to share their secret, which Gafni, *olov ha-sholem* and God rest his soul, had kept until his dying day, and whom the Warsaw dailies, weekly news-magazines, popular gossip rags and tv programs were full of this last week, making a national celebrity of him in anticipation of his funeral tomorrow, which with all the dignitaries and bigshots planning to attend was more like a state funeral. Had Gafni stayed in Poland, he too would have lived forever. But he chose to live in Israel and be buried in Poland, reversing the centuries-old tradition of Jews living in Poland and in their old age making the journey to Jerusalem to die and be buried in the Holy Land, for according to folk belief, at resurrection the dead in the Land of Israel would be the first to regain life and would not have to suffer the discomforts of rolling underground for weeks until they reached the Land of Israel. And only afterwards, when all the revived Jews who had been buried in Eretz Yisroel had already established little businesses and opened shops, kiosks, and resumed their crafts and trades in the thriving market (dry-cleaning of earth-stained shrouds a possible leading enterprise), and inns and hotels to accommodate the soon-to-come droves of visitors to Jerusalem, only then would all the other Jews of the world come cruising in underground specials organized by post-resurrection travel agencies (frequent flyer miles not honored at this time) through tunnels and caves and arrive in Israel in a postmortem catatonic state and only then be brought back to life once they set foot in the Land of Israel, too bad all the kiosks and concession stands are already taken.

Shmulik Gafni, Yankl Shtroy supposed, was no shopkeeper. Gafni didn't care about immediate resurrection. He wanted to be buried next to his father, in his beloved Poland, which kicked him out of the university where he had enrolled the year before the war began, after being made to stand in the back of each classroom with all the other Jews, while his Catholic fellow intellectuals sat in their seats and jeered the Jews, and then fleeing his beloved homeland, going east to the Soviet Union, where he fought the Germans first with Polish partisan units who hated and killed Jews, and then with the Russian partisans, and finally returning to Poland and seeing the carnage of July 4, 1946, when he decided that he belonged to another homeland, the homeland of his people's prayers.

Yankl Shtroy had read in local news reports that Gafni's widow, Malina, planned to bury Gafni with fanfare in the newer cemetery, where none of his relatives were buried. The Polish authorities agreed. Gafni wasn't consulted. He wanted to be buried next to his parents. And he surely didn't want cardinals and priests present at the gravesite.

But Yankl Shtroy had a plan. He didn't mind that a Jew was being buried in Warsaw. As a *Chevra Kadisha* member he needed some practice. What bothered him was the presence of the goyim at the cemetery. Not so much the goyim, because after all, goyim can come to a Jewish funeral. But it annoyed him that a cardinal would be there. Who knows? They might slip in a snatch of a requiem. That was the *shikse*'s doing, Yankl Shtroy suspected. And he wasn't going to let a Jew like Gafni, he didn't care how secular or how famous he was, to be buried with one of them present. And cameras and speeches for press coverage as well.

It wasn't as if Yankl Shtroy was a rabbi. Far from it. But he maintained honestly the Jewish tradition, and as head of the *Chevra Kadisha* didn't even want a whiff of Catholicism at the grave. Not even a hint of a whiff. Not even a suspicion of a hint. What are they butting in for? Because Gafni's *shikse* is a Polish Catholic? She wasn't being buried, was she? Or is it because they want to show how liberal they are? How Zionist they are? How pro-Jewish they are? Yankl Shtroy was sure it was the *shikse* who had asked for them. Yes, it was her doing. And anyway, who was organizing this burial? The Polish government or he, the longtime head of the *Chevra Kadisha*? A lifetime position with the Jewish Burial Society, eternal, if you will and so to speak. And who would say Kaddish? The Cardinal? Or maybe the President of Poland, who was there to get some publicity for himself and display his solidarity with Israel now that communism was gone?

All right, so Yankl Shtroy wasn't a rabbi. But at least he was connected. By day, he made a modest living conducting tours of the tiny Warsaw synagogues, mostly for goyim who came from abroad, and for Germans, may the earth swallow them up along with all the murderers, who stood stiffly and unmoved at the restored shuls, and an occasional group of American Jewish youngsters — oh, how the Poles hated them but loved the many Jewish dollars they brought in — who made what Yankl Shtroy called the New Holy Jewish Trinity and Triangle Tour of Jewish Sites of the World: New York, Auschwitz, and Jerusalem, stopping by to imbibe a bit of Polish Jewishness, a vaccination against the ultimate Jewish Polishness experience at the Big A.

Yankl Shtroy had learned a bit of English, and a favorite answer to a favorite question, "How do you make a living?" was: "By not dying," which they laughed at, but who had the last laugh? And by night and in his spare time Yankl Shtroy ran the Warsaw Jewish community's *Chevra Kadisha,* which had nothing to do with Polish Jews except making sure that the old gravestones remained upright, that they would be straightened and repaired after vandals regularly desecrated them, that weeds didn't swallow them up, may the earth swallow up all the enemies of Israel! For although Jewish death in Poland had been turned on its head, the weeds still followed the old tradition and overgrew the tombstones, which his *Chevra Kadisha* took care of.

Yes, nature was turned upside down for Polish Jews. But foreign Jews kept him busy once in a while. If the government knew what was happening with the local Jews, they didn't say. If they knew, they wouldn't advertise it. They didn't want mass immigration of Jews. Six or seven thousand were enough, thank you. And the Jews themselves in their local papers — Cracow, Lodz, Warsaw, Lublin — didn't say a word. Every Jew was sworn to secrecy — without ever taking an oath. It was a natural concomitant, almost genetic, to the phenomenon. There may even have been a bit of superstition to it, a bit of *ayin ho-reh, tfu tfu tfu,* the evil eye, figuring that once the news was in print, the magic would be gone, like Samson's shorn hair, and their permanent longevity would cease, and they would begin dying like flies once again.

Still, somehow word leaked out and Jews came. From Russia. America. Israel. A few from England. Especially the older ones. The old and the sick. Dying to breathe pure Polsku air so they could live. These pilgrims for eternal life were never open about their agenda. They never said a word. As if they too were sworn to secrecy. They sort of, just, like, you know, kind of, so to speak, wanted to come back home after all these years, they so much missed *der alter heim,* their old homeland. But it helped them like a *teytn bankess,* like cupping helps a corpse. They died even quicker. Which gave Yankl Shtroy and his friends something to do.

No wonder all the goyim were flocking to Gafni's funeral. They wanted to see something they hadn't seen in ages, perhaps ever. A dead Jew. An authentically dead Polish Jew. Something not seen in Poland in decades. Since July 1946, Kielce, fourteen months after the war, when the Poles alone, unaided, murdered seventy-six Jewish survivors, may the lifestuff slowly be sucked from them until they choke and their tongues hang out black, Amen!

No wonder they were making a circus out of Shmulik Gafni's funeral. AUTHENTIC POLISH JEW DIES reads the real and imaginary headline in the marquee of Yankl Shtroy's mind. Maybe they were secretly hoping that Gafni's death would break the ice and his fellow Jews in Poland would henceforth be unable to resist imitating him. Yes, that was it. With the cardinal at the head of the delegation, trying to cast an evil eye: *Pater noster*, we humbly invite all Jews to follow in Professor's Gafni's courageous footsteps, Amen.

SHMULIK Gafni arrived safely. He was here, safe and sound. Well, at least safe. But what to do with him now, and before tomorrow, was the problem. A problem Yankl Shtroy and his two assistants would have to solve, and quickly too.

Gafni insisted on being buried in Warsaw, but his wife insisted in involving the Polish government. Those *momzerim*, in order to get publicity for themselves in the newly post-communist era and show how civilized they were, used the poor man's death for their own political purposes, to make themselves kosher in the eyes of the world.

What to do? Yankl Shtroy mused. What to do? What to do? He had lived by his wits so long he hoped that his wits would not desert him now.

He paced the room of his tiny office, hoping that the rhythms of his pacing, four strides to one wall, four to the other, four back — inducing a self-hypnosis with the repeated what to do? what to do? — would inspire a solution to the conundrum.

One thing was certain. He must not let Gafni be buried with them present.

Now that he thinks of it, around the official Polish authentication he will be able to get, with the following ruse. On his official stationery he would type with his pre-war typewriter an official translation of the death certificate, stamped "Official Copy." In Poland, as elsewhere in Europe, the official rubber stamp — the *shtempl* — had a mighty mystic power. And he would put a few flourished signatures beneath his own to get the coffin through the gate. Hmmm, he sang to himself as he paced and saw the walls bouncing before him, this one, that one, this one again. The coffin would get through the gate. Of that there was no doubt. Just as there was no doubt that Shmulik Gafni was dead. Yes, yes, now he had it. The coffin would get through the gate. For the state funeral. Indeed, it was a state funeral, even though it wasn't advertised as such, and was scheduled to take place at 2 pm. And it would take place. The coffin would be there. Now Yankl Shtroy had it. It came to him at once. His wits hadn't deserted him, although he had deserted his witz, having dropped the "witz" from his former name Shtroywitz. Yes, he had lost his witz in Poland; what better place to lose them? Now he had it. Brilliant. The perfect solution. Everyone would be satisfied and happy. Yes, the coffin would be there.

Still, Yankl Shtroy would not, could not, permit a Jew to be buried like that, even though Gafni had gotten married in a civil ceremony, for he could not marry a *shikse* in Israel, to an unconverted Polish Catholic girl and had fathered a son who was ostensibly snipped even though he wasn't Jewish. Moreover, Yankl Shtroy couldn't figure out which mohel in Israel would agree to circumcise a goyish boy in a religious Jewish ceremony. Or maybe the boy wasn't circumcised after all. Yankl Shtroy didn't do an inspection tour. He had never set foot in Israel, although he had traveled there in his thoughts and in his prayers and had seen enough pictures to make himself believe he had visited. He had never left Poland, for those who leave, you know what happens to them, although some said one could leave for up to two weeks, but there was no guarantee. So he decided to see it only in his dreams. And, anyway, he was needed in Warsaw. Now that Polish Jews were no longer dying, it meant that the Messianic era was approaching and soon all the dead would rise and he would be needed to put bones together again. But enough of speculation. That was for tomorrow. But today was today.

Yankl Shtroy didn't spin out not dying into a philosophy or make it an obsession. It wasn't part of his daily thought process. In fact, if he gave it a thought at all, he considered more not dying than its (il) logical obverse, living forever. That probably would have frightened him. It didn't go with his modest lifestyle. Not dying was something he could live with on a daily basis. But as a concept, living forever was for him too grandiose. It would even have meant buying a new suit once in a while, which under no circumstances would he do. He wasn't a conceited man. The enjoyment of life was one day at a time, not eternity.

That's it. His mind was made up.

A man should be buried where he wants to be buried, not where his *shikse* wife decides. And that is why Yankl Shtroy decided to do a little hijacking himself.

Yes, the coffin would be there.

But not Shmulik Gafni.

19

YANKL SHTROY, HANDS WET,
AND GAFNI'S FINAL DEED

IN Gafni's coffin, along with the last breath that accompanies the dead like a good angel until he is laid to rest, floated the memory of Gafni's final act, which was why when Yankl Shtroy did the purification rites, washing the body according to Jewish tradition, he saw a faint smile on the dead man's face. He wondered how a man could die with a smile, but then amended his thoughts to say, If a man is born with a cry, he can die with a smile. In the rhythm of this optimism, he continued thinking: Better to die with a smile than with a wail. Let the mourners wail — the corpse should feel good.

Now it can be revealed why Gafni died with a smile.

Let us wind the clock back, or counter-clockwise to coin a term, paying no attention to Daylight Savings Time or Standard Time, for moving backward in time is saving enough.

In the hospital room Gafni was fading. Weak, dispirited, he was attached to the plastic intravenous lines which fed him liquids, not to cure him or prolong his life, but to make him more comfortable and reduce his pain. Into this room Malina had brought her father. What motivated her is another question. But not for another time. For now. When the extraordinary step of rolling back time is taken, we don't have time for another time. Only now. It might have been nastiness. Nastiness is often self-exculpated when one gazes into a mirror. But lately Malina didn't like looking into mirrors. She convinced herself it wasn't nastiness; on the other hand, neither did she suspect any possible link between Gafni and her father.

Shmulik was asleep when the man entered. When he awoke and his eyes finally focused, he saw what he saw and a wave of clarity, instant recognition, swept over him. All the jagged mirror pieces of his history coalesced into one looking-glass through which his unforgiving eyes penetrated. Yes, for a moment Gafni passed out. The shock of it. The pathos of his present condition. Oh, if only he were Samson. But strange things happen when one passes through a mirror, for when he woke Gafni was stronger, his mind in singular focus. Why had Malina done this? he wondered. But, in retrospect, it fitted in perfectly with her recent behavior: antagonistic, erratic, false, a changed personality, as if the Polish witch goddess Yadwiga had sprinkled her with curses.

Wait a minute, thought Gafni. If she knows nothing about the link between her father and me, it couldn't be nastiness. Is coincidence nastiness? But still, her true nature, her native Polishness, had emerged lately. The apple does not fall far from the tree, goes the Yiddish proverb. Gafni recognized the brute at once. How instant was the recognition? It was as if the man were on a dimly lit stage. Bright lights that could outshine sunshine suddenly lit the stage. That was the light in which Malina's father now sat, and a surge of something — juices, proteins, volts, Gafni didn't know what — coinciding with that light, filled him from the gut up.

Shmulik was surprised at his calm, for in hundreds of dreams he saw himself reacting immediately, like heroes of films, unthinking, turned into a vortex of controlled rage. But he was calm. He also knew he was weak. But he felt himself filling with energy, hope, resolution. He watched the IV dripping liquids into his veins. Not liquids, he told himself, energy. There is no doubt why I am here. Now. Today. And he thanked God that the had met Malina and married her, for only the coinciding of his path and her path had brought about this destined moment that could have never happened in this world without the two separate destinies that now collided. Thank God for Yiddish, he said.

That is why I am here.

Now.

The decades had not changed his despicable face, the hair that stood up like spears, the long jaw, the nose bent slightly to the side, the washed-out blue eyes. As Gafni stared at his face, the years rolled back and he saw himself becoming younger and younger.

Malina excused herself. She was going to get something to eat. She asked her father; he muttered he wasn't hungry.

"Jan," Gafni hissed.

Startled, the man looked at him.

Gafni said another name or two.

The man gripped the armchair.

Shmulik wanted to say, "It's me," did say it, in fact, then realized: If I know him, he doesn't necessarily have to know me.

So from his bed he said:

"I'm a friend of Tadeusz."

The man's expression did not change.

Still in bed, Gafni drew closer, drew closer, closer.

"From the Patriotic Society."

The man said nothing.

Gafni drew closer, still in bed, closer, still in bed, still in bed, in bed, bed …

The face of the old man now blended with the face of the young man then, like a negative slid over a contact print.

He drew a breath, the other man.

"Gardening in Kielce."

Perhaps a faint twitch of the bent nose.

This will do it, Gafni thought, do it, Gafni thought, thought: "July 4, 1946."

One blink, two blinks of the eyes, face still a stone mask.

Rising, slowly and quickly, rushing like an arrow to the target, his will quicker than his body, which will soon follow, savoring the slow, fearsome pace, Gafni said, chanted, keened:

"I'm my father's son. My uncle's nephew. My people's *nokem dam.*" Words aimed like a precise line of fire, a hail of bullets, not mitigated by the slow, dreamy pace of the words. Of course, the man with the now frozen, washed-out blue eyes, face still a mask, did not know that the last two words, uttered in Hebrew, meant "blood avenger."

The man tried to get up.

"Sit down," Gafni ordered, but the man half rose, wanting to know if he could overcome the paralysis of will with which the Jew in bed had hexed him with a quick run to the doorway. But his will was slow, Shmulik Weingarten's quicker. With a leap over the edge of the bed, without pausing, Gafni tore the IV from his hand and ran toward Malina's father.

"It's me," Gafni said again and now the other man understood, as Gafni came from one side, the father's son from another, the uncle's nephew from a third, now the man was surrounded, he had nowhere to go, and from up above, descending, Gafni's people's *nokem dam.* Blood avenger.

Gafni approached swiftly, even quicker than that, and yet in lugubrious, deliberate slow motion. The face of the man came closer, larger and larger and redder, and with one motion that did not pause for an eyeblink from the moment Gafni leaped from the bed — why had she brought her father here? he asked himself and at once replied: in answer to my lifelong prayers — and not a pause in the movement from the moment he tore the thin plastic tubing from his forearm to twirling it around the astonished man's neck, his graggle tamped by Shmulik's liberating primal cry as he wrapped and tightened, his hand a swiftly moving clockwise circle, and the other man's fingers to his throat in a desperate, feeble attempt to pull at the cord as Gafni pulled tighter and tighter until the man's eyes popped and his tongue, purple, now black, protruded.

Gafni returned to his bed. It cannot be said he felt better. It cannot be said he felt worse. His health was not this concern now. He felt muted. Done.

He lay down.

Saw his father, alive, smiling at him.

Shmulik smiled back.

WHO said, "There is no comedy in heaven"? Who made that gloomy, morose, assessment? Who sang that lachrymose song?

Mark Twain, that's who.

But he was wrong.

There was still room up there for a laugh or two.

20

AT THE END, A SHORT WHILE AFTER

AT the end, a short while after — maybe even during — the real Shmulik Gafni was being buried where he wanted to be buried*, with a burst of extra-terrestrial, pre-resurrection life force, the eyes of the late Shmulik Gafni bored through the coffin, through the tightly packed earth, looked eastward from the old Warsaw Jewish cemetery in the Praga district on the other side of the Vistula where the poor Jews are buried to the cemetery at the end of Genshe Street, same earth and stones, where the rich and more prominent Jews were laid to rest up to World War II, and where Malina wanted her husband buried, and where the official funeral was now (t)(f) aking place, and if we haven't yet sent you an invitation to attend, consider yourself invited, we need some decent folk here, even though invitations are never extended for funerals, it isn't a wedding or a Bar Mitzva you know (if Gafni could smile, he would smile at the irony of it, the comedy of it ... there ... see? ... Gafni is smiling ... for the second time since he died), and like Samson he gathered for a moment the strength of the eternal life of present-day Jews in Poland and, unlike Samson, without the beneficence of benisons, for can the dead indeed pray? For is it not written in the Psalms, *Lo ha-metim ye-hallelu-ya* , "the dead cannot praise the Lord"?, and there was no precedent he knew of for the deceased to utter prayers, but he did discover the answer to one of the questions he had asked as a child, to which the only reply he got was raised eyebrows and a short burst of laughter, hard to tell if sympathetic or sarcastic, maybe a bit of both, the question young Shmulik asked, "Do the dead get thirsty?" Some would say that the question was irreverent: some, that the guffaw was. In any case, Gafni finally found the answer the hard way, but find it he did: They do not. And with the power of his

---

*Knowing that the Catholic clergy would be present at Gafni's funeral, Yankl Shtroy and the others at the *Chevra Kadisha* secretly buried the beloved professor of Yiddish according to Jewish tradition in the other cemetery next to his parents. All ten men who knew Gafni recited the Kaddish along with Yankl Shtroy. When they returned to the little *Chevra Kadisha* building, they took an empty coffin and filled it with 150 pounds of the cheapest frozen fish. Let them bury that with the priests in attendance to the crocodile tears of Gafni's fat *shikse*.

alive-for-a-moment tunnel vision, the "late" with quotes, for at the moment he has reverted to so-called late but not really late, although he was late for his formal funeral, if not showing up at all can be considered late. Shmulik Gafni now looked up and saw gravediggers, wondered who or what was being buried at that gravesite, but disregarded that trifle for the cardinal concern of his life, even more important than all the disparate scholarship he had published, saw whom he saw and uttered, "Give me not eternal life, I'll pass on that," a rather tautological remark, don't you think?, given his rather immutable condition, considering that a negative request wasn't really a prayer, and certainly was not a praise of the Lord, as neither was the remark that followed: "Give me instead just one moment of special strength that you didn't give me when that beast sat in my hospital room," and with one last ray of apocalyptic rage sucked the killer into the black hole.

The person whom Malina engaged to conduct the faux-Gafni funeral, an overweight visiting student rabbi from the Very Liberal Movement* based in Jooptown, South Africa, fulfilling his one-credit, one-month mitzva tour, stumbled on the name (given the coffin's contents we can understand, even forgive), for the fat fool fumbled, "We give back to the earth the beloved Shmulik ben Yosef Fishman."

"Gafni," came the chorus.

"Gafni," the obese faux rabbi soloist amended.

What with the effluvium, foul aroma, godawful stench that exuded from the box, one can easily understand the slip. Naming Gafni Fishman when his real paterfamilias — remember? — was Weingarten can be explained psychologically, for just before the officiant's remark, the American cultural attaché who for some reason was present (the invitation to attend the funeral, addressed to the Polish Ministry of Cultural Affairs, was mis-sent to the American Embassy. Yes, now it can be revealed that the messenger was the miscreant. He scanned the envelope, saw Cultural Affairs, and with his limited English, read Polish as polish. Who had the most polished culture? he mused. America, of course. And so, to the United States Embassy the invitation to Gafni's funeral was delivered.), this cultural attache was a middlingly famous American novelist, who once translated an Agnon novel (*The Yemenite Girl*, for those of you who have forgotten), using a thinly disguised Icelandic pseudonym (it begins with C. Urtl). He was a man known for his outspoken stance, his mouth a loose cannon, who will remain unnamed in

---

*The VLM's motto: "We detox Orthodoxy, de-serve Conservatism and deform Reform."

deference to Ezra Shultish who despised him, but who was known for using Cicero in his epigraphs to show off his limited ken of classical culture, and is now making a cameo appearance, said rather indiscreetly in a stage whisper, "Something is fishy here."

Now "fishy" could be used metaphorically, also olfactorally. Given the cleverness of this novelist, he meant both at the same time.

And indeed, the American Jewish writer and federal civil service American culture functionary articulated what everyone felt, the strange, gamey *geshtank* that hung like a smelly blanket in the air, with no disrespect intended, mind you, for the deceased — was it the weekly perch special, non-filleted soon-to-be pickled herring, or cheap salt cod those inventive *Chevra Kadishaniks* had used? — but let's get that plain pine box six feet under pronto before we all pass out, please pass me that fan you're using, dahling.

But back to Gafni. And Gafni's widow.

Malina stood puffy-eyed next to the open grave. Puffy-eyed not from weeping but from globs of blub beneath the eyes, above the cheeks. In toto, she looked like a series of half-opened umbrellas, beginning with her wide, flat, slightly peaked black hat, her black dress with angled ruffles on the shoulders and matching waistband (in case you don't know, black is not the color of Jewish mourning), where she got those outré widow's weeds the devil only knows, she looked like a Greek village widow, only thing she lacked was a bent back but that will come soon enough, and if you can't picture that umber umbrella image (I can't!), try this: a big, black peanut-shaped balloon, pinched at the waist — there, that's better — with a fat and funny pale white face.

The man whom Gafni saw, the man standing between mal Malina and a callous Cardinal in mufti, stumbled, the man upon whom Gafni focused his underground laser zap of vision through several miles of earth, that man tumbled forward and down head first without warning as if pushed by a swift, unseen stormwind, dropped six feet and struck his temple on the pointed edge of the fish-filled faux-Gafni coffin, the same spot of temple where David's slingshot stone struck the gigantic Goliath and brought him down like a collapsed monolith, the pine coffin just now being showered and covered by a half ton of earth and rocks and stones.

Before the astounded gravediggers standing off to a side could react to the lone scream of the man's daughter, you all recognize the pitch of Malina's voice, don't you?, the driver of the big yellow back hoe, unaware of what had happened, pushed with one mighty thrust of the huge maw of his massive shovel the prepared mound of soft black earth and stones and rocks into the open grave, a shower of rocks and clods descended. By the time the gravediggers, engaged to fill a grave once emptied of earth and not defill it, and distracted by the unrelenting hysteria of his distraught daughter, could get to Malina's father, Shmulik ben Yosef Weingarten finally finally had his lifelong, now deathshort, foe in a fatal embrace.

When they finally finally pulled him out, defilling and later refilling the grave — for it would have been a disgrace even for faux-Gafni, even for foul fish, to have that piece of filth lie beside (him) (them) — Janusz the welder's tongue protruded, his skull was split as if by an axe, and, inexplicably, a length of IV tubing pulled tight as a hangman's noose was around his neck, making his black tongue hang out, loose and limp, like a lifeless viper.

21

THE PRESS CONFERENCE, MRS. GAFNI'S

AFTER her husband's demise, Mrs. Gafni, soon to be known as Professor Christiana Przeskovska, held a press conference.

Just look at her first name. Had it been invented, used as a name in fiction, Christiana would reverberate with phony symbolism, a puppeteer's ultra deluxe effort to score a point. But what can you do if that was her given name? Her middle name, Malina, was less obtrusive, and to her credit, that's the name she used when she met Shmulik Gafni in Nice and also in Jerusalem. But now, at the press conference, she bluntly stated, looking not at the reporters, as people are wont to do at such occasions, but at the tv cameras (read: at Poland, Israel, and the rest of the world):

"From now on, I would like to be referred to by my first name, my given name, my birth name, my primary name, my Christian name — Christiana."

As if anyone, any where, is going to refer to her anyhow, anyway.

22

WHEN THEY HEARD THE NEWS

WHEN they heard the news in Israel that Professor Shmuel Gafni, the King of Yiddish, was actually buried in Poland, that that really was his final wish, according to his properly signed, witnessed and executed will and testament, that no last-minute court injunctions were successful, and that there would be no intervention by anyone, not even the President of Israel, the protests and complaints commenced. They proliferated like seaweed on seashore. Newspaper articles and magazine features, photos and all, even sermons in synagogues, endless talk shows with politicians and demagogues on the traditional and the illegal, offshore, rogue stations. Why did he? How could he? How dare he? Let's report this to the Knesset, then the United Nations. Letters to the editor galore, more against, some for, no end of those, some in rhyme, some in acid prose, they were mostly cons, few were pros, some were amateurs ranting, others pros, experts in rumor planting, a stream of coffee klatsches in upscale cafés like Yehudit's and Apropos in Tel Aviv, phone calls, e-mail, faxes (when it comes to gossip, not a soul relaxes), shouts from rooftops (see opening pages, won't hurt to re-read them) — where are friends, defenders, when we really need them? — symposia and other forms of rages, buzz-buzz and blah-blah (of the latter quite a lot), while sipping decaf nectar and ambrosia from Metullah to Eilat.

But, then again, how many of us (needed or extraneous) can say that at our funeral, two of them no less (can you beat that?) and simultaneous — gaze down, good Gafni, from heaven's portals — how many of us can say at that our funeral we had a minyan of immortals?

About the Author

Curt Leviant is author of nine critically acclaimed works of fiction. He has won the Edward Lewis Wallant Award and writing fellowships from the National Endowment for the Arts, the Rockefeller Foundation, the Jerusalem Foundation, the Emily Harvey Foundation in Venice, and the New Jersey Arts Council. His work has been included in *Best American Short Stories, Prize Stories: the O. Henry Awards,* and other anthologies – and praised by two Nobel laureates: Saul Bellow and Elie Wiesel. With the publication of Curt Leviant's novels into French, Italian, Spanish, Greek, Rumanian and other languages – some of which have become international best sellers – reviewers have hailed his books as masterpieces and compared his imaginative fiction to that of Nabokov, Borges, Kafka, Italo Calvino, Vargas Llosa, Harold Pinter, and Tolstoy. The French version of *Diary of an Adulterous Woman* was singled out as one of the Twenty Best Books of the Year in France and among the seven best novels. *Kafka's Son* in the French translation was hailed on French television as a "work of genius" and by French critics as "a masterpiece."

But the most memorable praise has come from Chauncey Mabe, Book Editor of South Florida's *Sun-Sentinel,* who wrote: "Curt Leviant is one of the greatest novelists you've never heard of. His serio-comic novels, including *Diary of an Adulterous Woman* (the best novel I've read during the past ten years), should place him in company with Joseph Heller or even Saul Bellow…"